Praise for *Hand In The Till*:

"Continued brilliance, the characters still make you laugh and cry and fume the entire time you're reading," Colin Quinn

"Another excellent piece from Hansen. Darkly comic, I laughed out loud. Hansen brings the personal side of the continuing divisions in Derry with the dynamic interplay of his wonderful characters," Kate Rigby, *Little Guide to Unhip, Lost the Plot, Seaview Terrace*, among others

"Little and not so little brats from Hell, brilliantly staged, a surreal feat, gloriously dark and comically tragic. It's compulsive reading," Ashen Venema, *Course of Mirrors*

"Consummate black humor, skillfully crafted characters, inventive descriptions and a smart plot," Iva Polansky, *Fame and Infamy*

"Humor, the greatest weapon known to man when it comes to tackling institutional bigotry or social inequality. And Hansen takes that weapon and uses it like a pallet knife on this excellent canvas," James McPherson, *Lucifer and Auld Lang Syne*

"Bitingly, bitterly humorous. A strong voice and flowing prose, with a good pace and an idiosyncratic take on a bleak world," J.S. Watts, *A Darker Moon*

"The dialogue simply sparkles. Brilliantly funny even while a tad disturbing," John O'Brien, *Other Face*

"An absolute pleasure to read. The dialogue is spot-on, and the imagery stark and vivid. Shifts gears from the tragic to the hilarious with ease," R.A. Baker, *Rayna of Nightwind*

"Hansen has mastered the art of believable colloquial dialogue and his descriptive narrative puts you right there in the scene. The characters jump off the page and the read entertains. Yet another example of his excellent work," Delcan Conner, *Russian Brides*

"A black comedy indeed. A gift for dialogue and the ability to weave an intriguing tale," Katy Christie, *No Man No Cry*

"Puts you right there in that world with a masterly confidence, and the characters and setting are sketched with deft economy," NSL Lee, *Chosen*

"A masterful piece of work that deserves as much praise as can be piled upon it. A supreme writer with talent in buckets, buckets of talent and a gift that can never be achieved, only owned," Andrew Skaife, *God, the Son and the Holy Dwarf*

Praise for the ABNA 2010 Semifinalist *An Embarrassment of Riches*:

"A masterpiece," Colin Quinn

"As absorbing as it is hysterical," Publishers Weekly

"Wildly amusing…a cross between a roller-coaster and a carousel," Olivera Baumgartner-Jackson. Readerviews.com

"Clearly the work of a craftsman! (The characters) career around Derry with the grace of a drunken and horny bull," Chris Gerrib, Podpeople.com

"Classic, I-can't-stop-reading literature," Jonathan Henderson, Jonhenderscon.com

"Absolutely hilarious," Jessica Roberts, Bookpleasures.com

"Comedy as pitch-black as the moors of the Emerald Island itself," Riot, BurningLeaves.com

"Riotous entertainment," P.P.O Kane, CompulsiveReader.com

HAND IN THE TILL

Gerald Hansen

iUniverse, Inc.
Bloomington

Hand In The Till

This is a work of fiction. All of the characters, names, incidents, organizations, and dialogue in this novel are either the products of the author's imagination or are used fictitiously.

iUniverse books may be ordered through booksellers or by contacting:

iUniverse
1663 Liberty Drive
Bloomington, IN 47403
www.iuniverse.com
1-800-Authors (1-800-288-4677)

ISBN: 978-1-4502-8770-8 (pbk)
ISBN: 978-1-4502-8771-5 (cloth)
ISBN: 978-1-4502-8772-2 (ebk)

Printed in the United States of America

iUniverse rev. date: 1/14/2011

To Mom and Dad again

"Beware of false knowledge; it is more dangerous than ignorance."
—*George Bernard Shaw*

ACKNOWLEDGMENTS

I am extremely grateful to all who gave me such support for the first book, and to those who urged me on to whip this book into shape. I have been truly blessed. As usual, thanks so much for the editing and commentary to Erin Lynch and Gosia Kurek. And to the truly marvelous Colin Quinn and Lorna Matcham (my dear ExPatMaddie), who gave me the confidence and drive to continue, I thank you both from the bottom of my heart. Also very, very supportive were many brilliant authors on Authonomy.com, and first in line is Kate Rigby (you are a star for all you've done for me, and an excellent author!), followed very closely by Cait Coogan (I really am so thankful you sent that email), Lisa Candelaria Bartlett and Frank Robert Anderson. Thanks for gems of innovation, information and/or wisdom to Steven McEnrue (it all started with you), Ross Erin 'Louboutin' Martineau, Laurence 'O'Clock' Martinetian, Jeferson Medeiros, Anthony Darden, Niketta 'Fingernails' Scott, Leslie Ross, Estee Adoram, Miguel Tabone and James Zammat (I guess Malta will be in the next book), Maciej Rumprecht for the Polish tips, Mark Gondelman, Matt Kaminiecki and Tony "Rapel" Ramsey for listening to me babble on and on. Thank you excellent illustrators and great friends Swan Park and HyeJeong Park, and photographer supreme Marcin Kaliski. And of course, thanks so much to all my students and the marvelous people at both Manhattan Language and the Olive Tree/Comedy Cellar, NYC.

HOW TO PRONOUNCE THE NAMES (by popular demand):

Fionnuala: Fin-**noo**-lah
Ursula: **Uhr**-suh-la
Dymphna: **Dimf**-nah
Padraig: **Paw**-drig
Siofra: **Shee**-frah
Seamus: **Shay**-mus
Grainne: **Grohn**-yah

CHAPTER ONE

No thugs loitered in the damp beyond the windshield, but a syringe and soiled condoms littered the pavement. William Skivvins tutted his distaste as he parked his BMW on the cobblestones next to a burnt-out phone booth. It was covered with misspelled graffiti of kinky sex and hatred for Queen Elizabeth II.

He maneuvered his body to shield the vulgarity from his pride and joy, nine-year-old Victoria, sitting in the passenger seat with a face on her most would slap with glee. She was nodding that head and tapping her foot to some pop tune of the day blaring from her iPod headphones. William tapped her on the shoulder. Victoria heaved an inward sigh and turned down the volume.

"I'd feel better if you came into the shop with me, petal," her father said. He had to collect the previous day's takings.

"It's no bother, daddy. I'll stay here."

Victoria flashed him a smirk he mistook for a smile, then cranked the volume again. William ran a hand over his cropped hair and the blue tie which complemented his brown suit. For once, he had something to worry about more than the presence of germs: leaving his daughter defenseless in that hardened neighborhood of broken beer bottles and torrid murals of political violence which favored British tanks barreling over mobs of fleeing Catholics.

The 35-year-old entrepreneur owned five Sav-U-Mors, grim corner shops scattered across Derry City which sold everything from overpriced turnips to generic tampons. This one in the Moorside was the most grim. As members of the privileged Protestant class, William and his daughter were in enemy territory.

"Keep the door locked, then," he instructed in his precise voice which, together with his weekly manicures, ensured all male shelf-stackers and couriers kept their backs firmly to a wall when in his presence. "And don't utter a word to anyone. You know what they're like around here."

"Okay, daddy," Victoria said 'sweetly,' her blonde asymmetrical designer hairdo bobbing. "Oh, it's so hot here in the car."

She wriggled out of her school blazer, even more confident now that her pressed white shirt made her anonymous.

"Cheerio, then."

William exited the car. The moment he rounded the corner, keys flicking in his hand, Victoria was out the door. Her pert nose sniffed the rank air for action, Lady Gaga the soundtrack to her mission of violence. She was a marauder in a dangerous land, seeking casual violence against the indigenous people on that side of the River Foyle, those who were less cultured, less intelligent, less *human* than Victoria; her schoolmates, her uncles and cousins, her grandparents had taught her all about them, those who made up three quarters of the city and insisted the Pope was Christ on Earth.

Derry, Northern Ireland was a divided city, where the Catholic majority and the Protestant minority had spent decades waging war against each other. Although the Peace Process had begun years earlier, and the British paratroopers patrolling the streets with semi-automatic weapons and land-rovers were but a memory of the "Troubles" of the '70s and '80s, it was taking perceptibly longer for the two communities to harmonize.

They drank in separate pubs, shopped in separate supermarkets, got their perms in separate salons. But sometimes a step down the wrong street in the area found one facing a member of the opposing religion. And though Derry had been transformed into a most handsome showcase of European history, culture and technological progress, and both sides of the community were experiencing an unprecedented growth in financial luxury and sophistication, the Moorside seemed mired in a desperate past, the Euros pouring in from the EU having passed it by. This was where Victoria now hunted.

Her father had parked aside a row of ramshackle shops that Victoria presumed these particularly disadvantaged people visited for their paltry provisions. Her eyes eagerly scanned the doorways of the butcher's, the news-agent's, the chemist's, but there were no signs of life anywhere except an old drunk passed out against the wall of the off-license. Victoria supposed on this side of town few people had money to actually shop. She skipped over the tattered pant legs and considered the tramp. She had heard that in America teens set them alight and laughed at their flapping, burning bodies, but she had no matches.

She was heading to the car to get some when she heard a scrabbling from around the corner of the butcher's. She peered down the alley. Under clotheslines riddled with forgotten fashion, a girl with lifeless black hair and a yellow hair clip clawed glumly through a garbage can. The girl, about the same age and vaguely malnourished, Victoria thought, had a frayed PowerPuff Girls handbag dangling from her left elbow and clutched a black plastic bag that looked half-full of the spoils of her scavenging. Victoria could barely control her delight: the perfect victim. She muted "Poker Face" and went in for the kill.

"Look at the shape of you!" she snorted. "Rummaging through the rubbish like a wild beast! You're a disgrace to the human race! Coke or Pepsi?"

Siofra Flood froze with one hand in the garbage can, a look of mortification and dumb fear on her face. It was the question every Derry schoolgirl dreaded. The wrong answer could leave her with a clawed face, bruised lip, or tattered clothes covered with dog feces.

"I'm asking you a question, you vulgar creature," Victoria barked, taking a step closer. "Did you get your ears from a rubbish bin as well?"

"I heard ye!" Siofra replied with a slight tremble; the girl was a full foot taller than her, and had an almost demonic gleam in her eyes. "And which one are *ye*, hi? Coke or Pepsi?"

"Answer me first, or you'll feel my fist against your nose!"

They squared off amongst the broken beer bottles in the alley like two starved Rottweilers given a sniff at fresh meat. The question being asked had nothing to do with soda, but religion. *Coke or Pepsi?* meant Catholic or Protestant? *Friend or foe?*

Victoria was obviously Pepsi: not only did she have a West Brit accent and the How Great Thou Art school's gray and purple striped skirt, the white headphones trailing from her ears screamed their extravagance; few girls from the Moorside could afford an iPod. Siofra slipped her bulky CD player on its strap behind her back in shame.

"Scrounging through the rubbish for food to eat?" Victoria sneered. "You must be Coke, then; a filthy Catholic bitch!"

"Me granny Heggarty made me two boiled eggs for me breakfast," Siofra insisted, her cheeks burning. She had eaten one piece of butterless toast, burnt.

"What are you looking for, then, new clothes to wear? It looks like you need them to me, what with that bargain bin frock and those ratty tights hanging from your skeletal legs. Purple and blue don't even match, you know."

"Me...me mammy has me collect tins from the rubbish every time I'm out," Siofra finally admitted. "She's three months to live from the cancer that's eating her brain." Her guilt-trip comeback didn't seem to work. "And ye'd better leave me be, as she be's working off the last of her shifts at the Sav-U-Mor, right around the corner!"

She pointed feverishly out of the alley.

Victoria was surprised, but not shocked: in a city that small, everybody and everything seemed related to everyone and everything else, so such coincidences abounded. But she would never reveal that her father owned the Sav-U-Mor, let alone that he was probably speaking to Siofra's mother even as Victoria attacked her. And Victoria was certainly going to attack Siofra.

"If your mammy works there, it's odds-on you're a filthy Fenian," Victoria decided with a growl.

"And ye're a Proddy cow! With a face like a busted cabbage!"

"Your mammy can't save you now."

Victoria advanced quickly across the mucky path of weeds. Siofra pitched the garbage bag at her. Victoria jerked to the right, the bag plunged to the ground, and empty tin cans spilled out. Victoria lunged, grabbing a handful of Siofra's black hair and giving it a vicious tug. Siofra squealed as the hair clip popped off her head and clattered to the ground. Her fingers scrabbled against Victoria's face, but the nubs of gnawed fingernails had little effect. Siofra grabbed the headphones and tugged them from Victoria's ears.

The PowerPuff Girls handbag flew through the air and cracked against Victoria's head. Roaring for revenge, Victoria dealt Siofra swift kicks in the shin, then grappled her shoulders and threw her slight body against the garbage can. Siofra's head bounced off the plastic, and she stumbled to the mud. She struggled to prise herself from the filth and deal the girl a smack, but Victoria towered over her, and her pink-painted claws shoved Siofra back into the mud.

"Let's see what you have in that handbag of yours before I clatter the living shite out of you!" Victoria sang, maneuvering the purse off Siofra's jerking elbow.

Siofra whimpered in the dirt, and Victoria dug through the scant contents. It was British imperial history repeating: one who had so much pillaging from one who had so little. Victoria retrieved a mango lip gloss, a bobby pin and a fifty pence piece.

"Pure rubbish!" She tossed them to the ground, then delved into the handbag once again, tugging out a pack of 10 unfiltered Rothman cigarettes. Disgust registered on her face as if she held a handful of human teeth.

"Just as my daddy says." Victoria's voice rang with a righteousness at odds with her age. "All you Catholics smoke and drink yourselves into early graves."

"Them fags is for me granny Heggarty!" Siofra cried. "She sent me to the news-agent's for to get em for her!"

"Likely story," Victoria snorted, making to stomp on the pack with her sparkly Jellies.

"*Naw!* Me granny'll murder me!"

Siofra moaned in dismay as she watched the packet disappear under Victoria's heel. Victoria tossed the handbag aside, then threw herself on Siofra, grabbing the girl's spindly arms and pinning them over her head against the dried curry which trailed down the side of the garbage can. Siofra struggled to break free, and out of the corner of her eye spied a stinging nettle sprouting from a crack in the wall and swaying inches from her tormentor's twisted face. Siofra jerked her body to the left, and the leaves were two inches, one inch, from Victoria's pastel cheekbone.

Unaware, Victoria wiped the spittle from her lips and hissed, little fang-teeth bared: "Filthy, fag-smoking, Coke-slurping—"

Victoria started as she caught sight of something glinting on Siofra's flailing left arm. Confusion flickered in her eyes for a second—what she was seeing was impossible!—and they honed in on it, verifying its existence. It was happily wrapped around the little creature's wrist, taunting her with its presence on one so undeserving. While Siofra clawed the air, trying to wrench Victoria's head into the nettles, Victoria erupted into anger.

"Give me that now, you hateful toerag!"

"Naw! Naw! Not me Hannah Montana watch!"

Siofra's wails for mercy echoed down the alley, and Victoria's fist sailed through the air to stave her head in.

CHAPTER TWO

THIRTY YARDS AWAY AND AS MANY MINUTES EARLIER

Fionnuala Flood's bleached ponytails flew as she punched prices into the till, nerves and cheap bracelets jangling. The old aged pensioner hauled her purchases from the shopping basket onto the mini-conveyor belt and blabbered on into her face. Fionnuala's eyes flickered in panic from the goods to the clock. Nineteen minutes after eight. Mr. Skivvins was to arrive at half past, and she still had so much to do.

"...A bloody disgrace, so them hooligans is," Mrs. O'Mahoney whinged, "lounging around on me garden wall, outta their minds with drink and drugs, ringing me doorbell at all hours of the day and night, laughing at me infirmity and shoving dog shite through me letter box. Stepped on some the other week and ground it into me hallway carpeting, so I did, and nothing seems to be getting it out, not old coffee grounds nor mayonnaise nor wet teabags mixed with fag ash. Pure desperate, so it is."

"Och dearie me, aye, Mrs. O'Mahoney, a disgrace indeed," Fionnuala rattled off with mechanical sympathy, nod after nod, shoving the Spaghetti Hoops, the corn pads, the light bulbs into a plastic bag. She grabbed for a can and her heart fell in sudden dread. It was labeled Brussels Sprouts. Fionnuala knew it contained anything but. What she had once called her Cash Cow Cans were now the bane of her existence. She grabbed the can off the counter and tossed it underneath.

"Ye kyanny eat them Brussels sprouts; them is past their sell-by date," she explained.

Mrs. O'Mahoney was surprised. "I'll get meself another tin," she decided, making to stagger over to the shelf.

"The entire shipment's gone off! I was just about to clear them from the shelves when ye came in."

"How about them carrots, then?"

"All wer vegetables! Unfit for human consumption! That's ten pounds seventy-three pence ye owe me."

Mrs. O'Mahoney clicked open her coin purse to count out seventy-three pence. Fionnuala seethed inwardly and forced the bag at the woman.

"Never mind paying! Take the lot on me."

"Och, sure, I kyanny allow ye to—"

"Aye, ye can!"

Mrs. O'Mahoney's field of wrinkles broke into a smile.

"That's wile civil of ye. Pop a pack of fags in the bag as well, then, would ye love? Rothman's unfiltered. And I want a pack of twenty."

"Och, for the love of…"

Fionnuala tore a pack from the shelf behind her and thrust it in the bag.

"Ta very much!"

Fionnuala pushed a delighted, shuffling Mrs. O'Mahoney towards the door and guided her forcefully onto the sidewalk, then flipped the sign to CLOSED and locked the door. Now was her only chance, and she was cutting it close.

Right before Mrs. O'Mahoney came in, Fionnuala had gone to the back stock room and filled two cases with cans of each vegetable they sold. She now hauled those cases across the cracked linoleum toward the shelves of cans on display. She snatched her empty green and red tartan shopping cart from under the counter, flung the pricing gun on the top flap and raced towards the shelves. She fired the pricing gun over the cans in the cases.

For months, Fionnuala had been raking it in: buying cheap contraband stock from the Eastern Bloc at bargain bin prices from a creature with hollow eyes and shaky hands at the market under the Mountains of Mourne Gate in the city center, selling the goods at the shop mark-up, and slipping the difference into her handbag at the end of every shift. But the day before, Mrs. Feeney had flounced into the Sav-U-Mor, a can of Brussels Sprouts clutched in her fist and demanded to know what she had sold her. When Fionnuala had stared, stunned, at what she thought was a bizarre former communist delicacy inside the can, she realized with a sinking heart that something had gone terribly wrong. And when Mrs. Heffernan struggled in half an hour later with a can of carrots that contained anything but, Fionnuala realized the last few cases she had bought must have fallen off a truck from a very distant land indeed.

She threw the cans of tainted Cauliflower into the satchel beside her, took ten of the shop's from the case, and soon a new, and hopefully edible, row of cauliflower gleamed out. She cleared the cans of Brussels sprouts, the clock ticking in her mind.

Although Fionnuala Flood was a woman who never settled for what she had (even though it was more than she deserved), pure greed hadn't been her only motivation. Cigarette clinging with grim determination to her lower lip, she worked her way through the new potatoes, the carrots, the turnips and the mushy peas. Her gray face, with its horsey mismatched teeth, usually drooped in despondency, but now it was bobbing like a Thai hooker's. The brightly-colored bargain-bin clothes she seemed to favor as if to make up for the grayness only magnified the passage of time on her body, her bulk straining the seams as she reached up and down; she had never learned that the overweight should avoid tight clothing.

She was delving into a case of baked beans when she tensed at a rattling at the door. A key turned much too swiftly in the lock. Her co-worker, Edna Gee, waddled in breathlessly, an alarming mix of floral print paired with plaid.

"What have ye got the closed sign on display and the door locked for? Skivvins'll go mental!"

Edna gawked at the sight of a frozen Fionnuala, one arm stretched to the shelf, the other jammed into the shopping cart.

"What in Jesus' name—?"

"Dear Lord in heaven above!" Fionnuala seethed through a smile as false as her hair color. "I'm gasping for me tea! Get yer lazy arse to the back room and put the kettle on, would ye?"

Edna's eyes flashed in suspicion at the piles of cans.

"Them shelves was near bare yesterday, and the deliveries isn't due till the afternoon. What are ye up to?"

Edna moved closer to inspect.

"Nothing!"

"Me hole!" Edna snorted. "Ye've got a rabbit-in-the-headlights look in yer eyes, and this from a woman who can kill with a glare. There's something untoward going on here as sure as the Pope be's a Catholic."

She reached down.

"Get yer paws away from me cart," Fionnuala snapped, smacking Edna's hand.

The realization finally dawned in Edna's dull eyes.

"Holy Mary Mother of God! Ye're stocking yer own gear on the shelves and—"

"Back off, ye daft crone," Fionnuala warned.

"Ye've discovered a way to line yer pockets and put one over on that tight-fisted scourge Skivvins at the same time!"

Edna's plump, veined face suddenly brightened with connivance. She sidled conspiratorially up to Fionnuala and whispered, "Ye sly, sleekit cunt, ye! Go on and let me in on the scam, would ye, love?"

"Ye must be joking!" Fionnuala snorted. "And don't ye 'love' me. A drop of yer piss would scald anyone, ye aul cow."

Fionnuala balked when Edna was hired for the Sav-U-Mor the year before: not only had they been enemies since elementary school, Fionnuala long suspected one of Edna's many sons was responsible for digging up her father's grave years ago and kicking his skull around the cemetery as a soccer ball.

"*Aul?*" Edna roared. "I'm not the one prancing round town in bleached ponytails like one half me age."

"We be's drowning in a sea of debt," Fionnuala cried, switching tactics. "We've mounds of bills, and I've all them wanes with mouths begging to be filled." She placed a hand on Edna's shoulder and forced a tear from her eye. "Edna, ye've not a clue what a misery me life's been."

"Thousands would believe ye, not me, but," Edna snorted, shaking the unwanted hand off and then inspecting her shoulder as if she suspected Fionnuala had stolen some fabric off her coat. "Take them crocodile tears of yers and shove em up yer arse! Sure, two of yer lads be's locked up in Magilligan Prison, yer eldest girl be's off in Malta living the life of a degenerate, and that Dymphna of yers be's shacked up with her Protestant fancy man on the Waterside. Ye've no need to fill their mouths. I'm all for shoving me hand in the till; I've spent a lifetime engaging in it, like. Some of us, but, need money more than others." She planted a hand on her hip, looked Fionnuala up and down with disapproval, then spat out with resentment, "We've not had a sister-in-law win the lotto and throw an extra house at us. The whole town knows how ye ran after her money—"

"Naw!"

"Persecuted and tortured by ye, that poor aul soul Ursula Barnett was, chased off to America, never to be heard from again—"

"*Naw!*"

"There be's a river in Egypt for the likes of ye. Denial, pure and simple. Anyroad, ye've made me look a right eejit." Edna's voice rose in hysteria. "Side by side we stand behind that counter more hours than not, and ye've never let on, not a clue did I have ye've been lining yer pockets all this time by fiddling with the stock. How long has this been going on, then? That's what I'd like to know. If Skivvins found out, he'd never believe I didn't have a hand in it and all. And I know ye only too well, Fionnuala Flood. Ye'd be sure to point the finger of blame at me, and ye know I'm still on probation for that shoplifting offense last year. Give me a cut of the action," and here her lips curled into a cruel threat, "or I'll be on the phone to Skivvins."

She slipped her hand into the plaid and freed her mobile from the folds.

"One word to Skivvins," Fionnuala seethed, smacking the phone out of her hand, "and I'll bleeding throttle the fecking life from ye, ye minger! And ye don't know me in the least."

"Lemme at the evidence, ye thieving bloody stoke, ye!"

Edna clawed for the cart again, and Fionnuala pushed her away.

They grabbed opposite sides of the handle, scuffling in a field of cans, the goods rolling down the aisles. Their lumbering forms groaned with the exertion, their smocks would've billowed if they hadn't been stiff with filth, and they shoved clumsily into the bruised vegetable bargain display. It careened over, sending overripe cabbages and turnips raining down upon their struggling bodies.

"Fecking useless stoke!" Fionnuala seethed, her fingernails slicing through the air to latch into the flab of Edna's jowls.

The bell over the door tinkled again, and William Skivvins pranced in, cufflinks glistening. His left eye twitched, first in confusion, then in rage at the scene before it. He gave a sharp intake of breath, and then the roaring began.

CHAPTER THREE

Holding a squirming Siofra in the mud with one hand, Victoria admired the glittering prize she had just shackled to her wrist. Her favorite Disney Channel star, Hannah Montana, all conditioned blonde hair and sweetness, warbled into a microphone inside the petals of a daisy that was the watch frame, and a little guitar happily ticked off the minutes.

"How dare you! How dare you afford one!" Victoria seethed into Siofra's whimpering face. "I've been trying to get my hands on one for months. They're sold out all over the Internet! Did you steal it? Snatch it off the wrist of someone whose family actually *works and can pay for one?*"

As Siofra whipped her head from side to side, the treasures that hung from her ears were revealed. Victoria was quick at registering Hannah's toothy smile, the glimmer of pink and gold, the musical notes.

"You've the matching earrings as well?" Victoria gasped.

"Leave me earrings be! Themmuns is mines!" cried Siofra. "And give me back me watch!"

In her life of entitlement, Victoria shuddered at the affront of one of the lower classes having something she didn't, and now it was three things she didn't have.

"I'm going to take them from you too. Just as you must've taken them from someone more deserving!"

Her hand shot out and she pummeled Siofra with slaps, then tugged the earrings from her lobes, hoping they were pierced and she'd see some blood. Siofra yelped and thrust her body towards the nettles, which were proving increasingly useless the more that was snatched from her.

Even as Victoria clasped the daisy delights onto her ears, her joy was overridden by the perplexity of how this little prole had them in her possession.

"How did you get them?" she demanded of the girl struggling to prise herself from the field of muck.

"Give me em back," Siofra moaned weakly. "Themmuns is mines! *Mines!*"

"How could a penniless toerag like you afford them? That can't be."

"I didn't nick em."

"Tell me who you nicked them from now or the beatings are going to get worse!" Victoria warned, fists balled. "The poor soul missing them is probably a classmate of mine! Tell me! Tell me!"

Even menaced as she was, Siofra couldn't hide her pride: "I got em from the Hannah Montana fan club website. Them is a limited edition. Number 1215."

Victoria snorted her disbelief. "You need a credit card to buy from a website, and you don't even have a job."

Siofra leaped up with a roar, and her fingernails sliced through the girl's mop of hair and clamped onto her skull. She drove Victoria's head into the pile of nettles and cackled with victory as she scrubbed the pert nose into the spiny leaves.

My face! My face is full of nettles!"

Victoria's shrieks pierced the air, but she felt no pain yet, only Siofra grabbing for the earrings. Her elbow shot back and cracked against Siofra's breastplate. Siofra grunted, and Victoria whipped around, her fist pounding into Siofra's stomach. Siofra collapsed again, wincing with pain and heaving for air.

"My hives will soon disappear," Victoria said, her fingers running over her face. "But your pitiful life will stretch before you until your body is dumped into its coffin. And it'll be a wooden one, I've no doubt. If not cardboard."

"I've memorized the ratty features of yer ugly face," Siofra wheezed from the mud, revenge shimmering in her watering eyes. "I'll kick yer thieving Proddy arse the next time I see ye, ye effin gack!"

Victoria made a show of inspecting the time on her new watch. "Half-past eight exactly, I see," she tittered. She looked down upon Siofra with a mix of pity and disdain, the tingles creeping across her cheek. "You're a half-human Fenian beast. But you've brilliant fashion sense."

Victoria pointed her mobile phone at Siofra's spitting, disheveled form and, giggling gleefully, snapped a photo of her face wracked with pain just as Siofra trod on a shard of broken glass. The Protestant girl ground her heel into Siofra's CD player, cackled as it cracked under her weight, shook her head so the earrings jangled against her neck, and barked with more hilarity.

"And my daddy's car is bigger than your daddy's car as well!" she sneered. "But thanks very much for my new gifts!"

Victoria flitted out of the alley toward the safety of the BMW, pressing fingers with concern up and down her cheeks.

Siofra stifled her sobs as she swabbed at her bloody heel with a filthy tissue she had plucked from the garbage, mortified to be crying and barefoot in public and cursing the fact that her daddy couldn't even drive.

Another unknown but much smaller girl chanced by the alley and stopped, stricken, at the sight before the garbage can.

"Are ye right there, wee girl?" she asked, scanning the blood, the tears, the scattered lip glosses, the cracked CD player and broken handbag strap. She reached out a hand to help Siofra up, but Siofra slapped it away.

"Coke or Pepsi?" Siofra demanded.

CHAPTER FOUR

"What on God's green earth," William Skivvins roared, "are you deranged women playing at?"

"That one's been meddling with the stock!" Edna panted in a voice hoarse from decades of sucking down thirty cigarettes a day. "I caught her at it red-handed, her tote brimming with contraband, snatching at the tins on the shelves as if she were at the make-up counter during the January sales at the Top-Yer-Trolley!" Derry's Wal-Mart.

"I never! I never!" Fionnuala insisted.

Mr. Skivvins struggled to make sense of the scene before him.

"Where did all these tins of vegetables come from?"

"I haven't a clue," Fionnuala said.

"Ye kyanny take the thieving out of her," Edna said. "She's one of them Heggartys. It's in all themmuns's blood!"

"Och, and what about the band of hooligans ye spawned from yer filthy, scabby—"

"Enough!" William barked, feeling soiled. "Why can't you comport yourselves in a more age-appropriate manner? It's like playtime at the schoolyard in here."

The women didn't have the presence of mind for shame, choosing instead to glare defiantly at each other. William marched to the shelves and inspected the cans. He plucked a can from Fionnuala's case. At first glance, it was like millions of others that had rolled off the production line of any industrialized nation's factory. Closer inspection revealed the metal to be rusty and disfigured, and the label to be plastered on the can in a slipshod manner. He slid his fingernail into the edge of the label, and it curled off, fluttering to the floor, where all could clearly see the Scotch tape on its back.

"From the inferior quality of these cans," he said with a menacing calmness and eyes locked on Fionnuala, "and the likelihood that the labels have been tampered with, they have clearly not come from our supplier. What have you done?"

Fionnuala opened her mouth to reply, then closed it, then opened it again, then clamped it firmly shut. She couldn't let him know the full extent of her deviousness.

"That's how they was delivered," she insisted. "I've done nothing, save stock em, price em and sell em, as ye're paying me to do."

Skivvins stood in contemplation of the situation, his upper lip twitching, and his manicured nails clacking on the top of the counter. Finally, he seemed to reach a point of no return in his mind.

"I don't think I'll be paying you to do that for much longer," he said quietly.

"I've not done nothing!"

"To tell you the God's honest truth, I haven't a clue what you've been up to, nor do I care to invest the time or mental energy to figure it out, Ms. Flood. I've a litany of complaints the length of the River Foyle from customers about your threatening and rude behavior. I suppose it's no more than I expect from someone born and bred in the Moorside."

"Ye don't know me!" Fionnuala barked mechanically. "I was born in Creggan Heights, so I was."

"Almost as bad. You are one in a very long and tiresome line of degenerates in my employ who've spent a lifetime celebrating casual violence and petty crime, perched on the brink of drug addiction and alcoholism, the dreadful effects of which I have the misfortune every day to see. And to smell, too."

"Ye don't know me! Ye don't know me, so ye don't!" Fionnuala kept insisting, and the more she screamed it, the more he gave her looks which said he was certain he did.

"Needless to say," Mr. Skivvins said, flicking the cuffs of his shirt sleeves straight, "your employment at Sav-U-Mor is terminated as of this moment."

"Please lemme explain!"

"You're sacked, you thieving creature!" he roared at Fionnuala's twitching face, while Edna doubled over with silent mirth.

"Och, ye can shove this manky job up yer saggy arse," Fionnuala said. "Dead-end? Dead right! I'll be down to the council board for wrongful dismissal, but, mark me words!"

Fionnuala clawed the strings of the tattered smock and tore it from her. She threw it into Skivvin's face, then scrabbled around for her cans, the tears rolling down her face as she stuffed them into her shopping cart. Skivvins and Edna watched her silently, arms crossed firmly, eyes persecuting her. Fionnuala went behind the counter, and Skivvins, alarmed she was making for the cash in the register, pranced over.

"Och, I'm collecting me special tote, just," Fionnuala snapped through her tears. She hauled it over her shoulder, grabbed the shopping cart and made for the door.

She shoved her horsey features into Edna's face.

"And ye haven't heard the last of me, as God's me witness!"

Edna harrumphed, a superior look on her face, and said in a strained voice and with a sudden sneer in her smile, "I suppose I should give ye this in any event. I'd just bin it, otherwise. I only bought it to wind ye up, anyroad."

Fionnuala started down in incomprehension, unable to make out through her tears what Edna was shoving into her hand. Never one to turn anything down, though, she grabbed it and stormed towards the door. Edna turned apologetically to her employer.

"I'll be happy to work the extra hours until ye've located new staff, like. I hadn't a clue about her shenanigans, sir."

Fionnuala leaned against the brick wall in the buckets of rain that now emptied from the heavens. She was drenched in seconds. As the adrenaline coursed through her veins, as she heaved great gasps of anguish, she felt the noose of desperation tightening around the jowls of her neck, now with no source of gainful employment, and all the unpaid bills stretching before her like a long and winding endless road she had yet to climb.

Sniffling, she looked in confusion at the bright yellow envelope Edna had handed her. She tore it open as a passing truck splattered filth over her clothes. She blinked at the sparkly balloons and dancing bears in party hats on the card. *All The Best From One Who Loves You!* it exclaimed in colors of glee. Fionnuala whimpered, distraught, as tears erupted from her eyes anew and she shredded the mud-spattered card. The pieces fluttered to the sidewalk. She felt the blade of the ax that was her 45th birthday whizzing down to chop her bloated neck in two, and things would only get worse.

CHAPTER FIVE

On a desolate block in the wastelands of the Derry dockyards, MacAfee left his comrade Scudder in the driver's seat of the van, engine rumbling, and pushed himself through the pelting sheets of rain to the Pence-A-Day storage units office window. He had to ensure the flighty girl he had rented the lockup from the week before wouldn't see them unloading the gear. There she sat oblivious in her stripy top and dangling earrings, an H-bomb-cloud of red curls hovering over both her head and her massive breasts. She had a cellphone glued to an ear, one eye on a glossy celebrity magazine, the other staring intently through the filth of the window like a tiger ready to pounce.

The sight of her aroused MacAfee even as it disturbed: another example of the best of the Irish more interested in leafing through British publications, shoveling British crisps between her teeth, rather than joining the cause and freeing herself from the shackles of British cultural imperialism.

MacAfee turned to see what was causing the traitor such intense interest. The Protestant church across the street was being renovated, and the girl was hungrily taking in the backsides that strained the seams of the construction workers' overalls as they strut over the scaffolding. *Filthy slag,* MacAfee thought, *probably dying to fiddle with herself under the desk, and doing that with her wane screaming for a much-needed nappy change in its pram not two feet away!*

He crept back to the van outside Unit 12B, the shards of rain biting into his flesh, and nodded to Scudder.

"The daft cunt be's too busy staring at them workers' arses across the street to pay us any mind," he told Scudder through the unrolled window. "Let's unload the gear, and sharpish."

As Scudder prised himself out of the van, he raised a bushy eyebrow and ran fingers through what was left of his hair.

"Gagging to get her hole filled, is she?"

"Fancy yer chances, do ye, boyo?" MacAfee smirked, going with his mate to the back of the van.

"Let's see if we can't invite her for a spit roasting, twisting her round on the ends of wer knobs," Scudder suggested. He had the key to storage unit 12B's padlock and unlocked it, while MacAfee opened the back door of the van. "Like yer woman from the Jumping Hare last week."

"Shall we not focus on stockpiling the gear first?" MacAfee said, removing the old sheet that covered their load. "And mind ye don't trip on yer ego."

They reached into the back of the van, both smelling faintly of spent cigarettes and the previous night's drink. Just as their vision was mired in the past, so too were they walking fashion clichés of the decades which had formed them and beyond which they had yet to venture intellectually: MacAfee had a bad bleach job spiky with gel and a skinny brownish-pink leather jacket; Scudder an untidy beard—a regrettable choice when coupled with the few wisps of hair that clung to his misshapen scalp—and a denim shirt, jeans and a Thin Lizzie jacket that looked liked they hadn't seen the inside of a washing machine since the band's heavy metal had last graced the airwaves.

"What do ye think the odds are all them workers be's Catholic?" Scudder said with a nod at the church, taking a crate with Arabic lettering across it from the van. "Putting their skills to use for the Orange scum in the name of earning a few quid."

The Orange of the Irish flag had been appropriated by the Protestants as 'their' color; the Catholics chose the Green. Neither religion seemed interested in the White. Catholics working for Protestants angered MacAfee to no end as well, but he simply shrugged.

"Waste of their bloody time, so it is," he said, hauling out a carton of ski masks and placing it in the space. "Maybe we should blow up that Proddy church and all."

"When are we meant to receive that shipment of Semtex, then?" Putty-looking explosive material.

"Held up, so it was; some palaver about a spot of trouble in flimmin Budapest or Bucharest or feck knows where. Haven't spoken to yer man from the market in ages. Meant to be delivered in a case camouflaged as assorted tinned vegetables, it is. Let's deal with what we have now, and worry about that later, but. We've weeks until we need it, sure, for wer, what would ye call it?" His brain struggled for a moment as he hauled the detonators into the storage unit. "The *pièce de resistance* of wer operation."

"Piece de…Feck off, ye smarmy git, ye, or I'll shove the barrel of one of these assault rifles up yer intellectual hole. Next ye'll be telling me ye actually read books for pleasure."

The crate of AK-47 assault rifles thumped to the ground of the storage unit, and MacAfee slid a case of Soviet-made rocket-propelled grenades beside it.

"Ye know full well what I'm on about, but," he said.

"Och, aye surely. Blowing up the Top-Yer-Trolley during the annual sale and plastering wer names all over the dailies."

Scudder rubbed his hands in anticipation of the destruction of Derry's premier superstore, the carnage it would cost, then he struggled to pick up a rotting crate of ammunition rounds. The crate broke and the ammo scattered across the wet concrete.

"Christ almighty on a cross!" MacAfee wailed, scrambling for the rolling bullets. "Gather all them up before that wee girl in the office clocks us! One glance at wer gear, and we'll have to kill her before we've even had the chance to shag her."

They jumped for the ammunition, while inside the office, 19-year-old Dymphna Flood yelled down the phone:

"An hour, I've been waiting for ye to bring me some salve for the flimmin wane's nappy rash! Roaring out of itself with grief, so it is, and it's doing me head in! What would possess ye to guzzle down the drink at that swank Proddy pub with yer mates at," she glanced at her watch. "Half eleven in the morning? Aren't ye meant to be in one of yer classes?"

"Australia v. England, that's what," her fiancé Rory said through the roaring and laughter and clinking pint glasses. "I was passing the pub on me way to the chemists for to get the salve, and me mates inside caught sight of me. I had to join em for a pint. Only the one, mind. It's not me fault the match is being held in Sydney, and it's half-three there."

"If ye don't get yer drunken arse over here with that salve, it'll be the last match ye clamp eyes on, I swear to the merciful Lord. I'll gladly throttle the life outta yer son and all. And the next time ye have yer way with me in the bed, make sure it's more than a grunt and it's all over!"

She clacked the phone shut and seethed silently for a moment. She looked across the street and cursed the torrents of rain that had made the construction workers lumber out of her line of sight. Compared to those big-boned Catholic laborers, her Rory Riddell was an emaciated Protestant rake. Instead of their broad, cheery faces, she was saddled with a weasel: beady black eyes poking out from under the bangs of his greasy black bowl cut, the scraggly growth above his thin upper lip that was meant to be a mustache, his spindly limbs drowning in the oversized athletic jerseys—Umbro, Italia, Real Madrid, Brasilia—he never left the house without. Big bones and big grins was what she longed for; Rory had neither.

Dymphna kicked the stroller that held the bastard child responsible for the ludicrous engagement heading toward a mixed-marriage made in Hell. Six-month old Keanu erupted into another cackle of wails.

Ten months earlier, Dymphna thought all her Christmases had come at once: she had nabbed the engagement ring, vacated her slave-labor job shelling out fast food at the ChipKebab, moved from the decrepit Flood semi-detached council house in the Moorside into the swank bungalow on the Waterside, and anticipated a future lolling on a chaise lounge before a muted TV screen, nibbling Belgian chocolates and painting her toenails hot pink while she hummed along to something foreign—perhaps Yanni—as she imagined cultured people did.

Her reality was somewhat different: Rory's mother, Zoë, greeted her with a look behind her harsh Burberry frames as if both heels of her Christian Louboutins had just trodden in dog shit, and promptly put her to work at the family business for a slave-wage. Dymphna was a stranger amongst the high-end knickknacks she couldn't understand in the house in the Orange neighborhood, where she rolled the stroller past curbs painted the colors of the British flag and dodged rocks the neighborhood children threw her way; Rory was "doing a course" at MacGee University, which, as far as Dymphna could tell, meant getting bladdered with his mates at all hours of the day and night and little else. They shared an uncomfortable bed; he hadn't touched her flesh in weeks, which actually didn't come as a relief; she had needs of the flesh that needed tending to. And then there was the child. Keanu suffered from a long and winding list of infections: urinary and ear, impetigo, gastroenteritis, and a smattering of cold sores. The only part of his biology that seemed to function properly was his lungs.

Dymphna glared at the present she had bought for her mother's birthday.

She punched numbers into the office calculator and worked out how many hours of her own hard graft it had cost. Her resentment grew. Why was it so bloody expensive? She picked up the box and read it. She learned all about the foot spa's six rotating hydro jets to pamper tired, listless feet, its soothing heat source, and, her interest increasing, the reflexology rollers and splash guard. When she got to the massaging gel pads and toe-touch controls, she was on the verge of gifting it to herself, but knew Fionnuala deserved it, after all the torture following the Barnett's lottery win the year before, and then Dymphna shaming her mother further by moving in with Protestant bastards; plus, if Dymphna kept the foot spa for herself, what else could she possibly give Fionnuala for her birthday?

Dymphna had tried the sentimental route the previous Christmas, with a framed photo of her and Fionnuala's first grandson Keanu posing in Santa caps, but her mother had seen it for what it was: cheap. And Fionnuala had spared no breath pointing this out after one brandy too many during the Queen's Christmas speech. It didn't matter what Dymphna gave her; Fionnuala never seemed overjoyed. Dymphna was actually intelligent enough to realize she wasn't Fionnuala's favorite child; that honor was always reserved for boys, especially those in prison, and the Flood family had two, Lorcan and Eoin—their incarcerations, one for grievous bodily harm, the other for drug dealing, had done nothing to dampen Fionnuala's love for them; in fact, their absence seemed to make her heart grow fonder. Dymphna even suspected that young Padraig and Siofra, and maybe even Seamus, who was only five and still didn't have a personality as far as she could tell, came before her in the queue. Even the eldest, Moira, who was a degenerate—

Dymphna jumped as the text on her cellphone pinged. She saw with some trepidation it was from her mate Kate, a receptionist at the Health Clinic. Dymphna had paid a frantic visit there a few days earlier. Kate had access to the confidential test files patients normally needed to trek to the clinic and hear the results of from the mouth of the doctor herself, but Dr. Khudiadadzai was a Pakistani who, of course, couldn't be trusted, and also cast disapproving glances down her stethoscope. Dymphna had asked Kate to fill her in when the results were ready.

She read the text, her eyes darting helplessly from side to side. She bit into her fist as the whimpers of a small forest animal escaped her lips. Forgotten was the foot spa.

She lit a cigarette and puffed it to the butt, then punched her best mate's Bridie's number into the phone, her fingers fluttering with panic and distress. The phone went straight to voicemail. As usual, lately.

"Right, ye feckers! Bridie here," Bridie's hearty and friendly, if slurred, voice said. "I'm filling me gullet with drink at the moment and kyanny be arsed to take yer call, hi, leave a message ye slaaag, cheerio!" *Beep!*

"Och, Bridie, it's terrible, so it is!" Dymphna wailed down the phone. "I kyanny get me head round it! Kate from the clinic's after texting me and letting me know I'm six weeks up the duff. With another half-Proddy bastard, would ye credit it! Am about to slit me wrists here, I'm desperate for someone to talk to, and me fingers be's bloody from dialing yer number. Phone me, would ye, ye daft bitch?!"

She clicked the phone shut, feeling somewhat guilty for having lied to her best friend. She wasn't pregnant with a second half-Protestant child, because the father of Keanu was really—

Dymphna squealed as the door flew open and an alkie staggered in, eyes crazed with cheap gin, hair finger-in-a-socket-like. He brandished a sharpened screwdriver in his left fist.

"Lemme at me lockup!" he seethed.

"Och, Mr. Tomlinson," Dymphna said, deflating. "I near shite meself at the sight of ye."

"Ye've changed the lock on me unit, and I kyanny get at me belongings."

Most clients of Pence-A-Day were Protestant, as it was on the Waterside of the town, but Zoë Riddell, her bleeding heart quaking with the liberalness of it all, had arranged a scheme with the City Council so the financially-challenged would be subsidized by the government and pay pennies on the pound. Mr. Tomlinson was one such client, and even though he had touched Dymphna up on the playground once when she was a primary schoolgirl and was sputtering his frustration all over the foot spa and waving the screwdriver close to her nose, Dymphna relaxed: he was one of her own.

"Ye've not paid the rental in months, but," Dymphna said; she knew his case. "Ye're seven pounds in arrears."

"I told that daft Orange mother-in-law of yers—"

"She's not me mother-in-law yet," Dymphna said through gritted teeth. She swiped at the wavering point of the tool. "And get that flimmin thing outta me face, or I'll swipe ye in the gob. Would ye look at the state of ye! Wild looking, so ye are. Why've ye let yerself go so?"

He was torn between weaving back and forth in anger and ogling her shapely bosom.

"Gimme the key," he pleaded.

"I kyanny," Dymphna said. "Mrs. Riddell keeps em locked up."

He began to sob, and suddenly her heart went out to him, startling herself with the realization that some people's lives might actually be worse than her own. Plus, he was Catholic.

"Och, I don't give a flying feck," Dymphna decided, getting up from the desk and grabbing the lock cutter. "I owe no allegiance to that smarmy Proddy bitch with them two dots over her name. Can ye imagine such airs? C'mere you with me, and I'll let ye in. What do ye need with such urgency from yer lockup, anyroad?"

"Me methadone!" he barked, scampering after her as best he could on his jittery legs.

"Yer…?" Dymphna's step faltered, seeing him as diseased.

They had almost reached the door, and Tomlinson turned to mutter his gratitude but spit up all over Dymphna's top instead. She screamed down at the mess splattered over the stripes, the tears stinging her eyes from the stench of gin and bile.

"Terrible sorry, love. Let me clean ye up," Tomlinson sputtered apologetically.

Dymphna was about to protest, but couldn't shake from her mind a vision of deadly viruses coursing through his bodily fluid. She didn't want to put a finger near it; let him reinfect himself.

"Aye, right ye are," she grimly gave in, passing him an oily rag. "Mind ye go gently, but, over me fun bags."

His grunting and the glazed look in his eyes as he brought the rag towards her cleavage, plus the memory of that playground visit made her think better of him pawing her—

"Hold on a wee moment there."

—and also, to her dawning horror, the liquid was seeping through the polyester of her top. Her hands flapped helplessly at her sides as squeals of panic stuck in her throat. She was terrified of Tomlinson smearing his bile into her flesh and causing his disease to seep into some unknown pores of her skin. She couldn't embarrass him by letting him know why it was gripping her with such fear.

"Get it off me, just! Get me top off me this minute!" she begged, her feet stomping wildly, and in the corner Keanu erupted with new shrieks.*"Get it offa me, ye mindless geebag!"*

Tomlinson's glazed eyes danced with sudden glee, and he tore the top from her, Dymphna's breasts spilling out like the screams spilled from her mouth.

Through the window, Scudder and MacAfee stood in alarm at what they thought they were seeing: a shambling, sex-crazed tramp tearing the top off the girl, tears of fear rolling down her face, her trying feebly to ward him off with a lock cutter. They were all for group sex, but not forced. They flew inside the office, roaring with rage.

"Hands offa her!"

"Away from the wee girl, ye minging alkie nonce perv!"

"I'll clatter the fecking shite outta ye, ye fecking rapist!"

Scudder hauled Tomlinson's grimy hands off Dymphna, MacAfee's fist landed in his stomach, and Tomlinson reeled as their steel-tipped boots shot toward him.

"Naw! Leave the aul one be!" Dymphna pleaded. "He's helping me, just!"

Scudder and MacAfee started, and as the two strangers unhanded the cowering and whimpering Tomlinson, Dymphna felt the clammy pile of sick that had trickled down her jeans seeping through the denim.

"Me jeans! Me jeans! I need to get em offa me and all!"

Dymphna stepped feverishly out of her sling-backs and tugged at her zipper. MacAfee and Scudder exchanged a disbelieving look. The three lumpen men in a swiftly-decreasing horseshoe around her couldn't believe their luck as she peeled the jeans off and panted there before them on the varnished wood of the office floor, her fingernails scrabbling in relief over her bare flesh, her bra and panties and what lay beyond the culmination of all their pervy dreams. Leers broke out all around, and Dymphna was about to explain and apologize and praise the Lord for the quick action to ensure she was disease-free when—

"Dymphna! What the bleeding feck?! Three at once?"

Dymphna looked in alarm past her drooping bra strap. Rory stood at the door, his jaw agape, chemist's bag clasped in a hand that curled into a fist.

"Me mammy was spot on about ye!"

CHAPTER SIX

Where the name of all that's sacred has that wee girl got to with me fags? Flimmin useless gack, so she is! As lazy as her mother.

Maureen Heggarty, 74, weak with age and nicotine withdrawl, creaked open the door to her grandson Padraig's bedroom and was knocked back on her cane, stunned, at the air inside.

She had rejoiced a year earlier when her only daughter Fionnuala moved her into the Flood family home in the relative splendor of the Moorside. The two-story semi-detached house, 5 Murphy Crescent, had long been the Flood home until the Barnett's lotto win three years earlier. Ursula had foolishly bought it from the city council and claimed it as her own, to the uproar of her brothers and sisters, and especially her sister-in-law Fionnuala. Fionnuala had badgered—*persecuted*—the Barnetts into handing over the house before they escaped to Wisconsin, USA. Maureen had watched the proceedings from afar in her council flat in Creggan Heights with slight disapproval. Now 5 Murphy Crescent was an unsightly mess of loose pebbledash that squatters bypassed with a renewed sense of dignity at their lives, and Maureen had been uprooted to become indentured housekeeper and day carer of the Floods youngest spawn: 5-year-old Seamus, 8-year-old Siofra and 11-year-old Padraig. All the appliances had been sold off to pay bills, and it was less a home and more a warehouse which stored their sleeping bodies at night.

Maureen still hadn't made her mind up if Ursula handing over the house was righting a misguided indiscretion, extreme generosity, or rewarding bad behavior, but Maureen always thought back to the gift with a sense of admiration. Had Ursula known exactly what she was doing? Maureen wondered at night, saddling Paddy and Fionnuala with two council taxes, two electricity bills, two gas bills, two sets of windows, bathrooms and fireplaces to scrub, two sets of plumbing to fix, and two gardens to tend. Ursula was either a saint walking among the living or a sleekit, sly bitch, and Maureen knew which version she preferred.

A right smelly bastard, that Padraig, Maureen mused now as she forced the tip of her cane through the wild-fox stench and the filth that littered the threadbare carpeting. And years of looking at her second youngest grandson hadn't made him easier on the eyes: the bright orange hair gene was certainly her son-in-law's fault, as were the invisible eyelashes, translucent eyebrows and the albino skin. He had lately affected a sarcastic, menacing glint in the eyes that had her fearing for both his sanity and her safety.

Maureen wrenched the window open, and realized that for the odor she was partly to blame. She had fallen behind in the washing; it had to be done by hand in the kitchen sink because there was no washer and dryer. Maureen knew Padraig had run out of fresh underpants the Tuesday before and had been wearing his swimming trunks since. And only Lord knew how long his socks had been plastered to his feet.

She caught sight of curry- and tomato sauce-encrusted plates and bowls scattered beside his bed and was surprised. She thought Fionnuala had sold off all the china the week before.

"For the love of God, wee boy," Maureen muttered to herself, "ye think ye'd have the strength for to carry yer own dishes down to the scullery!"

She stuck the tip of her cane under the bed, dreading what she might uncover. It clanked against something hard. Leveling herself on the stiff bedcovers with her hand so she wouldn't topple over, she ran the cane up the length of the item. It was about half a foot tall.

Maureen's brow wrinkled with suspicion. She calculated the time and effort it would take to configure her brittle bones into a crouch to look under the bed, and decided to unearth the items with her cane. She nudged out a black plastic box with a big X on it. Confused, she scratched her cane under the bed for more. She uncovered another plastic box, this one white and sleeker than the first. A minute later, they were joined by what looked like those new shiny videos, (DVDs, she thought they were called) *Grand Theft Auto, Resident Evil,* and *50 Cent: Bulletproof.*

She stopped there. The further her cane dared, the more serious her crime as an accomplice would be when the police came calling. Maureen couldn't be bothered sitting down just to get back up again, so she stood there on her cane, inspecting the peeling wallpaper, until the bathroom door finally opened and Padraig bounded into the room, wrapped in the remnants of a towel.

"What in the name of all that's sacred be's themmuns?" she demanded.

"I found em!" Padraig brayed with an ease that only a lifetime of lies could affect.

"Ye must think I was born yesterday!"

For Padraig, nothing was further from the truth. He looked at a smattering of gray wisps of hair atop a pink scalp like melted plastic, skeletal arms and legs which clattered inside a fluorescent green track suit like poles in a tent, blood red frames circling a death's head of a face, accentuated, even at this early hour, by a slash of red lipstick. He didn't even have to look "up;" Maureen was barely as tall as the 11-year-old himself.

"I didn't ask ye where ye got em from, anyroad, I asked ye what the bloody hell they be's."

"That be's an X-Box, and—"

Maureen froze at the 'X,' visions of tits and arses dancing in her mind. "What in the name of all that's blessed be's an X-Box when it's at home?" she chanced.

"For video games, Granny."

"Is that what themmuns be'se?" She pointed her cane at the covers celebrating blood and gore.

He nodded.

"And what be's this white contraption, would ye mind telling us?"

"It be's a Wii, Granny."

"Don't ye get sarky with me! Tell me what it be's!"

"It's a Wii," Padraig insisted.

"Wee? Ye mean like 'little' wee or 'toilet' wee?"

"Naw, Granny, it's W-I-I."

"Ye're having me on!"

"It says right there on the side of it, like. It's for games and all. Ye've got to stand for them ones, but."

"X-Box, Wii, no mind, both be's foolish, goofy names. Dreamed up, I've no doubt, by some silly Yank corporation with more money than sense. Cost a pretty penny, making them with more money than sense prise open their wallets and all. High-priced luxuries posing as must-haves for every family, me arse! Why are ye looking at me like that, wee boy? I'll clatter ye round the skull! Ye're not getting much use outta them games, hidden under yer bed as they be. Up to no bleeding good, so ye are! Just because yer mammy lets ye run riot is no reason why I kyanny clatter the shite outta ye, ye thieving spastic!"

Smack! Smack! Smack!

Padraig yelped as the cane beat on his head. Now that she had done what was expected as a grandmother with a good moral compass, Maureen turned with a secret smile. Wee Padraig was indeed a treasure, she thought (physical attributes aside): he had started off with casual violence against pensioners, graduated to petrol bombs, and was now migrating to petty crime at the tender age of eleven; it was obvious to her the nefarious Heggarty blood flowed through his veins.

Five year old Seamus, a collection of black curls perched atop wobbly legs, padded into the bedroom, rubbing sleep out of his eyes and clutching a shapeless thing that had at some stage been fluffy and an animal, but which one nobody could now recall.

"Is Padraig after doing a boo boo?" he asked.

Maureen was about to put on the pretense that Padraig had indeed done something wrong, and berate him further to heighten the youngest child's sense of morality, when they jumped as a unit at the front door flying open and Siofra's tortured wails.

"Granny! Granny!"

"Me fags!" Maureen put the chairlift on the quickest speed.

Siofra was at the bottom of the stairs. She was drenched to the bone, her lips puffy, her eyes watery. Maureen pried herself out of the chairlift and demanded: "Where's me fags?"

"Me Hannah Montana watch has been nicked, and the matching earrings and all!" Siofra wailed. "A thieving Proddy cunt beat the living shite outta me and grabbed them offa me!"

Padraig sneered, Seamus was still making his way down the stairs, and Maureen set her lips even as she puffed away on the cigarette.

"Is this yer way of trying to let on you've no change from that ten pound note I gave ye?" she asked.

Siofra released some coins into the outstretched hand. Maureen inspected them; she wouldn't put it past her granddaughter to orchestrate some torn tights and a roll in the muck for the sake of slipping some cash into her PowerPuff Girls handbag. Which, Maureen suddenly noticed, did seem to be battered, the strap torn. Still, she said:

"There's fifty pence missing."

"It…it must've fallen outta me top in the fight. It be's the God's honest truth, but!" Siofra sobbed.

"Where's the bin liner?" Maureen asked. "How many of them cans did ye collect on yer way to the shops? Yer mammy needs twenty more for the Sav-U-Mor shelves the morrow, and if ye haven't got em she'll clatter the living shite outta ye."

Siofra looked at her empty hands in confusion.

"I'm wile sorry, Granny. I must've tossed the bag away in me haste to get to safety."

"Are ye telling me ye kyanny look after yerself on the streets?" Maureen finally asked, bewildered. "What if wee Seamus had been with ye? Ye would've been putting yer younger brother at risk from all sorts."

"What's up with Siofra?" Seamus asked, finally reaching the bottom of the stairs.

Siofra cursed. Now they were in a semi-circle surrounding and inspecting her. The looks in their eyes branded her a victim.

"I'm mortified, Granny, aye, I am. The toerag was twice the size of a boat, but. She must be one of them what eats three whole meals a day. A giant Proddy beast, so she was," she insisted.

Calmed by the tobacco intake, Maureen could now check her granddaughter out. Siofra might be a heinous little beast, but the grandmother in Maureen felt her heart swell at the laceration on her young flesh and the bloody lip, and the gash on the foot which Siofra felt compelled to display. Siofra's sobs of anguish reached near hysteria. Taken aback, Maureen wasn't sure where to put her eyes, so she chose an empty corner over the girl's left shoulder where a hall stand had once been. Victims of violence was one thing the Heggartys traditionally were not, and although Maureen knew sending an elementary school child out into the wasteland of the estate with cold cash on her was madness, she thought all Fionnuala's litter had popped out of her womb with street smarts intact.

The anger eventually reached Maureen's brain. "What's the wee stoke's name? I'll set me sons round to their house on the Fountain Estate to beat the shite outta the wee cunt's mother!"

Siofra and Padraig stared at their grandmother through the cloud of smoke; all their uncles on their mother's side had rigged the green card lottery years ago and abandoned the dreary town, having long ago emigrated to America, Australia and South Africa, where they worked as bartenders in Irish pubs.

Padraig vowed: "Go on you and point her out to me when we're out down the town together, Siofra. I'll clatter the shite outta her."

Siofra looked at him with gratitude.

"That's that settled, then," Maureen said with a note of relief. She jerked with sudden shock. "Jesus, Mary and Joseph! Is that the time? Late for to get me ears syringed at the Health Clinic, I'm going to be, and youse wanes is going to be tardy for school and all! Throw them uniforms on and get yerselves off. You, Padraig, clutch the hand of yer delicate rose of a sister there on her way to school. That one kyanny fend for herself on the streets. And mind youse scrounge up something for yer mammy's birthday celebration the night. She's given me the key to their house so's we can make her favorite for tea. She told me to pick her up after her shift so's I can escort her around the corner and youse can all scream and act the fool when she walks through the door, like. How in the name of God that's meant to be a surprise, I haven't a clue; them is her instructions, but."

In five minutes, Siofra and Padraig had flung their uniforms on and launched themselves down the street towards their respective schools, Siofra staring down gleefully at the fifty pence piece still clutched in her sticky palm. Maureen was wrapping Seamus up to fend the rain off of him when the letter box clanked, a version of knocking on the door.

"Of all the times!" she muttered, forcing herself to the door.

"A package for Dymphna Flood," the courier said from the depths of his motorcycle helmet. Maureen remembered when every merchant clattering the letter box, from the postman to the milkman to the coal man to the rag-and-bone man, had been the son of a nephew or the uncle of a cousin. Maureen hadn't a clue where the new companies shipped their employees in from nowadays, but the fact that this courier was a stranger made her task now so much easier.

"That be's me," she said.

Seamus looked up in alarm. "Granny, but ye're not—"

She nudged the child to the side with her cane, then signed for the package and slammed the door on the unknown bastard's face.

Maureen inspected the brown paper with suspicion. It was addressed to her shameless slapper of a granddaughter, Dymphna, who had moved out of 5 Murphy to cavort with the Enemy, and it had a peculiar postmark in a language Maureen didn't understand. But the stamp was of a sunset and said Malta, and she certainly knew the return addressee: Moira Flood. Maureen let out a squeal as if they had just called the final number on her bingo card at the St. Molaug's senior center. Seamus waved his shapeless thing happily and gurgled along with her.

"Mary mother of God!" Maureen gasped with wonder. "It's been a long time coming, but it's actually seen the light of day! As God's me witness, I kyanny believe I'm holding it in me hand."

"What does it be, Granny?" Seamus asked.

"Poison, wee boy!" she said as her eyes danced with glee. "Poison pure and simple from the pen of yer oldest sister, Moira!"

Although her body shivered with delight, she felt queasy even uttering Moira's name.

"The filthy bean-flicking perv?" the little boy quoted, eyes beaming in recognition.

"I should take a bar of soap to yer mouth for uttering the words of yer elders and betters, but, aye, the filthy bean-flicking perv," Maureen confirmed, patting him on the head; he had been taught well. "I kyanny wait to see the look on yer mammy's face when I show her. Priceless, it's gonna be!"

She hugged the package to the clunky buttons of her duffle coat, grappled Seamus' hand and hobbled out of the house toward the mini-bus stop as quickly as her osteoporosis could take her. A smile played on the slit of lipstick. For once, standing in the queue for the mini-bus in the horizontal rain, the ride through the panorama of bludgeoned mattresses and mutts copulating in mud, the drunken roars of abuse at the nape of her neck from the back seats, the endless wait on the unsightly and uncomfortable orange plastic chair of the Health Clinic, all would be a delight. Dr. Khudiadadzai could take her time calling her into the room to get her ears syringed; Maureen would be drinking in every word of every page, and she couldn't wait to claim a seat in the front row of the performance of tears and outrage that would be unleashed once Fionnuala set eyes on the book about the Floods.

CHAPTER SEVEN

Paddy Flood's elbow was shoved from behind, and his tikka masala Cup-O-Noodles splattered up his overalls, down the still-steaming kettle and over the staff room floor.

"Och, for the love of—!"

"Sorry, mate," Paddy heard in his left ear. It was not the voice of a friend.

As the culprit slipped away with a snigger, Paddy imagined his steel-tipped boot sailing through the air and cracking against the fat bastard's jaw, cracked teeth spilling out of a mouth that poured blood. He settled for mopping up the scalding ochre noodles with a stiff dishrag and a hand that trembled with repressed rage. Paddy, the wrong side of 45, youthful brawn a memory that sagged like his stomach, slicked black hair graying, was too exhausted after four hours of slopping up fish guts and scales to stick up for himself. And it had proved useless in the past.

Behind his clenched shoulders, the oily overall-clad workers of the Fillets-O-Joy fish packing plant were bunched around the tables, oversized rubber gloves cast to the floor beside clunky boots, tearing at sopping paper that held fish and doner kebabs and battered sausages and chips, digging into foil containers of curry chips and mushy peas, their loud still-boozy voices ringing out. The acid stench of vinegar and sweat stabbed the air, the gnashing of teeth and slurping of lips as they tore at the carbohydrates and flesh. Paddy peered sadly at the remains in his styrofoam cup, then, dodging the daggers and sneers aimed at him from under the hairnets and grimy peaked caps, made his way to the lone chair at the empty table next to the stench of the staff lavatories that was reserved for him.

"Fecking lord of the manor," he thought he heard through teeth that held sausage batter captive at the next table.

Paddy was as ravenous as he was hungover and still reeling from the abuse done to his locker that morning (*Hang the Snob at our Job* and *Flush Cunt*) to care about this emergency union meeting. And the irony wasn't lost on him that everybody else had handed over five quid to the chip van that pulled up to the plant parking lot every day at twelve, while he was saddled with noodles Fionnuala had bought at the Top-Yer-Trolley in a jumbo budget packet of twenty-four.

"Right, quiet youse down," said the union representative, Callum Sheeney, and he too was looking at Paddy as if he had some bold-faced cheek to be sat there with genuine members of the working class. "We've not much time, so let's get started, shall we?"

Callum turned down the transistor radio blaring out tinny renditions of pop tunes six years old.

"Death and dismemberment be's plaguing wer plant!" Callum roared. Paddy slurped a noodle. "Them new machines be's putting both wer jobs and wer lives at risk. We've had the forklift what grappled Liam McGillicutty's foot and hauled him twelve feet into the air before releasing him to the shop floor and his deathbed. And mind Gertie Feeney, her right hand mangled in the grinding machine. Three hours, it took, to find that finger of hers in the jumbo shrimp. And poor aul Gallagher, yer man who couldn't make head nor tail of the new automatic freezer locks. Hours, it took, before they could free him from his icy coffin, and then a further week to defrost fully."

Arms and legs shifted uncomfortably, Paddy's more than most. The duties were meant to change weekly according to some mysterious roster: unloading fish from boats, sorting them by species, putting them in brine and storing them in ice, manning the conveyor belts of the packing machines, and dumping fish meal and bran into the mixing and grinding machines for fish feed. Danger seemed to lurk in every corner of the plant, but the last task was the most dangerous, because of the relentless pull of conveyor belts that led to mysterious lead caverns which sliced and diced through bone, grizzle and offal. For the past year, the roster had Paddy on the mixing and grinding machines. Or cleanup.

"We know all this, aye, what are ye on about?" someone spoke up.

"Would ye believe the plant received yet another of them flimmin grinding and mixing machines the day? And there's two more packing machines on the way. It won't be long before they've replaced us on the floor, or, even worse, sent us all to intensive care. We kyanny go on like this, waking up every morning thankful we've all ten fingers and toes, grateful for the chance to breathe God's air another day."

Paddy thought back to the many times at the conveyor belt he had felt a pang of pain and stared down the length of his arm in horror, wondering where the hell his hand was. He always found it there at the end of his wrist, but Paddy knew well enough why he was willing to take the risks the plant presented, and what a greater danger might be: the blades of an industrial grinder were no match for Fionnuala's tongue.

"It's time for industrial action!" Callum roared.

"Ye mean...?"

"Aye, a strike!"

A roar erupted as if Ireland had scored a final goal against England, and fists banged on tables in unison.

"*Strike, strike, strike!*" their bleacher-chant rang out.

Cod jumped on melmac, tea spilled from styrofoam, but amidst all the excitement, Paddy's brain felt a slight unease as he followed the plan of a strike in his mind from A to B to C, and, his already bloodless face turning more ashen, slowly computed the thing missing from this socialist wet dream: a voice of reason.

He raised a timid hand. Eyes rolled the length of the room, and arms sprang around chests. Callum fought to affect a friendly smile as he nodded for the pariah of the packing plant to speak.

"Am I correct in thinking," Paddy said, "that while we're striking we're to receive no pay?"

"Of course not, naw."

"God bless us and save us! I kyanny feed me wanes if we're to spend wer days traipsing around in a flimmin circle outside the plant instead of collecting wer weekly paychecks!"

He appealed to his former friends.

"Have youse not given that one moment of thought?"

"Och, go on away with that!" someone spat.

"Ye're taking the piss, surely?" spat someone else.

"The bold-face cheek of the jammy bastard!"

"Youse Floods is minted!"

Persecuted and crucified, more like, Paddy thought grimly to himself.

"The community will rally around us," Callum put in. "At least, around those of us what needs help. There are sure to be food drives at the churches, raffles arranged to assist us in paying wer rents. Some of us, of course," he raised an eyebrow, "have no rent needing to be paid."

"If Paddy Flood's against it," roared somebody. "I'm all for it!"

"Aye, me and all!"

"And me!"

"Put it to the vote now, shall we?" Callum called out. "All for?"

Hands shot up in the air around Paddy in such unison and with such force it was as if he had stepped into a BNP demo.

"Against?"

Paddy inspected his empty Cup-O-Noodles, his arm unable to move, as silence reigned in the staffroom. Callum glared triumphantly at him.

"That's settled, aye? Monday we strike!"

The roars of the lumpen masses rang out, and Paddy deflated, while all around him the hoarse manly chants broke out anew, visions of a socialist victory, a finger to the capitalist death machine dancing in his co-workers' minds, and all the while the only thing Paddy saw was his miniscule bank balance disappearing and rage spewing from Fionnuala's lipstick. Chairs scraped, the workers lugged the gloves onto their hands, slapped one other's shoulders and asses, and all walked out to finish their shifts before clocking out and then downing a few pints in the pub and then going home to eat. Fish.

CHAPTER EIGHT

"And then, and then," Rory sniffed, "I saw them three filthy aul men circling her half-naked body, and the worst of it, Mammy, was the look of *thanks* on her face as they moved in to have their way with her."

Zoë lifted a well-moisturized hand to his face.

"You're giving my mind images it'll never erase," she said stiffly. "Please stop."

"How could she do it, but, ma? *How?*"

"It was always a ludicrous pairing. I told you from the beginning I would have happily paid for a termination to stop this charade of happy families."

"I know she be's a C—"

"Her religion has not a jot to do with it. I've always found the girl particularly repellent. Slovenly, ill-mannered, and worst of all, dim-witted. The name she insisted on for the child is evidence enough of that. She could be a Gnostic monk for all I care. The good Lord alone knows what your offspring will grow up to be with a gene pool like that."

Zoë's face softened, and she coddled Rory's sobbing head in her scant bosom.

"If anything," she sighed, "I blame myself for raising you so well, *too* well. I always taught you to take responsibility for your actions, even those brought about by the stupidity of downing vast amounts of alcohol."

Truth be told, Rory could remember only snippets of the lager-fueled encounter that had brought him and Dymphna together: a styrofoam container of curry chips, the meter of a taxi cab, fingers ripping at buttons, a traffic cone standing in the corner of the shabby sitting room, a glimpse of the Bleeding Heart of Jesus staring down at them from above an unknown settee with springs poking out, the torn elasticated band of his crusty briefs.

"I do understand," Zoë cooed on, fingers caressing the grease of his black hair, "the pride and excitement you must have felt when this girl told you she was carrying your child. Any other lad your age would have run a mile, but thanks to the virtues I've instilled in you, you stepped up to the plate and took responsibility for your moment of weakness."

The inevitability of it all was staring Rory squarely in his acne-cluttered face as it sidled uncomfortably against his mother's breastplate: he and Dymphna were a joke as a couple. And now that home truths were being revealed, he chanced with a snivel:

"She kept insisting I wasn't the father, ma. The mortification of it! There she is, with me wane inside her, and she be's blathering on to anybody in

31

town who would listen that the father be's Mr. O'Toole, her boss at the Top-Yer-Trolley. Ages, it took me, to make her see sense, force the engagement ring on her finger at the ChipKebab. Why was she so ashamed of me being the father? Am I such a toerag? Why, Mammy, *why?* And adding insult to injury by claiming O'Toole, of all men in Derry, was the father. Him with the mincing steps and limp wrists!"

The silence lasted so long, Rory feared his mother had gone mute. He chanced a look up and was greeted by two horror-stricken eyes behind the Burberry frames. Zoë's fingers shackled themselves into his scalp, and she pried him from her breast.

"What's this about Henry O'Toole?" she demanded. "What are you telling me?"

"She, she, I, I..."

"I knew it," Zoë seethed, "I knew it the way a mother does. That red hair, those blue eyes, that chin. The child bears no resemblance to you or me or any of the Riddells. It's a Flood and an O'Toole, through and through."

"Mammy, but, but... O'Toole be's an arse-bandit, a nancy-boy poofter."

"He's a prancing, leering goat! Couldn't keep his hands off my tights at last year's Derry Entrepreneurs Christmas do at the Gleneagles Hotel after a few shots of whiskey down his throat. I felt soiled until New Year's. Where is the repellent creature now?"

"O'Toole?"

"Dymphna!"

"In our room, packing."

While folding her smalls, Dymphna flinched through her tears as the door to the bedroom flew open and Zoë came barreling towards her.

"Out! Out of my house now!"

"I'm trying, sure," Dymphna said. "I'm after clearing out—"

"My bank account? My money's the only thing you're after! Let me have a look in there."

Zoë pushed Dymphna to the side and scrabbled through the clothing in the suitcase on the bed.

"My 7 For All Mankind jeans?" Zoë said. She shook her head as she removed them and dug in for more. "Thousands, I've spent, on designer gear for you to tart yourself up in since you forced your way into our home. And this is how you thank me?"

Rory eyed Dymphna with a mixture of disappointment and suspicion and moved to the bed to help his mother. Flush with mortification, Dymphna bit her lip and watched as fingers clawed through her bras and tights and private belongings. She longed to explain she was doing Zoë a favor by taking the jeans as they made her arse look saggy, but didn't trust herself to talk back to a woman who could afford such a fancy toothbrush.

"Rogues on parade," Zoë muttered, inspecting with disgust, then tossing to the side, the portrait of the Flood family posed before the washing machine in their kitchen. It was taken with a disposable camera months before Lorcan and Eoin had been sent to prison, Fionnuala smiling proudly from a tattered chair in the middle. Zoë dug further in the suitcase but reached the bottom, to her disappointment and Rory's relief, without incident.

"The ring," Zoë demanded.

Dymphna looked down at her engagement ring.

"Rory give it me, but!" she pleaded. "It be's the symbol of wer love!"

"Love. That's a laugh, indeed. It was bought on my debit card. I know only too well the likes of you, Dymphna Flood. The moment you step out that door, you'd be over to the pawn shop to flog it for drinking money or worse. The ring, please."

"Rory!" Dymphna pleaded.

Rory just stood there, stone-faced, slightly behind his mother. Dymphna sobbed as she tugged the ring off and reluctantly handed it over.

"The key to the office if you please," Zoë continued. "I don't want you rummaging around the lockups, stealing all the belongings our clients are entrusting us to keep under lock and key."

"What about me job?" Dymphna asked. She hated it, but she was at least paid a wage and could come out of the engagement with a steady source of income for diapers.

Zoë raised a waxed eyebrow. "You can forget that as well. It's clear to me the one thing you're not going to die of is a work-related illness. And certainly not while you're in the habit of using the office as a personal... pleasure dome."

Dymphna threw the key in her hand. She forced the top on the straining suitcase and sat on it to clasp it shut.

"And I do believe you have forgotten something," Zoë said, with a nod in the corner.

Dymphna thought for a moment she meant the foot spa sitting on the nightstand, but disappointment flickered as she realized Zoë was indicating Keanu. Dymphna placed him over her shoulder, hauled the suitcase up with one hand, the foot spa with the other and made her way through the door.

"If you so much as glance at my son again, I'll throttle the life out of your bones with my bare hands," Zoë said as they descended the stairs, "then dance with glee on the Y-shaped coffin they're going to have to bury you in."

Dymphna couldn't help but feel their careful eyes on her back, as if the Riddells expected her to snatch one of the Lladró figurines that lined the landing wall and make her way out the door with it. How that might be possible, as full as her suitcase and hands were, she couldn't imagine. While Keanu spit up down her back and she struggled to locate the front door knob through teary eyes, Dymphna appealed to Rory with the look of the last urchin in an orphanage.

"Rory?"

Her feminine charms had deserted her in his mind. He was having none of it.

"Go," he said.

Dymphna threw the now shrieking child into its stroller, tossed the foot spa on top of him and stormed out the door. Four steps on, she was wondering how quickly she could get Child Protective Services involved, what financial services they might offer and where to stop to clean the sick off her back.

When the door slammed (it did slam), Rory burst into tears, and Zoë cradled her love in her arms.

"There, there, my sweet child," she soothed. "You're well rid of that filthy Fenian beast. Mammy knows best for you, yes she does, Mammy knows best…"

But behind the Burberry frames, Zoë's eyes flickered with guilt.

CHAPTER NINE

In the computer room of Our Lady of Perpetual Sorrow Girls' School, Miss McClurkin, dried egg on her blouse, was flipping through the newspaper. Her droopy eyes resisted a glance at the Positions Available section. The girls were supposed to be researching forest animals, but most were on pop star websites, whispering amongst themselves.

Siofra Flood was searching for cardboard coffins. According to the Internet, they only had them in China. Siofra was perplexed. Did the girl who had stolen her Hannah Montana fan club exclusives think she was Chinese?

As her little fingers clacked on the sticky keyboard, Siofra was well aware of the bareness of her left wrist, the lightness of her earlobes, as she thought back to what else the horrible girl had said: 'people who work for a living can afford things;' Siofra's mammy and daddy did nothing but work, and still they could afford very little; that 'Catholics smoke and drink themselves into an early grave;' sure, her granny Heggarty was never without a fag hanging from her mouth, and she was ancient and Catholic!

Siofra's best mate Grainne Donaldson suddenly clutched her arm with excitement.

"Would ye look at that, Siofra?" she marveled in a whisper, flipping her computer screen so Siofra could see it. "Hannah Montana's traveling all the way to Ireland for to throw a concert next month!"

Although Hannah Montana was now calling herself Miley Cyrus, she would always be Hannah Montana to the little girls. That the teenaged American TV and singing sensation would be in their part of the world was like Christmas morning, an Easter Egg hunt and the final of *American Idol* all rolled into one.

"Effin magic!" Siofra gasped.

Grainne stared at her ears.

"Siofra? Where's them Hannah Montana earrings of yers? And the matching wristwatch?"

"I lost em," Siofra spat.

Grainne pondered this for a second, then got back to the matter at hand, her face sparkling.

"Och, Siofra, it's gonny be brilliant! We can sneak past security, so we can, and get into her dressing room, and she's gonny invite us for a Coke and maybe one of them Yank hotdogs, and then autograph wer arms and maybe even give us one of her scarves or maybe even an old guitar she don't play no more! And she can teach us how to put makeup on! Och, I'm gonny wet meself with excitement!"

Siofra's head nodded and nodded and nodded. "Aye, me and all!" she squealed.

"Girls!" Miss McClurkin warned.

They scowled but made a performance of turning to their screens. Siofra stole glances over at Grainne's computer, and as her eyes drank in the information of the concert details, she pouted. "She doesn't be coming to Derry, but," she hissed to Grainne. "She be's coming to flimmin Belfast, and it's miles away, sure. How could we...?"

Grainne chewed on her fingernails in sudden worry, her eyes searching Siofra's for guidance.

"Och, we'll catch a bus somehow," Siofra decided. Grainne's face lit up with relief. "What I'm more concerned with, but..." Grainne's face fell again.

"Is that we'll travel all the way over there and won't get the chance to meet her."

Grainne's lower lip trembled.

"We're her biggest fans in Ireland, but," she said. "How could she not invite us into her dressing room?"

Siofra chewed on the eraser of her pencil as her brain cells trundled. Her eyes skimmed the room of classmates, wondering which of their resources could be of help to her. Her eyes alighted on the hated Catherine McLaughlin, dutifully scribbling down notes about the wildebeest that was on her screen. Siofra's eyes shined with sudden connivance.

"Ye see iPod Girl over there?"

At the first show and tell session of the school year, Catherine had been fool enough to bring her father's iPod in, and ostentation was something the children of the Moorside couldn't stomach. And her father had recently been made an Inspector with the Police Service of Northern Ireland, which made her even more hated! Although many show and tells had come and gone, the children still called Catherine 'iPod Girl,' usually while they were holding her sputtering head in a toilet bowl of the school restroom, or tripping her as she passed in the playground.

Grainne nodded haltingly.

"Ye mind that iPod Girl told us her mammy be's a journalist for the *Derry Journal*? Or she used to be, anyroad, before the madness seeped into her brain. Ye mind what she brought for the last show and tell save one?"

Grainne thought for a moment, then nodded. They had been bored stiff at the sight of the laminated card that iPod Girl blabbered proudly on and on about, and disappointed as well, as calling her Laminated Card Girl would be too much of a mouthful. Now, however, she seemed to remember...

"I think she called it a press pass. What be's a press pass when it's at home, but?"

"I'm not rightly sure," Siofra said. "I wasn't paying her babbling much mind, sure. From what I recall, but, it's some sort of plastic card that magically opens doors when ye wave it at them."

Grainne inspected Siofra.

"They have cards like that?" she asked. "Ye mean ye can wave it in front of a house door, and it'll click open so's you can enter and nick their DVDs?"

"And their Pokemons, aye," Siofra said. "Something like that. What I'm talking about be's, but, that we can wave it to get on the bus to Belfast, then at the backstage door and step right into Hannah's dressing room and introduce werselves to her. We need to get Catherine to steal it from her mammy and hand it over, just."

"And as her mammy's away in the head, she won't have a clue that it be's missing! Bleeding effin marvelous!"

They clutched each other and squealed and jumped up and down even though they were seated.

"Siofra Flood! Grainne Donaldson!"

Miss McClurkin looked at Siofra as if seeing her for the first time.

"Siofra?" she said. "May I speak to you for a moment in the corridor, please?"

"It wasn't me!" Siofra wailed.

"Don't worry," Miss McClurkin said. "It's nothing bad."

The teacher turned to the class.

"We'll only be a moment."

Siofra scowled as she scraped her chair on the floor and got up, hoping Miss McClurkin wasn't one of those 'lesbians' she had been reading about. She didn't know exactly what a 'lesbian' was, but the letters of the word looked so strange together, and her mammy and daddy spent hours calling her oldest sister Moira one (along with 'beanflicker'), and her parents were always angry when they said it, so Siofra was certain she wouldn't want to be alone in a hallway with one. She had tried to research 'lesbian' on the Internet, but had only come across one article that explained you could single them out because, unlike 'real' females, their ring fingers were longer than their index fingers. She followed Miss McClurkin into the hallway, vowing to inspect the teacher's fingers.

Miss McClurkin hunkered down before her, which didn't set Siofra at ease, and said softly:

"I want you to feel like you can come to me and confide in me if you are in any trouble."

"What are ye on about, Miss?"

"How are things at home? Is everything alright?"

She placed concerned fingers on Siofra's shoulder, and the girl froze against the clanking radiator.

"I-I don't understand them questions, Miss." Siofra squirmed out from under the *fingers*.

"It's just that lately, your schoolwork has been suffering. And your personal hygiene, well, let's just say that's an unresolved issue. But today, there is a trace of mud in your hair, your tights are torn, as is your handbag. And I can't help but notice the welt on your lip and the bruise that is slowly forming on your cheek. Is there something you want to reveal to me? I understand that things can be difficult when money is tight in the household. Perhaps your parents are on edge because they must work so much, or need to take their financial or personal aggressions out on the children. I took a university course in this, you know. So I know. And you show all the signs. So I'll ask you again. Has a grownup been causing you harm?"

"Aye, a grownup has," Siofra confirmed.

Miss McClurkin brightened. "Yes?" she urged. "Who?"

"You! Ye haul me out of the class like this to talk about me tights again, and I'll tell all of the Moorside ye're one of them secret lesbians!"

Miss McClurkin blanched as she recoiled from the little beast.

"Siofra Flood! That is a very serious accusation."

"And ye're harping on and on about me mammy and daddy clattering the shite outta me!" That happened often, but it was none of the nosy parker's business.

Miss McClurkin folded her arms, which afforded Siofra a good look at her fingers. The girl relaxed.

"Not doing yourself any favors, I see," Miss McClurkin said stiffly. "Your own worst enemy. Fine. I only wanted to offer the hand of assistance. I understand defensiveness, and I understand wanting to protect people who you think love you. I really do. But if I see further signs of what I suspect is physical abuse, I will have to inform the headmistress Mrs. Pilkey, who will then have to inform the police. Don't be alarmed. I'm only doing this for your own good, you know. Back to class, now, and I'll be keeping a look out for you, Siofra. I'm really, really here to help."

"Help yer hole," Siofra muttered, stomping back into the classroom and glaring menacingly at all heads that faced her way. They whipped around to their computer screens. Siofra would have been more angry, but as Miss McClurkin's fingers seemed normal, maybe her teacher really was only being helpful. Siofra would rather eat fruit than reveal she had been attacked by a Protestant bitch, however.

Grainne passed her questioning looks that Siofra shrugged off angrily. Siofra made a show of inspecting a ferret on the screen for a moment. When Miss McClurkin was back at her newspaper, Siofra clicked onto the WeBKidsInDerry social network site. She poked around for a while, her anger subsiding, then it rose again as she read a message. She clicked onto a link and stared, disbelieving, at a photo of herself splayed across the pavement. Her eyes shot down to the uploader's name: PinkPetals. Siofra jabbed desperately at the delete button, but the picture wouldn't go away. In fact, with one jab, the photo exploded to full-screen, and she was stuck staring at her pained, vulnerable expression displayed almost life-sized for all of Derry and, indeed, the world to see. She didn't give a shite about the rest of the world, but the thought of all her classmates seeing her...!

Her face burning with humiliation, Siofra scanned the room to ensure nobody had seen, then switched over to another page, seething with thoughts of revenge against PinkPetals. Siofra knew sooner or later she would meet the girl on the streets of Derry; there were only so many streets. But even more than a retaliatory beating, Siofra hoped that, once she had a photo of herself posing with her arm around Hannah Montana, she could shove it into PinkPetals face, as proof she was just as worthy to breathe the air as any Protestant cunt.

CHAPTER TEN

Paddy didn't notice her until his third trip back from the loo. She was sitting with two mates and their shopping bags in a darkened corner of the Sheepshank pub under the sign that warned Don't Abuse Our Barstaff; it was often ignored. Beyond the heaving, roaring masses, she was guzzling a vodka and Coke and devouring him with her eyes, a swizzle stick sliding suggestively in and out of her lips.

For months, Paddy hadn't seen the inside of the Rocking Seamaid, the Fillets-O-Joy workers' pub of choice. Once word spread through the packing plant that the Floods owned an extra house, invites for a pint after work, for a game of darts, for Secret Santa at Christmas, had abruptly stopped. There were sudden silences when Paddy approached a group clustered around the tea kettle, glares over the dividers of the staff urinals. Having an easy life was a social sin on par with wishing a police officer a pleasant day.

Paddy now did his daily post-shift drinking at the Sheepshank. It was probably the only pub in Derry he wouldn't run into people who resented him, as the management had once tried a gay-friendly evening, and custom had fled, horrified. The madness was quickly abolished, but three years on, anyone Irish caught entering or leaving the pub was regarded with suspicion. The immigrant workers of Derry, mainly Poles and Filipinos, seemed not to know the pub's shameful history, and it was their pay packets that kept it afloat.

Paddy had guzzled four pints of lager and two shots of whiskey in a nook that gave off a feral smell, dreading the scene that would unfold at home, and fretting that he might be sitting right where the arse of a mincing queen once had. Around him as the alcohol seeped into his brain, the strangers of Derry huddled in corners, their clothing odd and their tongues odder, the Poles barking, the Filipinos yapping their secrets.

Nobody trusted these recent arrivals to Derry City, where for generations the only non-Irish encountered were the occasional Yank tourist willing to overlook the reputation Derry still had of being a war-zone and come searching for their roots (they were sitting ducks for casual knifings and muggings), and the Chinese family who ran the takeaway down the Strand (chicken curry and chips was always the order; the moo goo gai pan and crab rangoon were too foreign). The new Poles and Filipinos were seen as cagey bastards and sleekit cunts, eyes searching for work and housing, brought to Derry for the first good economy in recent history. They had taken the jobs the Irish were happy to be rid of, but now work was in short supply, and resentment was starting to grow. When Fionnuala had been caught nicking toilet paper and urinal cakes from her job of scrubbing pub toilets the year before and fired, her position had been taken over by a Filipino grandmother. Fionnuala had retaliated months later: a quick elbow to the foreign creature's ribs, and she fell into the new fountain in front of the Guildhall. Fionnuala scampered off up Shipquay Street with a lightness in her step and a smile on her face for once.

The arses and crotches around Paddy jerked with the bass beat as another Eurodisco tune came on the jukebox—the Poles seemed to favor this genre— and his pint glass jumped on the table. He scribbled unsteadily on a beer mat how much the household's overdue notices totaled, and how much the next month's bills might swell to. He soon ran out of space. His wages for the next week, which he now wouldn't be collecting, had already been long since spent in his mind.

It might have been the whiskey, but Paddy was surprised he was thinking of his brother-in-law Jed Barnett, and regretting the events of the previous year which had sent Jed and Ursula fleeing to Wisconsin after the lotto win. Jed's friendship could always be relied on, as could, more importantly, a handout when necessary. Jed had always been up for a round on the golf course or many drinks in the pub, his easy manner and general kindness sorely lacking in anyone else Paddy knew. Jed always seemed content as long as there was a one-stop-shop for all his vices: booze, smokes and lotto slips. The Floods had turned on Jed the moment he hadn't splashed out the majority of his lotto 'millions' on them. Under threat of Fionnuala, Paddy had betrayed his best friend in Derry the past decade. But, Paddy considered, Jed Barnett was a Yank and therefore someone to be treated with suspicion, no matter that he had lived amongst them for ten years; Jed was a stranger as much as the economic migrants that now surrounded Paddy, and as he had been hounded back to his rightful country, a handout wouldn't be forthcoming.

Paddy finished the dregs in his pint glass and pushed his way through the strange-tongued beasts, made his way down the seedy corridor to the toilets and, inside, clutched the stained wall as he zippered down and a moan of drunken misery escaped him. Coming back, his wavering steps trampled on the trio's shopping bags, and he ignored their squeals of alarm.

"Bloody foreigners," he muttered by rote, without pausing to wonder if that was actually what he really thought. "Get yer foreign arses back to yer own land."

Paddy felt resentment swell as he staggered to the bar for another pint and eyed the Next, the BodyShop, the Sephora bags filled with quality not quantity; resentful that those foreigners had the advantages of youth (of a sort), friends, and, by the amount of shopping bags and the names on them, disposable incomes, resentful that he had to drink in this pub of degenerates and aliens, resentful that the Fillets-O-Joy job had been taken as something to tide him over after he left school at 16 until his real career began, and that that stop gap had lasted 28 years.

Then, as he handed over the coins for his pint to the frazzled barmaid, he noticed the look. The Polish women Paddy saw around town were blonde and shapely, and although the unfortunates in the corner would never grace a catwalk, he knew they must be Polish because they weren't Filipino. He couldn't see the two other women; their polyester backs were to him, one pink paisley, the other dalmatian spots. The bad case of static cling of the woman in question's low-cut zebra-print top revealed the curve of her ample but sagging breasts, and her eyes seemed locked on something of intense interest as she glided the swizzle stick in and out.

Paddy turned around to see what she was ogling, but there was only what looked like a bloody handprint on the faded wallpaper behind him. It was one of many, so that couldn't be what caught her interest.

The Polish stranger ran aqua fingernails through the sadness of her straw-like hair and revealed the smile of a tobacco-stained overbite over the rim of her vodka and Diet Coke at him. Paddy felt a stirring that had been dormant from years of Fionnuala slapping his drunken, groping hands away from her tattered nightgown at night. He self-consciously picked at a stain on his jacket and swaggered haltingly to the nook as something base and animal urged for release beyond his crumpled denim.

That she was no spring chicken was obvious, and the passage of time hadn't helped a face already disadvantaged in youth. The makeup troweled on made her look more harsh than an obviously difficult life had, classic mutton-dressed-as-lamb, but she was certainly younger than him. And her body made up for her shortcomings. Paddy never sought things out in life; he took whatever happened to come his way. This is perhaps why he was still saddled with a mirthless job, and why Fionnuala was the mother of his seven children. And as the woman's two friends turned slightly to inspect him out of the corners of their eyes, and they pressed in together and giggled in their strange language, Paddy—

—yelped as his right pocket vibrated. He tugged out his pay-as-you-go cellphone and saw a text from his daughter Dymphna: Hve u 4gttn mams bday???!

"Bloody Christ on a cross!"

The alcohol fled his brain in a state of shock. The sense of something of life-or-death importance had been nipping at a distant corner of his mind, but the shock of the impending strike had dislodged it. The jangling coins in his pocket wouldn't be enough to buy the gift Fionnuala would be expecting, and she had been dropping hints for a month. Gripped by panic, Paddy looked around him, searching desperately as if the pub were the Quayside Shopping Center. Time was of the essence, as Fionnuala clocked off from the Sav-U-Mor at three, the shops in the city center were all shuttered up, and he had enough presence of mind to recall that Maureen and the children were planning a surprise dinner at five. A matching set of pint glasses? A collection of beer mats? Fionnuala loved her gin; perhaps he could distract the barmaid long enough to reach behind the bar counter and—

—then he spied it. Paddy had reached a state of drunkenness where the ridiculous seemed logical. To his drink-soaked brain, it was the perfect gift, and it seemed to be barely hanging on the wall. If he could pry it off and make out the door with it unseen, the price would be perfect as well. A hoard of construction workers had just piled into the pub, and the bar staff was frenetic with the orders barked out at them. Paddy grabbed his workbag and sidled up to the dartboard, stealing glances over at the bar. The staff wasn't watching, but someone else was.

The dartboard hadn't been used in years, and Fionnuala had won the darts championship at the Sav-U-Mor Christmas do the year before and proudly dusted the plastic trophy on the mantelpiece when she could be arsed with housework; Paddy could almost hear Fionnuala's squeals of delight when he presented her with the dartboard (he was deranged with drink). A few rusty darts lay on the shelf of the case like museum exhibits. Paddy scooped them up and slipped them into his workbag. The case hung by mangled hooks to the wall. As he reached up to dislodge the case from the nails in the wall, the Polish woman got up, revealing skinny acid-washed jeans paired with ruby stilettos that marched towards him.

To Paddy's alarm, he felt a pair of hands slip under his sweaty armpits to assist in the theft, and the warmth of something akin to deflated airbags against his back. He heard whispered in his ear: "*Pozwól, że ci z tym pomogę.*"

"Eh?"

"I help, yes?"

"Right ye are," he said.

They slipped the case off the wall, and Paddy reached into his bag for a

filthy pair of overalls to drape over the case so he could hustle it out of the
pub unnoticed.

"*Jesteś bardzo seksownym facetem.*" she said with a giggle younger than her
years, much. "Mean in our language is sexy man. *Ładny tyłek.* Nice arse."

Paddy's bloodshot eyes weren't sure where to look. Belonging to a hot-
blooded man as they did, they wanted to gawk at her breasts, but red flags
sprung up at the sorry state of them beyond the static cling and zebra print,
they wanted to peruse her lips, but those were in need of Chapstick. This
Pole had a skewed concept of personal space, and his body felt the warmth of
hers dangerously close. Blood pulsed into regions long relegated to those of
long-lost adolescent dreams.

"Er, for me wife," Paddy said, motioning to the dartboard case he was
having trouble hiding in his overalls.

"Wife," she said with an arch smile, as if there were no less of an obstacle
and no more of a pleasant challenge. "I tie, yes?"

She snatched the overalls from him and fashioned the left leg and right
arm into a bow of sorts.

"Now easy to be carrying, yes?" she said.

"Er, ta. I must be on me way home now, but," Paddy muttered. "Ta for
yer help, like."

"*Do zobaczenia,*" she said, not 'goodbye,' but 'until we meet again,' as, in
a town that small, this was obvious.

As Paddy shoved through the stench of old ale and thumping Eurodisco,
he was thinking less of Fionnuala's birthday and more of the 'youngster's'
cracked but exotic lips. He wondered what path had just been carved out for
him, where it might lead, and if the Polish had heard of breath mints.

Awkwardly gripping the dartboard, Paddy opened the door, looked back
to see if he could bag a glimpse of the woman's bony arse, but the acid-washed
denim was lost in the bodies and the music. He turned from the turbulence
inside to the turbulence of drunken hoards of teens outside.

"What're ye doing in that pub for pervs? Fecking arse-bandit!"

A skull in a hoodie cracked against Paddy's head, and he crumpled to
the cobblestones. Headbutting, the uppercut of the underclass. As the thug
wrenched the dartboard from Paddy's hand, his mate kicked him in the head
for good measure and finished off the abuse with half a can of lager splashed
over Paddy's head.

"Nancy-boy poofter!" They flipped him off and lurched drunkenly around
the corner, roars of laughter from the depths of their hoods. "Pedo scum!"

Paddy whimpered from the pain and the stench of old urine as he picked
fist off his tongue and struggled to tug himself from the street, knowing at
once the attack was the Lord's wrathful retribution for his future sins of the

flesh. Paddy staggered home to the Moorside, where he was certain more wrath awaited him.

CHAPTER 11

On the lookout for rocks hurled at them, a beloved sport of the local youngsters, Maureen urged her daughter around the corner from 5 Murphy Crescent to the Flood's house. It was slow going. Maureen warned Fionnuala to put on a brave face for the sake of the children. Seamus, Padraig and Siofra had prepared long and hard to mark their mother's birthday, at least that was the story, and Fionnuala's waterworks over her sacking would undermine the festivities.

"Give me some of them tablets of yers for to calm me nerves," Fionnuala demanded. Maureen scrabbled through the handbag that seemed to sway permanently from her elbow. "Thank feck we've Paddy's paycheck coming in, and yer pension and all."

Maureen handed over a few pills that Fionnuala wolfed down there on the pavement. "I told ye them Cash Cow cans was a bloody foolish idea," Maureen said. "Ye wouldn't hear anything of it, but. What possessed ye to unload another pile of them rejects from the Sav-U-Mor in wer scullery just now? Not a fit place to eat, that scullery, a tinning factory floor that would be closed down by the Health Department, it looks, with them old tins, the new tins, the flimmin glue, the pigging labels. The hours me and the wanes frittered away in that scullery to put yer gacky get-rich-quick scheme into place the past few months—"

"For the love of God almighty, would ye quit harping on about it, Mammy!" Fionnuala barked as they passed the dead weeds that were the front garden. "It's me special day, like. And I paid good money for them tins. I wouldn't let yer man Skivvins near em."

Across the door, a hastily-erected banner exclaimed in magic marker: HAPPY BRITHDAY MAMMY!! On the dust of the hall stand next to Fionnuala's mass book and rosary stood two large envelopes with the Magilligan Prison postmark: sons Lorcan and Eoin had remembered. As Fionnuala ripped open the envelopes, she wondered briefly, as a mother would, what shape their arses might be in. Her heart ached as she looked down upon the scrawled X's and O's. Her shining stars were prison bait, and she had to make do with the detritus of her offspring. Fionnuala turned to her mother and moaned, ever the martyr: "Och, how I pine for me two strong handsome sons. What sins of the past am I suffering for now, Mammy?"

"There's another card for ye there," Maureen said with a nudge. "From yer sister-in-law Ursula, so it is."

Fionnuala was incensed as her lips mouthed out what she saw on the front of the card: Reaching Out Across the Miles To Wish You A Happy Birthday!

"Jesus, Mary and Joseph, that jumped-up bitch has a bold-faced cheek, mocking me with a card. I'll reach out across the miles for to claw her eyes out!" She tossed the card aside, unopened, then murmured, "Mind you, her lotto millions would come in terrible handy for paying the bills right now."

"Chasing them Barnetts from Derry probably is one of them sins of the past ye were just on about," Maureen said. "The torture ye put Ursula through, even after she paid off yer mortgage for youse, would make a marvelous book, but." She smiled. "Calm yerself down. The wanes is all waiting for ye in the scullery,"

Maureen guided a glowering Fionnuala through the tired wallpaper of the corridor towards the kitchen, where the noise inside—the blare of pop music (Rihanna with that one about the umbrella, if Fionnuala wasn't mistaken) and kiddie squeals—made even that world-weary birthday girl tingle in anticipation.

"Surprise, Mammy!" chorused Padraig, Siofra and Seamus from around the filthy kitchen table, forks aloft before guilty faces pillaging gristle and bone. Their bobbing heads were half-hidden under crown-shaped crepe-paper birthday hats with shiny bits they had unearthed from the attic, and there was more fear than joy in their eyes as they peered up at her. The table groaned under half-scoured platters of ham hocks, hairy, and raw on one end, burnt on the other, a smattering of fish sticks, blackened cheese on toast, singed turnips, lumpy mashed spuds, and what looked like baked beans.

"What a lovely surprise indeed," Fionnuala cooed with little claps of glee, though it was not lovely, and the only surprise was the sight of Dymphna grinning like a simpleton with her half-Orange bastard in its stroller at her side, a tray of food on her lap. The surprise turned to rage as Fionnuala spied Dymphna's suitcase by the washing machine.

"We was weak with hunger, Mammy," Padraig chanced.

"Where the bloody feck's yer father?" Fionnuala said through a fixed grin, pulling up a chair and stabbing out her fag on a plate. She had only pushed the insult to the back of her mind; there was time aplenty in the lives of the greedy wee bastards to unleash the appropriate punishment on them when they least expected it.

"I texted him, Mammy. No reply, but," Dymphna piped up through the grinding molars and blank stares.

Fionnuala forced down a forkful of watery and cold turnips. Why was Paddy not there to celebrate her special day? He was her rock. A teetering, drunken rock that always stank vaguely of fish and that was frequently denied entrance to her garden of delights to be sure, but a rock nevertheless. For Fionnuala, her forty-fifth birthday was always meant to be the magic one. The Heggartys had a habit of dying while ninety years of age, and the extended family never let a chance slip by to pound this point home. Her father, two of her aunts and one uncle had all died uncannily at that age. So although most people would celebrate their sixteenth, their twentieth, even their fiftieth with aplomb, for Fionnuala, forty-five marked the smack-dab middle of her life.

When Fionnuala imagined this day throughout the years, she had envisioned an array of talented children—a fashion model, a soccer player, perhaps a third one of Pan's People, a dancer on the TV show Top Of The Pops—gathered around her in a circle of gratitude, one of those fancy cakes with many tiers she had seen on an ad on the side of a bus, perhaps a chocolate fountain gurgling in the background, children whose exciting and lucrative careers were splashed across the pages of glossy magazines, a source of pride, and whose income helped maintain the restaurant she owned, something exotic and upmarket, like a pizzeria. In fact, the life she suspected Ursula Barnett was now living. Fionnuala looked around the table in despair. Her appetite had fled. She placed the fork down and glowered at her shameless slapper of a daughter, Dymphna.

"Kicked ye out on yer backside, has yer Proddy fancy man?"

"It wasn't me fault—" Dymphna said through a mouthful of spuds.

"Aye, and I'm the Queen of Sheeba. Let's get to me gifts, shall we?" she decided out of maternal duty rather than zeal.

Fionnuala got to work. The presents, such as they were, were wrapped in some of Maureen's old true crimes magazines and done up with duct tape, photos of crime scenes and serial killers looking up at her. For her mother, Siofra had freed the faded palm leaves of the previous year's Palm Sunday from behind the Bleeding Heart of Jesus portrait in the sitting room and fashioned them into a flower or an animal of sorts. Fionnuala tossed it on the table and demanded:

"What's up with yer face, wee girl?"

"An Orange bitch clattered seven shades of shite out of her," Padraig eagerly piped up.

Fionnuala was about to unleash a torrent of verbal abuse on Siofra, shrugged and said: "Serves ye right, ye witless spastic."

Siofra kept grinding down the food like an automaton.

"Open the one from me, love," Maureen urged with a nudge in Fionnuala's ribs. "Ye should be gasping for what's inside right about now, if I'm not mistaken."

Fionnuala was grateful for the bottle of gin, though it was generic, and as she unscrewed the top and guzzled down, her relief was tempered by the feel of Dymphna's thirsty eyes on the bottle. Seamus wobbled over from the table.

"I've a gift for ye and all, Mammy," he said. "Ye kyanny unwrap it, but. It's me bedtime prayers, all in me head. Just like ye wanted me to do em."

Fionnuala wiped the gin from her chin, shuddered with ecstasy as the warmth filled her, and faced her youngest with a row of teeth awkwardly fashioned into the smile of a caring mother.

"Let's hear em, son."

Seamus took a deep breath and with the measured concentration that would try the patience of a saint said: "God bless me and make me a good boy, to loven serve God, God bless Mammy and Daddy and Granny Heggarty and me brothers and sisters, specially them what be's locked up in prison, not me sister Moira, but, as she be's in the clutchees of Satan, and God bless all me uncles and aunties, except me Auntie Ursula. Amen."

Fionnuala's smile was now genuine as she removed a baked bean from his forehead.

"That's me wee dote," she said, turning to her mother. "Mammy, Seamus does indeed be a wee dote, aye?"

Maureen, one hand clutching a fish stick, the other a teacup filled with Paddy's stash of whiskey, nodded. Fionnuala reached for Dymphna's gift and unwrapped it glumly, but screams suddenly spewed from Keanu as Fionnuala knocked the stroller aside and heaved the multitude of plugs from the lone electrical socket to power up the foot spa.

"Mary Mother of God! Just what me aching feet needs!"

Dymphna teleported to her side with a pitcher of water.

"Ye're to fill—"

"Ye must think I'm simple-minded, you," Fionnuala snorted, peeling off her socks. "I know what to do with a foot spa, sure!" She had watched enough infomercials on them.

The wanes tore themselves from their plates and gawked in a semi-circle as the horror of their mother's middle-aged toes disappeared into the bubbling water. Fionnuala moaned in rapture, and Paddy walked into the scullery.

"Daddy!" squealed the younger children.

"Happy birthday, love!"

He was, Fionnuala noticed as he planted a kiss on her forehead, empty-handed. Her face fell, and she unleashed her belt of a tongue.

"Where the bloody hell have you been up to now? Och, don't bother yerself the mental strain of spewing out a pack of lies. The stench of drink offa ye be's overpowering." She took another swig of gin and wriggled her toes deeper into the frothing water. Paddy sidled up to the table, grabbed a ham hock and dug his tarnished teeth into the flesh.

Sparks crackled from around Fionnuala's heels and shot through the air. The children shrieked as Fionnuala leaped from the machine that suddenly shuddered and convulsed. With a few more sparks and some smoke, the foot spa died. Fionnuala heaved a labored breath and glared accusingly at Dymphna.

"I thought ye was giving me a present, not putting me in a coffin. Did ye purchase that murder contraption from the Mountains of Mourne Gate market stalls?"

Dymphna forced a nod.

"Just as I suspected, pound wise and penny foolish. Ye couldn't spend the extra three quid to buy the real McCoy at the Top-Yer-Trolley for yer mother's birthday instead? Useless, so ye are."

She faced Paddy.

"Where's me gifts?"

"I've something special for ye, I left it in me locker at the factory, but. I'll give it to ye after the weekend."

"Och, wise up you. Now's not the time for joking." Her voice was laced with menace.

Padraig sidled uncertainly up to his mother.

"Daddy went in on them gifts what says on em they be from me," he said.

Paddy's secret look of gratitude at his son from behind the cheese toast was tempered with worry; he had no clue what might be revealed under the face of Jeffrey Dahmer. Fionnuala's wet feet tramped through the unwrapped newsprint that littered the floor, and she approached the final gifts with rising excitement. Her fingernails sliced through the paper, and even Jay-Z rapping from the radio couldn't drown out her squeals.

"Bath salts! From the Dead Sea!"

While Padraig beamed strangely at his mother's side, Paddy spat out gristle and eyed the gift with surprise—

"And Elizabeth Taylor's Passion perfume! And ye've got me her White Diamonds scent and all!"

—unease—

"And…Merciful Jesus, me eyes kyanny believe it! A Burberry scarf!"

—and alarm. The kitchen was enveloped in a mist of Elizabeth Taylor's most costly, and Fionnuala was oblivious to the daggers of the upstaged that Dymphna, Siofra, Maureen and even Seamus tossed at Paddy and Padraig.

She made a quick check of the label and thread count to ensure the scarf was genuine, then wrapped the magnum opus around her neck with a giddy giggle much younger than her years and posed right, left and center, hand on her hip, tears of delight welling in her beaming face.

"Lemme at a mirror!" But the closest one was in the upstairs bathroom, so she cast an approving look in the toaster instead.

"I knew ye wouldn't forget," she bubbled to Paddy, asphyxiating his neck and detonating kisses on his chewing face. "Och, ye're a wile and lovely man, so ye are, and Lorcan and Eoin can rot in their cells, so they can, with a son like you."

Padraig wriggled under her hugs, and Maureen wanted to spew. A lopsided rhubarb pie, Fionnuala's favorite, materialized from the fridge courtesy of Siofra. Fionnuala saw to her annoyance they had seen fit to splash out on candles, the number of them taunting and blinding her.

After the candles had been blown out and the pie served, Maureen cleared her throat and said with the air of one christening a luxury liner: "One last gift." She reached into her handbag and pulled out the book. "Came by post the day. Addressed to Dymphna, it was. I opened it by pure mistake."

Fionnuala looked down in her hands in confusion; she knew the last place to find a Heggarty was browsing through a Barnes and Noble, and it was a most inappropriate gift for her. "What in the name of God possessed ye to...?"

Then she noticed the words *A Novel of Family and Greed by Moira Flood.* The forks flew from their fingers at the rage in her voice.

"Cunt-slurping bitch! Novel, me hole!"

Lotto Balls of Shame screamed the letters of the title up at her. The bright yellow cover showed a gravity-pick lottery machine, with little heads of the main characters emblazoned on the winning balls in the chute. At a glance, Fionnuala could tell who was who: Ursula with her eggplant-colored bob, her husband Jed with his cowboy hat and goatee, Paddy with his slicked-back black hair, Dymphna with her bright orange curls, and Fionnuala herself with her bleached ponytails. Ursula and Jed were beaming with glee, whereas Paddy and Dymphna were scowling across the balls at them. Fionnuala's image was tilted to the side, and her face was stretched with rage, a smoking cigarette hanging from her lower lip. The cover was insult enough. Why had the illustrator made her look so much older than she was?

"What is it, Mammy?" Siofra asked.

"It's called a book," Maureen cut in. "Apparently written by yer disgrace of a sister Moira. All about how yer mammy, with a wee bit of help from all youse, chased yer auntie Ursula and uncle Jed to the States by causing them grief of all sorts. I'm on chapter seven."

"Does she have me in it?" Padraig asked.

"Aye."

"Me and all?" Paddy asked.

"The whole lot of youse. Names cleverly disguised, but."

As they clambered around in amazement, it never occurred to Fionnuala to crack open the book's spine. She flung it the length of the scullery. It hit the window and shattered the glass, shards landing in the filthy cookware piled high. The book toppled sadly into the baked beans pot.

"A rip-roaring read so it is," Maureen continued. "There be's a wee note in there from Moira and all, about how there's to be a swanky do held in Malta to mark the book coming out. Free drink and finger foods. Two months hence."

Fionnuala tore the scarf from her neck and glared in accusation all around her.

"Wipe them foolish, goofy smiles offa yer faces. Are youse not concerned with the filth she must've written about youse?"

But they were shame-free, even Paddy, knowing they had been bit players in everything that happened the year before; Fionnuala had orchestrated the grand schemes and pulled their puppet strings. Fionnuala singled out Dymphna.

"And you! She sent that filth to *you*. Have ye been in contact behind me back? Ye traitorous bitch, ye can stay around the corner at 5 Murphy with yer granny and the wanes."

"B-but, Mammy," Dymphna began, tears brimming, "I hadn't a hand in it. Moira and me was always close, but I kyanny comprehend how she thought to send me the book. And the wanes have told me there be's no amenities at 5 Murphy left, barely a kettle and toaster, and with a wee infant to care for—"

"Amenities? Catch yerself on, ye jumped up geebag! A few months on the Waterside, living in luxury, and ye've ideas above yer station. I don't know what be's worse, ye living in sin with an Orange bastard or ye living in luxury with his Orange bitch of a mother. Madness be's eating at yer brain if ye imagine I'd welcome ye with open arms, the disgrace ye've dragged the family through. I kyanny keep me head up when I pass the neighbors, so I kyanny. The thought of yer sister Moira brings the sick shooting up me throat, aye. She had the decency to clear off outta town at least. I kyanny stomach, but, staring at yer bloody face in the same room!"

That face burned out at the family, and Dymphna furiously shredded the scrap of toilet roll she was using as a napkin, the tears streaming into her turnips, while around her the others went back to shoveling the rhubarb and candle wax down their gullets.

"Have ye not a clue what yer traipsing around with yer Proddy fancy man and yer half-Orange cunt of a bastard have put me through?"

"Why do ye hate me so much, Mammy?" Dymphna sobbed.

"Och, would ye wise up?" Fionnuala steamed, smacking her across the face. "I don't hate ye, ye daft cunt, ye!"

Fionnuala faced her mother.

"How could Moira do it, Mammy? How?"

Maureen, who had long been tortured with her daughter's antics, knew exactly how, but kept her lips pressed into a circle as if concerned.

"A fine birthday celebration this turned out to be," Fionnuala barked. "Scatter!"

They did. With the house bathed in quiet and the plates still on the table, Fionnuala led a lager-fueled and strangely skittish Paddy up the stairs, where she would allow him to perform his birthday bedroom duties to calm her down. Her mouth formed a smile of lust, but her Liz Taylor-scented head was already clicking with thoughts of revenge.

CHAPTER 12

Before moving to Wisconsin, Ursula Barnett had known nothing of crystal meth addicts. One year on, she could single them out as easily as she could someone misquoting scripture: the rashes and receding gums, the chemical stench from their unbathed and skeletal bodies. And she was only too aware of their need for the cash of strangers to feed their filthy habit. The proportion of the state that seemed to be infected was alarming, and she was now sharing the roulette table with at least three.

"Double zero," said the caller, and expletives erupted from those around her, souls both lost and losing. Ursula had seen that look of desperation in their eyes before, many times, in her husband Jed's eyes. She glanced over at his stack of chips, and was not surprised to see it was now a smattering. One of the degenerates bumped into her, and Ursula self-consciously brought her hand up to the string of pearls she had draped around her neck for the occasion.

That she was overdressed for the casino on the Indian reservation was an understatement. When Jed suggested the trip, Ursula had visions of tuxedos, jet setters, the 'in-crowd,' perhaps a chandelier and a French accent or two.

She wasn't prepared for what greeted them the moment she lifted the petticoat under her black velvet evening gown and sashayed through the battered doors of the crackhouse: sticky carpeting that made every step in her high heels a chore, clouds of cigarette smoke, shrieks of infants as desperate mothers rolled them through aisles of penny slots in their mission to win rent; the only 'in' this crowd might ever be was rehab, Ursula thought grimly.

"I gotta shit like a motherfucker," said the man to her right, pawing at the few chips he had left.

Ursula quietly unclasped the pearls from around her neck and locked them inside her handbag, which she clutched on the cigarette-burned felt before her as if it contained the only copies of her children's birth certificates. The woman to her left, with scraggly hair and what looked like bedroom slippers on her feet, hacked into a beverage napkin. The caller spun the wheel again.

Ursula configured her eyes across the bets to beg Jed for release from this torture. She couldn't meet his eyes, hidden under the shadow of his cowboy hat and glazed with excitement and free casino liquor as they were, following the ball clattering round and round on the track of the wheel. Ursula noticed he was clutching the pint-sized Baileys and cream as if it might grow wings and fly away any minute, yet was allowing next month's mortgage payment to fly from his fingers, right back into the croupier's bank.

"Thirty-three black!"

The man beside her scooped up his chips and staggered, not to the restroom or to cash them in, but to the adjacent craps table.

"Let's pray ye take some of them winnings and purchase yerself a bar of soap," Ursula sniffed, happy to be able to breathe freely again.

He fixed his bloodshot eyes on her as best he could, but Ursula knew the secret weapon of her Derry accent: she could insult people all she wanted, and they wouldn't be able to understand a thing. Bedroom Slippers Woman lurched forward and ejected a torrent of foamy bile into the bev nap.

Ursula could stand it no longer. Feeling soiled and in desperate need of a toilet, she scurried off and made her way frantically through the endless rows of slot machines. Tears welled in her eyes, whether in sadness at the sorry state of humanity around her or her own despair or the smell, she didn't know. She asked a youthful couple for directions to the restroom. They told her to go to Hell.

Ursula bit her fist to stifle a cry, and on she pushed, trying to look as dignified as the passage of time and the gaining of weight could make her (though compared to the indigenous population that wasn't drug addicted, she was slender). She hurried through a row devoted to 'luck of the Irish' nickle slots, and the leprechauns, claddagh rings, harps, pots of gold and rainbows mocked her. This was nothing like the Ireland she had left behind: even before the tragedy of their lottery win in Derry, harps and rainbows had been in short supply. And after...

Jed had 'only' won £500,000, but once they bought their dreamhouse and matching Lexuses, there wasn't much left. Ursula's family refused to believe this. The Floods' endless demands for handouts the Barnetts couldn't afford had driven them mad.

What was more of a misery: surrounding herself with a family who resented her, or nobody? Ursula was now an uprooted stranger in an even stranger world. Her time in Wisconsin seemed to be spent sitting in the car doing Sudoku, pencil in one hand, calculator in the other, Aida on the CD player, and Jed digging them out of the snow of the endless winter. Then putting on her parka and helping him push.

Ursula and Jed had used the money from the sale of their new house in Northern Ireland to fund their escape to Jed's hometown in the middle of nowhere, where the only visitors to their depressingly functional home were Jed's brother and business partner Slim (a most ironic nickname) and Slim's wife Louella. Jed seemed fine with the fields of wheat? barley?—Ursula hadn't a clue what surrounded them. But if she glanced at another cow, she was going to spew. Ursula needed people, apparently even ones who hated her. Her family were vicious people who resented and hated her, to be sure, but people nevertheless.

A sign announced WOMEN. Ursula inwardly thanked the Lord for finally guiding her to a restroom, yet wished He had supplied her with a pair of tongs to touch the door handle. Desperation made her wrench the door open with the exposed flesh of her fingers and, out of the corner of her teary left eye, she was vaguely aware of a figure brushing her elbow. Ursula pushed inside and was taken aback at the stench of antiseptic and stringent homelessness.

The door flew open behind her.

"...Hell you think you are? Shoving your way in before me? The days of the back of the bus are over."

Ursula looked back at the woman in alarm. The glare from her goggled eyes invited Ursula to brawl. The right hand on the hip of her brown corduroy culottes trembled with the excitement of inciting a scene, and the left hand scratched her forearm incessantly. Ursula tried to look anywhere but at the pink cowboy boots littered with rhinestones and floral print top with love handles spilling over, but that brought her eyes directly to the horror of the woman's fingernails. They were huge, clawlike things painted garish shades of purple and blue, covered with glitter and stenciled with Gothic lettering. The right index fingernail was pierced, and a little golden ring dangled from it.

"I-I'm wile sorry," Ursula said apologetically, her eyes unable to pull themselves from the fingernails. "I didn't see ye at the door."

"Because I was too *dark*? You wouldn't push your fat ass in front of me if I was one of *your* people! I know how your white people's eyes see me, ghetto trash, a second-class citizen!"

"*Me* people?" Ursula asked, pointing to herself in puzzlement. How did the stranger know she was Irish? It dawned on her the woman meant white people.

"Looks like you're loaded. Gimme a fiver."

Ursula stepped back in shock at the woman's breath. She clasped her handbag to her breast, hiding her giraffe brooch of cubic zirconia. From the woman's stance, it was clear she thought the world owed her a living, and from her outstretched palm, that she considered Ursula the world. Nothing could be further from the truth. Ursula had only brought $25 with her, and that she had lost at the bingo session two hours earlier.

"I don't have it."

The woman snorted.

"Yeah, right, you don't. Rich white bitch. Nothin but lazy trash from the ghetto, you think we be. Yeah, I be from the ghetto, but ain't nothin lazy bout me. I be poundin the pavement every day lookin for work, got blisters the size of golf balls to prove it. White man won't give me no job, give em all to his white ass friends. Bet you never tasted dogfood. Or shit in a bucket cause the asshole slumlord won't fix the plumbin. I be looking for work."

Ursula wondered where this 'ghetto' of hers might be. She had lived on the plains of Wisconsin for a year and hadn't seen anything resembling a town, let alone a city. For all the woman's claims to poverty, Ursula knew she must have afforded the gas to get to the casino. And she struggled to think of a task in any job description that might be performed by hands with such nails; they seemed custom-made for only opening envelopes containing welfare checks.

"Ye had funds enough to get them nails done, I kyanny help but notice," Ursula sniffed.

"In membrance of my son De'Kwon, taken to the heavenly Lord at sixteen."

She thrust the stenciled nails under Ursula's nose so Ursula had no choice but to read the Gothic font. R-I-P D-e spelled the right hand, '-K-w-o-n the left. Ursula saw as well the henna tattoo in need of a touch-up on the flab of the woman's upper left arm, her son's face in its do-rag glaring out with menace, and R.I.P. on a scroll underneath what looked like what might have been in the past two hearts. Ursula's own heart went out to the stranger, as no mother should have to grieve a child's death. She was on the verge of touching the woman's shoulder, but fear of infection made her relent.

"Och, I'm wile sorry—"

"White man drugs killed him," the woman announced.

Ursula's lips disappeared as if pulled by a string, her compassion waning.

"An overdose, are ye telling me?"

"Samplin a batch to sell in the hood, then keeled over."

The kindness dissolved from Ursula's eyes.

"A drug dealer, then?"

The woman shrugged.

"Spend a day in my nails," she said, "and then talk to me about a hard ghetto life you sure as hell ain't never stepped foot in. Let's see what you got in that designer purse of yours."

Ursula had bought it at the Target Labor Day sale. She knew, knew, *knew* that she should just turn around and walk away from trouble. Isn't that what Judge Judy always said? But anger flashed through her, as it so often did, and, after months of being holed up in the tundra with nobody but the parish priest who didn't understand her to talk to, the frustration bubbled over, and she could hold her tongue no longer.

"Och, for the love of God, catch yerself on, miseryguts. Me life was spent in a poverty-stricken war-zone. Did ye grow up with a telly? A microwave? A car? Heat in the winter? A phone?"

The woman's dreads bobbed up and down, and she was staring at Ursula as if she were a lunatic: of course she had grown up with those necessities; it was the USA, after all.

"We hadn't any of them luxuries. There be's people worse off in the world, and by the standards of the rest of the world's poor, ye're rolling in it. So don't ye be whinging on at me about this fantasy ghetto of yers. C'mere a wee minute while I tell ye about me life in a war-zone, rubber bullets flying through the air, soldiers trampling through wer front garden with rifles, barricades of burnt-out cars at the bottom of wer street, tear gas clouding the air, friends and family shot down in the prime of life, not because of drug-related drive-bys, but as we were born in the wrong location. When ye take a gander outside yer door into a war-zone, then ye can start telling me about a hard life! Can ye look me in the face and tell me ye've had a life as full as misery as mine? Ghetto, me arse!"

The woman peered at Ursula as if seeing her for the first time.

"What language you speakin?"

"Och—"

"Open the bag, bitch, or I'm gonna beat you down!"

Even as Ursula wondered when 'beat up' had been replaced by 'beat down' in the current vernacular, the woman raced toward her, menacing her up against the door of the toilet stall. Ursula's eyes shot towards the frustratingly still restroom door, and she wondered feverishly why this restroom was as unvisited as the High Limit lounge outside; weren't the bladders of the multitudes bursting from all the free liquor they were guzzling down on the floor? But Fionnuala Flood had spent the previous year trying to get her claws into her handbag, and Ursula hadn't let that happen. Ursula looked well-fed and content, but the harshness of the Derry Troubles and the acid tongues of her relatives had given her a steely constitution to combat danger.

"Ye kyanny scare me, woman!" she said, her purse flying through the air and smacking the crack addict in the face.

The purse flung from Ursula's hand, and the contents sprayed onto the floor. The woman wobbled over and collapsed on the filthy tiles. Ursula scrabbled to collect her belongings: the rosary beads, the Minnie Mouse bingo stamper, the pearls, the wallet with her credit cards and coins scattered on the tiles.

"I'm gonna find you and kill you!" the woman promised from her location of the floor, fingernails clacking on the tiles. "I'm gonna find out where you live! I'm gonna hunt you down and slit your throat while you sleep in your bed!" She was too high, drunk, fat or lazy—Ursula couldn't decide which—to raise herself from the floor.

Ursula raced out of the restroom onto the floor of the casino, desperately searching for a security guard. There seemed to be one at the bar laughing with an aged cocktail waitress with a ladder running up the left leg of her pantyhose and lipstick on her front teeth. She hurried over and pointed frantically in the direction of the restroom.

"Some aul crone has just gone and clattered me in the ladies' loos! Outta her mind with drink, so she was! Och, I'm afeared for me life, so I'm are, pure heart-scared."

The guard stared at her uncomprehendingly. The waitress took a step back. They exchanged a glance at the strange words coming out of Ursula's mouth, then looked at each other conspiratorially. Ursula ground her teeth, as she had no doubt they thought the wit had seeped out of her brain from alcohol.

"If you'll just come with me, ma'am," the waitress twittered, placing a kind hand on her shoulder. "I'll be happy to take you to the food court and get you a coffee, nice and black and free."

"Och, get yer hands offa me. I'm not deranged with drink, that's how I was born talking. It's not me head that needs examining, it's that lunatic creature in the ladies loos ye should be after."

She was about to threaten a lawsuit, if only to see some alarm on their faces over more than her accent, but she realized that that was the Fionnuala Way (and perhaps the Way of the woman on the tiles).

"Can youse not come to me aid?" Ursula pleaded, wringing her hands.

She was relieved to see Jed's cowboy hat winding its way through a maze of cocktail waitress trays towards them, bobbing through the craps tables.

"Och, I'll handle it with me husband, here he comes now. Go on away off, youse," she dismissed the two. They gratefully hurried off. "Jed! I'm over here!"

"Hi, honey," Jed said. "I was looking for you."

"Och, it was a wile terrible trial, so it was," Ursula said, but suddenly stopped her blubbering as Jed placed a hand in worry on her shoulder. She felt safe now he was by her side, even drunk and probably out of funds as he was.

"What is it, dear?" Jed asked, genuine concern in his voice. His big, strong hands stroked her own.

"It's over now," Ursula decided, the danger now definitely gone, and the thought of further confrontation making her ill. Judge Judy would have been proud. "What made ye come seek me out?"

"Uh, yeah, could you write me a check for a hundred?" Ursula now kept tabs on the bank account to ensure there was at least some money in it.

Ursula had to indulge Jed. He had tried to sacrifice his life for her the year before, after all. Plus, Jed Barnett was damned with constant good humor, which irked Ursula to no end at times, but which endeared him to almost everyone else, and which comforted her now.

She guided him to the very long line of the cashier's, twiddling her giraffe brooch and shaking her head, bemused, at the panic she had felt minutes earlier. With Jed slouching by her side whistling the theme from *The Jeffersons,* she was no longer gripped with fear; the casino employees' annoying looks and suspicions were forgotten, and the ghetto beast and her empty threats already a thing of the past. In this world of many people, Ursula was certain she would never set eyes on the woman again.

Ursula scrabbled through her purse and located her tired checkbook. Another hundred dollars would probably never be seen again, but Jed didn't ask for much often anymore. He had learned to bet only what they could afford. She reached for her wallet, as she would need to show her driver's license.

"Hey, honey, you shoulda seen the big win I had after you left the table. I put almost all my chips on nineteen, you know, Gretchen's birthday, and— Ow! You're hurting me!"

Ursula's fingernails sliced into his arm. Her face drained as a dread gripped her.

"Me driver's license has gone missing!"

And she knew, the way one does, that it had found its way into those RIP-stenciled fingernails.

"Jed! She knows where we live!"

CHAPTER 13

Dymphna sadly inspected the hand-held shower hose attached to the bathtub tap. After almost a year in the splendor of the Waterside, she had gotten used to the Riddell's state of the art walk-in steam affair that fit two, its ceiling rain shower and soft lighting, the all glass surround, water pressure that fairly took the flesh off her bones, and aromatherapy option (Dymphna was partial to the ylang-ylang). The shower had frequently been a social affair for her and Rory when set to 'steam.' They would never again share another sexy scene loofahing Christian Dior gel into each other's crevices in the steam, Dymphna thought glumly, staring with hatred at the sliver of soap bleeding down the side of the tub.

When Rory coerced her to be his fiancée, she had found it frustrating to have the same male body next to her in bed night after night (especially that body), but recently she had been finding it comforting. Now she had nobody. She knew she could go to any pub in the city center and take her pick of the fit young lads in their Nikes and soccer shirts, but—

As she forced her bare feet from the ratty carpet to the icy tub, her tingly nipples and a slight sense of nausea reminded her of the shameful secret growing inside her, the horror of her sordid little family expanding. She took careful aim with the hand-held shower. Thin rivulets of tepid water dribbled over one foot, then one hand of goosebumps. Dymphna moaned as she shivered, and she looked with a further sense of doom at the bathtub itself, with its filthy ring and mildewed tiles. She damned the misunderstanding at the Pence-A-Day storage units which had led to her expulsion from both a ready-made support system for a newborn infant and an unborn child and a house which had the Internet actually *inside it*.

She had suffered a fitful, sleepless night at 5 Murphy Crescent as Keanu screamed at her side and her granny Heggarty snored in the next room, wondering if she should chance and how she could afford the bus ride, ferry ride and taxi ride over to England for a termination, and the taxi ride, the ferry ride and the bus ride back. She cursed the lunacy of Irish legislation which still had abortion illegal, just as she had ten months earlier.

"It's all coming back to me now," she thought grimly, "This is what me whole life was like."

The rooms of 5 Murphy Crescent were more dank and dingy than the romanticized memories of when she had been forced to live there with her granny Eda (her parents had been furious the then-unborn Keanu was a half-Proddy bastard). The misery of life in the semi-detached council house came flooding back to her, the hot water bottles, shivering and weighed down, a prisoner to the mattress, under the weight of seven smelly blankets, the coal bin, the tiny fridge which could only hold three eggs and a half pint of milk, the smell of a pensioner's wee.

"And now I'm back in the Moorside," she sighed to herself. "And me life is only gonny get more miserable."

She had been positioning the showerhead at her trembling flesh in a wide array of angles, yet was still barely damp.

"Och, this flimmin attachment is useless, so it is," Dymphna finally realized. She would have to forgo the middle-class pretensions of a shower and revert to running a common bath, another step back into her past. She dismounted the tub and wrapped herself in the silk bathrobe with the ZR monogram she had secreted in the bottom of her suitcase under her smalls.

She tugged the rubber tubing from the tap and glumly watched water of a yellowish hue fill the tub. She wished she had thought to nick some of her mother's Dead Sea bath salts. And then she recalled what she had finally seen clearly on her mother's face when Fionnuala had entered the kitchen the night before: disappointment, annoyance, a hatred reserved especially for her. Her mother was right, Dymphna suddenly decided, the shame overwhelming her: she was a jumped up wee bitch, with ideas above her station; this was the world she had been born into and to which her flesh belonged.

She slid her hand in the pocket, pulled out her cellphone and frenetically dialed Bridie's number. There had been a time they were inseparable as mates; if you kicked one, the other would limp. Once again, she received Bridie's voicemail message. She rattled the cellphone, hoping this would bring about a different result. The beep unleashed a torrent of tears from her.

"Och, Bridie, why don't ye answer me calls, ye daft cunt?" she cried down the line. "From bad to worse, it's getting. Rory's mammy kicked me out. I'm relegated to living at me auntie Ursula's old house with me granny and the wanes, me mammy hates me and…Och, Bridie, for the love of God almighty, answer me, would ye? Maybe ye're at work? I'm slavering for one of them TakkoKebabs from the ChipKebab, and some Chicken Dippers with that garlic sauce. I'm gonny be down the town the morrow and I'll pop in to see ye, and ye can have a wee gander at Keanu, ye've not seen him, aye? And a round of gossip and all. We've ten months of it to trawl through, aye?"

She clicked the phone shut and flung it at the sink, and it knocked the ashtray to the floor, butts flying. But as Dymphna sniveled on the edge of the tub, an insurgent thought bubbled up from an unknown corner of her mind: she wouldn't settle for what she had been born into. She would land a job at the ChipKebab with Bridie and become financially solvent; then she would somehow get Rory back, tell him about his new child growing within her, and he would be overjoyed; she would move back into the bungalow; she would even learn to love Zoë's organic spinach and courgette pies. She might even give up lager and groping strange lads' arses. And then her life would be perfect.

As the teenager gingerly lowered herself into the mire, her fingers reached squeamishly for the sliver of soap, but Dymphna had a feeling she would arise from the tub a different creature altogether, swathing the silk robe around her dripping body somehow reborn—a woman.

CHAPTER 14

While scouring burnt spud bits from the side of a pot, Fionnuala discovered she was humming Celine Dion's "My Heart Will Go On." It was no wonder, as the song was playing on the radio next to the teeming sink, and *Titanic* was her favorite movie of all time.

"Near…far…wherever you are…!" Fionnuala sang into the grubby suds.

The fallout of her birthday, her sacking, her unflattering image on the cover of Moira's book, all made the pan pipes of the song tug on the strings of her anthracite heart. Fionnuala felt a tightening in her throat as she made her way through an eggbeater, three teacups and a spatula and was carried off to an Ireland she was hard-pressed to find in the drudgery of the gray bricks beyond the net curtains (and even that she was hard-pressed to see, as the broken window had been duct taped with cardboard). Fionnuala knew that Celine's Hollywood version of the Celtic wonderland of Eire existed somewhere, but she had visited it only in her heart.

Behind her, Paddy padded in and placed his hands around where he suspected her hips must be, singing in baritone, *"We'll…stay…forever this way...!"* He nuzzled his three-day growth against his wife's neck, and yelped as Fionnuala cracked her elbow into his rib.

"Are ye mental, ye eejit?" she scoffed.

There was a limited amount of physical affection Fionnuala could stand, and during the birthday bedroom antics of the night before, Paddy had gone over her limit. Then she remembered Paddy and Padraig had been the only two who gave her presents that cost more than a tenner, and her heart softened.

"Them gifts was grand and lovely, so they were," Fionnuala said. In the sitting room the phone began to ring. "An extravagance, mind, especially as we've only one income coming in now. Ye weren't meant to know I'd get the sack before ye bought em, but. How in God's name ye had two pennies to rub together baffles me still. Ye hand yer paycheck over to me every fortnight. Ye've not been down at that betting office again, have ye? Throwing away yer hard earned dosh on them dogs?"

Paddy set his face to one of seriousness, while the house phone continued its incessant ringing. "I've something to tell ye," he said. "I meant to tell ye yesterday, but with all them festivities, and wer Moira's book showing the light of day and all..."

Fionnuala's hands, deep in the filthy dishwater, froze. The front door opened, then slammed shut.

"If ye're telling me that Burberry scarf be's a cheap knock-off!" she warned, a pink latex glove dripping slime at his nose. "I don't want to go prancing down the city center looking like one of them chavs!"

"It's sweet feck all to do with them gifts," Paddy said, though on this subject he didn't seem able to meet her eyes. "It's about me job at the plant."

"I swear to God Almighty, if ye've been sacked and all—"

Padraig interrupted her rage from the sitting room. "Mammy! There's a call for ye."

"Jesus Mary and Joseph," Fionnuala huffed. "Can I not get a minute's head peace?" She peeled off the gloves, marched into the sitting room and wrenched the phone from Padraig.

"Aye?" Fionnuala barked. She listened with her right ear for a second as a woman on the other end blabbered on like a mad thing in a West-Brit accent that set Fionnuala's nerves on edge, and soon found more interesting things to listen to with her left ear. She watched Paddy lean down and hiss at Padraig (as if she wouldn't hear him! Was Paddy a simpleton?):

"Where did you get the money for all them gifts from, hi? I'm all for shoplifting, especially as the scarf makes yer mammy bearable, but if we're to have a third son banged up in the slammer—"

"I'm but eleven," Padraig said, that strange look in his eyes; Fionnuala could see it from where she was standing in the next room. "The peelers don't lock up wanes at eleven years of age, so they don't. Set yer mind at rest, but, da. I didn't nick em."

"Dealing drugs, then? Following in yer brother Eoin's footsteps?"

Again that stare.

"Would ye quit looking at me like that, wee boy?" Paddy suddenly roared.

Fionnuala could take the woman's voice no more. She wailed like a wounded beast into the receiver: "Fionnuala Flood, did ye say? We're on wer way to her funeral now. Knocked down like a common animal in the street while on her way to Sunday mass, so she was. By a lorry. Ten feet in the air, her body flew."

She sobbed a few times for good measure, then slammed the receiver down and filed back into the kitchen.

"Another of them collection calls?" Paddy asked.

"Aye," Fionnuala said. "We've the gas people hounding us now. That's sure to keep em confused for another week at least. I hope I made the bloody minger feel like shite. Imagine terrorizing people like that to bring home a paycheck. Some have no dignity. Now what's all this palaver about the wane's strange looks?"

"He's been doing it for weeks!" Paddy said.

"What way am I looking at ye?" Padraig asked.

"Ye know flimmin well the look I'm on about."

"Daddy...but, as God's me witness, I haven't a clue what ye're on about!"

"That narrow, evil squint, yer eyes glinting and threatening me with all sorts of malice."

Fionnuala bent down and inspected her son, really seeing him for the first time in weeks; she had had other things on her mind.

"Aye, ye're dead right there, Paddy!" she gasped, and Paddy nodded righteously behind her. "It's not normal!"

She turned to her husband: "I've been uneasy about that wane since he started pelting rocks at teetering old pensioners, and I've told Father Hogan about it in the confessional and all. So help me Heavenly Father, Paddy, he better not be turning into one of them serial killers like what me mother always be's reading about. Scundered, I'd be, pure red in the face."

She faced her son and smacked him across the cheek: "Have ye started torturing wee animals yet?"

"What are youse on about?" Padraig squealed. "I'm doing nothing with me eyes! Nothing, I tell ye!"

"What've ye come round here for anyroad?" Fionnuala asked. "To hack into wer sleeping bodies? We've been up for hours, more fool you."

"For the use of the loo. Dymphna's been in wers for ages, so she has, and I'm bursting for a slash. And I've a wile bad headache and all. Have youse any paracetamol? We've nothing round ours."

"Yer granny's a walking chemist's, sure!" Fionnuala said, flabbergasted.

"Aye, she told me she's nothing for wanes, but."

"Ye think we've the dosh to splash out on tablets for headaches we might have in the future? And surely yer sister's outta the jacks by now. Get yerself back round the corner. Ye're giving me the heebie-jeebies. And don't ye turn around and flash me one of them unnatural looks of yers on yer way out."

The moment the door slammed, Fionnuala's hand whipped though the air and connected with Paddy's face. He yelped and clutched at the pain.

"Are ye mad, woman?"

"I didn't want to show ye up in front of yer son. Where's me birthday gift? I heard ye talking to that mental creature about how ye hadn't a clue where they come from. Had I known ye had no hand in procuring em, ye sure as bloody hell wouldn't've had yer way with me last night."

"Och…" Paddy wavered before her on the peeling linoleum, still massaging his cheek.

"Out with it, man!"

Fionnuala inspected his mouth that was like a goldfish's on a floor, then clutched his arm as a sudden, terrifying revelation hit her.

"Jesus, Mary and Joseph!" She made an impromptu sign of the cross. "God bless us and save us!"

"What's up with ye?" Paddy asked.

She hesitated. "Och, ye'll think me a wile eejit…"

"Come out with it, woman."

"That look in yer son's eyes…it was…*unchristian*, so it was. Paddy, ye don't think…should I be contacting Father Hogan at St. Molaug's?"

"What are ye on about?"

"So's the priest can…" She looked around the kitchen appliances for eavesdroppers, then mouthed: "Cast out the demons?"

His laughter was sharp, her fists sharper.

"Sure, all the wanes the day be's giving looks like that," Paddy said, fending off her blows.

"Sign of the times, me arse!"

"Catch yerself on, woman. Take wer Padraig to the Health Clinic before ye show yerself up taking him to St. Molaug's."

Fionnuala seemed unconvinced and dismissed her husband to the soccer on the TV as she had much to think about and many dishes still to slog through. She shuffled in misery to the sink, irritated that Celine Dion had been replaced by Gwen Guthrie's "Ain't Nothin Goin On But The Rent." She snapped the radio off and dug her fingers into the dishwater. Music was but window dressing to mask the misery of their lives anyway.

Is this me lot on this pigging Earth? she thought *Scrounging and scrimping and—*

Something sliced into her flesh. It was glass from the broken window.

That bitch Moira and her flimmin book—

She located the beans pot where it had fallen the night before. She made sure Paddy was still glued to the telly.

Perhaps a wee look inside…

But the book was gone.

"Where the bleeding hell? What spastic in their right mind…?"

Before the TV, Paddy jerked at the sudden appearance of Fionnuala hovering over him with a glare. Beer splattered from the can over his jeans.

"Ye get on that mobile of yers and ring up yer man Callum Sheeney from the Fillets-O-Joy," she intoned.

The blood drained from Paddy's face as he jumped up from the cushion.

"What are ye on about?" he asked, fear flashing in his eyes. "Ye mean ye kn—"

"Or whichever of them lads be's responsible for the roster at the plant. Ye're to phone whoever and demand all the overtime that be's going."

"A-a-a-as ye've been sacked? To help with paying the bills, ye mean?"

"Aye, that and all," Fionnuala said. "As well, but, to fund the holiday we're going on."

"H-holiday?" He looked at her as if she had just announced she was pregnant. Again. "August is months away, sure."

"I mean the trip we're taking to Malta."

"Where the bloody feck be's Malta?"

"No filthy beanflicker of a daughter is going to show me up for all the world to read and then live to tell the tale. We're heading up to Malta the lot of us, even that devil-child of yers and Dymphna, for that do Moira be's throwing. Rocks, I'm gonny be throwing at her gacky skull with them flimmin intellectual specs perched on the end of it. I kyanny wait to rip them smarmy, snide specs off her fecking jivin face and rip into her with me tongue. She kyanny get away with it unscathed, Paddy. She just kyanny. Ye mind the likes of me when I heard them Barnetts wouldn't hand over some of their lotto win to us?"

Paddy blanched at the memory of Fionnuala's face as it had been, stretched in rage for months.

"That'll pale in comparison to the wrath I'm to unleash on that ungrateful wee cunt-slurper Moira when I see her. The holiday's to be yer birthday gift to me, so I'm not taking naw for an answer, and so help me Jesus, ye better be right there with me in the front line when I descend upon her undeserving bones and give her the lashing of her life with all the bodily force the Lord will allow, bless Him. And maybe next year ye won't forget yer wife's bloody birthday, ye demented cunt!"

CHAPTER 15

Struggling up Shipquay Street with Keanu strapped to her breasts, Padraig glowering at her side, and clutching Maureen's shoulder to haul her up the steep incline, Dymphna felt a freedom she had long been denied as the indentured servant of the Riddell household. Her depression in the tub of the day before seemed to have passed.

"Them beans from yer mammy's party is repeating on me," Maureen moaned. "The shite's been spewing from me body ever since. Dehydrated for two days, I've been."

Dymphna giggled to herself over Keanu's shrieks and smiled to a gang of hooded teens on the corner, rolled cigarettes hanging from their scowls. The fact that the sun was blazing in the sky yet they were being pelted with horizontal rain seemed to cause her no ill will to the world at large. At long last she was free!

They rounded the corner of the city walls, pushing past shopping bags coming at them from all directions and strollers thronged with screaming children, and shuffled through the discarded Styrofoam containers and vintage vomit which was the fast food joint's panorama. Dymphna stopped and looked up and down the cobblestoned street in surprise.

"The ChipKebab's missing!" she gasped.

"Och, did I not tell ye? A multinational corporation bought it the other month," Maureen explained. "I mind during the Troubles of the '70s and '80s," (here Dymphna and Padraig tensed; how the dottery old ones could whine on and on about the city's violent ancient history which had nothing, they thought, to do with their modern lives) "all them foreign corporations was terrified of setting up shops on wer streets for fear they'd be blown to bits the moment they were erected. The whole of us stranded by the world here in Northern Ireland heard about McDonald's and Burger King for decades; never set eyes on a BigMac, let alone bite into one. Ye had to take the ferry to England for to get yer fill of PizzaHut and Colonel Sanders and whatnot. Loads of shameless slappers with unwanted wanes..." she stared pointedly at Dymphna, "...had to traipse to Liverpool for both their terminations and ChickenMcNuggets. Came back with empty wombs and enough Big Macs to store in their freezers for months. If they had had freezers back in them days, which none of us did. Youse wanes the day have not a clue how good youse have it."

Padraig couldn't help but ask: "Granny, but...what did youse eat back then, hi?"

"There was one fish and chip van on the Lecky Road and a café on the Strand," Maureen sniffed. "Did a marvelous shepherd's pie, so they did, the spuds lovely and moist with crunchy bits on top. Blown up by the UFC in 1976, it was. The ChipKebab now be's called Kebabalicious. Fecking goofy name. Same hooligan service, but. I'm parched, the tongue be's hanging outta me with hunger, and I'm gagging for a slash all at the same time. Let's get werselves inside so's I can perch meself on that swanky new loo of theirs. They've still got a mirror inside it and all, would ye believe?"

Dymphna was impressed; she'd have to have a look at the mirror. They parted as a drunk with garlic sauce rolling down his chin barreled out the door and waved hello. The trio and a half entered. Maureen and Padraig raced for the restroom. Dymphna felt the zits forming on her face as she pushed through air sodden with grease.

Same old grease, but this certainly wasn't the ChipKebab of old. Dymphna marveled at the new cleanish surroundings, the shiny purple and orange tiles (especially those on the ceiling) with little graffiti so far, yet she was comforted by the sight of the disheveled teens with badly-bitten fingernails and ludicrous caps slouching at the tills. Some things hadn't changed during her six month exile on the Waterside.

Beside every girl at a till was an unemployed boyfriend with a soccer jersey and cold sores who stood babbling on about nothing of interest, and glared with menace at any male whose eyes rested on their girlfriends' breasts longer than necessary, and whose only use outside Kebabalicious seemed to be siphoning down food from the girls' home fridges, snatching their paychecks at the end of every week, spending it all on lager and drugs, and, in return, giving them a jolly good rogering when they needed it. All except Bridie's till.

Dymphna watched Bridie scratch her fat arse before she handed over a portion of chips to a customer, and she fought the urge to dry retch.

I'm gonny boke, she thought, but "Bridie! Bridie!" she said, waving eagerly.

Bridie looked up from the till. Dymphna whipped her head around, looking for the cause of sudden distress on Bridie's face. She saw nothing but a torn promotional poster for weekly line-dancing sessions at the Leisure Center taped to the front window. Perhaps a hoard of lager louts had passed and gone to the upmarket McDonald's next door instead. Dymphna balanced Keanu on the table next to the choking victim poster and made her way to the counter.

"What about ye, Bridie?" Dymphna asked (the typical Derry 'how are you?').

"Bout ye, Dymphna."

Dymphna reached across the purple counter sheen and hugged her best mate. Bridie didn't press back. Dymphna wondered briefly about this but, seeing the size of Bridie now, she wouldn't want anyone touching her either.

"Ye're looking wile...healthy, hi," Dymphna managed.

"I'm on a diet," Bridie said through a fixed grin. "Small portions. What's yer order? It's grand and lovely to be seeing ye after such a long time, there be's a line forming behind ye, but."

"Shift yer arse to yer woman's till there, boyo," Dymphna demanded of the youngster behind her. She leaned in conspiratorially across the straw dispenser. "Did ye not get me voicemail? I haven't seen ye in ages, holed up in that Proddy Hell as I was. Up the scoot, so I'm are, and kicked outta the family home. I've nothing on at the moment as I've been sacked from the lockups job and all. Are there any jobs going here? It would be a wile craic if we was working together again, like. Don't ye think?"

The expressions on Bridie's face didn't seem to follow logically from what Dymphna was saying. For example, a look of horror was now disfiguring Bridie's face, while Dymphna could think of no reason why that should be. She continued.

"I mind when I was carrying Keanu the thought of going off with lads made me ill. This new wane's got me feeling randy, but. I'm gagging for a shag. How about you and me meet at the Craiglooner after yer shift? We can down a few pints there, then head off to that new club Starzzz for a twirl on the dancefloor, maybe pop a winger or two. It'll be just like old times, hi!"

"Me shift here starts the morrow morning at nine."

"O'clock?"

Bridie's eyes shifted helplessly from side to side.

"Shall we see how it plays out, just? What's yer order?"

Dymphna hadn't had time to peruse the new menu, and she was still waiting for Padraig and her granny to come back from the restroom to tell her what they wanted.

"Och, it's been a terrible wile trial for me, lately. Rory was of the mind I was giving me hole up to three aul ones at once in the Pence-A-Day office. It's all down to me looks, ye know. It wouldn't be in all this trouble had I a face like a busted cabbage. Good looks be's a wile awful curse, Bridie. Ye should count yerself lucky, so ye should," Dymphna said earnestly, flicking her orange curls.

"For feck's sake!"

Dymphna was taken aback, thinking Bridie's rage was directed at her. But Bridie wasn't looking at her. She was staring at the restroom, where a mob of angry, desperate punters were banging on the door, Maureen moaning and twisting on her cane on the outskirts.

"Would ye hurry up in there," Padraig roared, fists pummeling the door. "There's an aul one out here ready to flood her knickers!"

"Virgin Mary mother of God!" Bridie huffed. "Not more of them junkies passed out in the jacks! Ye should see state of the new tiles after themmuns use it as a shooting gallery, hours it takes to scrub and sanitize. Had to call the ambulance twice this month so far due to overdoses. Go on and help me prise em out, Dymphna."

Bridie got the master key from the hook, pulled on latex gloves and raced over, Dymphna reluctantly in tow. They pushed through the crowd, and the door rattled with the force of Bridie's substantial blows. Maureen battered the door with her cane.

"Hi!" Bridie yelled. "You in there! Rouse yerself now! Clear on off outta wer jacks or I'm ringing the peelers on ye!"

The key flicked in the lock, and Bridie tugged open the door.

"Filthy, mingin beast!" Bridie's contempt was all-consuming.

Dymphna wrinkled her nose in disgust at the unconscious figure inside and followed Bridie in. Maureen noticed the mirror was gone. The figure was not a junkie, but an archetype of the ruin that too much alcohol could breed: a young man looking older than his years, clothing rumpled and stained, scabs on his knuckles from where he had bumped into walls while out of his mind with drink. The skeletal limbs looked familiar, however, and unease crept though Dymphna as Bridie approached him with her latex gloves. When the unfortunate's face was revealed, she grabbed Bridie's arm. Bridie shook it free.

"Bridie, but!" Dymphna gasped. "That's me Rory, so it is!"

CHAPTER 16

Edna Gee had been to the Health Clinic for her annual shingles vaccine, and was fuming over that new Pakistani doctor refusing to inject it in her arm. She opened the Sav-U-Mor door and hobbled in, each step a chore.

"About time," Skivvins snipped, rattling his Rolex under her nose.

"If ye would get a replacement for that Flood creature—" Edna huffed, heaving her handbag onto the counter.

"No time to chat. Things to do."

Skivvins threw her the keys and pranced out. Behind the counter, Edna struggled into her work smock and winced. She didn't trust that Dr. Khudiadadzai or her ability with a hypodermic needle; the pain in her backside was torturous. What sort of injury had the doctor done to her? She rummaged through her handbag and found her compact. She had her plaid skirt pulled up, her floral knickers down on one side, straining to view the injection in the compact mirror, when the door flew open.

Two men with ski-masks barged in. Edna screamed, unsure what they were after, the till or her virtue. They went straight for the canned carrots. Edna watched in puzzlement. They glanced at the labels one after the other, tossed the cans to the floor, then rifled through the mushrooms and parsnips.

"What in God's name—?"

"Silence, aul one!" growled the taller thug.

Edna's arms snapped around her chest, and she bristled at the affront. *Aul one, indeed!* Anger and frustration rising, the intruders made their way with increasing violence through the beans, peas, carrots and sweet corn, cans clunking to the floor and rolling through the aisles.

Edna boiled. She had spent hours fixing up that canned vegetable shelf after her fight with the Flood woman a few days before. And they needn't have bothered disguising themselves, the foolish gacks, Edna thought, as at a closer look at their jackets—the Thin Lizzie one and the New Wave one—she knew exactly who they were: the two layabouts who huddled together in the nook of the Rocking Seamaid where Edna met her Pub Quiz team on a Tuesday night.

Edna didn't know these eejits' names, but Thin Lizzie was the uncle of the girl behind the meat and cheese counter of the Top-Yer-Trolley who had left her husband for a drunk, New Wave the cousin of the man who did the karaoke down at the TenderHorse before he was banged up for drug dealing. Edna had heard gossip they were resurrecting an offshoot of the IRA, and irritation rankled the pride Edna felt for their activity: certainly Britain should give up its hold on Northern Ireland, and the four counties should be reunited with the South, but at what price, what bloodshed? Her uncle's left leg had been paralyzed by a rubber bullet in '74, and Edna still couldn't get over it.

"If youse would tell me what ye're looking for…" Edna chanced.

Thin Lizzie reached into his jacket and pulled out a gun. Edna shrieked as he waved it menacingly at her, and New Wave followed suit, a second gun materializing from the side of the brownish-pink leather.

New Wave snorted under his ski mask.

"The fecking eejit of a cunt we get wer…goods from down the market accidentally sold cases of cans meant for us to ye. Took hours of beating to get it outta him. Yer man be's laid up in intensive care at Altnagelvin now for his foolishness."

"The same can be arranged for *ye* and all," Thin Lizzie put in, the room receding from Edna in her mind as he verged upon her with the barrel of the gun pointed at her forehead. She blessed herself and whimpered a quick prayer beside the Jelly Babies. "Where the bloody feck be's wer cans? Have ye put em in the back?"

"Naw, them cans doesn't be in the back," Edna sniveled, cold steel inching towards her nose. "I've no part in this! Ye've me fear-hearted! Leave me be!"

"Ye're the Flood woman, aye?" New Wave asked.

The insults never stopped.

"God bless us and save us, naw."

For a moment, it seemed the pause button had been pressed, then New Wave motioned to Thin Lizzie.

"Enough," he said. "She doesn't be the one we're after."

Thin Lizzie lowered the gun, and Edna deflated in relief against the laxatives.

"Och, youse put the fear of the Lord into me, right enough," Edna said, her body still shuddering. "All ye had to do was open yer mouths and ask me, sure. Yer woman was sacked for her silly game with them cans the other day. Dragged em all home with her. Fionnuala Flood be's her full name. Her husband works down the Fillets-O-Joy. From the Moorside, so they are."

"Och, that we know, sure. Which house exactly, but."

Edna trawled through her frenzied mind for some memory; Fionnuala's lair was the last place she would ever visit.

"She never shuts her bake about 5 Murphy Crescent. Youse're sure to find her or some sign of her there."

The two exchanged a look through the eye holes of their ski masks.

"Let's clear outta here," New Wave said.

Thin Lizzie hesitated, seemingly on the verge of giving one of Edna's breasts a quick fondle, but sanity prevailed and they raced out the door.

Now that the adrenaline was fleeing her shaken-up system, Edna felt the dull throb flooding into her backside again. She shuffled over to the sea of cans littering the linoleum and grimaced as she bent down to pick them up. A good neighbor would've been on the phone immediately to alert Fionnuala of the danger she was now in. A good neighbor. Wiping dirt off a can of new potatoes, Edna smiled through her pain.

CHAPTER 17

Bridie and Dymphna pried the empty cider bottle from Rory fingers, tugged his floppy limbs from the toilet seat and, as Maureen pushed inside past them, they dragged what was left of him through the crowd and into the stockroom. Bridie was relieved the manager was 'making a deposit at the bank;' usually he chose that excuse to get his leg over his best mate's wife down the docks—he'd be gone a while.

She stole glances at Rory's glazed, swiveling eyes as Dymphna tried to slap some sense into him, and Bridie's heart secretly fell. Getting so wasted showed Rory was devastated by the breakup; he must really care for Dymphna.

"Wake up, ye daft eejit, ye! Wake up!" Dymphna implored as she clattered him about the head. It lolled against a carton of urinal splash guards.

"Perhaps some black coffee would be more beneficial than battering the shite outta him, hi," Bridie said stiffly. "I'm away off to get some."

"Ta," Dymphna said, looking up gratefully. She didn't have a clue what to do on her own.

Waiting for the coffee dispenser behind the counter to fill a jumbo cup, Bridie knew it would now be more difficult for her to get her claws into Rory, but she was a woman on a mission, with the mental resources to help her get what she wanted, which is precisely what her former best mate Dymphna lacked. She wanted to ensure Dymphna's engagement ring eventually found its way to a more deserving finger, hers.

Bridie reentered the stockroom and smiled as she handed Dymphna the coffee. Rory was still unconscious.

"Och, the poor aul soul," Dymphna said, affectionately wiping drool from Rory's chin with her sleeve. "It's breaking up with me that got him into this state. Ye know, Bridie, I was scundered when he asked me to marry him.

Especially as he's a Proddy and wee Keanu isn't even his. Now, but... I've been wile lonely sleeping on me tod."

Bridie sought the Lord's help to maintain the composure of a concerned friend, then jumped as Maureen's body blackened the doorway.

"The hunger's gnawing a hole in me stomach," she complained. "Did we not come here to fill wer throats? Though the stench of yer man there be's putting me off the thought of food."

"Can ye not see we've more important things going on at the moment, granny?" Dymphna griped. She reached impatiently into her purse and shoved Zoë's credit card at her. "Get yerself and the wane what youse want. I'll take a burger of sorts." She turned to Bridie. "Have they something like that on the menu here, hi?"

"Aye, the Cowalicious-On-A-Bun." Bridie felt a fool uttering the name.

"Get me one of them. And a small mineral, *diet,*" Dymphna said, arching her eyebrows at Bridie as if to say, 'ye see, there's no shame in it.'

Maureen was looking at the platinum Amex in revulsion. "There be's something unseemly about using a Proddy bitch's credit card."

"Have ye money on ye? Has wer Padraig money on him? Ye think I have money on me? If it makes ye sleep better at night, ye're using it *because* she be's a Proddy bitch."

This did seem to make sense. Maureen shuffled off.

"Try to get this coffee down him," Bridie said, handing Dymphna the steaming coffee and secretly hoping the stupid girl would end up burning the lips off him. Bridie could nurse those lips back to health.

Rory entered the land of the conscious, if not the sober. His eyes creaked open, and he slurred a few things the girls couldn't make out, no matter how close they placed their ears.

"Bridie, I want him back, so I do," Dymphna said. "Spindly limbs, spots and all."

Bridie could keep silent no longer. "Are ye sure it's him, or is it his mammy's bank account and yer flash life on the Waterside ye're after? Once ye moved in with them Orange toerags, we saw neither hide nor hair of ye this side of town. Too good for us, were ye?"

Bridie wanted to smack the look of innocent shock off of Dymphna's face, but had no chance as Maureen barged into the stockroom again.

"That fecking Orange cunt's gone and put a stop on this card. The wee girl at the counter said the machine told her to take hold of it and ring the Filth."

They all shared a wry chuckle; as if phoning the police were likely.

"Musta been the nappies and formula I bought with it yesterday that alerted Zoë," Dymphna mused. "That pigging Keanu, cause of all me heartache."

"And," Maureen continued, "that brother of yers is making a wile show of himself over by the soda machine—"

Padraig himself poked his head in the stockroom. "Me head!" he moaned, clutching said item. "It be's like knitting needles shoved behind me eyeballs. Please, Dymphna, take me home to Mammy, would ye?"

Bridie thought the child must really be suffering, asking to see that hard-faced cow Fionnuala Flood.

"We're trying to conduct a conversation here between husband and wife," Dymphna said, motioning to Rory's glazed eyes that still stared at nothing.

"Youse isn't married, but!" Padraig said.

"Near as dammit," Dymphna intoned. Bridie simmered.

"Yer man there kyanny speak nohow," Padraig squealed in desperation. "Legless, so he is."

Bridie put a hand on Dymphna's shoulder. "Perhaps ye should be off," she suggested. "It's gonny be hours before ye get any sense outta this one. And the manager's sure to be back soon. Youse kyanny set up camp here. I'll look after him for ye, Dymphna."

"Ta, Bridie, ye're a star, so ye are," Dymphna said with gratitude. She squeezed Rory's hand one last time and got up from the concrete floor. "Lets get ye home, Granny, and see if we kyanny scrounge up something for ye to get down yer bake. And some painkillers for ye and all, Padraig."

"Not them beans on toast again," Maureen huffed, wobbling away.

"I saw cases of tinned vegetables collecting dust in a corner of the scullery. Now where the feck did I set that flimmin Keanu?"

"Och, naw. Them tins of yer mammy's vegetables kyanny be eaten by humans."

Their voices trailed off. Bridie shut the storeroom door. Rory groaned and, finally, lucidity shone in his eyes. She gently brushed his bowl cut bangs to the side with her left hand She attempted a smile of warmth and relief, configuring her eyes into a look of compassion. She posed with her right elbow on a drum of industrial-strength decalcifier, hand under her chin, pinkie raised in the air.

"Och, quite a fright ye gave us, boyo," Bridie breathed, tinkling with dainty laughter (rather at odds to her usual bawdy cackle). "That was some bender ye were on."

"Wh-where am I?" Rory asked.

"Ye passed out in the loo of Kebabalicious," Bridie explained.

His eyes, which were like two raisins in ovals of blood-spattered snow, narrowed even more.

"Aren't ye Dymphna's mate Birdie?"

"Bridie," Bridie corrected. "Aye, Bridie McFee from Ineshowen Gardens. And yer Dymphna was here to witness yer fall from grace and all."

His eyes swiveled, and Bridie bristled at the alarm and mortification in them.

"Dymphna? Where is she?"

"One look at ye and she raced outta here like her quim had been set ablaze. Said she couldn't be dealing with the likes of ye, ye fairly turned her stomach, so she said. Happy to see the back of ye and yer fascist mother. Had to drag ye in here meself."

Bridie treasured each line of disappointment that formed on Rory's face. A head bearing a purple and yellow cap poked inside the storeroom.

"The manager's back, youse, hi."

Bridie pulled a face; she had still to scrub out the sundae topping dispensers and would have to take a shortcut in her plan to nab Rory for herself.

"I think…" Bridie ran her finger down the length of his hand shuddering on the concrete as she made a show of conjuring up an idea there on the spot. "I know just what ye need to fill the empty hole in yer life."

"Not…Alcoholics Anonymous?" Rory inquired, his voice trembling.

Bridie threw back her head to cackle, caught herself, and tinkled instead.

"Catch yerself on, hi! Alkies Anonymous be's some peculiar Yank invention for those what kyanny handle their drink like hard men and women can. Naw, I'm talking about the self-respect and emotional fulfillment that comes from line-dancing It's a wile craic, so it is. Me group meets down the Leisure Center on a Wednesday." It was the only place in Derry a pig-ugly girl like Bridie found appreciation and respect and actual admirers, due to her perfect Boot-Scootin-Boogie, Cotton-Eyed-Joe and wide array of fringed fashion. Where better to show her popularity off to her new conquest?

Rory stared at her, aghast, though he was partial to Shania Twain's "That Don't Impress Me Much."

"Scribble down yer phone number." She forced a pencil into his hand. "There's no backing out. Ye're to cleanse yerself of the demons tormenting ye through the pleasures of the dancefloor. Ye might just discover one of them demons be's called Dymphna Flood."

Rory did as instructed. Like most women, Bridie McFee knew how to handle men. And she, too, had an empty hole that needed filling.

CHAPTER 18

Catherine McLaughlin (iPod Girl) skipped happily past a charred refrigerator and some bludgeoned mattresses towards the school playground. Her red hair shimmered in a stint of uncharacteristic sunshine. She eyed the rusty merry-go-round and imagined all the fun she'd be having on it. She'd just have to ignore the filthy words spray-painted across it and stop worrying about what they meant, as her daddy instructed. And steer clear of the splinters from the huge hole that had been hacked into the platform by a sharp instrument of sorts.

She froze with sudden fear, and her Hello Kitty backpack smacked against her shoulder blades.

Between her and the plaything stood the dreaded Siofra Flood and her sidekick Grainne Donaldson. Catherine whimpered. At the sight of Catherine, the two clunked towards her across the litter-strewn tarmac like cheaply-built mini-robots, their movements a close approximation of friendly schoolchildren. Catherine feared they had become pod people.

"'Bout ye, Catherine?" Siofra called out.

Through there seemed no malice in Siofra's voice, Catherine cowered against the see saw. She wriggled out of her backpack and nudged it towards them, now feet away from her.

"Take it and leave me be!" she pleaded, the straps quivering.

Grainne reached in her pocket—Catherine tensed for the blow—and pulled out a mangled packet of pickled onion potato chips. Siofra held out a tattered roll of Fruit Pastilles.

"Ye wanna be mates, hi?" Siofra asked, her voice as sweet as her personality would allow.

Catherine blinked, unsure whether this was her wildest dream or worst nightmare come true. As her lower lip trembled in confusion and Hello Kitty sagged to the ground, she realized what was odd about them: they were smiling.

"T-them doesn't be poisoned, does they?" Catherine asked.

Their eyes flickered with a brief annoyance, then the freakish smiles stretched wider further disfiguring their faces. Catherine wished they would just give up the charade; it was like two Halloween masks staring at her.

"Naw," Siofra said. "Lookit, they still be's unwrapped, sure."

Catherine tentatively reached for the snacks, knowing she was leaving her backpack unattended on the tarmac, which might be what they wanted.

"We've wanted to be mates with ye for donkey's," Grainne explained.

"I'm wile sorry we beat the shite outta ye so many times in the past," Siofra said. "Jealous, we musta been. Now's the time to make up for it, but. Could ye not forgive us for wer sins against ye? I've been paying attention to Father Hogan's sermons at St. Molaug's, so I have."

Grainne nodded eagerly.

"Aye, me and all."

The Flood family sat in the next pew to the McLaughlins every Sunday, but the feeling of comfort and reassurance Catherine received from weekly mass was always tempered by their sniggering and their abuse of the hymnals; there was something not right about the Floods' presence in a house of God. But perhaps Siofra had indeed heard the call of the Lord. Catherine was prepared to give her the benefit of the doubt. She unwrapped the Fruit Pastilles (she'd eat the chips later alone; pickled onion was her favorite) and offered them to Siofra and Grainne. They took one each to put her mind at ease about poison.

Siofra said: "The other night, I had a dream of an angel."

Catherine's face lit up with interest, and she began to relax as she chewed.

"Ye don't say?"

"Aye," Siofra said, chewing as well. "It was wile strange. I told Grainne all about it the day, so I did. I was in Heaven, minding me own business, jumping happily from cloud to cloud, when an angel appeared before me, hovering about the next cloud but one. 'Siofra Flood,' goes the angel, 'I've something to tell ye, something to help ye avoid the clutches of the Devil. Ye might be in Heaven now, but don't think ye're safe. The Devil be's terrible powerful and be's everywhere, so he does. Even here in Heaven.'"

Catherine's eyes widened like saucers. Grainne took another candy.

"I looked around the clouds, suddenly afeared. Where was the Devil hiding in heaven? I started to cry, so I did, but the angel flapped her wings, it was a she, ye see, and she goes, 'Don't cry, Siofra, I'll show ye what ye need to avoid the road to Hell,' She reached into some pocket of her angel garb and pulled out a press pass. 'Ye're to find one of these press passes,' the angel says, 'and when the Devil approaches ye, ye just wave it at him and he withers and be's in terrible pain and be's forced to go back to his lair in Hell.' I was happy. 'Ta very much for telling me,' I says, 'that's wile civil of ye,' and I reached out me hand to take it. But the angel snatched it away and says, 'Naw, Siofra, this be's mines. Ye're to find yer own. I'm letting ye know what ye need to avoid eternal damnation, just.' And away she flew, playing her harp. And then, from another cloud, I saw a pitchfork and some horns and a pointy tail. It was the Devil, plain as day, and he was coming for me, and I hadn't the special press pass to protect meself. And I was heartscared and sobbing and begging yer man to not drag me down to the burny pits of Hell."

Catherine was hanging on every word, fascinated and scared.

"And then?" she dared to ask.

"And then she woke up," Grainne snapped.

The three stood in silence for a moment. It was certainly strange, Catherine thought, but she knew the Lord worked in mysterious ways. Wasn't there the woman down in Cork who had seen the Virgin Mary in a bowl of raisin oatmeal? She reached for another candy, but Grainne had finished them all.

"And why is ye telling me this?" Catherine wondered.

"Doesn't yer mammy have one of them press passes?" Grainne said, her voice ringing with impatience. "Ye brought it in for show and tell, sure."

"A-aye, but…?"

"Ye're to get yer mammy's press pass and give it to me, to save me from the Devil," Siofra announced.

Catherine couldn't have been more surprised if they asked her to be best mates with her. *Oh!* They just had. Catherine's face grew with alarm. Her mother hadn't been well since Catherine's collapse at her first Holy Communion the year before. She had had to step down from her job as a journalist, and was pumped full of medication.

Catherine wriggled with discomfort as she aired some dirty laundry: "Just after me mammy went away in the head, she used to sneak outta the house with her press pass and use it to gain entry into posh events in town she wasn't invited to. Strangely, she behaved at em. That press pass be's locked up in me daddy's safe in his study now. I kyanny get at it. He's the keys on him all the time, sure."

"Yer daddy has *a study*?" Grainne looked in disbelief at Siofra. Siofra nudged her to be silent.

"I suggest ye find a way to get them keys to unlock the press pass," Siofra said, "if ye wanny save yer new best mate from the Devil's cloven hooves."

"…that be's thieving, but…"

"Aye, and?" Siofra asked, hand on hip.

"Thieving be's a sin against God," Catherine whimpered.

"Ye can visit Faller Hogan in the confessional on a Wednesday evening and confess afterwards, sure," Grainne said. "Then yer sins be's cleared by God. Like a magic trick, so it is."

"Me penance, but will last hours and—"

"Coke-drinking cunts!" "Fenian bastards!" "Minging arseholes!"

They jumped as a unit at the yells and whipped around. A hoard of girls, seven or more, raced across the tarmac towards them, young faces stretched with hatred.

"Themmuns is Pepsi-slurping gits!" Siofra screamed.

"Themmuns've balloons with em!" Grainne wailed. "Let's clear outta here!"

The three girls screamed and scattered like sheep caught in a war-zone, knowing the liquid in those balloons came from no tap. An arsenal of balloons sailed through the air, and roars of laughter rang out as fountains of piss exploded all around the see saw. A balloon hit Grainne in the face, the plastic ripping and liquid exploding.

"I'm soaked in Proddy urine!" Grainne wailed, racing for the doors of the school.

Catherine cried as something putrid and brown sailed through the air.

"They've dog mess and all!" she screamed, splats erupting around her on the tarmac.

They scrabbled towards the doors, and still the bloated missiles kept coming. Siofra and Grainne banged on the filthy glass.

"Let us in! Let us in!"

Catherine fell on the gravel leading up to the steps, tears pouring down her face as she scraped her knee. Blood seeped through her white tights, and the hateful bastards pointed and roared with cruel laughter. And moved in, balloons exploding and feces spattering on her struggling body.

"Leave her be!" Siofra roared.

"Leave her be! Leave her be!" mimicked the girls as the door flew open and the startled janitor dragged Catherine inside.

"Och, fer the love of God!" Siofra heaved a grunt of fury and raced back, dragging Catherine by the arms and hauling her up the steps. A balloon ruptured against Siofra's back, the urine trickling down. She hauled Catherine into the safety of the school.

"Clear on off outta here!" roared the janitor into the yard. "Get yerselves back to yer Proddy school and leave wer wanes be!"

The girls roared with laughter, flipping them all off, and raced out of the playground.

"Are youse alright?" the janitor asked, lips taught with anger.

"I'm drenched in Proddy wee, so am are," Siofra said. "I'm gonny spew."

"Another attack from them jumped-up minted cunts from the How Great Thou Art, no doubt!" the janitor fumed. "Hours, it took me, to clear up all the egg they flung on the windows of the science lab last week."

He stormed off down the hallway, presumably to get a bucket and mop to clear up this new filth on the playground. Grainne and Siofra had hearty constitutions and were used to such violence, but Catherine slumped against a drugs awareness poster, sopping and shell-shocked. She had the presence of mind, however, to pass Siofra a look of gratitude.

"Ta, for saving me," she said weakly. The jury was still out on Grainne, but perhaps Siofra Flood was her new best mate after all.

"Get me that flimmin press pass as thanks, just," Siofra said.

As they struggled down the hallway to the girls room to clean the mess off them, Grainne blabbering on and on about her new Little Miss Princess top being ruined, Catherine wondered why Siofra seemed distracted. She couldn't know Siofra had recognized one of the seven, and was fuming with thoughts of revenge. The ringleader of the group, the girl who had flung the most dog mess and the biggest balloons, including the purple one that had exploded on her back, was none other than PinkPetals.

CHAPTER 19

Paddy dozing at her side, Fionnuala sat in the waiting room of the Health Clinic, flipping through her favorite glossy celebrity magazine and resenting not only Brad Pitt and Angelina Jolie, but also her existence in that room at that moment. There were many things she could be doing with her precious time, and taking Padraig to the doctor's, especially this doctor, wasn't one of them. Dr. Khudiadadzai had asked Fionnuala if she wanted to accompany the child into the consulting room, but Fionnuala wanted to be as far away from him as she could.

"He's been doing me head in, outta his bleeding fecking mind," Fionnuala had explained to the doctor when she asked what was wrong with her son. "I'm half-afeared we'll have to haul him off to Gransha." The mental institution on the hill.

Fionnuala was irritated by the sound of the receptionist clicking on her keyboard, and of the pensioners in the orange chairs nattering away to each other. Then she pricked up her ears:

"…aye, and ye see that Mrs. Gee from up in Creggan? Letting on she be's skint, while me niece tole me she be's minted."

"Ye mean yer woman down the Sav-U-Mor?"

"Och, naw, I mean the elder Mrs. Gee, her mother. Why she allows her daughter to slave away at the counter of that minging tip, if she does indeed be rolling in dosh, I kyanny comprehend. The mortification!"

Fionnuala percolated. Her fingernail clawed out the left eye of a grinning Angelina on vacation in the Caribbean, and, having learned that Malta had sun as well, Fionnuala reached for her special satchel. She had learned many things from her visit to the travel agent's down the Strand that morning, including that to get to Malta they would have to go "down," not "up," as it was an island in the Mediterranean. And that the Mediterranean was a sea under Ireland, and that it was located below the entire continent of Europe. Fionnuala fumed over Moira choosing the furthest point of Europe from Derry to move to.

Most of what else Fionnuala had learned was not good. The scene was still vivid in her mind, but she felt no shame for the tongue lashing she had given the trainee travel agent, a wee girl who should've stayed in school as she was a dim-witted simpleton, as Fionnuala told her, and whose eventual tears and threats to call the police Fionnuala scoffed at.

Fionnuala had erupted when the girl told her the thousands of pounds such a trip would cost. Weren't there seats for two or three pence on budget airlines? She saw the ads on the telly all the time. It wasn't Fionnuala's fault she had just recently learned about the betrayal of her daughter, and the need to bag cheap seats for three adults, four children plus an infant six weeks later. What the stupid girl couldn't realized, Fionnuala had harped on, was that their trip to Malta was more important than all others' who had already made reservations to travel there just to luxuriate in the sunshine.

When the girl suggested the cheaper alternative of ferries coupled with Eurorail, and the excitement of traveling through the Chunnel from England to France, Paddy had to pull Fionnuala's rage-infused, sputtering body away from the desk. But Fionnuala had snatched brochures and things from the plastic displays up front as Paddy ushered her out. She pulled out one of the maps from her satchel now.

"That's a grand and lovely bag, sure," the pensioner who apparently knew Mrs. Gee's niece offered. Her friend smiled and nodded in agreement.

"Och, that's wile civil of ye to say," Fionnuala smiled, running her hand fondly over the frayed stitching of the straps, though she didn't need a doddery old pensioner to tell her the obvious. The Celine Dion-Titanic-"My Heart Will Go On" Tour 1997 satchel was Fionnuala's second most-prized possession, after her Kenny Rogers "The Gambler" teaset.

For their 15th anniversary back in 1997, Paddy had gotten her tickets to the Celine Dion concert in Belfast. They had dumped the seven brats off on Ursula and Jed and taken the bus over. Her memories of the night were misted by the passage of time, and she had long repressed spewing up in the lap of the women sat in the auditorium next to her (too many trips to the bar in the lobby), but she remembered as clearly as if it were the day before the chivalry Paddy had shown as he had cracked open the skull of the heroin-addicted ticket tout who had grappled her left breast outside the venue, and the many pounds he had handed over at the souvenirs stall in the lobby for the satchel.

As the two pensioners cooed admiringly, purple rinses bobbing, Fionnuala wittered proudly on about the features of the bag.

"Here's Celine's face on the one side, ye see, holding her microphone. And ye see on the other side here, there be's the Titanic ship itself. There's a wee mechanism where, when the bag be's empty, the ship be's sailing as it was before it hits the iceberg. The more ye stuff in the bag, but, the more the ship tilts, until when it's full, the ship finally sinks into the water. A limited edition, so it is."

"Whatever will they think of next?" marveled one pensioner to the other.

One reached for Fionnuala's wrist, but Fionnuala flinched as she thought she was going for the bag. Nobody was allowed to touch it.

"And did ye know the Titanic was built down the road in Belfast?" the pensioner asked. "The centennial of its launch be's quickly approaching."

"Aye," said the other. "2012. Celebrations aplenty, there's meant to be."

"Och, I'm not an eejit, sure," Fionnuala snapped; she had been counting down the months. Fionnuala was grateful the two were called into the nurse's room. She turned to the map and began to study it.

Eurorail Exotic European Excursions, Senior (over 60) and Youth (Under 26) Fares. EU Child Fares and Age Limits said the top of the map.

Paddy woke up with a moan.

"Is yer man still in there with that doctor?" he asked.

"Do ye see him here?" Fionnuala snapped.

"What are ye doing with them maps?" Paddy asked.

"I'm trying to work out the most economical way to transport the lot of us across the Continent. I'm already prepared to shame meself into claiming I'm a pensioner to get the seniors' rate. Ye're to do it and all. It's the wanes I'm worried about, but. Ye see here…? All them nations we've to go through lets wanes what be's under five years of age in free of charge."

"Seamus be's five and Siofra be's eight," Paddy said. "We kyanny get them in for free."

"We kyanny fork over thousands we've not got just so's the wanes can gawk at the Eiffel Towers. Sure, there's pictures of them plastered all over the Internet in the library, and they can march down there and goggle them till the cows comes home. I've another route in mind."

Paddy look at the map further and noted that the Eastern Bloc countries let children under ten travel free. He stared sadly as Fionnuala's eager finger bypassed the simple journey from France to Italy, from Sicily to Malta, and propelled a journey that wound through Belgium, Germany, the Czech Republic, Slovakia, Hungary, Slovenia, Croatia, Bosnia-Herzegovina, Montenegro and Albania. And then, he supposed, a ferry to Malta. His wife was desperate. She had no idea that, with her being sacked and his last paycheck quickly running out, finding food would be more of a priority than prancing off on a dreamtrip to Malta. He had to tell her about the strike.

He cleared his throat, already smarting from the back of her hand that had yet to hit his cheek.

"Have ye not wondered, love, why I'm sitting here next to ye like this on a Monday? Why I'm not at the plant?"

"How the bleeding feck should I know? One of them roster changes, I suppose. And I asked ye to get more overtime. Even traipsing across the Continent on ferries and trains is sure to cost a bundle."

"The workers was afeared of all them new mixing and grinding machines both chomping off wer extremities and replacing wer positions, like. We're on strike."

The receptionist flinched at the violence on the plastic chairs.

"A strike? *A strike?* Are ye outta yer flimmin mind? How are we meant to eat? How are we to pay them bills? Ye fecking useless gack, ye!"

"I voted against it, like," Paddy managed, arms shielding her blows.

"How are we meant to afford wer trip to Malta?"

Finally Fionnuala's fists were still. Fionnuala boiled in her chair, nostrils like a raging bull, as she struggled to get her mind around the black pit of destitution into which she had just fallen. The receptionist relaxed the finger hovering over the security button.

"We're putting that flimmin 5 Murphy up fer sale," Fionnuala decided.

"We can try," Paddy said meekly. "In this market, but? It's never gonny happen."

Fionnuala considered.

"Aye, and we'll be dead of starvation long before the closing date, anyroad."

She fixed her eyes on him so he was of no doubt the importance of her next utterance. Her voice rang with foreboding: "As God's me witness, you'll be marching proudly past that picket line the morrow."

"But, a scab...?" Paddy asked weakly. "How could I ever face me workmates? And breaking the picket line be's against everything we stand for as members of the working class, sure."

"Och, catch yerself on, spouting that ancient union working class shite! From the whinging and moaning from ye the past few months, ye've no mates to speak of on the factory floor anyroad. Betraying themmuns should fill ye with joy."

Dr. Khudiadadzai entered the waiting room, Padraig dragging his heels behind her. Although he didn't want to look at his son's face, Paddy was grateful for the distraction. They jumped up and faced the doctor, hope in their eyes.

"Well?" Fionnuala demanded.

"Mrs Flood, I've run numerous tests on your son, taking into account his headaches and his straining of the eyes. I'm afraid the tests are inconclusive."

"What the bloody feck does that mean?"

"It means that—"

"It means ye're bloody useless!"

"I would suggest you take him to an op—"

"And I suggest ye get yer flimmin useless arse back to Pakistan where ye belong! Invading wer country with yer foreign degrees and bloody foolish accents! I kyanny comprehend a fecking word coming outta yer mouth, ye sarky skegrat, ye!"

Even Padraig cringed in mortification. Fionnuala grabbed her satchel, her husband and her son in that order and stormed out of the clinic. She whipped around to Paddy as they climbed down the stairs.

"Hell will freeze over before I let ye prance around them factory gates waving foolish placards in the sunshine, not while ye've seven mouths to feed and a holiday to fund."

"Sunshine?"

"Ye're entering that factory the morrow if I have to drag yer limbs across the picket line meself!"

Paddy went to the pub.

CHAPTER 20

Mrs. Pilkey, headmistress of Our Lady of Perpetual Sorrow, had been ravenous all morning long, but there were so many things to take care of she hadn't a moment to rest. She finally settled at her desk at 2:30 and slipped out of her heels with a sigh of content. Hunger gnawing a hole in her stomach, she unwrapped a chocolate croissant with bony fingers that could barely contain themselves. She was an angular woman, all elbows, ribs and protruding teeth. Those teeth opened wide in anticipation.

"Ye kyanny barge in there! She be's in a meeting! A meeting, I tell ye!"

Mrs. Pilkey distanced her tongue from the golden flakes in dismay as the door flew open and in barged a man who looked like a forgotten '70s porn-star, all paunch and scraggy mustache, a tiny redhead dangling from his huge right fist. The secretary waved her hands frantically from the door frame, mouthing 'I tried to stop them, Miss.' Then her finger circled her ear wildly to indicate mental instability.

Mrs. Pilkey shooed Magella back to her hutch and greeted the intruders with a mouth that looked as if it had just tasted something it hadn't much enjoyed, though of course it had yet to taste anything. She ran a hand through her black hair, captive in a chignon with a chopstick driven through it.

"What is the meaning of—?"

"Inspector Liam McLaughlin here. Sorry to disturb yer *meeting.*"

He motioned archly to the croissant and flashed his credentials under her nose. She raised a hand to her chest.

"Are you here on…official duty?"

"Me daughter Catherine here and her two helpless mates were set upon by thugs in yer schoolyard the other day. I can see by the confusion yer face that ye've no idea what I'm on about."

Mrs. Pilkey was indeed confused; it was the first she had heard of Catherine McLaughlin having 'mates.'

"You'd better have a seat, then. Catherine, is it?"

Catherine nodded haltingly and dragged herself in shame to a chair facing the headmistress. The child stared at the croissant. Inspector McLaughlin remained upright, pacing back and forth like he was down at the police station, informing the troops of the details of a fatal drunken stabbing the night before.

"They was attacked by a pack of vicious hooligans who pelted them with dog shite and balloons filled with human urine. Poor wee Catherine's been living a misery ever since. Kyanny put her head down on at night, as she wakes up screaming. Plagued with nightmares, so she is. Nightmares of evil urinating balloons with legs chasing her over endless hills of feces. Are ye not informed of all the bullying what occurs in yer own school?"

Mrs. Pilkey winced. "We prefer to call it child-initiated contact." She took in the girl, who was ogling the croissant as if she had just been released from a refugee camp. Mrs. Pilkey edged some papers over it. *Does he not feed her?* she wondered with a flash of irritation. Inspector McLaughlin continued:

"Can ye not see the wane be's traumatized? Post-traumatic stress disorder! Textbook case!"

Mrs. Pilkey was a business administrator brought in three years earlier mainly to balance the school budget, and as such she knew little about teaching and less about children. She fiddled with a staple remover, wondering how to handle the problem on the chair. She toyed briefly with the idea of sharing the croissant, but…perhaps with kindness instead? She screwed her feet back into her shoes, checked Catherine's hair for signs of lice, then placed a tentative hand on the girl's shoulder.

"What did the perpetrators look like, love?" Mrs. Pilkey asked, wishing the kindness in her voice was more convincing. She should have paid more attention during that sensitivity training course.

"I kyanny remember," Catherine said. "Afeared, I was. Pure heart-scared."

Inspector McLaughlin roared: "The thugs was yelling out anti-Catholic slurs. Must be from How Great Thou Art. More to the point, where be's yer security measures? Yer guards and dogs? Yer flimmin CCTV footage? According to me daughter, me officers should've been sent out on at least seven incidents of child-on-child abuse since the school year began. None of yer wanes wants to approach us, but. We kyanny protect the community if nobody be's prepared to shame themselves to come forward, and we kyanny prosecute crimes if there be's no evidence."

Catherine and her father looked around the office.

"What's that noise?" Inspector McLaughlin demanded.

Mrs. Pilkey willed her stomach to silence. Father and daughter glanced at the papers on the desk.

"Then," Mrs. Pilkey said, "perhaps you should speak to the headmaster of How Great Thou Art. They were the instigators, after all. When did this occur, Catherine, love? Can you remember that?"

"Yesterday," Catherine said with a pout.

"Sunday?" Mrs. Pilkey touched her chopstick. She wasn't surprised that such an attack had taken place on the day of the Lord, more that the children had visited the school when not under duress. She clacked the staple remover like it was a little black mouth with silver fangs.

"You must realize, of course, that as it was the weekend, we are technically not liable. If fact, the children were trespassing."

"I know loads of wanes from this school, and I'm well aware they doesn't be innocent wee lambs. I've seen them down at the Richmond Shopping Center, alarming packs trolling the streets, their threatening behavior and cruel taunts directed at the aged and the infirm, their casual shoplifting. Even so, they deserve protection from hate- and bias-crimes. If ye kyanny protect wer wanes in yer own schoolyard, I'll have to take steps meself to ensure their well-being. I can arrange officers to come down and patrol on an hourly basis."

"Could you please leave the room, Catherine?" Mrs. Pilkey asked. "Ask Magella the secretary to, er, give you something."

Catherine did so gladly. Mrs. Pilkey leaned across her desk.

"Police officers parading through the schoolyard?" she scoffed. "I think not. Parents would yank their children out of the school, and our staff would be teaching to empty chairs."

"Because it would show how violent the school be's?"

Mrs. Pilkey looked at him as if he had just stepped off the banana boat.

"Because fully three quarters of your force are Unionist sympathizers! You think the parents of my charges want their children rubbing shoulders with *Protestants?*"

"Have ye not a clue that be's part of the same problem? One city, two communities. The Peace Process began yonks ago, and still the people in this city divides everything by Green and Orange, Coke and Pepsi, Derry and Londonderry. You, but, be's the gatekeeper between what the new generation, the wanes of the day, thinks and does and the backward thinking of the aul ones and their parents. Have yer heard of that new school where there be's some sorta goings-on hoping to lead to Proddys and Catholics holding hands in unity for the future? And more Catholics be's joining the police force as time goes by, I'll have ye know."

Clack-clack-clack! What the Inspector had brought up was a thorn in Mrs. Pilkey's angular side. She had done research about the integrated schools movement in Northern Ireland, the social experiment of the past twenty years which sought to implement cross-denominational student bodies, and if this is where the police inspector was heading, it was making her uneasy. There was one such overly-progressive school in Derry, and they had not only the mixing of religions, but also the mixing of the sexes...who had heard of such a foolish thing? It was an institutional policy she found distressing.

"Actually, Mr. McLaughlin, I was only playing devil's advocate. My personal beliefs are moot. I can't disregard what others in the community, especially the parents of my charges, think. They are adults and their minds can't be changed. I must live in the real world."

"Ye get this sorted," Inspector McLaughlin warned. "Any more harm comes to me wee Catherine and her mates, and there's gonny be more police officers marching up and down that schoolyard than you've had, er, hot dinners."

Not these fantasy mates again, Mrs. Pilkey thought. The inspector stormed out of the office. Mrs. Pilkey pounced on the croissant and tore into it like a wolfchild.

Groaning in the luxury of sustenance, Mrs. Pilkey twisted under the expanse of her oak desk, fingernails clacking like castanets on what used to be a lacquered sheen. She ran through the Rolodex of her mind for someone who could help her solve the generations-old problem of schoolyard sectarian violence and abuse and cursed the staleness of the croissant. She'd never again buy from that Sav-U-Mor next to the schoolyard.

Then she remembered the school district Christmas party and the hanky-panky by the photocopier, the local small business owner and entrepreneur of some standing in the Protestant community, a member of the Parents-Teachers Organization, who had a daughter about the same age as Catherine McLaughlin. He had been charming and, more importantly, recently-widowed. And with her husband spending long hours away on the road, Mrs. Pilkey was quite looking forward to having a reason to share a Cabernet or two with him.

She found his number and punched it into the phone.

"Hello, Constance Flynn here," she twittered, removing an imaginary piece of lint from her suit and running her fingers down her left thigh. "Is that you, Mr. Skivvins?"

Her voice tinkled with girlish laughter.

"No worries, all the copies are safely destroyed. The reason I'm ringing is…I think you might be able to help us with a small problem we've been having at the school. And I'm certain that adorable daughter of yours Victoria could be a great help as well. How is she doing at How Great Thou Art? Well, I'm sure. She's so bright and *such* a sweetheart. This is what I was thinking…"

CHAPTER 21

In Paddy's sobriety-deprived mind, Fionnuala was perched on his back as if it were a parapet of Notre Dame and she a gargoyle, hissing him on to betrayal. He plodded over the cracks in the sidewalk with little plants growing out of them. He had spent 28 years of joyless, hungover mornings taking that route past the rubbish dump and around the gasworks, the packing plant yard wall, concrete and festooned with rusty barbed wire, looming. He heard angry chants as he approached the gate and, peering through the corroded railings, he gawped. Hoards of his co-workers were stomping around the tarmac, brandishing signs which read: MACHINES +3 FINGERS -2 and MORE MACHINES = FEWER TOES.

"*What do youse want?*" hollered Callum, the union rep, through a megaphone.

"Respect and financial security and all wer limbs!" roared the others.
"When do youse want it?"
"Now!"

What Paddy hadn't expected was the fish and chip van doing a brisk trade in bacon sandwiches off to the side. And the troops of riot police, heads hidden under helmets with visors, see-through shields hanging at their sides, batons clutched in fists. Paddy saw that at the moment they were just keeping an eye on things and that they had parked their vans in the spaces reserved for the handicapped.

He was wondering how to slip past the chanting mobs and into the doors of the factory unnoticed when a convoy of air brakes fizzled behind him. Paddy turned. A fleet of mud-spattered buses roared past him and through the gates. Fury from the lumpen masses laced the air. The riot police thrust themselves to the front of the factory doors as the buses squealed to a halt. The workers banged their signs on the sides, jeers and threats spewing from their throats. The buses deposited hoards of strangers in acid-washed denim, who fled across the tarmac through the tunnel of riot shields and scampered into the front doors, fear on their faces, but also the resolve to bring home a paycheck to feed the mouths of their foreign children. The crowd approached, faces red and stretched with anger, veins bulging in throats as they yelled:

"Scab! Scab! Scab!"

Rocks and half-eaten sandwiches flew through the air. Paddy chose his moment and, head bent, the flesh of his cheeks burning with shame, raced through the blitz, dodging stones and bacon thrown his way. He slipped through the enraged mob and sidled through the factory doors. Roars at his back, the clanking of rocks on the glass, he took a place in the line that wound through the factory floor towards the changing rooms. Tables were set up, the first manned by Fiona, the owner's niece who had become floor manager three months earlier and, of course, was loathed by all. She was quickly taking down details of the temporary hires. Paddy shuffled towards her, and their eyes met, sharing the shameful knowledge they were two of the very few who had sacrificed loyalty and solidarity for a pay packet.

"'Bout ye, Paddy," Fiona said. "No need to take down your details, boyo. Clock in as usual, just."

Paddy nodded, mortified.

At the next table, Fiona's aunt Lois was handing out hairnets and caps, boots, gloves and overalls.

"I do believe ye've got yer own gear," she said with a smile he wanted to punch off her face.

Paddy shuffled glumly to the men's changing room and was surprised to see he was alone. The 'temporary hires' must all be women. He slipped into his overalls, then dragged himself into the line where the scabs were divided into groups, and Lois' eldest son—Paddy couldn't remember his name, but knew he was the one who had just come back from five years of bartending in Australia—gave each huddled group their duties. Paddy hoped he wouldn't get the mixing and grinding machines again.

"Youse are to go to the fish sorting, youse to cleanup, youse to the mixing and grinding machines…" A translator in a Beatles-cut sharkskin suit with a skinny tie stood to the side with a clipboard, droning on in their foreign tongue. Paddy suspected he was a homosexual. *"Musisz pójść do sortowni nyb, musisz posprzatać, Musisz pójść do maszyn mielących i mieszających."* Paddy wondered if he would go mad working in the foreignness.

Then she stepped out of the changing room and joined his group. Even in her hairnet and cap, Paddy recognized her, the lipstick on her yellow teeth and the blood stilettos poking out from her overalls. It was the Pole from the pub. She eyed him with amazement; clearly he was the last person she expected to run into, Paddy being an Irish national.

"We work together?" she asked. *"Zajebiście!"* How exciting! Had he known what she said, Paddy would no doubt think it more dangerous than exciting.

The poofter pointed to their group. *"Musisz pójść do sortowni nyb."* They were assigned the fish sorting; that was something, at least. The group made their way past the air blast chiller spewing forth the cold, their teeth chattering and their limbs trembling to retain a semblance of body heat. The woman grabbed his elbow.

Working in the Fillets-O-Joy warehouse was like working in the mines, only without the lamps. Deep inside the mountainous cavern, the tiny slits of windows let in even fewer sunbeams than the perpetual rainclouds outside. Fish residue stuck to surfaces both horizontal and vertical as far as the eye could see. The whirr of industrial noise competed with the pop music blaring from speakers overhead at a rock-concert level (management thought this good for morale).

The woman pointed to herself as they lined up at adjacent crates overflowing with dead creatures of the sea. "Agnieszka Czerwinska," she said. "Agnieszka."

Paddy tried to pronounce it three times while pulling on his rubber gloves, but finally settled on 'Aggie.' She giggled and nodded.

He pointed to himself. "Me Paddy."

Aggie tried this on her lips, plumes of breath pouring from that mouth which still had Paddy wishing for the sudden appearance of a Listerine strip. She nodded and smiled; his name satisfied her.

Next to the crates were huge vats filled with ice into which they were to sort the fish. Paddy fought the urge to spew into the crates teeming with dead fish, their glassy cold eyes pleading up at him to be set back free into the Irish Sea.

Their hands plunged into the scaly depths and grappled the slippery bodies. He grabbed a handful of mackerel from the potpourri of fish and flung them into the Oily Fish vat. She grappled the tails of four jumbo shrimp and tossed them into the Shellfish vat. As he bent, Paddy was somehow aware of her eyes on his meaty backside filling out the seat of his filthy overalls. It met to her obvious approval. as when he faced her she ran a tongue of lust over her weathered lips. Seven plaice flew into the Flat Fish vat.

Aggie turned to Paddy and announced: "Cheer!"

It was not what he was feeling. He stared at her, confused, as he heaved two handfuls of cod into the Round Fish vat.

She pointed up to the iron crossbeams, "Cheer!" It was the last place Paddy expected to find cheer. Then he realized the loudspeakers were roaring out Cher's "Believe."

"Ah, *Cher*," he said, laughing.

Her eyes twinkled with the delight of making him happy. She sidled up to him. Paddy felt her rubber-clad fingers move the length of his thigh. He stared uneasily at the fish slime, blood, scales and oil she had smeared on his overalls. Paddy removed his left rubber glove and pointed to his tarnished wedding ring, but her face brightened.

*"No to swietnie!"*Aggie said, ecstatic. That's great!

She moved closer to him. Instead of his marital state being a deterrent, Paddy wondered if the prospect of a threesome with him and Fionnuala was turning the oversexed creature on. He had heard all those foreigners were kinky bastards.

Paddy kept pointing to the ring, and couldn't understand why she wasn't getting the message. In fact, with every jab towards the ring on his left hand, the more aroused she seemed. Paddy couldn't know that Poles wore their wedding ring on the right hand.

While Paddy struggled to remain true to his marriage vows inside the Fillets-O-Joy plant, outside in the quietening parking lot, the riot officers received a call to vacate the factory and make their way to Our Lady Of Perpetual Sorrow, as anarchy was now on the verge of kicking up there.

CHAPTER 22

TWO HOURS EARLIER

Siofra sobbed as she strained to see her mother's face through the cloud of cigarette smoke. "They kyanny make us do it, can they, Mammy?"

Fionnuala's horror grew as she struggled with the words to reach the end of the letter from the school.

Due to the recent escalation of incidents regarding child-initiated contact between students from our school and the neighboring How Great Thou Art, your daughter and her class have been invited to participate in a refreshing new cross-community event we hope will become an annual delight: the Fingers Across the Foyle Talent Show. Along with a specially-selected class from neighboring Protestant school How Great Thou Art, your daughter(s) will compete in an individual or group act showcasing a talent of their choice. The Grand Prize is the Togetherness Basket, a wicker basket tied with a bow and brimming with bright Granny Smith apples and plump oranges, symbolizing the mixing of Catholic green and Protestant orange. The Runners-Up will receive two six-packs of Coke and Pepsi. We hope you will show your support and reach your friendly fingers across the River Foyle with us. Participation is mandatory.

Fionnuala turned to Maureen for help.

"What's this sentence mean, Mammy?"

Maureen inspected it through the fingerprints of her red specs.

"That ye've no choice but to join their madness."

"Naw, Mammy, naw!" Siofra wailed. "I'm not gonny mortify meself for pieces of god-awful flimmin fruit!"

"I'm well aware ye'd rather piss on fruit than eat it, but reel yer tongue in, wane!" Fionnuala snapped, stubbing out her cigarette on a plate. "Yer mammy's not finished reading the filth." Her brow furrowed as she suffered through the additional words:

PS: This talent show has been planned with not only the children in mind, but also the parents of both sides, as greater understanding and tolerance for differences in the community can only begin at home. To this end, we will also host a specially-catered mixer for parents of both schools at our teachers lounge next Friday. We hope you decide to come, especially those of you involved in the protest before the school gates the other day. There will be complimentary alcohol and hors d'oeuvres for all.

Fionnuala crinkled the paper with excitement. 'Complimentary' was one of the few five syllable words she knew the meaning of. She had to appeal to her mother again, however. "What's this mean, but, mammy?"

"That means snacks."

"No need to write it in bloody Foreign!" Fionnuala fumed. She faced the sniveling Siofra. "I was all set to march down to that school and give them a piece of me mind. I know only too well what them egg-headed gacks in charge of yer school be's up to. Years, it's been going on, ever since themmuns got rid of the morning prayers. Chipping away at youse, they be's, forcing youse wanes further and further from the purity of the Catholic church and into some land where religion doesn't matter a jot, where pervs and heathens and pagan Pakis and nancy boys and bean flickers and Proddy Orange bastards get their say as if they was God-fearing, upright citizens like the rest of us! The mingling of the religions, that's what themmuns be's after. Godless, so it be's. But can ye not wait til after yer mammy has gone to the drinks reception next Friday to voice me protest? The drinks be's free, ye understand."

Siofra stomped her foot and roared out of her: "Naw, Mammy, naw! Do it now! I kyanny show meself up dancing on the stage before rows and rows of Pepsi-drinking gacks!"

The screams from the girl were so blood-curling, Maureen feared the neighbors would be calling Child Protective Services. She looked up from her crossword and said to her daughter, "Ye can always attend the drinks reception no matter what ye do down at the school the day, love. And the wee dote did spend all that time and effort making ye that lovely goat? fer yer birthday."

Siofra sniffled her gratitude to her granny and wiped snot from her nose.

"It be's a mermaid."

Fionnuala reconsidered, her left eye twitching.

"Right!" she said finally, reaching for the phone to round up as many of her mates as she could. "I'm not gonny go on me lonesome, but. Fetch Seamus and Keanu down."

Ten minutes later, having received nothing but a slew of answering machines, Fionnuala strapped Keanu to her back, forced the walking stick into her mother's hoof, grabbed a hand of both Seamus and Siofra, and stomped out of the house.

When they got to Our Lady of Perpetual Sorrow, Fionnuala realized why nobody had answered her calls. They were already outside the school, spilling over the sidewalk and blocking the street, rows and rows of haggard housewives in crumpled raincoats and matted hair, arms locked, swaying, and singing out in untrained voices the old chestnut of defiance "We Shall Overcome." A few were fiddling with rosary beads, though what use those could be Fionnuala couldn't fathom.

She had no idea the Proddy mothers would be out in force as well, a group of them huddled next to the bakery on the opposite sidewalk and exchanging jibes with a few of the Catholic mothers unfortunate enough to be on the ends of the rows. She could tell they were Protestant by their makeup and upmarket fashion, and wished she had had enough sense to sling the Burberry scarf around her neck before she left the house.

Although there was a smattering of Catholic grannies and, it seemed, great-grannies as well, balancing on their walkers and humming along, the crowd was skewed younger than Fionnuala, and they were turning her stomach as their whiny soft-sell protest droned on. "We Shall Overcome" segued into "Imagine," a song to Fionnuala like claws on a chalkboard.

She nudged her mother in the ribs and laughed without an ounce of joy, motioning to a woman in a plastic raincap.

"Ye see yer woman over there? Always has her hand in the till, her. And yer woman beside her, works down the post office and laid into me when I was three pence short for a book of stamps. A fresh mouth, so she has, a fresh mouth if ever I've heard one. Fresh mouth!" Fionnuala had heard Judge Judy use the American idiom, and was trying it on for size.

Her daughter kept repeating the strange expression, but Maureen couldn't see anything fresh about the woman's mouth at all. In fact, the more she inspected it, she saw that even the teeth seemed to be trying to escape from it, and many had succeeded.

"Are ye not meant to be facing the school?" Maureen asked.

But Fionnuala had spied Niamh Cavanaugh with a few of her mates, half-heartedly clapping along and more interested in nattering away than protesting. Niamh especially made Fionnuala's flesh crawl. She was a volunteer for OsteoCare, a not-for-profit organization of community care whose members volunteered to visit the infirm and aged inflicted with osteoporosis and doled out friendliness and tea and a biscuit. Ursula had joined their ranks when she lived in Derry, so Fionnuala saw them all as holier-than-thou busybodies. Fionnuala had ceased contact with her friend Aileen Harris when she announced she had become not only an OsteoCare provider, but one of their managers. Fionnuala took crab-like steps to hear what they were saying. Mrs. O'Hara was blabbering:

"...there's a sale on irregular knickers at the B&S down the Richmond Center the day. The moment we're done here, I'm on me way there. The pair I've on me now are fit only for the bin, so they are, one side be's creeping down the cheek of me bottom, while the other side be's riding up me crack. A terrible pain, they're giving me, and ye ought to see the state of em when I tug them off me at the end of a night."

"Och, I wondered why ye was walking like that," Niamh said. "Ye know,

I think I'll accompany ye and bag meself a few pairs, and a few for Mrs. Ming and all. I'm to visit her the night."

"Ye're her provider for OsteoCare, are ye?"

"Aye, and she was telling me last week about the sorry state of her knickers and all. Poor aul soul has the dosh to buy em, all them sons of hers raking it in from their flash jobs abroad, but she kyanny leave the house, what with her ailment and all. One son be's a doctor of some sort in London, and must be sending her the dosh every week, like. A lovely new fridge, she has, and one of them flat-screened tellys and all."

"Ye don't say?"

Niamh suddenly turned to Fionnuala, who had been inching her head closer and closer to the circle. "Fionnuala! How have ye been keeping?"

"Grand," Fionnuala snapped.

"And how's yer Ursula?"

"She's not me Ursula," Fionnuala seethed, irritation lancing her brain at the mention of the cunt's name, the whiny chorus of "Imagine," the wanes babbling at her feet, the close proximity of the Protestant bitches. She rolled up the sleeves of her cardigan with two buttons missing and unharnessed Keanu from her back.

"Take youse yer wee nephew over the street there," Fionnuala decided, its inhuman grunts and squeaks causing her grief. She unloaded the infant into Siofra's struggling arms. "The violence be's set to kick off."

The children staggered away, and Maureen grappled her cane in mortification as Fionnuala burst through a pair of linked arms. "Leave wer wanes be!" Fionnuala roared at the facade of the school. "Protect wer wanes! Protect wer wanes!"

The lone copper at the fire hydrant looked up in alarm and reached for his walkie-talkie.

"C'mon, youse!" Fionnuala urged the slumbering sheep. "Let them intellectual twats hear the fire in yer bellies! *Leave wer wanes be! Leave wer wanes be! SAVE WER WANES!*"

Uncertainly rippled through the rows, but the few tuts and clucks were drowned as pockets of anarchy erupted in the sea of bargain bin gear and joined the chant, "*Save wer wanes! Save wer wanes!*" Maureen wobbled on her cane as she was elbowed by unlinked arms transformed into fists of rage aimed at the windows of the school.

Fionnuala whipped around to her troops, eyes blazing. "Enough of the John Lennon shite! He was an Orange cunt and all! Scoop up them rocks, ladies, and fling em at the Proddy bitches in their swanky gear! One pair of the tights themmuns wears takes the likes of us a week of hard graft to afford, sure!"

The Protestant contingent squealed and scattered as the crowd did just that, rocks ricocheting around their fleeing Giuseppi Zanotti heels. The copper's two hands flailed ineffectually at the sudden wave of bloodlust.

"Fling em at the school!" Fionnuala roared through her smile. They turned like a well-trained squad, cheerleaders of rage, housewives of hatred, stones sailing through the chill along with the chant *"Save wer wanes! Save wer wanes!"*

They stormed the school gates, fingers grappling anything they could and flinging it through the railings. Fionnuala's ears pricked at the sound of sirens, already at the Lecky Road, if she wasn't mistaken. She pushed through the roaring crowd and scooped Maureen up.

"Let's disperse," Fionnuala said, duty done and gathering the children. "The filth be's on their way, and I see no sign of life behind them windows. Nobody be's listening to us. As usual."

"Are we away off home, Mammy?" Seamus asked.

"Naw, wee dote," Fionnuala said, patting his curls as Maureen looked on in surprise. "The Richmond Shopping Center."

Certainly not to shop; she had no money. But she had seen Niamh's and Mrs. O'Hara's threadbare perms teetering down the street when the aggro erupted, and she had a duty to perform. They set off along the filthy streets lined with brightly colored murals of old violence.

Fionnuala ignored her mother's scolding about violence breeding violence, about the Peace Process and the dawning of a new day, about being mired in the past and the turning of new leaves and the Lord staring down in shame.

"Enough of yer mouth, Mammy," Fionnuala said as they shoved through the Sunday shoppers into the mall. "Go on youse wanes and play with the escalator."

Seamus and Siofra screamed with delight and raced towards the steel jaws. It was the closest they ever got to an amusement park ride. But Fionnuala spied Niamh on the Down escalator and called them back. "I've changed me mind. Play with them sliding doors instead." These could give hours of diversion as well. Siofra and Seamus clapped their hands eagerly. "Take Keanu, Mammy, and keep you an eye on the wanes."

Maureen did as instructed. She wanted no part in whatever lunacy Fionnuala was certainly up to. Fionnuala hurried to the escalator and positioned herself behind Niamh, staring down at her blue rinse bobbling up and down as she blathered on to Mrs. O'Hara a step below her. Fionnuala elbowed Niamh roughly in the back, and the woman grabbed for the handrail, but it hadn't moved along with the steps in months, and Niamh screamed as her body clattered down the remaining twenty-four steps. Fionnuala galloped over the shopping bags and the spilled oranges, and she hovered over Niamh's body, shuddering in pain on the tiles.

"Shocking, them young hooligans of the day be's," Fionnuala tutted. "I saw a hoodie reach out and shove ye, so I did, and off he raced, back up the escalator. Are ye feeling any pain?"

"Me hip! Me..ankle?" Niamh moaned. "I kyanny move, so I kyanny. Broken, they must be. Get the ambulance!"

Mrs. O'Hara twittered in distress, and Fionnuala fumbled for her mobile. Her smile was hidden behind a swinging ponytail as she made the call. After she hung up, she would ring Aileen Harris at OsteoCare, as a position for a new volunteer had just opened up.

CHAPTER 23

Mr. Skivvins and Miss McClurkin perched uncomfortably on the tattered pleather sofa in the headmistress' office. Mrs. Pilkey had called an emergency meeting of the Fingers Across the River Foyle committee. She was bewildered.

"I don't understand all this protesting, it's so Seventies. Why are the students and their parents complaining? I'd be delighted if I had a chance to win a basket of fresh fruits. And isn't soda the drink of choice amongst the young?"

"It's all energy drinks and alcopops that I'm confiscating from their backpacks," Miss McClurkin said. "And I haven't seen a piece of fruit in their hands unless they're launching it at someone they hate in the schoolyard."

"Victoria sat me down and had a talk with me," Mr. Skivvins said, doing his best to avoid the lure of Mrs. Pilkey's pacing legs. "She thinks we should offer a prize that is a bit more modern, something that will give the children more incentive to appear in the talent show, focus on performing to the best of their ability, and allow them to forget that they are competing against the enemy. If we change the attitude of the children, the parents will follow. Hopefully. And as for the parents, I do believe the drinks reception will be an opportunity to calm their ruffled feathers as well. I have the perfect prize."

Miss McClurkin had flinched at the word 'modern.' She was afraid to ask what perfect prize Mr. Skivvin's brain had conjured up, as his easy smile, caring eyes and general aura of earnestness immediately put Miss McClurkin on guard, and his suit was of the most peculiar cut. When Mrs. Pilkey had introduced him to her the week before, his outstretched hand had seemed curious to her: manicured and soft to the touch from expensive lotion. *A homosexual or a Protestant?* Miss McClurkin had worried. She had taken the hand with reluctance and done her best to shake it, but she now knew the answer to her question, as the man had a daughter at How Great Thou Art and eyes that were clinging onto every movement of Mrs. Pilkey's calves. Miss McClurkin found lust distasteful, and the lustful man continued with his madness:

"Victoria tells me there's an entertainer popular with the youngsters of today. Her name, apparently, is Hannah Montana, and she happens to be giving a concert over in Belfast in a few weeks time. The venue is owned by the cash-and-carry owner I buy all of Sav-U-Mor's stock from. He owes me one. I can put a call in and see if we can't get a few free tickets."

"Is this Hannah Montana age-appropriate?" Miss McClurkin demanded to know.

"She's from the Disney Channel," Mr. Skivvins said. "I've watched her show many times with Victoria."

"That's alright, then," Mrs. Pilkey replied, relaxing. "As much as it pains me to say it, Miss McClurkin, I believe he is right. Perhaps we should make The Togetherness Basket the Runners-Up prize, and free tickets to this Hannah Montana concert the Grand Prize."

As the man prattled on, Miss McClurkin swerved from unease to alarm to downright horror. The details kept spewing from his blindingly white teeth, Mrs. Pilkey bobbing her head eagerly like a spastic child at his side, and Miss McClurkin stared down at her two arms as if choosing which vein she would inject the heroin into. She could keep silent no longer.

"Have you both taken leave of your senses? Have you no clue to the left-wing manifesto of the Disney Corporation? Don't be fooled by the connotation of Disney with family values, cuddly cartoons and a Christian view of life. Nothing could be further from the truth! The same company condones same-sex partnerships by allowing them to extend health benefits to their partners. They allow such perverts to participate in the Fairy Tale Wedding program at their resorts, Disneyland and DisneyWorld, where the degenerates are permitted to ride in Cinderella's coach, followed by uniformed trumpeters into the castle, and waited on hand and foot by Mickey and Minnie Mouse. The mere thought of what shenanigans they get up to in the back of the Cinderella coach makes my skin crawl, and should even have you, Mr. Skivvins, reaching for the sick bucket and all. The Disney Corporation owns ABC, the American network known for its anti-Christian agenda, their news reporters frequently skewing broadcasts against Pope Benedict, branding him an attacking

Rottweiler. Many God-fearing Catholics and," Mrs. Pilkey glanced at Mr. Skivvins, "also those from lesser religions have been boycotting Disney's resorts for years, and with good reason. DisneyWorld is full of homosexuals flouncing around in costumes of their cartoon characters, allowing innocent children to sit on their laps while their unsuspecting parents snap holiday photos of them. The good Lord alone knows what sinful gropings and filthy arousals occur during those lap-sittings! I understand we have to change the prize, but I put my foot down at having children under our charge being entertained by a pawn of an institution promotes such low-brow, sexually-deviant culture. Mrs. Pilkey, I will be forced to hand in my resignation if the prize is filth! And don't get me started on violent video games!"

Mr. Skivvins adjusted the knot of his tie, his animated grin having faltered long ago. He turned to Mrs. Pilkey, confusion in his eyes. Mrs. Pilkey touched her chignon.

"You've certainly spent some nights worrying about Disney," Mrs. Pilkey said weakly. "We can't stop the march of time, Miss McClurkin. I know you are of the mind the sexually-charged culture of the day is leading our children straight down a path to eternal damnation, but perhaps we must face the fact that innocence is a thing of the past."

Mr. Skivvins said through pursed lips: "I've watched the show with my Victoria, and there is nothing degenerate or homoerotic or anti-Christian about it. It's a pleasant, happy family show about a little girl from Tennessee who leads a secret life as a pop star with her song-writing father, who is played by Billy Ray Cyrus."

Mrs. Pilkey brightened.

"Didn't he sing 'Achy Breaky Heart?'" she asked, warming immediately. "Yes."

"I quite like that one, spent many a night line-dancing to it in my university days. *Don't break my heart, my achy breaky heart*," she warbled.

"Billy Ray Cyrus?" Miss McClurkin struggled to maintain calm. "And you say the show has no homoerotic element?"

"The role of Hannah Montana is played by his daughter, Miley Cyrus, who is becoming a pop star in her own right. She has a brother as well in the program, Jackson. Let me put your mind at ease. When Hannah's not touring the country as a secret pop singer, she is a normal little girl, who likes going camping and going to the beach, and is afraid of spiders and the dentist."

"And who doesn't like going to church and has no healthy fear of the Lord, no doubt," Miss McClurkin sniffed. "And where is the mother in this charade of happy families, I'd like to know? I presume this 'caring father' is, dare I utter the word, divorced, as all Yanks appear to be these days? The American media is quick to celebrate alternatives to the nuclear family, forcing our children to believe jumping from one marital bed to the other is the natural arc of adult life!"

"Hannah's mother died of a terminal illness, if I remember correctly. Cancer, I believe it was."

Miss McClurkin was nonplussed, steadfast in her conviction.

"If she's a secret pop star, I presume she must lie to those close to her? Breaking one of the ten commandments—bearing false witness against her neighbors—every time she opens her mouth."

Glossy brochures and pamphlets abruptly appeared from Mr. Skivvin's briefcase and were shoved with irritating earnestness towards her.

"And I have here a poster of the concert."

Mrs. Pilkey inspected with suspicion the photo of a blonde teenager in a sparkly purple top, jeans, and a tasteful dark red jacket with many buttons, no sign of cleavage or belly buttons beaming out at them. She took an immediate dislike to her.

"Her teeth are too big for her mouth. Her lying mouth."

"She's a Yank," Mrs. Pilkey explained. "All their teeth are too big for their mouths. And unnaturally white, as we all know."

Miss McClurkin stole a glance at Mr. Skivvins' teeth.

"Those Yanks, I can't stand people who are so full of themselves," she said, then glanced again at Mr. Skivvins. "In a bad way, I mean," she added apologetically.

"I think you are missing the obvious, Miss McClurkin," Mrs. Pilkey said. "Mr. Skivvins' daughter could have been a fan of that harlot Britney Spears."

Miss McClurkin grew pale at the thought…

"Or Katy Perry," Mr. Skivvins put in. "Remember that song about lesbian sex which spent weeks at number one on the hit parade?"

…and shuddered…

"Or Lily Allen, every song of whose deals with sex and is littered with expletives."

…and gripped the arm of the sofa, finally calming.

"Or Amy Winehouse, extolling the virtues of drink."

"Given a Grammy by the Yanks! Rewarded for bad behavior!" was Miss McClurkin's knee-jerk response.

Miss McClurkin was relenting. She had long since resigned herself to the fact she was a one woman windbreak of decency against the tsunami of modern culture. She hadn't trusted anything that had come out of America since Donna Summer's "Bad Girls" in 1979. Who but a nation of degenerates would release a double album about prostitution and then market it to impressionable young minds? *"Toot Toot-Hey, Beep Beep,"* indeed!

Miss McClurkin sighed. "I suppose I've no choice but to agree," she said in a cold, dead voice.

Mrs. Pilkey and Mr. Skivvins high-fived over a pile of tattered faxes.

"Oh, and Miss McClurkin?" Mrs. Pilkey said as the teacher made to escape through the door.

"Yes, headmistress?"

"Any whiff of insubordination on your part, any plans of sabotage whispered into the ears of the girls, and, tenure be damned, I'll find a way to ensure you're down that Job Center sharpish."

Miss McClurkin left, shattered.

CHAPTER 24

Fionnuala turned down the heat on the pot of potatoes to simmer. She carried a tin-foil covered plate of beans on toast, leftovers from the night before, around the corner to 5 Murphy Crescent, shopping cart trundling behind her. She pried open the gate which sagged off one hinge and marched through the shame of the front garden.

"I'm now an OsteoCare volunteer," she announced to Maureen. "I've me first visit planned for old Mrs. Ming on Rossville Street the night. Taking Siofra and Seamus with me and all, I am, to show them what compassion be's all about."

As she dug her dentures into the beans, Maureen found it difficult to mask her shock. Care, compassion and Fionnuala were three words she had never considered in one sentence.

"A—?" she struggled.

"What the feck's yer problem?" Fionnuala scowled. "I've always been up for helping the aged."

Maureen carefully avoided her daughter's eyes.

"And how much are they paying ye?" she asked in an offhand manner, attacking the soggy toast with a fork and attempting a smile.

"Och, ye never have a decent word to say, have ye? Always thinking the worst. Volunteer means volunteer."

But although Fionnuala had no problem spewing out bold-faced lies to strangers, her mother was another matter. It was now Fionnuala's turn to avoid

Maureen's eyes, and it was their misfortune to turn towards what Maureen had shoved down the side of the chair.

"Is that where that flimmin book got to!" Fionnuala said, pointing accusingly at the battered and bean-juice-stained *Lotto Balls of Shame*.

"Kyanny put it down," Maureen confessed. "Fascinating, so it is. Och, don't bore into me with them eyes of betrayal. It pays to know yer enemy, so it does." Maureen had no trouble lying to her daughter; Moira was one of the old woman's favorites, if not the favorite, of the whole sorry lot of them. She was proud of her granddaughter's gumption to admit she was a degenerate, her bravery to leave the city and of her ability to write in cursive. "Perhaps before ye kill yerself trying to get the funds together to attempt this fantasy trip across the Continent to cause wer Moira grief ye ought to read a word or two of what she's written. I don't believe ye've even had a glance inside?"

Maureen flipped through the book to read a chance paragraph, then grimaced. "Perhaps I should choose a different page."

"Naw!" Fionnuala barked. "Read that page ye didn't want to!"

"If ye insist, love," Maureen murmured. She cleared her throat of beans and began. Fionnuala stared at her, fascinated.

"To call Nelly Frood an obese layabout would be an understatement. Although she had given birth to nine children in a row, that's where her labor stopped. Her sister-in-law, Una Bartlett, however, couldn't have been cut from a more different cloth. Civic-minded, loyal and industrious, the classy lady of Derry City rightfully deserved the multi-million pound win on the lottery which had given her a swanky new home with a view of the Foyle River, a chauffeur for her BMW, and an upscale nail salon to which she was the sole proprietor."

Fionnuala gave a wail like a wounded beast and buried her head in her calloused hands, the same hands which had proudly cradled her first newborn offspring all those years ago (at least that's how her selective memory now imagined it; Moira's labor had been long and arduous, and when the child had finally been spit into the world, Fionnuala had begged the midwife to get it the hell away from her). Closing the book, Maureen was shocked at the sobs arising from those worn knuckles. The last time she'd seen her daughter cry was in 1995 when Ireland won the Eurovision Song Contest.

"This," Fionnuala sobbed, "be's the thanks I get for the nine months I carted her around in me womb. Betrayed by me own spawn of flesh! Ungrateful cunt! Nine months of torture I had to endure! Nine fecking months!"

Maureen didn't know where to look, her daughter having conveniently forgotten the douching with fizzy lemonade and the sucking down of forty cigarettes daily in an effort to miscarry, which had led to Moira's premature birth at eight months. Maureen roused herself from the chair and, under duress, placed a hand on comfort on her daughter's shuddering shoulders.

"Calm yerself down or you'll give yerself a coronary. Sure, nobody reads books nowadays anyway. It's all video games and movies."

But Fionnuala had heard some people did read for leisure, and not just for daily necessities such as shopping lists and arrest warrants.

"Aye, but what about all them nancy boy poofters with no mates and Orange cunts with more education than sense," Fionnuala said, her wracking sobs refused to subside. "Self-important wankers with their smug turning of the pages as if they know more than the rest of us."

"Themmuns kyanny even tell ye the amount of times Derry Football Club won the title, or how many fish fingers comes in a packet, but," Maureen said, trying to make Fionnuala feel better.

"I kyanny get outta me mind, but, the image of wer Moira hunched over the typewriter, pecking away on the keys the hatred for her own mother. I don't know what makes me more ill, the vision of her pinched lips as she types away the poison, or the thought of where them lesbo lips finds themselves at night."

They both turned with relief as Dymphna slouched into the sitting room, a screaming Keanu over her shoulder, a can of beer in her hand.

"And this one!" Fionnuala said with contempt, wiping her eyes. "What time do ye call this to be rousing yerself outta bed? Yer granny there's already on her second meal of the day."

"Aye, and I'd be on me third if this one had gotten itself from around the corner and into me gullet in a timely manner," Maureen harrumphed pointedly.

Dymphna perched herself on the edge of the couch, lip up a cigarette and reached for the remote.

"Isn't it high time ye prised yerself from in front of that telly and made an effort to find some gainful employment?" Fionnuala rattled on.

Dymphna looked up at her in shock. "Me arse has barely settled itself on the settee, and I haven't even had time to turn the telly on, sure. I kyanny miss Judge Judy, so I kyanny."

Fionnuala herself had sat before *Judge Judy* many a time, a notebook on her knee and a pencil in her hand, ready to scribble down tidbits on how to scam money from unsuspecting do-gooders. The program was a treasure trove of inspirations. Those Yanks really knew how much a good deed never went unpunished. But Fionnuala was now in no need of inspiration; she had her own scam planned with her new OsteoCare victims, and could almost feel the Maltese sun on her face and Moira's flesh under her fingernails.

"Although why ye should even waste the time pounding the pavement looking for employment in this town, I don't know. A waste of good shoe leather, so it is. All them places ye've been sacked from, there's not an employer left who would give ye a chance. Useless, so ye are."

"Never fear, Mammy," Dymphna said as brightly as her misery would allow. "It won't be a job I'm needing when I get meself back in the Riddell's good books. I've a date with Rory the morrow night."

"That's about as likely as me turning Proddy," Fionnuala said. "I tell ye this, but, ye better beat them odds and nab yerself a job, as ye've to pay yer own way across the Continent."

"I don't feel comfortable going to Malta to ruin Moira's big day, but," Dymphna revealed carefully.

Fionnuala's eyes bored like two rusty pneumatic drills towards Dymphna's.

"I'm not taking naw for an answer."

"Och, leave the wane be," Maureen said. "And what are ye still doing here anyroad? Ye've already fed me. Why've ye yer shopping cart with ye? Away off down the town for the messages?" *Messages*, Derry for shopping.

"Ye think I've money?" Fionnuala snapped. "Naw, I need to cart that case of tins from the Sav-U-Mor round the corner to ours. Filled with revolting shite, themmuns might be, but a cupboard shelf collapsed this morning and I need themmuns to prop it up. I never thought them manky tins would be more use to me than that daughter of mines guzzling the drink over on the settee; the proof be's in the pudding, but."

Fionnuala headed to the kitchen to get the cans, and Maureen turned to Dymphna, sobbing before a shrieking Judge Judy.

"I know that one be's a hard-faced bitch," she said. "She be's yer mammy, but, and only has yer best interests at heart. A heart of slate, mind, but a heart nevertheless."

CHAPTER 25

Ursula closed the book, tears of joy threatening to spill from her eyes. She looked up to the heavens, a smile gracing her face for the first time in ages. During the dark days of the fallout from the lottery win in Derry, she had only wanted one kind word, one, spoken towards her. And now here were words, many kind words, written. She wanted to circle them all with a pencil and count them.

"Thank you, Moira," she whispered. "Thank you, dear God."

It was true there were some kind words directed towards the character of Nelly Frood in the book as well—her being a working-class mother struggling to raise a litter of ungrateful and violent hooligans on a budget and blah, blah, blah—but Ursula assumed Moira had stuck them in only as life insurance against Fionnuala's wrath. It was so nice of Moira to send her a pre-release copy, together with a note that was as kind to Ursula herself as Moira had been to Una Bartlett in the book. Ursula now knew that, in Malta at least, somebody really did love her. The cozy fantasy life of *Lotto Balls of Shame* saved in a special part of her mind forever, Ursula set the book aside and forced herself back onto the ledge of nervous exhaustion and free-floating anxiety that, ever since her ID had been stolen by that creature in the casino, was her reality.

She froze in horror at the beeping from their new motion-sensitive alarm system. Someone had entered their property! Ursula crouched behind the curtains and whimpered at the forms she spied waddling down the path, sure it was the woman from the casino with a male friend. Casino Woman had scrubbed herself up, cut her nails and made herself resemble a respectable member of the human race, and a white one at that. Ursula wasn't fooled.

The doorbell rang and Ursula screamed.

"I'll get it, dear," Jed said from some depth of the house. "It's only Slim and Louella."

He looked into the living room on his way to the door, and his heart fell at the frazzled look on Ursula's face, the hair she had let go to pot, the nibbled fingernails.

"Aw, honey," he said. "It hurts to see you looking so bad. I can always tell them to go away. We can play cribbage another night."

"Naw, it's fine," Ursula said. "There be's safety in numbers, after all."

He looked at her as if stricken with buyer's remorse, but truly his heart welled with affection and the need to protect. He had spent a military career protecting the nation, and now he was protecting his wife. For someone who had grown up in a warzone, Jed thought, Ursula was quite vulnerable.

Jed's watch beeped and he gulped a pill as he headed for the door. Jed had bottles of pills for high blood pressure and the like strewn all over the house, and a timer on his watch that went off when he had to take one. He got a bit confused as to which one and how many he should take every time it beeped but he hadn't collapsed yet, so he supposed he must be doing something right.

Ursula got up from the floor and swallowed a pill of her own (she wasn't without medication either). Jed opened the door and greeted his brother and his wife.

"Hey, Jed!" Slim said. "The store was packed today."

"Great news!"

Jed had invested in Sinkers, Scorchers and Shooters, Slim and Louella's store which sold fish tackle and bait, hot sauce and a small selection of arms. They were considering branching out to beef jerky.

Ursula plastered a smile on her face as she hugged as much of them as the length of her arms would allow. *Beauty is skin deep*, she kept muttering to herself. She could have used a session on the Stairmaster herself, but there was, she sniffed, a difference between overweight and morbidly obese. A year earlier, though, Slim and Louella had accepted Ursula with open arms—albeit flabby ones—and for that Ursula would always be grateful. Company was difficult to come by in Wisconsin, and it was more than her family did. The cribbage game at the kitchen table, bowls of popcorn and pretzels and kielbasa and crackers and cans of beer spread amongst the cards, would keep Ursula from fantasizing about Casino Woman's impending attack. She only wished Louella didn't cheat.

As they popped the tabs on their beer, Ursula sipped a chilled chardonnay out of a wine glass and shuffled the cards. Their black poodle, Muffins, yipped at their side, trying to get at the snacks. They played away, dealing and cutting flipping cards, calling out how much they amounted to, moving pegs around the scoring board. Money, of course, was being bet, and dollar bills and tarnished quarters piled up before them. Ursula kept a close look at the progress of Louella's peg around the board. They discussed cheese varieties and Dr. Phil episodes, and which flavors of beef jerky the store should stock. And then the discussion turned to the new security measures.

"I thought you were gonna get an electric fence?" Slim asked through kielbasa and cheese. "Five."

"Nine," Jed said. "I thought it was a bit too much, though." He took a gulp of beer.

"Aye," Ursula said, "And when I thought about it, nine and seven is sixteen, I had a vision of wer poor Muffins fried to a crisp as she did her business in the yard." She reached under the table with the hand not holding the cards and fed Muffins some popcorn.

"It must be terrible," Louella said, "being under all that pressure constantly. Nineteen. Not knowing if that crazy woman's going to come knocking at your door."

"Twenty-three," said Slim. "You shoulda gone to the police."

"Well," Jed said, "Ursula asked me to bring her, twenty-five, a gun home from the store so she could feel safe."

"Aye, twenty-eight," Ursula said. "I wanted one with a pink pearl handle. Jed was too mortified to order it from the suppliers for me, but."

"Thirty!" Louella squealed with delight. "That's two extra points for me!"

She counted her peg two spaces around the board with glee, and scooped the kitty to her breasts, Queen of Kitchen Cribbage.

"So he got me a Glock," Ursula said, staring into Louella's eyes. "Who cut these cards?"

"Why don't we order a pizza," Louella suggested.

Ursula looked down at the empty bowls and was surprised even as she realized she shouldn't be.

"I want pepperoni," Jed said.

"I want sausage and mushrooms," Slim said.

"I want extra cheese," Louella said. "And jalapenos."

"Foreigner!" Slim joshed.

"And make sure," Louella said, "it's a deep-dish with one of those cheese-stuffed crusts."

"I'll pay," Ursula said.

She reached for the cash on the table, but their hands shot out.

"Leave that, honey," Jed said. "We're using all our cash to bet. Use the credit card."

Ursula excused herself and moved to the hallway to phone. Louella winning again was making her angry and she needed a self-imposed time out. She phoned PizzaPielotta, pitying the poor fool who would have to ride through the miles of tundra to feed them for the sake of a two dollar tip. She put in the order, had to repeat it three times so he could understand, then said as clearly as her annoyance would allow: "I'm using a credit card."

The PizzaPielotta man took her details. There was some muttering on the line, then he said: "I'm sorry, ma'am, your credit card isn't going through."

"Och, catch yerself on," Ursula said. "We've a $5000 limit, sure."

"It's been declined."

Ursula hung up, relieved she had moved to the hallway; she would have been embarrassed if Slim and Louella had heard. Ursula stabbed the numbers to the credit card company on her phone. She was furious and hungry herself now.

"Aye? Hello? I've just heard me credit card be's declined, and I know we've not charged anything on it."

"I'm so sorry, ma'am."

"Och, nothing to be sorry for. Ye've not done nothing. Have ye?"

"Er, no. Why don't you give me your account number?"

Ursula barked the numbers in the phone and fiddled with the plug of a lamp as she waited. Barbra Streisand's "Woman In Love" played in her ear, and just as it got to the good bit, the man came back on.

"Yes, we had to place a temporary hold on your card as there's been suspicious activity on it."

"It's been here in me handbag all the time, and I can assure ye me handbag never be's far from me side."

"Not that card, ma'am. The other card."

Unease filled Ursula. She wished she were still listening to Barbra Streisand instead of this man.

"The other card?"

"Yes, the card you opened last month."

"I did no such thing!"

"Yes, you did ma'am. You opened another credit card, and we extended a $5000 line of credit to you. It was gobbled up in three days."

Ursula hung up, frenzy in her brain, and ran into the kitchen, where she screamed. The cards in Louella's hands scattered to the floor.

"She's gone and stolen me identity!" Ursula wailed. "She be's Ursula Barnett now! With $5000 worth of gear bought on me credit!"

As Jed and Slim stared at her, Louella slipped her peg two holes up the scoring board.

CHAPTER 26

"And what will you be doing for the talent show?" Miss McClurkin asked the next girl in line.

"Irish dancing," was the reply, the eyes brimming with excitement.

Miss McClurkin heaved the sigh of a martyr as she dug the point of her pen into the paper on the desk before her.

"Marvelous choice," Miss McClurkin said in a voice devoid of emotion. The clueless girl scampered out of the office.

"What's your talent?" Miss McClurkin growled to the next.

"Irish dancing."

Miss McClurkin struggled to find her center. The pen flew, and she was unable to look the girl in the eye.

As the twenty-fifth girl exited her office, Miss McClurkin reviewed the list with dread. She had one girl who would play "Danny Boy" on a recorder and twenty-four girls Irish Dancing. She envisioned the endless stream of stiff arms, flailing legs, clacking shoes and treble jigs, and realized she would have to bring either a stiff drink or a small pistol to turn on herself on the day.

Next in was Siofra Flood and Grainne Donaldson, with Catherine McLaughlin at their side. What sweet little Catherine could be doing with those hardened thugs the teacher couldn't imagine. Miss McClurkin inspected Catherine's arms for bruises of coercion, her eyes for a sign of panic. She saw none, but didn't know if the girl was intelligent enough to speak to her with her eyes.

"And what about the three of you?" Miss McClurkin demanded, no longer able to keep up a pretense of civility. Was this to be a group display of Irish Dancing?

"Me and me mates Grainne and Catherine are to sing and dance to Lady Gaga's 'Poker Face.'" Siofra announced.

Miss McClurkin froze with surprise. Of course, she wasn't "with it," as she believed the youngsters now termed it, where the day's popstars were concerned, but she had spent a long night with a flagon of white zinfandel after her outburst of prudishness in the headmistress' office, and the alcohol had helped her see she should perhaps allow the world to march its way to eternal damnation. Just the name of the artist, let alone the title of the selection—she was sure it had something to do with gambling—made her squirm with unease. And, yes, she was sure she had overheard a trio of housewives at the frozen foods section of the Top-Yer-Trolley cackling on about Lady Gaga being a disgraceful role model for young girls. Hadn't they discussed something about tarty fashion sense, bad mothering, promiscuity, mental instability and writhing with live snakes? Hadn't the "singer" even, sin of sins, gotten one of those divorces? Or was that that Britney Spears?

Miss McClurkin was certain Lady Gaga and her "Poker Face" song were elements not befitting an institution like Our Lady of Perpetual Sorrow, but at that moment, she would gladly have invited Satan himself to perform naked cartwheels onstage; anything to avoid another entry of Irish Dancing.

"What a delight," she said, cooling; at least that little terror Siofra Flood was showing some imagination. "But I'm afraid I'm not familiar with this tune, er...'Poker Face?' Would you be so kind as to give me a printout of the lyrics so I can ensure they are appropriate for the school?"

"Lyrics?" Siofra asked.

"Words."

"Och, the words be's fine."

"Nevertheless, I must insist on a printout. And, these dance moves... Nothing too suggestive, do you understand?"

The three girls exchanged a look of confusion.

"Suggestive, Miss?" Grainne asked. "What be's that?"

"Never mind," Miss McClurkin said with a quick shake of the head. "We'll see during the rehearsals if modifications need to be made."

They shuffled uncertainly; the children of Our Lady of Perpetual Sorrow could rarely understand a sentence that left the teacher's lips, though Miss McClurkin seemingly spoke the same language they did.

"Off you go, girls," Miss McClurkin said, a smile on her lips and a dance in her fingertips as she wrote down Pop Singing and Dancing on the entry form.

They scampered towards the door.

"Oh, and Catherine?"

Catherine turned.

"I'm happy you're making mates."

Catherine looked down shyly at her Jellies and murmured, "Ta, Miss."

She joined her two partners in crime in the corridor. Siofra grappled her by the tie and shoved her against the water fountain (broken for years). Grainne clapped with glee.

"Now we're best mates," Siofra said to Catherine's terrified nostrils, "and ye're in wer group for the talent show and all. We're gonny beat them Pepsi-slurping gacks from How Great Thou Art hands down, and then we're off to Belfast to see Hannah Montana. I won't be able to sleep, but, if I don't have that press pass in me hands. I don't wanna see her like a wee ant on the stage from miles away. I told ye to get it for me days ago."

"I-I'll get it for ye when we win," Catherine whimpered.

"Naw! The morrow!" Siofra barked.

"Me daddy, but...the safe...the keys...me mammy..."

"Me fingers better be's clutching it the morrow, or ye won't be able to dance on that stage with yer new mates as ye'll be laid up in Altnagelvin with yer legs in casts!"

"I'll get it to ye! I'll get it!"

"Swear on the Holy Father and the Virgin Mary!"

"I...I swear."

"On the Holy Father and the Virgin Mary!"

Catherine swore on both the Holy Father and the Virgin Mary as instructed so her lungs could get some air, but as Siofra released the grip on her tie, she didn't have a clue how to make that promise reality.

CHAPTER 27

"It's time to begin, now count it in! 5-6-7-8!"

The electro-fiddle-bass beat of the old Steps tune shook the speakers, and tens of cowboy-booted feet raced to the tattered linoleum of the Leisure Center dance floor around Rory. Bridie had excused herself to the restroom, and Rory was downing the free coffee at a table next to the bingo machine as if his body could store the caffeine for use later on. The sweat was lashing down his body, his arms and legs aching.

Rory had been skittish about his first line-dancing session and the force of Bridie's fingers around his wrist, but she had thrust a spare cowboy hat on his head and hauled him onto the floor, and his limbs could do nothing but comply. He had mastered and then performed to "Cotton-Eyed-Joe," "Mambo Number Five" and a Shania Twain b-side the running-a-hand-across-the-brim-of-your-cowboy-hat move, the lassoing-a-calf-for-slaughter move, the reaching-for-your-holsters move, the gun-shooting-a-moving-target move, the hiking-up-the-chaps move, the thumbs-locked-in-the-belt-loops-move (rather similar to the holster move), and, with his feet, the shuffle-right-four-steps-then-shuffle-left-four-steps, the cross-the-legs-then-kick-to-the-back, the cross-the-legs-then-kick-to-the-front.

"My rodeo romeo, a cowboy god from head to toe…"

Rory was under no illusion about why Bridie had insisted he join her at the Center, and it had little to do with steering him away from a life of alcoholism. She thought he would become her 'rodeo romeo,' her 'cowboy god from head to toe,' but if that hideous cow in her fringed corduroy skirt thought she would get her fat fingers anywhere near his tackle, she was sadly mistaken; he'd rather douse his eyes with bleach. And he had noticed she was chucking down the Guinness as if Prohibition were going into effect the next day while she demanded he remain alcohol-free. Rory stirred his coffee and glumly awaited her return before he could claim a headache and make his escape home.

Inside the lavatory, Bridie took stock of her face in the mirror as she carved her mouth with lipstick: the hair of no discernible color, the cold sore, the pimples from grease thanks to long shifts at Kebabalicious, the burns from smoking cigarettes in the wind. Bedding Rory Riddell seemed a long shot, but wasn't it about time the Lord finally smiled her way?

Bridie McFee was a bitter old spinster at the age of twenty two. Even when younger, she knew she didn't have the physical attributes Dymphna Flood had. She had realized as the nights in the Craiglooner pub piled up and the alcohol took its toll on her already disadvantaged body that it was becoming more and more difficult to catch the eye of a lad. When she had been about seventeen, the young fit ones had quit looking at her, then the young ugly ones at nineteen, and, now, at twenty-two, even the old alkies and social outcast junkies wouldn't look her way.

She was mired in a dead-end job slinging Cowaliciouses-On-A-Bun across a counter to drunken young ones who flung insults at her and taunted her for doing the McJob she was doing even as they grabbed the bags from her, and who she recognized as being in primary school years earlier. Time had passed and they were now of legal drinking age (or almost, anyway) and Bridie's life was becoming increasingly stuck in the forgettable. Was it any wonder she had grown to loathe Dymphna and her DD cups?

Dymphna was too dim-witted to realize what a find she had in Rory, Bridie thought, and the only ammunition Bridie had to make Rory see sense and shift that engagement ring from Dymphna's finger to her own was her line-dancing skills and her intelligence; she had taken night classes at the Foyle Community College a year earlier. It was only when she had started learning knowledge that she realized what a simpleton not only Dymphna was, but also all their mates from school she had wasted her childhood and then youth getting drunk and dancing around their handbags at Starzzz nightclub with.

Bridie thought the evening was going well. Rory had rattled on between songs about how he had started drinking months earlier, when he had heard around town that Dymphna was claiming to all who would listen that her poofter boss Henry O'Toole was the father of her child when he knew it was him; how he had proposed to her out of a sense of duty; how he had moved in and the baby had been born; the embarrassment when she had insisted the child be called Keanu, the pressure from his mother Zoë to rid himself of her; the ribbing of his mates for settling down with a Catholic, and a slag at that. Bridie was enraptured. She wasn't sure if it was what Rory was saying, or if it was the sight of his crotch before her as he shuffled back and forth. Her mind was excitedly trying to make out what could conceivably be the shape of his ass in those shapeless jeans, the thought of his spindly arms wrapping around her.

Me face might be a disappointment, but thank feck I've been on me small portions diet, Bridie thought, running her well-bitten fingernails over the embroidered cows grazing in a field of her shirt and exiting the lavatory. She plastered a leer on her face as she made her way through the syncopated arms and legs on the dancefloor towards Rory. Time to shift the chatter to sex and bag her man; lads were always up for getting their leg over.

"I kyanny understand why ye hit the bottle last week," Bridie said. "Ye're a star on the dancefloor, you. A regular John Travolta. And I'm sure ye're a man of many more talents besides, like."

She undressed him with her eyes. Rory looked down, all bashful.

"Ye mean…?" he asked.

Bridie raised a filthy eyebrow. "Aye," she said, eying his crotch, though it was too dark in the corner for Rory to notice this. "Ye know what I'm on about."

"I suppose Dymphna told ye all about it?" he asked.

In fact, Dymphna had always said sleeping with Rory was like rolling around in a sack of sick, but Bridie didn't want Rory getting a complex; he was fragile after all.

"Aye," she said, nodding eagerly and sidling closer to his limbs. "She never lets up about yer prowess, but I want to hear all about it from yer own lips."

Her eyes searched his face eagerly, and it was all Bridie could do to force her hands to remain Christian. Rory was surprised. He had only told Dymphna briefly about his expertise with the Rubik's cube when he young, the trophy he had received for it from the Protestant Youth Center, and she had seemed bored to tears. But if she had told her best mate…

"The things women talk about!" he said.

"I'm all ears."

"Well, if ye really wanny hear all about it…"

Bridie's eyes said she really did; and her quim was atingle at the sneak peek Rory would allow her into the bedroom antics she, fingers crossed, would soon be sampling.

"Some says technique be's important, but speed be's what matters to me. It only takes me a minute and half and then I'm done. I've spent years practicing in me bedroom, as I think it's madness to waste half an hour twisting and turning away when there be's more important things I could be doing. There be's a special website where ye put up yer video of ye doing it quickly for all the world to see, and I'm proud to say me video be's ranked number two. Brilliant, aye?"

No wonder Dymphna was disappointed in the bedroom. Bridie's ardor for Rory began to chill.

Rory went on, warming to the topic: "I started quite late, ye know. Fourteen, I musta been, would ye believe? The first time was with me da."

Bridie gawped at him as both horror and compassion filled her. This certainly explained Rory's lager-fueled meltdown, seeking comfort in drink. She reached out a comforting hand. "Yer da? At fourteen years of age? I'm wile sorry. Ye must've been terrible traumatized."

To her surprise, Rory pushed her hand away and tsked defensively. "If that's yer attitude, I'm not gonny continue. It annoys the feck outta me, this mortification young people the day feels for doing such things with their da, their reluctance to admit the fun they had together as a family. Disgraceful, so it is. I blame the Yanks. Ye wanny know the details or not?"

Bridie had done a course in sexual deviance at the Foyle Community College, and had learned all about defensiveness, the love children still felt for their incestuous abusers, and that the need to protect and remain loyal to their violators could continue through to adulthood if they didn't get the correct therapy.

"Sorry for me insensitivity. Go ye on ahead," she urged, though she was dreading what he might come out with next. Rory stirred his coffee a few times, his anger subsiding. Then he faced her, seemingly having forgiven her.

"Me and me da was staying over at me granny's for the weekend, and it was raining and we was bored—me granny was up in the loo, I think—and me da suddenly reached into his bathrobe and pulled it out."

Bridie gasped, and Rory flashed his eyes at her, so she struggled to control the revulsion she felt.

"It was strange to me at first, but I soon got the hang of it and realized what a craic it was. Then me granny came in and demanded a go. She found it difficult at first to get her hands around it—they be's riddled with arthritis, ye understand, but she was soon twisting away, and I haveta admit I was glad she joined in as it seemed to take years offa her. After that first time, me and me da did it every chance we got. Weeks later, me mammy came in once unexpectedly when we was at it in the back garden, and she was gagging for a go and all. Ye wouldn't believe all the places we've done it together as a family: at the bus stop, waiting for wer order at the fish and chips shop, once even in the snack bar of a ferry to Liverpool, with all the passengers around us in a circle clapping and urging us on."

Bridie fiddled with a fringe. The poor soul was revealing such sordid secrets so casually, almost proudly, his sense of what was acceptable to most emotionally-functional families so skewed and bizarre. Her heart swelled with pity; the years of abuse had left him truly debased.

"I don't suppose youse've all done it together in yer family and all?" Rory asked, to her horror.

"No, I can't say as we've had," Bridie replied stiffly.

"I don't suppose there's many that does nowadays; it goes back to what I was telling ye before. Why all families doesn't do it together be's a mystery to me. Most Christmases of me youth, we was less interested in the dinner and more looking forward to doing it together in the living room, right before the Christmas tree with the carols playing the background. I've one special memory of the Christmas of 2001. We had loads of aunts and uncles and cousins over for the day, and they all joined in during the Queen's speech on the telly."

Bridie thought in sudden horror that perhaps she was gaining an exclusive glimpse into the sex lives of the typical Protestant family, and silently thanked her strict Catholic upbringing which sought to put a lid on the sins of the flesh. This revolting scenario of the Riddell's extended family was liberalism gone mad. She didn't want to appear to be a prude, however, and forced herself to nod understandingly, though her stomach queased with repugnance.

"Is it still going on?" she chanced. "Or is you too old for them now?"

"Me da was killed by an IRA sniper's bullet years ago, so that put an end to his involvement. But what I'd give for him to be alive and for us to share wer special time together one last time."

"Och, I'm wile sorry for yer loss," Bridie said, "but..but..."

"Out with it, hi."

"But the fecking bastard deserved it! He deserved everything he got!"

Rory's jaw dropped. A change overcame his face, like an iron curtain slamming down which had them on opposite sides of a very large divide.

"Ye're one heartless mental bitch, you!" he seethed. "I was of the mind ye were different from wer parents, one of the new generation, one of the forward-looking, Peace Process wanes what be's seeking to unite the community. I always thought it strange Dymphna would sleep with a Protestant like me. I was always of the mind, but, that legless as she was on the night, drink had played a part and she hadn't a clue, or didn't care I was from the Waterside. You, but, was well aware of me religion, and still ye kept urging me here to this minging tip with ye, you with yer hidden agenda."

Bridie couldn't comprehend his sudden switch from child abuse to politics, even with all those night classes she had taken. "Me..me hidden agenda?" she gasped. "Y-ye're brain doesn't be thinking right, Rory, and I understand from all the abu—"

"Ye're a closet IRA sympathizer, a soldier for the cause, biding yer time all night long, ready to spring on me and hurl abuse at me the moment ye could contain yerself no longer. Secretly delighted, ye musta been, that me poor aul da was a victim of sectarian violence. Ye're sick in the head, ye fecking mad cow, and ye better steer clear of me when ye see me down the town, or ye're gonny find yer eye skewered on the end of a sharpened screwdriver!"

Coffee spilling over the ashtrays, Rory lurched from his chair and fled through the calf-lassoing crowd. Bridie looked in shock at his retreating back, and looked down at her handbag. She would have no use in the foreseeable future for the three packs of condoms she had purchased.

CHAPTER 28

In the spitting rain, Fionnuala clanked the letter box, adjusted her bleached ponytails, and concealed her scowl behind a welcoming smile. Three feet below her horsey head, Seamus and Siofra shuffled with impatience.

"Mammy," Siofra whined. "I'm soaked to the bone."

"Och, ye're sickening the heart outta me, wane," Fionnuala seethed through fixed lips. "Plaster a silly grin on that miserable face of yers, or ye'll feel the force of me palm on yer boney wee arse. Ye wanny see the Mediterranean Sea or not?"

Siofra was more interested in having a good look at Moira's fingers.

"Are ye ready for the treasure hunt, wee dote?" Fionnuala asked Seamus, smacking a finger away from his nostril.

"Aye, Mammy! Wile fun!" Seamus answered by rote.

Fionnuala noticed the chocolate all over his face, swiveled her thumb in her mouth and brought it, spittle dripping, towards Seamus' face. She gouged into the tender flesh of his cheek as he squirmed with pain. Siofra stuck her tongue out at an old drunk staggering by clutching a dartboard he had no doubt nicked from a stall at the market.

Finally the door rattled open.

"Mrs. Ming! How lovely to see ye!" Fionnuala cooed.

Mrs. Ming regarded the woman at her door with alarm.

"Fionnuala Flood? What on God's green Earth brings ye here to me home?" she asked, one hand snaking to the neck of her bathrobe in fear, the other reaching to slam shut the door. But Fionnuala had already barged into the foyer, trailing the children in with her and unraveling her bulky cardigan.

"I'm yer new OsteoCare provider," Fionnuala recited, the words ringing false to her own ears.

Mrs. Ming, as well, seemed to be having difficulty comprehending the meaning of this sentence.

"Where's Niamh?" she asked.

"Laid up in Altnagelvin. Don't ye worry yerself about her. I've all the makings of a grand and lovely visit," Fionnuala rattled on as she dragged the befuddled pensioner into her sitting room and planted her on the settee. She reached into her Celine Dion-Titanic satchel swinging from her shoulder. "I've rosaries if ye want to pray, a MahJong set if ye want to play, a video of *On Golden Pond*..."

Although she suffered from cataracts, even to Mrs. Ming's eyes that satchel looked suspiciously light if it contained all the diversions this home invader said it did.

"I've brought me own tea and all," Fionnuala continued, brandishing a thermos, a teacup and a saucer from some unknown depth of the satchel. "Sweet and milky."

"Have ye not got a copy in that big bag of yers of the book yer eldest wane wrote? The degenerate?" Mrs. Ming said with a lightness that hid the spite as Fionnuala poured. "*Lotto Balls of Shame*, I believe it be's called? The whole town's been talking about it, but I hear it's not gonny be released until next month, but I'm sure ye've an advance copy. I wouldn't mind ye reading me out a few wee passages of that."

Fionnuala tensed as if the pensioner had clattered her across the face. She urged a smile to her lips as she forced the tea upon Mrs. Ming.

"I'm afraid not, naw," she said. "I left me copy at home."

Mrs. Ming gazed down in uncertainty at the swirling tea. Having spent eighty years clawing out a life for herself and her eleven children in the brutal grimness of life in the Moorside—with a war raging in the background for almost thirty of them—Mrs. Ming was no fool. Although Fionnuala now had Flood as a surname, Mrs. Ming was only too aware the tea had been made by the lone girl in the notorious Heggarty clan from Creggan Heights, and that the daughter of deceit had married up to a less violent family. Mrs. Ming and her brigade often clucked about Fionnuala at the Senior Center between cards on bingo night; Fionnuala's reputation for petty thievery had marked her out as someone who couldn't be trusted. Mrs. Ming kept a wide berth from Fionnuala when she ran into her at Sunday mass, and the sight of the sinner mouthing words of praise to the Lord filled the old woman with contempt. Fionnuala Flood had a bold-faced cheek entering St. Molaug's not only every Sunday, but all Holy Days as well, and now here she was blackening her sitting room and forcing an odd-looking tea at her!

But with the sweet little daughter beaming up lovingly at her side, Mrs. Ming considered, maybe she was being too harsh on the woman. Surely the little girl couldn't be that good of an actress at such an early age? And the younger child was behaving himself. Causing her cat grief, to be sure, but didn't her own grandchildren do that? Perhaps she should reconsider and show some decent Christian compassion and a bit of faith that Fionnuala had somehow changed. Stranger things had happened, for example the Troubles ending and the British paratroopers pulling out and leaving the town in peace. Yes, Mrs. Ming thought with a decisive nod of the head, people could change. She grabbed the saucer and took a sip of the steaming tea.

As the barbiturates took effect, Mrs. Ming's head bobbled, and finally she nodded off.

"About time," Siofra muttered.

"Right, wanes!" Fionnuala said. "Let's get werselves up into the loft, and sharpish. The aul one's only gonny be out an hour or so."

The children scampered up the stairs towards the trapdoor of the attic, Fionnuala panting behind them. The Titanic on her special satchel would soon be sinking.

CHAPTER 29

Her mother was in bed with another of her many bad turns. Catherine took her chance to obey Siofra's demands. Frigid with fear, she slipped her ear against the front room door. She heard the drone of some gardening program, the snoring. She pushed the door open. Her father was passed out on the couch, the day's newspaper crinkling as it rose and fell atop his chest. The girl crept across the carpeting, avoiding the two planks she knew creaked. Her little body trembled as she towered over her father's slumbering form.

Above the couch, Jesus glared down at her in disappointment from the Bleeding Heart portrait. The angels that floated on wispy clouds around His suffering body cast her looks of disdain from on high. He died for your sins, they seemed to be warning wee Catherine, and now you're going to throw it all away and plunge yourself into the depths of depravity.

Catherine's eyes welled with tears as she knelt at the side of the cracked leather. Her right hand shuddered through the air as it made to invade the private sanctum of her father's trousers. She slipped the tips of her sweaty fingers into the warmth of his pocket. Catherine grew more queasy, more squeamish, and more resentful of Siofra's demands the deeper her fingers crept into the warmth. Her fingertips brushed past the rumpled pound notes, past the half-eaten roll of breath mints. As her fingertips alighted upon a pound coin, she was sure she was violating the man who had raised her to be respectful, pious and true.

"I'm being forced to sin," she whispered feverishly to herself. "Forced to sin, forced to sin..."

She felt no relief as she located the round hard metal of her father's keyring, only a heightened sense of wrongdoing. Inspector McLaughlin grunted in his sleep and adjusted his leg, Catherine whimpering as her hand was taken along for the ride. She had to half-turn to avoid her fingers slipping out of his pocket. She wound her fingers around the keyring and tugged, tugged, tugged it up the length of her father's leg. The tinkling of the keys as they slipped out of his pocket sounded like the tolling of the bells of St. Molaug's at some old thief's funeral.

Heaving silent pants of misery, Catherine grappled the keys and clutched them firmly in her little fist. She slowly and quietly rose from her father's feet and tiptoed back across the carpet

Her father grunted and sputtered, and she turned around, frozen with fear. But he didn't wake. She couldn't help but glance at the portrait above the couch. The angels seemed now to be condemning her with their glares, letting the little girl know she would now never join their ranks in a heavenly afterlife. Catherine shuddered and left the front room to continue her journey on the road to Hell. Next stop: her daddy's study, and all the while her mind screaming with sin.

CHAPTER 30

Fionnuala thought her plan brilliant: if she kept her hands off the high-priced items on show in the house proper and ransacked the attics, it would be months, if ever, before the theft was discovered, as how often did pensioners scale the ladders, afflicted with osteoporosis as they all were? By that time, Fionnuala and her one-stop OsteoCare visit would be but a memory (if even that, in some of her clients' muddled minds).

Fionnuala followed the children up the ladder and popped her head into the darkness. She tugged out her flashlight and shone it into the cobwebs. Seamus was gnawing on asbestos as if it were cotton candy.

"Och, ye'll ruin yer appetite, ye daft gack," she said, smacking it away from his tongue. "Youse, be on the lookout for anything of value."

"How about this, Mammy?" Siofra asked, her little frame struggling to haul a typewriter from the floor.

Fionnuala was transfixed, shoving the child to the side and digging her claws into the treasure, then she remembered the technological transformation that had introduced those computers into everyone's home.

"Och, catch yerself on, wane!" she spat. "We kyanny get tuppence for an aul piece of shite like that."

"Mammy! Mammy!" Seamus wailed from a corner, holding up a coffee percolator. "This looks wile dear!"

Once again Fionnuala's eyes widened with excitement, then narrowed with scorn.

"Useless, youse wanes are! Them looks like swanky dishes over there. And there be's some rags. Wrap them up, youse."

While the children were packing the dishes, Fionnuala poked at the corroded coils of a space heater in a corner and was struck with the niggling sensation that something was wrong with the intelligence she had gathered. Those women who said Mrs. Ming was rolling in it must have been out of their minds; this attic was a graveyard of obsolete technology. If she took anything from it to the market, she would struggle to make bus fare to Creggan Heights, let alone fund a trip to Malta.

She scrabbled through a pile of dog-eared album covers, pausing for a moment at Kenny Rogers Greatest Hits. She pulled it out of its sleeve, but saw it was scratched. It could have fetched a pretty penny at the market. She flipped further through the albums, and read with interest the track listings of the Barry Manilow live collection, The Bodyguard soundtrack and the Sheena Easton greatest hits, then realized the LPs were too big to fit into even her bag. Although it would have given her great pleasure to listen to "Can't Smile Without You" and "I Will Always Love You" and "Sugar Walls" again after so many years, she felt her heart sinking and her frustration rise, and it wasn't because she couldn't locate *Bucks Fizz's Gold Collection*.

"Take them dishes and shove em in me satchel. And get to work on them Christmas decorations over there and all."

Next to the albums was a pile of VCR tapes. She brightened momentarily, then realized it was all DVDs nowadays. She shuffled through *ET* and *Robin Hood: Prince of Thieves* and *Sophie's Choice*. Then her eyes alighted on a workout video, *Ab Fab Abs and Boulder Buns...Eight-Minute Workouts to a New You!* She looked down and realized she had let her body go to pot. The only time her legs got a workout was when they were sprinting to catch a closing elevator.

"I think I might give this a go," she mused. She made sure Siofra and Seamus weren't looking, then slipped it into her bag. The video would be cheaper than joining a health club, especially as she was stealing it. How could she not find eight extra minutes in a day? She slid a copy of *Ghost* and then *Fame* into her bag as well, and already felt the pounds slipping away.

"Gather up them things and shove em in me bag," Fionnuala said, glancing at her watch. "We need to get werselves home, and quick. That aul one's sure to reach consciousness soon, and the spuds be's ready for dinner."

CHAPTER 31

Catherine crept up the stairs, knees trembling, tears welling. She held the key to her daddy's study aloft. She glanced into her parent's bedroom and saw her mother tangled in the bedclothes, her head buried face-first in the pillow. She inched past the opened door and reached her daddy's study. He sometimes took his work home, and she knew the door was always kept locked as he was shielding her and her mother from the violence of the crime scene photographs. She had caught a glimpse of the walls of the study through the ajar door once, and had almost retched on the spot at the photos of carnage.

She unlocked the door and staggered through the wallpaper of violence, gripping her stomach in displeasure, forcing her eyes to avoid the horrific scenes and focus on her daddy's safe. It was in a cabinet to the left of the desk, right under a well-thumbed Bible. Catherine approached it with dread. As she knelt before the safe, the unease coursing through her, she felt a shadow pass across the opened door. She squealed and whipped around.

Her mother stood there, hair matted, eyes strangely glazed as they had always been of late, a basket of dirty clothing balanced on her hip and a spatula in her hand.

"Oh, hello," Concepta said.

Catherine was horrified her mother had caught her in the private study, but she didn't even seem to be certain who she was speaking to, let alone where.

"L-looking for me Pokemons, just," Catherine said through gritted teeth.

Lying! Another mortal sin! It was indeed a slippery road to damnation.

"Wee dote," her mother said. She would have patted the girl's head had she not been clutching twenty pounds of filthy underwear. Catherine smiled at her mother until she wandered off down the hall, then she shoved the key in the lock of the safe, reached in and scrabbled through the documents and girlie mags until she found the press pass. There was no relief, only a sense of shame. She cursed Siofra Flood as she clicked the safe shut. But at least she wouldn't be bullied again at school now. Would she?

Before she hurried downstairs to replace the keys in her daddy's pocket, she made a quick trip to the bathroom.

Inside, Catherine flung open the medicine cabinet, pawed through the many prescription bottles that had started to proliferate there as of late and grabbed the toothpaste. She spent ten full minutes attacking the length of her tongue with a toothbrush to remove the black spot of lying she was sure tarnished it.

CHAPTER 32

They were assigned the mixing and grinding machines. Dumping inedible fish remnants into a chute twenty feet above the factory floor was a thankless task, but Aggie found at least two things to be thankful for: the cheeks of Paddy's backside flexing inches from her nose as they climbed the ladder. Far below them, the rest of their crew plodded to the conveyor belts, which would spit out fish feed to be packaged and wrapped and hauled onto pallets.

Reaching the catwalk, Paddy and Aggie grabbed a tub of fish remains and began emptying the slop down the chute. Paddy hummed "Gloria" (Laura Brannigan's, not Van Morrison's). He didn't know what was worse: the stench of murdered fish, the sight of the vats of viscera, or the feel of Aggie's leers.

Paddy and Aggie worked quickly as a team, and seven vats soon disappeared down the chute. That would keep those below busy for hours. Paddy took out his flask of whiskey and guzzled down. He offered Aggie a swig, and her face lit up as if he had flashed her.

"We do break, yes?" she asked, her glove wiping the whiskey and fish scales from her chin.

"Aye, I'm gasping for a fag," Paddy said.

They climbed down the ladder and rested against the cold steel of some machine. The women on the conveyor belt followed their lead—if an Irish national could skive off, so could they—and milled around, pulling out cigarettes and food from pockets and nodding towards Aggie, flaunting her friendship with a foreigner. They hissed into each other's ears and flung daggers their way.

Aggie unwrapped a greasy paper bag and thrust some dumpling-looking things under Paddy's nose.

"Pierogi!" she said proudly through the cigarette smoke. "You try."

Paddy couldn't imagine which shop in Derry she had bought them from; they looked like they had been shipped over on the cheap by her mother.

"Yum!" Aggie promised. "From my country. Make more big. More man."

She grappled what she could find of his bicep through the padded overalls and gave it a squeeze that lingered. Paddy was embarrassed not to take one of the creepy foreign things, so he did and chewed it fearfully.

"You sell...?" She threw fantasy darts with her hand.

Paddy had almost forgotten that desperate night at the pub. He mimed carrying the dartboard, opening the door of the pub, ducking fists, falling to the sidewalk, being kicked, and grasping the air for the stolen dartboard. The more violent the pantomime became, the angrier Aggie got.

"Bad! Bad men!" she snarled. "Bad!"

The conveyor belt women pointed and laughed at the idiot foreign man writhing around on the fish residues. Aggie turned, and her tongue rained a torrent of rage-fueled Polish upon them. Paddy spat the half-chewed vileness on the floor. The woman with the cleft chin and the one with the wart slunk back to the conveyor belt, but still Aggie's shrieks threatened to drown the Meatloaf shuddering the speakers. An especially hard-faced one had the nerve to snap something back, and Aggie singled her out with a jabbing finger and a further onslaught of abuse. Others came to Hard-faced's defense, and hands shoved and caps flew and bodies pressed against steel.

I'll see if I can't get transferred to a different group the morrow for me own safety, Paddy mused, nudging the pierogi under some fish scales with his boot. He was scared of Aggie's reaction if she discovered he hadn't cherished every bite. *Yer woman there be's one mad cow, a bunny boiler if ever I clamped eyes on—*

His cellphone vibrated in his pocket, and he rounded some pounding pistons to take the call. Fionnuala's bark in his ear was soothing by comparison: "Paddy! Me head be's spinning! Ye'd not believe the flimmin things I've just been told!"

"Calm down, love," he said, alarmed at the panic in her voice.

"I was down the Top-Yer-Trolley shopping, and before ye chunter on about us not having the funds, we was in desperate need of staples like loo roll and salt, especially the loo roll. We've held out long enough, sure. Anyroad, I ran into Ciara by the meat and cheese counter, and I was telling her about wer Padraig's evil squint and all the distress it's been causing me, and she told me it's not an exorcism that wane needs but a pair of specs! Would ye believe it? It happened to her nephew Liam and all, apparently. Och, Paddy, I'm mortified! Somehow I think wee Padraig being in the clutches of Satan be's a kinder fate. Wer Moira be's the only one of the family what got specs, and look at the shape of her. Ciara agrees; not a soul speaks to her Liam-no-mates since he got em. I kyanny stand them glares no longer, but, so I'm hoping I've yer blessing to haul him down to the eye doctor the day."

Paddy couldn't believe he was hearing correctly. The last time Fionnuala had asked for his approval before acting was when she needed him to check out her betting slip down the dog races the year before.

"If that be's what the wane needs, put him out of his misery," Paddy said.

"And don't forget we've that fancy free drinks do at the school the day after the morrow. I'm putting the finishing touches on me outfit, and ye better be there on me arm or there'll be hell to pay. I don't want ye pleading ye forgot after a few pints at the Rocking Horse. Och! I clear forgot, ye'll hardly go drinking with themmuns down at the plant as ye're on one side of the picket line and themmuns on the other!"

She rang off. Paddy re-rounded the pistons as the foreman materialized and bellowed into the sniping, poking melee: "What the bleeding feck is going on here? Catfighting when youse should be grafting hard! Get yerselves back to the conveyor belts! And put them fags out! Fags out! Work!" O'Leary mimicked these actions with his hands, irritated they couldn't understand something as simple as 'fags out.' They glared at him as they rearranged their outfits into a semblance of normality and shuffled back to their positions. Aggie stood by herself, her makeup a fright.

Paddy marched up and said, "Och, them bloody laws of the EU! How in the name of feck are we expected to work ten hour shifts without the comfort of a fag? Next ye'll be checking wer breath for the whiff of alcohol!"

O'Leary tugged a laser from his belt sagging with new gadgets and pointed it at a fish vat. Then he dealt with Paddy and Aggie.

"And why isn't the two of youse up on the catwalk?" he barked, laser in mid-lase. "Look at the state of this floor! A flimmin tip, so it is!"

Paddy and Aggie looked at the wet fish slime, blood, gut contents, scales, skin and oil.

"Hose down them aisles, or youse'll receive a written warning!"

"Och, for the love of—"

"Ye're quite welcome to join them eejits outside if the work's not to yer liking. The entire country of Poland be's gagging to work here, sure." O'Leary skipped down the factory floor, scribbling down temperatures in his clipboard.

Paddy and Aggie slipped their goggles on and trudged to the industrial hoses. Hot sweat clung to their cold flesh as they struggled to unwind them. Aggie grappled the heavy rubber, posed like Lara Croft, Tomb Raider, and turned on the hose. Her body slammed against steel as acids more caustic than her tongue exploded from the nozzle and drenched the factory floor. Paddy's hose spewed a torrent up the side of a grime-encased wall. The heel of his boot trod on the half-chewed pierogi, and his body skidded forward, the hose slipping from his fingers and writhing on the floor like a boa vomiting toxins. Aggie wailed as she was drenched in acids. Paddy's body collided with the conveyor belt of an adjacent grinder. His gloved hand caught on a stud of the churning belt.

"Help! Help!" he yelped. A line of overalls turned with interest, and not a few faces broke out with glee. Paddy's hand stretched closer and closer to the clomping pistons. The safety strap at the wrist held his fingers prisoner. He dug his teeth into his glove to eat it off.

"*Pomocy! Pomocy!*" Aggie implored, frozen in horror. "*Pomocy! Pomocy!*" Help!

The women at the conveyor belt folded their arms and widened their smirks. Rooted to the spot in fear and indecision, Aggie noted the cold panic in Paddy's eyes, the chomping of his teeth on the insulation, the scrabbling of his feet through the fish on the floor, the helplessness of his fingertips inching towards amputation.

She streaked through the line of catatonic workers and banged on the buttons of the control board. Lights flashed and sirens rang out, and the conveyor belt slowed to a halt. Aggie squealed as if she had won free dental checkups for life and ran to Paddy's shuddering body. She tore the tattered glove from the stud and threw her arms around his neck.

"I save you! I give you a life!" Aggie rejoiced, wiping dewdrops of flesh-eating acid from her forehead. She luxuriated in the glow of a job well done and, glancing at her watch, earning time and a half while she was at it. "Me your hero! Yes!"

As she planted kiss after kiss on his sweaty brow, Paddy realized with a heart sinking more than the Titanic on his wife's satchel that he now Owed Her One.

CHAPTER 33

"'Poker Face' is vulgar," Miss McClurkin explained. "Filth pure and simple."

Mrs. Pilkey scanned the page of lyrics the teacher had handed her, and her lips contorted with confusion. She had been bracing herself for F- and A- and B- and C-words, a litany of expletives which described the joys of substance abuse, promiscuity and casual violence; she had heard that was what the pop songs of the day dealt with, as well as being three major pastimes of the city at large, but she could find nothing of the kind on the printed page.

Mrs. Pilkey said, "I must admit I thought the song dealt with tending to a fireplace. I now see that is not the case. But perhaps you could point out to me which words you find offensive?"

"I should think it's obvious!"

"Not to me. Please point them out."

"If I must."

Mrs. Pilkey waited with a look that said she really must. Miss McClurkin took a deep breath and pointed out.

"There's *I'm bluffin with my muffin*, and *I'm just stunnin with my love-glue-gunnin*,..and, most distressingly of all, *baby, when it's love, if it's not rough, it isn't fun, fun.*"

"Hmm, perhaps you are right," Mrs. Pilkey said. "They are rather declassé. But I suggest that, as you are the one who has an issue with the lyrics, you deal with Siofra and the girls about this yourself. The entire class is practicing in the gym."

"With pleasure."

Miss McClurkin minced down the corridor like a convict enroute to a strip-search with a cellphone lodged up her hole. She bemoaned the flagon of wine which had made her moral compass spin too far in the wrong direction.

Inside the gym, pan pipes and fiddles blared from an army of CD players strewn across a floor in desperate need of a polish. Legs flew, skirts billowed, arms stayed rigid as 4x4s, and in one corner a girl with a recorder was close to hyperventilation. Next to the changing rooms, Grainne and Catherine stood around the CD player blaring Lady Gaga's electro-pop—"*Mum mum mum mah, mum mum mum mah...!*"—as Siofra showed them their moves.

"...and towards the end," she said to Catherine, "ye join me and Grainne and shake yer bum seven times, then pose with yer hands in the air like this. And then ye smile."

Catherine was disappointed. Grainne, as well, stood in a strop; she didn't know much about choreography, but suspected that a group dance should include more than one dancer.

Catherine opened her mouth. "I—I—I..."

"Och, spit out what ye want to say!" Siofra snapped.

"I haven't many dance moves, have I?" Catherine chanced.

"And I don't think ye've made great use of me talents either," Grainne slipped in.

Siofra glared at Grainne as if she had just thrust a sharpened screwdriver between her shoulder-blades.

"I'll give ye more steps, Grainne," she conceded. "You, but, Catherine, should count yerself lucky to even be seen in wer presence."

"B-but, b-but…"

"Och, out with it!" Siofra barked.

Catherine took a deep breath. "I stole from me daddy and lied to me mammy, two sins I committed, to get ye that press pass, and seven shakes of me bum and a smile is all I get to do?"

"Getting us the press pass was just to join wer group. If ye want more steps on the stage with us, ye've to get us that iPod of yer daddy's and all!"

Catherine gasped, and Grainne beamed. If she and Siofra had that most sought-after of luxuries, they would be the most popular not only in their class, but also with the older girls. They could share it with six headsets, enough for twelve ears; maneuvering through the playground might be difficult, but every stumble would be worth it.

"That iPod, but…" Catherine sniveled. "Me mammy gave it to me daddy for last Christmas. He's never without it when he be's washing the dishes or up in his study or doing the gardening."

"Yer daddy *washes the dishes?*" Grainne gasped, moving away from her.

"Me mammy, me mammy…she kyanny, as—"

"Aye, a mad aul bat, we know sure," Siofra sighed. Her brain cells trundled for a moment. "Okay. Ye've no need to nick it from yer daddy forever. Give us a loan of it for a day or two, but, so's we can walk down the town with it in wer ears so's everyone thinks it belongs to us."

Miss McClurkin approached, apology on her face.

"I have a rather delicate matter that I must bring up," she said. They regarded her in suspicion. "I'm afraid Mrs. Pilkey has decided that the lyrics of this 'Poker Face' are not fitting for a Catholic girl's school. I myself was extremely excited at the prospect of you performing the song. However, we must respect the wishes of the headmistress. What did you say, Siofra?"

"Nothing, Miss," Siofra scowled, swallowing her muttered obscenities.

"So, what I'd love for you girls to do is engage in an informal brainstorming session, so to speak, and devise an alternate performance piece."

The girls exchanged a look, perplexed.

"Does that be yer jumped-up way of telling us we've to sing something else?" Grainne asked.

Mrs. Pilkey nodded haltingly.

"I suppose it is, yes."

"Miss?" Grainne again.

"Yes?"

"Why do ye always be saying 'yes? Doesn't the word be 'aye?'"

"That be's the way wile posh people says 'aye,' ye daft gack!" Siofra whispered with a dig in Grainne's ribs.

"Might I point you girls in the right direction? It should be something the entire family enjoys together. Perhaps something by Abba, or…?"

Grainne jumped up and down, waving her hand wildly under the teacher's nose.

"Ooh, Miss! I've one! I've one! It be's one of me mammy's favorites."

Hope sprang eternal on Miss McClurkin's face.

"Yes, Grainne?"

"It's that aul one by Destiny's Child, 'Bootylicious,' it be's called."

"Absolutely not!"

Siofra thought she should name one of her mammy's favorites also: "'Hips Don't Lie' by Shakira?"

Miss McClurkin's face said it all.

"Why not but, Miss? It be's all about telling the truth, sure!"

Miss McClurkin thought the only truth 'hips' could tell would be about fornication.

"The talent show's not for another fortnight, so you've plenty of time. Just ensure you bring me a lyric sheet of whatever song you choose."

Miss McClurkin scampered off, but Siofra noticed three of the Irish Dancing girls rushing over to block the teacher's escape. The girls pointed in their direction, and Miss McClurkin had a wild look on her face.

"I'll bet ye anything themmuns is switching over to a pop song," Siofra said. "They've seen the teacher was paying their jigging no mind, and knows they won't be winning. We've to step up wer game."

Grainne and Catherine were scared and turned to Siofra for instruction.

"Och, I kyanny think that quickly and," She looked down at her wrist, but her watch was long gone. She looked at the clock on the wall. "And I've to meet me mammy down the town. We've pick up me brother Padraig and then pay me…me *third* granny a visit."

Grainne and Catherine stared; who had heard of anyone having a third grandmother? Siofra pointed to Catherine.

"You, but, have yer homework to do," she warned. "Get us that iPod or not only will ye not meet Hannah Montana, Grainne and me'll take great pleasure in dumping ye off in the playground of How Great Thou Art tied up in ropes."

As she ran off, Catherine looked over at Grainne for verification that this was the plan. Grainne nodded her head gravely, though this was news to her. She snapped off 'Poker Face' mid-chorus.

CHAPTER 34

"Please read these letters aloud for me," Derry's most overworked optician said.

Padraig stewed in the chair.

"Aye, surely," he scowled. "P-I-S-S-O-F-F."

"Come, come," Dr. Chattopadhyay chided. "Look at the chart and tell me what you see."

"I see I'm not gonny wear specs!"

Padraig's little fists beat upon the optician's white coat. Dr. Chattopadhyay took a step back so the boy was left punching air. The optician calmly polished his pupilometer. He was used to this reaction; the entire town seemed to have decided that corrective lenses had less to do with aiding sight and more to do with outing homosexuals. Years in the future, the optician suspected, when his youthful patients were bigger and stronger, they would probably thank him for his help to see the world by attacking him with a sharpened screwdriver and snatching his wallet when he was a doddery pensioner. He hoped he'd be practicing elsewhere. Years of occupation by British paratroopers seemed to have left even the children of these people with a hatred of authority. It had degenerated, bizarrely in Dr. Chattopadhyay's opinion, into distrust of uniforms of any type, from firemen to bakers. And he was wearing a white coat.

He completed the examination as quickly as the abuse would allow, and, as he had already heard from the boy's mother, instructed Padraig to choose a pair of government-subsidized frames from the National Health scheme. Dr. Chattopadhyay pulled open the drawer of embarrassment to reveal the selections, and when the boy peered inside, Padraig's fury and tears began for real.

Padraig shuffled into the waiting room with the specs perched on the tip of his nose. Fionnuala threw back her head and roared with bawdy laughter.

"Look at yer brother!" she urged Siofra and Seamus. "A right gack, he looks! An arse-bandit poofter! Point at him, youse, point at him and laugh like yer mammy!"

"Och—" Padraig spat, fists curled.

"Specky four-eyes, specky four-eyes!" his mother sang in a taunt, grabbing the younger children's arms so they could dance around him ring-a-rosies style. Siofra and Seamus were reluctant to join in the fun, letting the horrified receptionist know of their shame with their eyes. "Spoilsports, party poopers! *Every party needs a pooper, that's why we invited youse!* Och, youse is miserable, so youse is, no sense of fun."

Still, Fionnuala choked with laughter as she turned again to face her sudden disgrace of a son.

"Soon ye're gonny be prancing round town dressed in pink with yer nose buried inside the pages of a flimmin *book!* Ha, ha, ha! Oh, me stomach!"

"Aye," Padraig seethed, "and me first choice'll be *Lotto Balls of Shame.*"

For once he could see his mother's hand whipping though the air towards him. Smack! Siofra, Seamus and the receptionist flinched.

"Never utter them filthy words again, ye vile cunt!" Fionnuala had swiftly sobered. "And I kyanny understand the abuse flying in me direction. It was yer daddy insisted I drag ye down here. He wouldn't take no for an answer, so blame him for the road of misery yer life's about to take."

Fionnuala glanced at the clock on the wall, collected her Celine Dion satchel and thrust Siofra's PowerPuff Girls bag into the girl's fingers. She inspected Padraig with a sorrowful shake of the head.

"Och, I'm scundered, pure red in the face, to be seen on the street with ye, but I need every pair of hands available for to shift all the gear we're to clear outta that aul cunt Mrs. Gee's loft. Is yer hands big enough, or should we stop by the market and get a frilly wee handbag for ye, *tee hee hee?*"

CHAPTER 35

In the spartan filth of her cell/bedroom at 5 Murphy, Dymphna took careful aim with her weapons: blush brush, eyelash curlers and tweezers. Usually she just slapped the makeup on; she realized at sixteen she could have lipstick carving a path down her chin and would still attract a lad for the evening. But she was now on a mission to get what passed as her man back, those freshly-gleaming lips taut with resolve around the cigarette plunged between them.

Face perfect, she opened another can of beer and disengaged the old pair of tights holding her hair at bay. She shook her red curls free and attacked them with the blow dryer. Keanu erupted with shrieks from his stroller in the corner—he was always in his stroller as there was no other place to put him—and Dymphna turned up the radio to drown him out.

Singing along with Beyoncé, *"Cause if you liked it, then you shoulda put a ring on it,"* Dymphna envisioned Rory waiting for her at the Craiglooner. It was Dymphna's former local pub and scene of many acts of alcohol-fueled bloodshed. Scrubbed up, Rory would be, and maybe wearing the black track suit with the white stripes Dymphna had shoplifted for his last birthday. It was the only birthday they had celebrated as a couple. He was sure to be a bundle of nerves, unable to look at any of the glasses that surrounded him, the alcohol in them demanding to be drunk, and equally unable to look any of the patrons in the eye for fear they would discover he was Protestant.

"Woah, oh oh, oh, oh, oh...!"

Somehow through Beyoncé and Keanu and the blow dryer, Dymphna heard her cellphone ring. It was Bridie.

"Bout ye, Dymphna?"

"Ye've a bold-faced cheek!"

"Eh?!"

"How dare ye ring me up!"

"What are ye on abou—?"

"Don't come the innocent with me, Bridie McFee! Monica from Pricecutters told me she saw ye with me Rory at the line-dancing Wednesday last. Arms like an octopus, she said ye had, and that ye could barely do the steps with yer eyes boring into his arse on the floor! I kyanny erase from me mind the sight of yer eyes bulging at the size of the diamond on the engagement ring when ye saw it, and I kyanny forget the way ye've been treating me ever since I was forced back to the Moorside."

"Och, Dymphna, naw, but! Yer man Rory was in such a state when he woke up after ye left the Kebabalicious. Blubbering on and on about his life descending into drink, and he didn't know what to do with himself after yer breakup and the like. I was extending the hand of friendship, just, offering him a change from getting legless in the pubs. Trying me best to get youse back together, so I was. Does that be Beyoncé I'm hearing in the background, hi?"

Dymphna fiddled with the cord of the blow dryer as she struggled to understand if she should believe Bridie or not.

Bridie went on: "And ye know that Monica from Pricecutters be's one narky jealous cow. Always happy to spread the gossip and stir up the trouble, her. Sure, she lives for nothing but delighting in the misery of others, pure and simple."

In fact, Dymphna thought Monica friendly and trustworthy and pleasant, if she overlooked the teeth, but Bridie was always Dymphna's number one best mate. *Was? Had been? Was?* Dymphna finished the beer in one gulp and lit another cigarette.

"Ye know I've his wane growing inside me," she said carefully down the phone. "I've not told anyone else, Bridie, not me mammy nor me daddy nor even Rory, for that matter. I've always thought I could trust ye. Now, but, I feel I trust ye about as far as I could throw ye, and given the size of ye now, that doesn't be very far."

Dymphna shook her phone at the silence. Finally, Bridie replied: "Ye've got to trust me, Dymphna. And, wane growing inside ye or not, ye'd do best to steer clear of Rory Riddell."

"Ha! Fat chance, miseryguts, as I'm on me way to the Craiglooner now to patch things up with him. Took a week of phone calls to arrange. He finally agreed, but. And feck his new-found aversion to drinking. I'll be pouring the shots of whiskey down his gullet to make sure I end up back at his mammy's house. If only to keep him away from the claws of desperate ones the likes of you!"

"He doesn't be mentally fit!"

"Och, catch yerself on!"

"It's true, but, Dymphna! He revealed to me at the line-dancing that his da and his mammy and even his granny be's pervy shirt-lifters!"

"Och, ye're talking out yer arse! Ye're mad, you!"

"Years of abuse they've inflicted on his privates in the secrecy of their home! Deranged with confusion and guilt, he be's, defending them pedo violators and the filthy acts themmuns forced him into at a young age! I mind from that psychology class I took when I was going to the community college that ones who be's abused—"

One part of Dymphna's brain froze. There was no greater betrayal than braying about higher education. To her, being a student was unsettling and Protestant.

"Preparing for a PhD, are ye, ye hateful cunt?!"

Dymphna hung up, but could only fume for a second as her grandmother barged into the room in the wake of her cane.

"Not now, Granny!" Dymphna implored, choking back the tears, though she knew it must be something very important for her granny to travel all the way up the stairs.

"Have ye moved on to dating men what be's aul enough to be yer father now?" Maureen asked, eyes flashing with interest.

"What are ye on about?"

"I've just come from the bingo, and there was two highly suspect men lurking round the front garden. From the coal company, themmuns said they was after I asked em what the hell they was up to. I saw no uniforms or van, but, nor any evidence of soot on em. Peering up at the windows, they was, with a strange gleam in their eyes. I thought themmuns might be after yer delights. I told em to clear off as ye've already one wane too many, and a Proddy fiancé to boot. That put the fear of the Lord into em, sent them running down the street, so it did. I hope ye don't mind, but I've only yer best interests at heart. Ye're too lovely a wee girl, you, to waste yer youth on aul chancers like that."

"I haven't a clue who ye might be on about," Dymphna said. "What did themmuns look like, like?"

"Degenerates! One in filthy denim from head to toe, the other a leather perv, and orange leather at that, if ye please!"

"I'm clueless, Granny, as to who themmuns might be. Ta, but, for getting rid. And now that ye're here, would ye give me a lend of twenty quid? I've a date with Rory to see if I can't get back in his house. Twenty extra quid, but, might be enough to buy the drinks what will tip the scales in me favor. I know me being here is causing all sorts of grief."

"Perhaps to yer mammy, but I'm happy enough to have ye here, wee dote. And grateful yer mammy spends most of her time round the corner. Aye, I've twenty quid stashed away for me wash and set next week, but for yer future it be's better spent. And that wane needs a nappy change, love."

Maureen struggled out, and Dymphna checked herself out in the mirror. As a crowning glory, she gingerly applied the fake tan. Abused or not, Rory would be hers.

CHAPTER 36

"Mammy! I gotta go numbers!" Seamus complained.

Two floors below them, raspy snores from a Fionnuala-induced slumber vied with the canned laughter from the TV. Mrs. Gee had been easier to dupe than Mrs. Ming, as she was at least a decade older and didn't realize the Floods were strangers, let alone that she had osteoporosis and a Carer.

"I told ye to go before we left the optician's," Fionnuala fumed. Her flashlight beamed under the eaves and revealed an old crate next to some pigeon droppings. "Relieve yerself in there."

Seamus toddled over a crossbeam in the gloom. Fionnuala turned the light on the older children. Siofra, using her skirt as a wheelbarrow, dumped a load of tarnished cutlery, a soccer trophy and some old coins at her mother's feet, then hurried back across the beam. Fionnuala scooped the loot into her bag. Padraig struggled up with a record player in his hands and a life-sized cardboard cutout of Donnie and Marie Osmond under his arm. Fionnuala squealed with delight; the latter was something she'd buy herself if she chanced upon it at the market.

"At least them nancy boy specs has given ye the power of locating things in the dark," she conceded. "Right lad ye are. It's all CDs the day, but I'm sure we can find some DJ that needs a turntable. What I'm wondering is how we're meant to transport them large items across town without some nosy parker—"

"Mammy!" Seamus' cry cut across the darkness. "Mammy!"

"Can ye not shite in silence, wane? Leave me head peace—"

"Mammy, but! I'm afeared to go in the crate. It be's full of bottles, and they be's cold!"

Fionnuala was set to roar abuse at the toddler, but a memory she had long sought to repress flooded back to her: sitting on the mini-bus weighed down with Top-Yer-Trolley shopping bags while behind her two filthy poofters lisped on and on about vintage wine and the incredible prices it fetched. They must have been tourists, as Derry had no homosexuals.

Arms waving for balance, Fionnuala raced the length of the crossbeam like a bargain basement trapeze artist. She hauled Seamus, mid-squat, off the cobweb-draped crate and tugged out a bottle, brushed away clumps of dust, and scrutinized it with the beam of the flashlight. Her lips curled with distaste.

"Would ye look at the color of that? Shite brown! It's mingin aul wine that's gone off, so it is. Unfit for human use!"

She was about to fling it back in the crate and tell the boy to finish his business inside it when she scratched her fingernail at the label and unearthed the design from decades of crud: bronze and silver coins, brown ribbons and red, white and blue stripes. They hadn't even had the decency to write the label in English, Fionnuala thought.

Premier Fils, she struggled to read, and then *Absinthe Superieur—1945*, and then, barely able to control her excitement, *180 Proof.*

Fionnuala shook her head with wonder. *Mrs. Gee be's a right secret pervy alkie bitch*, she thought, *hoarding away a stash of illegal, hallucinogenic filth, and French filth at that!* That wouldn't stop Fionnuala flogging it around the town to the highest bidder.

"Come youse here now!" she barked.

By the time Padraig and Siofra reached her, Fionnuala already had a third of the crate in her Celine Dion satchel, the trembling in her fingers growing with each bottle shoved inside. After seven bottles, there was no more room. She snatched Siofra's PowerPuff Girls bag from the girl's elbow and forced the eighth inside.

"Mind me lip gloss!" Siofra wailed.

Fionnuala was already screwing the ninth and the tenth deep into handbag, the stitching straining.

"Fling that over yer shoulder and let yer mammy have a look," she instructed Siofra.

The girl did as told. The bottles poked out, a third exposed to the eyes of any alcoholic they were likely to run into on the way home. Fionnuala's eyes shot around the murky depths of the attic.

"Grab me them old newspapers," she told Seamus.

Fionnuala unloaded the bottles from Siofra's handbag, wrapped them in the yellowing newspaper, and shoved them back in. She disguised six more bottles and pushed one into each of her children's six hands. The final bottle she wrapped and clamped under her left arm.

"Let's be on wer way, wanes," she instructed, hauling the Donnie and Marie cutout under the arm with the absinthe and the record player under the other. "And if youse drop one of them bottles, youse'll be resting in the grave next to yer granny Flood."

The children had difficulty climbing down the stairs with their little fists full, but finally they all stood on the upstairs landing, wincing up at their mother's backside lumbering towards them, the bulging, clanking satchel straddling her shoulder, Celine Dion's toothy grin beaming out. Siofra could take the sight no longer and scampered downstairs. Then she screamed.

"Mammy! The aul one's shuddering something terrible!"

Fionnuala jumped down the ladder, and she and the boys galloped down the stairs. In the sitting room, Mrs. Gee's body convulsed on the settee, her lips blue. Padraig eyed her with interest, Seamus with fear, the tears lashing down his face.

"What's wrong with the granny, Mammy?" he screamed.

Even though the victim was Edna's mother, the frail woman convulsing in pain had the power to wipe the scorn off Fionnuala's face. Her brain cells trundled to figure out what action should be taken.

"Let's hoof it, wanes," she decided.

They were half-way through the front garden, fearfully scanning the houses in the dusk for the twitching curtains of witnesses, when Fionnuala stopped in dread.

"Och, I've left me fags on the mantelpiece! Evidence, they be's, and £5 a pack at that. Get youse around the corner and play with a fence or some such and *look natural*."

She sprinted inside, and the children rounded the corner, their limbs straining.

"I don't care what Mammy says," Siofra told Padraig as they converged at a lamppost and pretended to play with it. The swag fell to the pavement. "I like them specs of yers. Dead posh, ye look."

That was the problem. Padraig fumed.

"Mammy be's away in the head if she thinks she can shift this shite down the market," he said.

"I've been wondering," Siofra continued. "Could ye get me an iPod with that special credit card of yers? I've asked this daft gack in me class to nick me her daddy's, but I can only get a lend of it. And ye know me CD player was broken the other week."

"About me credit card, the other day I tried to buy—"

He yelped as a rock cracked against his shoulder.

"Fanta-pubes with the specs!"

"Specky-four-eyes! Specky-four-eyes!"

A hoard of well-heeled children appeared from behind a mural of victims of the Troubles and closed in on them, hooting with laughter. The Flood children scattered, diving behind a row of garbage cans as stones cascaded around their heels.

"Mammy's gear!" Siofra gasped. Everything lay unattended on the sidewalk, save the three bottles swinging from Siofra's elbow.

"Blind Fanta-pubed Fenian geebag!" sang the ringleader, tossing a rock with the flick of a wrist accessorized with a Hannah Montana watch. Rocks ricocheted off the cans, and the Catholic children hunkered down, Seamus whimpering and shuddering. The mob disappeared down the street as quickly as it had come.

"Who the bleeding feck—?" Padraig demanded, twitching in anger.

Siofra poked her head over the garbage can, simmering with fury. *Pink Petals again!* Siofra could hate her brother and his glasses all she wanted, but heaven help anyone else who did. At least they hadn't come with balloons.

"Shh," Siofra said as they hurried up to the pile of loot around the lamppost. "Here comes Mammy."

"Mammy! Mammy! I'm heart-scared!" sobbed Seamus, wrapping his arms around as much of her legs as he could.

"Och, ye daft toerag," Fionnuala snorted, kneeing him off. "Five minutes, I was gone just."

"Did the pensioner die?" Padraig asked a bit too gleefully.

"Thank feck, naw. I had to wipe wer fingerprints off everything we touched in the event she does, but," Fionnuala explained. "Och, miserable, it was, just like dusting."

Halfway home, Fionnuala's Catholic guilt got the best of her. Making a mental note to never crush three of Maureen's tablets into the tea for the next OsteoCare visit, she stopped at a pay phone, surprised to see it functioning and, after wiping gooey residue from the receiver, dialed 999. "Send youse an ambulance to 89 Lockview Crescent. There's an aul one having a fit."

While their mother was in the phone booth, Siofra turned to Padraig.

"I've a plan to get that hateful Proddy bitch Pink Petals back," she said. "I'll be needing yer help, but."

Massaging the lump forming on his back, Padraig nodded eagerly; and considering the length of his youthful offender's record, the more violent the revenge, the better.

CHAPTER 37

Rory was indeed wearing the black track suit with the white stripes and sat hidden in a nook. Dymphna was glad as it would give them the privacy she needed. At first, he complained of a headache that might cause him to end the night early, but then the trips through the cleavage and elbows to the bar began. Pints of lager were downed. And Maureen's twenty quid paid for the shots of whiskey. Dymphna finally explained the mix-up at the lockups, Rory apologized for doubting her and for his mother's behavior, Rory asked how his son was faring, Dymphna asked how his courses were going. Then they discussed the latest housemate evicted from *Big Brother* and Derry FC's chances for the League of Ireland finals. As speech grew slurred and movements clumsy and trips to the loo more frequent, Dymphna told him how lonely she felt in bed, and asked if he felt the same. It seemed he did.

Dymphna couldn't bring herself to ask about his special relationship with his father, his mother and his granny. She didn't want to show herself up or ruin the mood, and she was sure Bridie had made it up as she was a jealous cow.

It was interesting, then, that four hours later, Bridie was the one shoving two drunken idiots clutching aluminum containers of Kebabalicious curry chips into a mini-cab. Perhaps it was the power of the drink.

"Get yerselves home," Bridie roared with drunken glee. "And don't forget youse've made that dinner date for the morrow! Och, it gladdens me heart to see the two of youse at it like dogs on the street!"

Dymphna slobbered all over his neck, her fingers scrabbling around in the darkness, the radio blaring the Spice Girls, the driver's eyes glaring at them from the rear view mirror.

"Lemme at it!" Dymphna begged, tugging at his belt, his zipper, her fingers desperate for his manhood.

He needed Bridie's octopus arms to fend her off.

"Come back to mine!" she begged. "I want to ravage the arse offa ye the night!"

"There be's loads of people cooped up in that house of yers, but!"

"Och, ye can have me in the back garden, sure. We've a shed there."

"I kyanny," he slurred. "We've wer dinner date for the morrow anyroad. Make sure, you, we've the house to werselves."

The mini-cab pulled up to 5 Murphy, and Dymphna spilled out onto the pavement, her tights a mess of ladders, eyeliner blackening the lower half of her face, booze glowing in her startled eyes, one bra strap hanging. She couldn't locate her keys in her curry-spattered handbag She pounded on the letter box.

"Lemme in!" she begged, then turned, wanting to smile seductively and wave and perhaps flash a breast or two at Rory in the mini-cab. But it had already sped down the street and was on its way to the Protestant side of town. As she clutched the house for support, Dymphna was too drunk to wonder *What in the name of feck was Bridie doing at the Craiglooner?*

CHAPTER 38

"Effin brilliant!" Grainne gasped, while Catherine squirmed with worry. It was morning, and the girls were sitting in a circle on the gym floor, surrounding pots of glue, safety scissors, crayons and fingerpaint, and fashioning pipe cleaners into seahorses and cardboard into smiling jellyfish. Siofra had just laid out her plan to wipe the smirk off Pink Petals' face. And win the competition as well.

"But—"

"None of yer narky shite," Siofra said to Catherine. "Ye of all people should be delighted that vile Protestant cow's gonny get what she deserves, after the nightmares ye've had since the attack in the schoolyard. And the mortification of getting yer daddy involved and all. Hand me that glue, would ye Grainne? There'll be no need for yer daddy to visit Mrs. Pilkey again once we've put wer plan into action. Pink Petals is gonny steer clear of wer side of town for the rest of her life, her."

"She might suffer from nightmares after it just like me, but, and—"

"Where's me and Grainne's iPod, by the by?" Siofra asked.

Catherine lowered her head.

"Anyroad, we've wer plan and we're sticking to it. I'm changing the subject now. Me oldest sister be's one of them lesbians," Siofra proudly revealed.

"What does that be?" Grainne asked.

"Have ye not heard of them? They be's on shows on the telly all the time, so me daddy says. Wile trendy, so they be's. Dead brainy and all."

Grainne looked doubtful as her blue fingers painted what she hoped resembled waves on a refrigerator box.

"Me sister Moira wrote a book about wer family, did ye not know?" Siofra confided. "It's to be in the shops next month. We're gonny travel to Malta for to visit her, so we are. Me and me brothers has been doing special secret work with me mammy to get the funds together, like. Ye'd not believe the fun we've been having. Like a Harry Potter movie, so it is."

"Does Malta be further than Belfast?" Catherine asked. That was the furthest place in the world she had heard of.

"Aye, miles further. Would ye believe to get there we've to travel on a bus and a ferry and a train?"

Catherine stared in wonder as she hacked away on the cardboard with the safety scissors. Grainne looked up.

"I've been on a plane," she announced. "Me mammy took me to Spain for to get me a suntan for me First Holy Communion."

"Aye, and mind how that turned out. Ye fell asleep on the beach and came back with yer face all blisters. Planes is for eejits with more money than sense," Siofra quoted her mother. "Ferries and buses and trains be's effin magic!"

Grainne's fingers curled around a pipe cleaner in frustration. When she thought something was great, Siofra was always the one to cut it down. When she had loved pickled onion crisps, Siofra insisted prawn cocktail ones were better; when she loved Hello Kitty, Siofra had switched to the PowerPuff Girls. And all this babbling about Hannah Montana and Lady Gaga, Grainne couldn't reveal she secretly enjoyed Justin Bieber more. How was the poor girl to realize that Siofra was, in some respects, her mother's daught—

"Girls!" boomed Miss McClurkin, and the children jumped. "You've certainly been busy! Just what have we here?"

She looked their creations up and down, a look of wonder on her face.

"What are these?"

"Flowers, Miss!"

"And these?"

"Waves!"

"And these?"

"Creatures of the sea, Miss!" Grainne said. "We've jellyfishes and crabs and regular fishes and all sorts."

"And, ooh, I love this banner! Where is...er...this Hapynnes? Is that perhaps some village in Scotland one of you visited as a family?"

"It's the Happiness Boat, Miss," Siofra corrected.

"This is all delightful," Miss McClurkin said, making a mental note to step up the class' spelling syllabus. "It shows real initiative. I just wonder, though, how this all fits with your song. And what is your new song, if I may ask?"

"We've changed wer minds about the pop song," Siofra said.

Miss McClurkin's face fell.

"Irish dancing on the Happiness Boat...?" she chanced with a rising sense of despair.

"We've come up with something brand new!" Siofra said.

As she told Miss McClurkin their plan, the teacher's face lit up. She clapped with joy.

"Wonderful, wonderful!" she marveled. "What amazing, caring girls you are! You have captured the spirit of Fingers Across the Foyle marvelously!"

Siofra and Grainne beamed, but Catherine couldn't face the teacher's eyes. She knew they had done no such thing.

CHAPTER 39

Jed raced towards Ursula's unhinged shrieks from the living room, expecting to find her atop the coffee table fending off Casino Woman with a lamp. He secured the perimeter from the threshold, his years of military training kicking in, but saw nothing suspect. Just Ursula in a state of disrepair on their Raymour and Flanigan sofa, *Biblical Word Search* at her side. He and Muffins entered as a team and hurried to her side.

"What's up, honey?" he asked; he would've knelt if his knees weren't giving him such problems.

"I kyanny take it no longer, Jed," she said, tears of frustration and fear rolling down her cheeks. "I've to get meself to Derry for a visit."

Jed stared as if she had stripped off her clothes and demanded he take her there on the polished wood. But react first, regret later, that was the Ursula way, and after decades of marriage he was used to it. His face softened.

"Honey…"

"And ye're coming with me."

His face hardened. Jed took off his glasses and polished the frames with the bottom of his checkered shirt. He would rather battle Casino Woman than face Ursula's family again. As unbalanced at Casino Woman sounded (he had yet to meet her), at least with the Floods Jed had the advantage of knowing the enemy. And there was a reason they had cleared out of that hellhole of Derry so quickly their luggage wheels had left skid marks.

"The medication the doctor gave you might be affecting your brain, dear."

"I'm so afeared for me life. What if that lunatic murders me in me sleep and when me body be's shipped back to Derry—I'm not to be buried in the tundra here, by the by—and me family celebrates by lining up round me grave just to spit on it? Ye mind how, when me mammy passed on, themmuns tossed the flowers I got her off the grave and danced on em? If me days on this Earth be's numbered, before I go, I've to patch things up with me family."

Cruel to be kind, Jed forced himself to state the obvious: "Face it, Ursula. It's never gonna happen."

A tortured sob arose from Ursula's throat. "I won't be able to meet me maker in peace if I don't at least try while I'm still drawing breath."

Jed was thankful he heard his cellphone ringing in the kitchen. He grasped Ursula's hand, the hand he had been so excited to grace with an engagement ring all those years ago, and said: "We'll discuss it later, after you've calmed down at bit."

At the door, he turned.

"And, honey, don't book any flights without talking to me first."

He made his escape.

Ursula's sobs turned to sniffles, and she inspected the dust on the brass Mayfair Steamer Cube Trunks from Restoration Hardware that served as end tables. She had been too frightened lately to waste energy dusting. Ursula realized how expensive the trunks were and how lucky she was to be able to afford them. Many people in the world couldn't. She and Jed had a delightful modern home in Wisconsin, but Ursula felt their new American furniture was alien. Muffins licked her toe.

Ursula was surrounded by people and things that meant nothing at all to her, and she secretly suspected the hatred Paddy and Fionnuala threw at her showed some love. She had tried to give her family everything she could, but for the Floods too much wasn't enough.

Now she was a strange-speaking foreigner in the backwoods of Wisconsin, where people sat on 'sofas,' not settees, where people had 'children,' not wanes, where the meals of the day (in the order they were eaten) were called 'breakfast, lunch and dinner,' not breakfast, dinner and tea, and where a decent portion of fish and curry chips was impossible to find.

She had scoured the local food warehouse for turnips and ham hocks, her comfort food, to no avail. Ursula had never seen shopping carts so large. Everything in Wisconsin, and by extension, America, was large. Large and empty. Large and empty and alien.

Ursula suddenly realized this is what Jed must have felt like amongst her family in Derry. It was perfectly understandable how he had turned to drink back then; she was feeling quite thirsty herself. Now Jed was getting his life in order (except for that online gambling he had begun), and hers was spinning into madness.

She knew why she had insisted Jed retire in Derry, why she had put up with ten years of the sniping, the sarcasm, the oneupmanship of a people clawing out a living as if from stone, the memory of decades of sectarian violence unable to free itself from their collective memory, why she had tolerated the danger that lurked from hoodies on every corner, the filth, the relentless rain, the shocking price of postage stamps. During her parole in Wisconsin, Ursula was watching Jed blossoming in his late-late-middle age as a small business owner, Slim getting better at cribbage, Louella getting craftier at cheating, and Muffins putting on the pounds. For Ursula herself, there was nothing here but the passage of time and the effects of gravity on her aging body.

She was missing out on the things she thought she would be entitled to as a family member, and a generous and loving one at that; the time she had invested now time wasted. She would miss out on the weekly visits to Eoin's and Lorcan's prison and their eventual releases; would never see Padraig's or Siofra's or Seamus' graduations; never be part of Dymphna's or Eoin's or Lorcan's or Padraig's or Siofra's or Seamus' weddings, and now, given the shockingly liberal laws of the EU, maybe Moira's as well; would miss the births of their first, second, third and fourth children and however many more might come after that; never beam proudly in her Sunday best in St. Molaug's church at her grand-nephews' and grand-nieces' baptisms and First Confessions and First Holy Communions, gifts and cards painstakingly selected, bows carefully tied and xxx's and ooo's love Great-Auntie Ursula carefully written. When she had joined St. Molaug's choir years before in Derry, Ursula had envisioned warbling away and staring down proudly at her family in the pews as the years passed and the hymnals grew more tattered and the lines grew on their faces, the young ones turning into old ones.

Ursula scratched the dog's head as the tears welled.

"Only me body be's here in Wisconsin," Ursula sobbed to the poodle. "Och, Muffins, ye and Jed be's the only ones I feel love from. Except for youse, I'm all alone in the world, so I'm are."

Muffins stared blankly at her. Perhaps the dog couldn't understand her accent either.

And if the Floods wanted no part of her, Ursula thought with increasing resolve, if she were to spend the twilight years of her life in this perplexing and godforsaken place, she wanted to at least see the family home, her beloved 5 Murphy Crescent, one last time. After the Flood's outrage when she bought it with the lottery winnings, she had eventually just seen it as bricks and mortar, an albatross around her neck. Now she realized she had been too hasty gifting it to the Floods before she and Jed had fled to the US. She now knew exactly why she had bought the house and how much it meant: the stairs she had crawled up as a child, the coal bin in the back, the bay window shattered by a rubber bullet in '73, the wallpaper stained with tear gas, the boozy laughter nevertheless ringing out from the sitting room within the pebble-dashed walls as the violence raged outside, she and her mammy and daddy and all her brothers and sisters passing around the whiskey and popping open the cans of lager, the ribbing and hilarity and cigarettes lit off one match, the years passing, Three Dog Night, then Rod Stewart, then Billy Joel replacing one another on the radio in the background, the TV shows switching from black-and-white to color—

She screamed as the house phone on the Cube trunk erupted into life. Ursula eyed the receiver with suspicion. Had Casino Woman somehow secured their now-unlisted number? In the brass of the trunk, she caught a glimpse of herself: haggard, a feral gleam in her eyes, the roots of her eggplant-colored bob in desperate need of a touch-up. Ursula answered the phone.

"Mrs. Barnett?"

"Aye?"

"Eric here from the credit card fraud department. I hear you've been having trouble with some of our operators?"

She had hung up twice when people from the Indian subcontinent had answered. Then she had called back to demand somebody who spoke real English phone her. This Eric seemed like he spoke English the way God intended, at least in the American section of His creation. Ursula reeled in her accent as best she could to be understood.

"Have ye me details before ye?"

"Yes, I do. You are claiming some suspicious purchases?"

"Indeed I am, aye. Some *woman* stole me driver's license the other week and opened a new card in me name, then maxed it out $5000 worth. I've been wanting to know what's been purchased on it. Could ye help me out with that?"

"I can indeed. Let's see, I've got it before me now. We've got a $300 X-Box 360 here."

"A…Does that be something pornographic?" Ursula dared to ask; she knew Casino Woman had stolen her identity, but she was suddenly thinking of Jed.

"Oh, not at all, ma'am," Eric said with a condescending laugh. Ursula wanted to hang up a third time. "It's a game console for kids. I also see here a Wii purchased on the same day."

"A…?" Why had the miscreant opened this credit card and purchased items that were no part of any sane person's life? Well, perhaps it was understandable. "What be's that?"

"Another game console, this one for $400. That accounts for $700."

Ursula couldn't bring herself to ask if these games things could be played with foot-long fingernails.

"And then there's a computer, a flat-screen television, five iPods, that's another $3000. If you don't mind me saying, these are all things very popular with teenagers. We find that many times, credit card fraud is perpetrated by members of the immediate family between the ages of twelve and eighteen, kids with no jobs who want to be like every other kid on the block, so they somehow secure credit cards from wallets or purses laying unattended around the house. Or while the owner is in the shower or bath. Do you have teenagers?"

"Me sons and daughter be's grown, and their wanes be's but toddlers. And it wasn't any of themmuns anyroad. It was some aul lunatic who tried to attack me in the ladies' of a casino."

"Maybe some nephews or nieces?"

Unease began to fill Ursula; she had plenty.

"Not to speak of," she said in a stilted voice. *I think most of them be's banged up in prison, anyroad,* she thought

"And then, *oh!* This is strange."

"Aye? Aye?"

Ursula suspected the next purchase would be for an elaborate weave or nine fingernail piercings.

"After all those high-gadget things a teen would buy, I see here a large purchase a few days later of Dead Sea bath salts, Elizabeth Taylor's Passion perfume and the matching body scrub, her Sparkling White Diamonds perfume and eau de toilet, and then a Burberry scarf. The scarf is the deluxe cashmere mega-check that retails for $500. All items for the more, er, mature woman."

Ursula asphyxiated the phone with her fist. She knew only one mature woman who loved Elizabeth Taylor scents more than she, and she wasn't from a ghetto, at least not the American version of one. She silently counted to ten, then asked:

"Was them items bought, by any chance, around April the 20ᵗʰ?"

"Why, yes!" he exclaimed. "April the 20ᵗʰ exactly."

Ursula never forgot Fionnuala's birthday; it was the same as Hitler's.

"Does this mean you know who might have opened the card?"

"Naw," Ursula insisted. Trouble in the family remained in the family; she had it ingrained in her from an early age. "But could ye tell me where them purchases was made?"

"It looks like it was, hmm, it looks European. Um, LeDerry. Perhaps France?"

"Le..?" Ursula felt uneasy. "That wouldn't be Northern Ireland, would it?"

"Uh," She heard clicking on the keyboard. "Yeah!"

"That's not LeDerry! That's L'Derry. Londonderry!"

"If you say so, ma'am. Are you sure you don't have a suspect we might check out?"

"Ye've been most helpful," she barked in the phone, then slammed the receiver.

Ursula immediately felt ill. She crouched on the sofa, rocking and moaning and thinking pains were attacking her organs. For weeks she had lived a misery in her electrified fortress, too terrified to even leave the house for a trip to the beauty salon, and all along the danger hadn't been from the ladies room of a casino. She had been attacked by the usual suspect, Fionnuala extending her claws across the entire length of the Atlantic to snatch the straps of her handbag. The Flood-free life Ursula had envisioned when trudging across the rain-drenched runway to board the plane at Belfast International Airport had been suddenly snatched from her. Even in Wisconsin, USA, she wasn't free from Fionnuala's greed.

Although she lived six times zones away, Ursula didn't need to do the math to know what time it was in Derry; she was always on Derry time in her mind. And it was 9:00 PM. *Coronation Street*, the Flood's favorite nighttime soap opera, had just ended, so they were sure to answer the phone.

She dialed Paddy's number. She got Fionnuala.

"Aye?!"

"Fionnuala? It's Ursula."

"That's all I bloody well need!" Ursula heard Fionnuala mutter, and she steeled herself against the spitting sarcasm sure to erupt.

"I was hoping for Paddy." Each word was a chore.

"Hope all ye want. He's doing *overtime* at the factory as we're in desperate need of it. What are ye on the line for? For to *gloat*? Or for to snatch more bleeding food from wer fecking mouths?"

Fionnuala still had not forgiven Ursula for claiming Caretaker's Allowance for Paddy's mother, Eda, while the Barnetts were luxuriating in their lotto win. Conveniently forgotten in the peculiar maze of Fionnuala's memory was everything Ursula had done for Eda while Fionnuala had never lifted a finger.

"I'm calling to inform youse that I'll be visiting Derry, just," Ursula said.

"And why the bloody feck would we give a cold shite in Hell about that?" Fionnuala demanded to know, although inside herself she was pleased at Ursula's stupid sense of fair play; in war, surprise is a great advantage, but Ursula apparently wanted to fight on an even battlefield, letting her in on the movements of the troops. *More fool her, the silly aul cunt.* "I'll be surprised if ye find a pilot that's willing to man the plane to take ye here. Nobody wants ye in Derry! We was all dancing with glee to see the back of ye. Sit on yer fat arse in Yank-land and rot, ye grabby bitch, ye!"

"Speaking of—"

Fionnuala slammed down the phone, steaming, and turned back to the sewing machine. Her hand clutched for the mug of tepid tea, and she gnawed at a slice of burnt toast piled with pats of butter. Ursula coming to visit was indeed important news, but she would have to file it away for contemplation later on.

At the moment she had the next night's drinks reception at the school to think of, hobnobbing with the movers and shakers of Derry, the majority sure to be Protestant cunts and bastards who would no doubt be desperate to look down their noses at her. Thank feck she had her Burberry scarf. The rest of her outfit was the problem. She had arranged rhinestones on an old black jacket and was about to sew them on. She kept staring at the rhinestones under the harsh strip-lighting of the kitchen. They spelled out D-Y-N-K, and something about that didn't look right to her, but she ground her foot to the pedal. She still heard Ursula's voice in her ear.

The click-click-click of the sewing machine mirrored the click-click-click of Fionnuala's mind. She feared what Ursula might look like when she marched back to Derry after her months spent in the mythical land of verandahs and heated swimming pools. Ursula would no doubt be desperate to claim the victory of aging with grace.

In America, they had the institutions and plastic surgeons and exercise plans to keep youth eternal. Fionnuala had seen it before. Paddy's older sister, Roisin, lived the life in Hawaii, and Roisin had shown up in Derry a year earlier, her bronzed, oddly-taut body matching the youthfulness of the cornrows that had clanked against her pristine face. Nothing could hide the crevices in Fionnuala's forehead, nor the droopy eyes of exhaustion framed by spidery crows-feet And Fionnuala didn't even want to contemplate the state of her gut splayed under the sewing machine.

Fionnuala knew Ursula had the funds for a transformation to make the decades of the pull of gravity upon her body disappear. She probably had a personal trainer in some flash Yankee health club with carpeting and shiny state-of-the-art machines. In Fionnuala's world, gyms were curiosities, healthy eating unnatural.

She held up the jacket and nodded with satisfaction. It looked like the genuine article. She could pass for Protestant in it! She peered past the sparkling rhinestones and flinched at Padraig glowering at her through his yellowish-opaque frames. The look from him would've struck the fear of the Lord into anyone who hadn't given birth to him.

"I kyanny take it no more, Mammy," Padraig said. "All sorts of grief, I've been getting, in the playground, on the way home from school, because of these flimmin specs. I want ye to get me that laser surgery!"

Fionnuala roared with laughter.

"Contacts, then."

"Och, stop yer sobbing, ye daft cunt. We kyanny afford contact lenses for an eleven year old. Yer granny is decades older than ye, and she's still got specs. And nobody gives her grief because of em. Mind, there was that time she was attacked coming outta the butcher's last year..."

"Could ye not at least get me ones that doesn't be wile-looking pig-ugly? Ones that doesn't be from the National Health Scheme? I look like a right spastic! I kyanny blame me mates for beating the shite outta me. I wanna beat the shite outta me meself, sure!"

"Are ye away in the head, wane? Why in the name of all that be's sacred would we waste hard-earned dosh on specs when themmuns gives em out for free? And what the feck does the color of them specs of yers be anyroad? Piss yellow?"

"Feck you!" Padraig roared.

Fionnuala pounced from her chair. Her hand pounded against his ugly, enraged face with a satisfying *smack!*

"I'm leaving home," Padraig sobbed. "And youse better beware, I've tossed petrol bombs in the past, if ye recall."

"Go ye right ahead! C'mere til I tell ye, I've had it up to here with yer insolence. Get the feck outta wer home and never come back! And I want ye outta 5 Murphy and all!"

Padraig blinked, wondering what 'insolence' might be.

"R-right then," he said, making uncertain moves towards the door.

"Before ye go, but," Fionnuala said, waving him back into the kitchen.

Padraig took a crablike step, trying to hide the hope behind his lenses.

"Strip them clothes off yer ungrateful bones before ye go. We bought em ye! Starkers, ye're gonny leave the home!"

Fionnuala grabbed at his hoodie. Padraig screamed and kicked.

"Get offa me! Offa me now, you!"

Fionnuala knew she could sell the clothes half price down the market, and his strange new sneakers looked like they would fetch a bundle. The cotton slipped through her fingers, and Padraig escaped out the kitchen door.

"I'm telling me da!" he roared. "I'm going down to the factory now to tell him all about yer abuse!"

"Aye, good luck with that, boyo. Like ye can wriggle through the picket line. I'll be waiting for ye to strip the clothing from ye when ye—"

The windowpanes shook as the door slammed shut. Fionnuala lit a cigarette, picked up her new jacket and inspected it from a different angle. A smile of pride wound around the butt.

CHAPTER 40

Her granny was at the bingo, Dymphna and Keanu at the Top-Yer-Trolley late night shopping, and Seamus in a room playing with his shapeless thing. She didn't know where Padraig was.

Siofra had counted the money she owned and kept in a special yellow coin purse in her PowerPuff Girls handbag, proud it now totaled £4.07. Then she shimmied a few times before the mirror, singing Hannah's "The Best of Both Worlds" into the community hairbrush, but soon tired of that. She made her way downstairs and into the kitchen to inspect the newest case of cans her mammy had brought home from the Sav-U-Mor a few weeks before. She was surprised to see it missing. But the case from months back was still in the corner next to the sink. Siofra smiled. Perfect. She was about to delve inside when the letter box clanked. Then someone hollered through it: "Siiiiofra!"

It was Catherine. Siofra ran to the door and opened it.

"Bout ye, Siofra."

"Aye, bout ye. Come on in, you."

Catherine inspected the hallway, her brow furrowed. There didn't seem to be anything in it except the carpet. She reached into her Hello Kitty handbag and passed over the iPod.

"Here's the iPod."

Siofra squealed and clutched the treasure to her chest in glee. She turned it round and round in her fingers, marveling at the white sheen and cute white headphones.

"Och, it's wile civil of ye, Catherine!"

Siofra plugged the headphones in her ears and luxuriated in the feel of them. She mimicked walking down the street with it in her right hand. She felt very posh. She felt American.

"Ye've only got a lend of it," Catherine reminded her. "Me daddy'll go mental if he finds out it be's missing, and he always uses it on a Sunday for to help him with the gardening."

"All I need be's to let it be known round town I've one. Ye'll get it back after I wear it a few times on the mini-bus."

Catherine bit her lip in concern.

"Ye sure?"

"Aye, I promise."

"On Hannah Montana?"

"Aye, I promise on Hannah Montana."

Catherine's face brightened.

"And I get to do extra dance moves, aye?"

"Aye. Not as many as me and Grainne, but."

Catherine clapped her hands and jumped up and down.

"And when we win and get to Belfast and get backstage, we can ask Hannah her favorite color!" she bubbled. "And her favorite food!"

"I heard it be's spaghetti tacos."

"I wanny eat spaghetti tacos!"

"Them Yank taco shells be's terrible dear, but. I've seen em on the shelves of the Top-Yer-Trolley with me mammy. She wouldn't buy em for us."

Catherine nodded in understanding: everybody in school knew everything from the States was excellent but expensive.

"How does this thing make music so's I can hear it, but?"

"It be's easy. Lemme show ye how."

She showed her, and Siofra squawked with joy as Abba flooded her ears.

"It's all me daddy's music, mind," Catherine said. "Ancient music. Good, but."

She showed Siofra how to shuffle, how to repeat, and how to turn it off.

"I've to be on me way home now, Siofra. It be's wile late. Me daddy'll be fearing for me safety on the streets."

"Och, it takes but five minutes to get to yers. I want to show ye what's to help us win the talent show."

"But—" Catherine looked in fear at her Dora the Explorer watch.

Siofra wondered for an angry second if Catherine was making a show of looking at her watch so that Siofra knew she had one, but just as quickly decided that wasn't the case. She calmed down.

"A minute it'll take, just."

She grabbed Catherine's wrist and led her into the bare-bones kitchen. Catherine's eye followed a trail of crusty tomato sauce across the warped linoleum to a sink heaving with dishes and up a crack in the filthy window that led to a spiderweb in the ceiling and down a frayed wire below which dangled the bare light bulb over her head. She followed in silence to the case of canned vegetables that seemed to give Siofra much delight.

"Me mammy brought a new case in to us the other week," Siofra explained. "It be's gone now, but. Never mind, as I opened a tin and it was boring yellow wax-stuff inside, just. What be's in these cans be's loads better! Effin deadly, so it is, and in each one something different!"

Catherine peered inside the case. She saw a selection of cans, some dented, some rusted, all with shabby labels haphazardly affixed, some curling at the point where the paper met. Catherine read a few of the labels, and she couldn't mask her disappointment.

"Siofra, but. They be's baked beans, mushy peas, carrots and like, just." Was Siofra having her on?

"So ye might think!"

Siofra brandished a can opener proudly; using it made her feel adult. She ostentatiously hacked open a can of 'carrots.'

"Go on and have a look inside, then, you."

Catherine did, then recoiled, eyes spitting tears, nose affronted.

"Ewww! What does it be?"

"Pure mingin!"

Long before Mrs. Feeney and Mrs. O'Mahoney had demanded a refund on the cans of waxy stuff, a smattering of customers had come into the Sav-U-Mor clutching tins from a case of assorted vegetables Fionnuala had bought the week before. Fionnuala had quickly cleared the shelves and brought them home. Around the kitchen table, the Floods opened a few and all peered inside, wondering what they were looking at. They dug through the potato skins and empty microwave packets of the garbage and located all the original labels they had peeled off and replaced as a family. Paddy sent Padraig to the Internet at the library, and the boy's search in the Google translator revealed that Disznóbőr Vér-Val Tojásrántotta meant the 'carrots' were pigs blood in scrambled eggs from Hungary.

They also learned that the Шоколал Охватываемые Сало 'baked beans' were Ukrainian chocolate covered pigs fat, and the 'mushrooms' were Chinese fried popsicle bonbons with pea-milk flavoring. Even Fionnuala blanched when Padraig revealed that she had sold five cans of 'cauliflower' that were Qayigyar Qamiqur—seal brain fritters. And many more horrors besides.

With these props for their performance, Catherine knew the Happiness Boat would be anything but. Except for Siofra, perhaps. Still, if her involvement made her popular and got her backstage...

"Ye wanna see inside another?"

"Walk me to the corner, would ye?" Catherine asked. Her daddy told her Siofra's street was one of the most dangerous in town. "We can each take a headphone and listen to music while we walk."

"Scaredy-cat!" But Siofra relented, and they were out the door, skipping through the gate of the front 'garden.'

"You can dance, you can jive...having the time of your life...!"

Siofra was about to tell Catherine that Miss McClurkin was right; these hoary old chestnuts from Abba were indeed great, when the iPod was smacked out of her hand from behind. The headphones popped from their ears, and the iPod flew through the rain, clattered onto the street. and disappeared under the wheels of a passing car.

Tommy Coyle, the ten-year-old hoodie thug from across the street, cackled with cruel glee as he slipped around the corner. Catherine stood agog, almost wringing her eyes with her fists as they couldn't believe what they had just seen.

"Siofra! *Naw!*"

"Aye, Tommy, ye're a hard man, so ye are!" Siofra called out angrily.

The girls ran into the street and knelt before the remains of the iPod, little black and steel mechanical-looking things sprinkled across the cobblestones. Siofra plucked the squashed case and inspected the tire track on it with worry.

"I don't suppose we can fix it?"

The tears burst from Catherine's eyes.

"Me mammy already be's going further outta her noggin with her mental disease since she discovered that press pass be's missing the other day. I woke up last night and caught her taking a wee on me bedroom floor, so I did. I'm gonny let ye in on something I've never told a soul." Here she clutched Siofra's shoulder for comfort. "Me daddy batters the shite outta me something terrible. He set to me with the belt when the press pass went missing, thinking I had something to do with it. A huge buckle, the belt has, and, och, I kyanny go on with the details, too painful to reveal, they be's. Siofra, help me! Help me! I kyanny let on to me daddy I nicked his iPod as well. He's sure to put me in intensive care in Altnagelvin, and who knows what me mammy will leave on me bedroom floor the night!"

Siofra trembled at the anguish on the girl's face.

"Can ye not contact the Filth about yer daddy?"

Catherine stared.

"Me daddy *be's* the Filth! Ye know that, sure!"

Siofra led the shattered Catherine to the sidewalk because another car was barreling towards them. A steely resolve descended on her young face.

"I'll get ye another," she said. "Don't ye worry."

"How, but, Siofra? *How?*"

"I don't know how now. I promise, but, on Hannah Montana, I'll think of something."

Catherine slowly dried her tears and they parted, Siofra hugging her next to the Coyle's threadbare hedge. Siofra waved and Catherine waved back. As Siofra entered 5 Murphy, she reflected that, as miserable as her life seemed, some had it worse.

CHAPTER 41

"Jestes sexy!" Aggie growled, the excitement making her unable to conjure up any of the little English she had learned. She flung off a scale-encrusted glove and ran her forefinger up the length of Paddy's sagging upper arm. She pursed her chapped maw.

The rest of the crew had clocked off hours earlier. Desperate for overtime, Paddy and Aggie had volunteered to scrub out the fish feed vats and man the machines that could be run throughout the night. They were alone in the factory (except for O'Leary doing the accounts in the office miles away). The Polish woman was about as seductive as an old alkie pleasuring himself on a park bench, but Paddy felt his manhood stir.

"Pocałuj mnie teraz!"

The puckered shape of her lips and their movement towards his through the plumes of hot breath let him know she was insisting he kiss her.

Paddy was torn, but what could he do? Without her, he would have a stump for a hand. And he had spent a soccer season of nights staring at Fionnuala's spine in her tatty nightdress directed firmly at from him across the sagging mattress, and a man had needs a hot water bottle couldn't satisfy. Before this, getting his leg over behind Fionnuala's back had never been an option, and it was equal measures his love for her and the gossip he knew went on in the aisles of the Top-Yer-Trolley that kept him loyal; many a Derry marriage had been annulled—divorce was out of the question—due to information shared next to the frozen fish sticks. Paddy pressed Aggie against the pulsating cold steel of the grinding machine and felt the warmth of her lips. The churning of the machines drowned out Padraig's young gasp, hidden as he was behind one of them.

Aggie flicked her hair and let escape a guttural giggle Paddy assumed was more arousing in her mother tongue. He concentrated instead on the shape of her bosom waxing and waning under the fetid overalls.

"*Zerznij mnie!*" Aggie gasped, pointing at her nether-regions. Paddy was of no doubt what 'zerznij' might mean, as she circled the forefinger and thumb of her right hand, and poked her left forefinger in the circle a few times, her eyes staring into his and her eyebrows raising conspiratorially to ensure he understood what she was demanding.

"Och, sure, we kyanny," Paddy said weakly.

She pointed excitedly to the rumbling mass of steel that was the wall of the grinding machine.

"*Zerznij mnie na tej maszynie!*" Fuck me against that machine!

Paddy feared his heart might give way, the excitement of sex compounded with the rumbling of the machine.

He shook his head at the machine. "Not there!"

She pointed eagerly into the corner.

"*Albo moze w tym kacie!*" Or maybe in that corner!

Aggie fell against him, her fingers flying towards the straps of his overalls as she covered his grimy face with kisses. Paddy shivered as the overalls slipped to his knees, then to his gray sagging socks that had once had elasticated support and been white. She squealed like a sow at a trough of new slop as his powerful working class hands ripped through her polyester.

Aggie pulled away and shrieked in surprise, pointing into the darkness.

"*Ktoś nas podglada!*" Someone is here! "*Kim jest to dziwne stworzenie?*" Who is that strange creature?

Paddy saw what was indeed a strange creature that had materialized with little fists bared beside a conveyor belt. Paddy burned for a moment with fury as to why Aggie had not informed him she had a son. He stifled a guffaw at how nancy-boy-poofter the child was; they certainly bred them effeminate across the Iron Curtain, he thought, then did a double take as he realized it was Padraig with his new glasses. He was torn between shame, confusion and shock that Fionnuala would let him out on the streets looking like that.

"Jesus Christ almighty!" Paddy said.

Padraig glowered with hatred and betrayal, glaring up at one, then the other, then the first again through his greasy fingerprinted lenses as his lips struggled to make words.

"Daddy! What is youse playing at? How could ye do it, da?"

"How in God's name did ye slip through the picket line, wee boy?"

"That's the least of yer worries," Padraig promised. "I'm off to tell Mammy ye've nabbed a fancy woman for yerself, and a flimmin wile-looking busted-cabbage faced gee-eyed skegrat fancy woman at that!"

"C'mere you now!" Paddy thundered, lumbering towards him as best he could, but Padraig had disappeared into the maze of grinding machines and the man of the Flood house was left standing with his overalls around his ankles and a noose around his neck.

"Gee-eyed skeg…?" Aggie wondered.

"That be's English for 'Polish,'" Paddy lied.

"You in trouble, yes?"

"Aye."

She pulled up her bra strap.

CHAPTER 42

"Food first, filth later," Dymphna promised Rory.

He peered eagerly across the microwaved lasagne through the flickering flames, barely able to locate Dymphna's face in the gloom. It was the Day of the Assumption of the Blessed Virgin Mary, a Holy Day of Obligation, and Dymphna had paid a visit to St. Molaug's. While the congregation muttered through the Liturgy of the Eucharist and hacked coughs into their prayer books, Dymphna crept over to the Prayers for the Dead candles stand, slipped a fifty-pence piece into the box and lit a candle. Kneeling, she muttered up a quick prayer to the Blessed Virgin for her Granny and Grandda Flood and her Grandda Heggarty; the three hadn't exactly been civil to one another in life, but Dymphna figured they could all share one candle in death. Then, with a quick genuflection, she made out the door with a box of votive candles under her coat.

The candles now lined the dining room table; they not only set a romantic mood, they also hid the filth, and stealing was easier than cleaning.

"And I miss wee, er, Keanu," Rory was saying through teeth surrounded by ground meat, nodding with some reluctance in the general direction he suspected the stroller lay.

Through the candlelight, Dymphna picked coyly at her pasta and took in what she was finding the increasingly sexy combination of his red soccer jersey, his white skin and his jet black hair. As she giggled and chewed, she found herself yearning for his piercing blue eyes, his lithe, athletic body, the three heads of his shower, and the pounds that bulged in his mother's bank account. She was relieved the dimness hid his pimples. This dinner would seal the deal. She would get her claws into him, then wait a few days to tell him about his unborn daughter; she knew it was a girl, the way an expectant mother does.

Their glasses clinked, and Rory leaned his face toward hers through the flames. The letter box clanked.

"Who the bleeding feck could that be at this hour?" Dymphna snarled; nobody in the family had outstanding warrants that she was aware of.

"Leave it," Rory said. "They'll soon be on their way."

Their lips met, and still the clanking continued, soon replaced by pounding on the door proper. Try as Dymphna might to concentrate on relishing the moist warmth of his lips, on the playful flickering of his tongue through the bits of ground beef, it was useless. She could stand the racket no longer, and her curiosity got the better of her. She unplugged her lips from his.

"I need to answer that flimmin door," she said angrily, wiping tomato sauce from her mouth. "If it's some aul gypsy woman begging for coins for her wane, she'll get me fist in her begging gob."

Rory checked out Dymphna's shapely hips as she marched out of the kitchen, and as he chewed he felt himself stir at the sight of her flicking her hands through her curly red mane of luxurious hair, still felt the passion of the kiss on his lips. He had been giving his mother too much credit; Dymphna, her mind aside, was indeed a great catch. And he had been about to let her slip away. When Dymphna sat back down, he would demand she move back in, and to hell with Zoë and her over-protectiveness and old-fashioned prejudice. He dug his fork into a chunk of beef.

Dymphna tugged open the door and flinched at the middle-aged man stood there with his bald head, greasy ponytail and rockabilly sideburns.

"And who the bloody hell is *ye?*" she asked, moving swiftly to slam the door on his ugliness. He shoved his shoe inside.

"Sorry I'm late, love. Dymphna, isn't it? Ye wouldn't believe the traffic, but. There was a pileup on the Craigavon Bridge. The bloody Filth—ahh, I smell the lasagne already. Brilliant! I love pasta, so I do."

He thrust a bouquet of daffodils at her and marched into the house.

"Hold on there a wee moment, mister!" Dymphna demanded, trying to shove him back out onto the street with the hand that wasn't clutching the flowers. "What gives ye the right to march into me house like this? I've never set eyes on ye in me life!"

He made his way into the kitchen.

"Christ on a cross, it's dark in here, but."

He turned on the light bulb, and Rory looked up from a forkful of pasta in alarm. The stranger took in Rory with surprise, and then confusion.

"Er, bout ye, mucker," he said uncertainly.

He faced Dymphna, who was clutching at his elbow and uttering strange grunts and squeals.

"Who be's this?"

"Who the bleeding feck is *you*, more to the point!" Dymphna seethed.

She grabbed him by the collar of his shirt and tried to pull him back into the hallway and thereafter onto the street.

"Paul McCreeney, sure! Ye asked me to yers for dinner last night in the back of the mini-cab. Do ye not recall?" He suddenly seemed furious with himself, stamping his foot, his hands curling into fists at his side. "I knew it was too good to be true. Out of yer mind with drink, so ye were. Begging me to abandon the mini-cab and take ye upstairs for a jolly good rogering, ye said, and up the arse and all, ye promised!"

Dymphna's shock was topped only by Rory's.

"What the bleeding feck?" he gasped, leaping from his chair.

"It was against me better judgment to take advantage of ye in the state ye were in, no matter how much ye insisted ye were gagging for it," the stranger went on, as Dymphna's horror rose. "More fool me, hi! Ye haven't a clue about wer date, have ye? Forgotten the moment ye put the key in the door and collapsed in a drunken, sleazy heap on yer STD-ridden bedclothes, I've no doubt!"

"Rory!" Dymphna wailed. "He be's away in the head, sure! Stop him from babbling more deranged lies!"

But Rory only stood and glared. At her. He lunged for his jacket draped on the back of the chair.

"No, Dymphna," he said, flush with rage. "I'm the foolish gack who's been out of his head. Believing all this palaver of how ye've changed, when ye're still the same sleazy, scabby slag me mammy has been warning me all about since the moment ye stepped foot in wer house."

Out he raced. The stranger made himself at home at the table.

"Shame to let this lasagne go to waste," he said, lifting up Rory's fork. "Microwaved, was it?"

"*Out!*" Dymphna shrieked. "*Outta me house now!*"

155

Bursting into tears, she wondered *what the bleeding feck just happened here?*

CHAPTER 43

Siofra had let the waterworks flow, and Dymphna unlocked her handbag and graced her palm with £5. Siofra now had £9.04. Grainne might help her with another pound or two, but there was a long way to go before she conjured up the additional £184.95 to replace Catherine's iPod. Options were slim: Padraig's credit card had been stopped, and he had already sold the five iPods he bought on it (what that money had been spent on was a mystery to her); her granny never had any extra money from her pension; her daddy was always at the factory; and Seamus and Keanu were too young to own money. That left her mammy. Madness as it was, Siofra had to ask. Earlier that morning, she had had a terrible nightmare of belt buckles approaching her through a field of hands with grabbing lesbian fingers and woken up bathed in sweat. Siofra rounded the corner before school to the house that had previously been her home.

Her mother was at the table in the kitchen in her bathrobe with the torn pockets, head hovering over the maps to get to Moira with a look of puzzlement on her face and a tea mug in her hand. Siofra spied an éclair from the swanky new café on Shipquay Street on a little plate, and her breakfastless stomach growled with excitement.

"Mammy?"

Fionnuala's head shot up.

"What are ye doing here? How did ye get in?"

Fionnuala's elbow dug into a corner of a map, and the éclair disappeared under Bulgaria.

"Mammy…"

"I know who I am, sure! What are ye after, wane?"

"I…I broke me mate's iPod, and…and I'm afreared her daddy's gonny batter her senseless if I don't get another for her."

"Not that I believe a word of them lies spewing from yer bake, but for argument's sake, what's it to do with me? If it be's a handout ye're after…!"

Her mother's eyes flashed menacingly.

"Mammy, but!" Siofra whined with an angry little stamp on a hole in the linoleum. "Ye mind last birthday ye sat me down and explained how ye and me daddy was skint and youse couldn't afford to get me a present and youse'd owe me? And I've been helping ye up in them aul ones' attics, nicking all that gear for ye to sell down the market, wasting me time when I should be practicing for the talent show. I need £184.95, and—"

Siofra was shocked at the speed of her mother jumping from the chair, rounding the table and clattering her across the face. *Smack!*

"Nicking?! *Nicking?!* I should take a bar of soap to yer filthy wee mouth for spewing such lies! Yer mammy be's doing no such thing. Theft be's one of the seven deathly sins. Breaking one of God's ten commandments! Clearing that gear from the attics be's helping the aul ones out, doing their spring cleaning for em, and payment for going out of wer way to visit em as nobody in their right minds would want to listen to em babbling on about their decades spent on earth. And if ye think I've 200 quid to throw away on iPods and such ye're outta yer bleeding fecking mind, not when we've this trip to Malta to fund and all wer bills to pay and all. Give me head peace, wane! Clear outta here and get yerself to school where I hope themmuns teach ye how to not be a grabby wee cunt!"

"I hate ye! *I hate ye!*"

"And the feeling be's mutual. Outta me sight, wane! I've still loads of strength in me wrist, sure!"

Siofra left, and Fionnuala took her seat, simmering at the bold faced cheek of the child. How could she have raised such a self-centered beast? She chomped into the éclair and revisited the maps.

The moment the slamming of the door told him his daughter had gone, Paddy padded fearfully down the stairs from his vantage point of the hall landing. He stepped into the fluorescent strip lighting of the kitchen, and for once the light seemed too bright. He was sure Fionnuala could read the guilt on his face. She barely registered his arrival, however. Perhaps Padraig hadn't had the chance to blurt out what he had seen in the factory, or perhaps his love for his daddy had made him reconsider? Paddy was suddenly grateful for the time he had spent/wasted kicking around the soccer ball with his son when there were professional games on TV he would rather be watching.

Paddy went to the larder and opened it. His lunch, prepared by Fionnuala earlier, sat there. He grabbed at the aluminum foil.

"I'm away off to work," he announced.

"Away off with ye, then. Cheerio. And don't ye forget the drinks do at the school the night. Eight o'clock sharp, I want ye there. Don't make me look like a gack by having to wait around for ye."

Paddy stood in indecision before her. If he told her before Padraig had a chance to? If he owned up, told his wife he found the Polish migrant worker repellent, that he felt he owed Aggie as she had saved his hand, and without two hands, he wouldn't be able to collect a paycheck and...

"Before I go, but..."

Fionnuala heaved the sigh of a martyr and dragged her neck up to face him. Paddy shuffled before her uncertainly, sure she could hear his heart pounding.

"There be's this woman at the plant. One of them Poles ye see down the town all the time as of late. They've shipped all the workers over from Poland, ye understand. And—"

"What in the name of feck are ye blathering on about?"

"Well, last night, we was working late for that overtime, if ye recall. And something happened that I kyanny quite fathom at the moment how. Anyroad, before I go any further, I've to tell ye she saved me hand from being mangled in the machine a few days earlier. Ye mind I told ye about that?"

"Dementia, ye think I'm suffering from now?"

"And I've to tell ye that you be's the only woman in me life that's ever meant anything to me. Proud, I was, when ye gladly took me hand in marriage. And in all them years, in all them years—"

"Ye're gonny be docked yer wages if ye show up late, so ye are. Can ye not wait for Valentine's or til I'm on me deathbed to let loose with all the sentimental claptrap?"

"What I'm trying to tell ye is—"

Fionnuala's eyes narrowed, then ballooned as a gasp of shock exited her mouth. Her hand shot out, her fingernails digging into the flesh of his upper arm with such brute force Paddy was of no doubt she finally understood.

"Jesus Mary and Joseph!" she seethed.

"Aye?" Paddy asked timidly, unable to glance into the anger that exploded in her eyes, and steeling himself for the abuse, verbal and physical, that was sure to follow.

"I forgot to take the pork knuckle out of the freezer for the tea the night!" she wailed angrily, racing to the fridge. "Midnight, it'll be before the wanes and me mammy can fill their stomachs!"

She waved him off distractedly as she hunted through the freezer.

"Mind ye close the door on yer way out."

Paddy lingered at the threshold, his lunch of three butter sandwiches clutched in his hand. Decades of marriage had made him an expert at identifying the merest trace of sarcasm in her voice. At the moment that voice was curiously flat. Perhaps too flat? Wondering if he were second-guessing himself, or if the lager from the night before were still dulling his senses, he finally turned and walked down the front hall. He couldn't believe somebody as conniving as his Padraig would let go an opportunity to cause friction in the family; the little bastard thrived on it. Paddy would check his sandwiches for bits of ground glass when he got to work. He walked out the door.

CHAPTER 44

Fionnuala's clumsy fingers dwarfed the stem of the martini glass.

"Bruschetta?" a woman with a tray offered.

Fionnuala inspected the caterer's tie with suspicion, then dared to view what the bull-dyke was shoving under her nose. *A fecking fancy foreign name for wee tomato sandwiches with no tops on em? Jumped-up intellectual cunts!*

But she grabbed one with an awkward curtsey, the caterer hurried off. Fionnuala picked off the leafy green bits before hoovering it down.

"The Proddies be's out in force, hi," Paddy said.

Fionnuala and Paddy were milling around the teachers' mail-slots in the room full of Brooks Brothers suits and cufflinks, pearls and cocktail dresses. Indeed, it seemed the Our Lady of Perpetual Sorrow teachers' lounge was hosting the invasion of the Orangefolk: Protestants of all shapes and ages were clamoring around the chocolate fountain and the ice sculpture, while the smattering of Catholic mothers and the odd father or two seemed relegated to the corner where the photocopier stood and the caterers rarely ventured.

The neighborhood children clearly hadn't embraced the new Grand Prize of Hannah Montana tickets as wholeheartedly as Fionnuala's daughter; word shared across the hedges and through the washing lines of the Moorside must be that the Fingers Across the Foyle talent show was rubbing shoulders with the enemy. Fionnuala wondered with a spike of fear if she and her family would be branded Unionist sympathizers. But if they were to be tarred and feathered later for taking part in the reception, she may as well fill her belly with drink now. Her horse-head lowered itself to the rim and she slurped down. She swiped another martini from a passing tray.

"There's yer man Skivvins from the Sav-U-Mor by that daft fountain," Fionnuala seethed, wiping her chin. "He be's to blame for all wer money woes, for the wanes looking gaunt as junkies due to the hunger gnawing at their stomachs. And that headmistress with him, that Mrs. Plinkie, or whatever the feck her name be's, be's one hard-faced miserable cunt. Ye mind I told ye she called me into her office and almost got wer Siofra excluded after that palaver with the fire extinguishers the other month? Look at her now, her hands all over yer man, and him an Orange Proddy bastard. Disgraceful, so it is!"

Across the expanse of the bobbing hairdos, the headmistress lowered her eyes and nodded in her direction. Fionnuala read her lips clearly: "I do believe that's the woman from the protest."

Fionnuala turned around slowly, both to hide her face and to shine her designer rhinestones at them. She should have brought her Celine Dion satchel; Celine was classically-trained, so she was high class. Trying to behave as someone in real designer gear would, Fionnuala scooped something with tentacles from a passing tray and placed it haltingly on her tongue. She blanched.

That wee girl better win this fecking competition, she thought as nausea surged up her throat. She wrapped the slop in a napkin useless in size and let it fall to the floor. Her toe nudged it under a chair, and she was suddenly irritated by Paddy at her side. It was the denim, the whiff of seaweed, the fingernails black with fish dinge, and the image of his stiffie plowing into a fetid Polish field at the fish factory.

"Could ye not have put on a shirt with buttons?" Fionnuala chided, elbowing him in the ribs. "And mind yerself with the drink. I don't want ye showing me up any more than ye already are. Sip, Paddy, *sip.*"

"Right ye are, love," he replied, as if he would.

"I'm away off to mingle," Fionnuala decided. "Ye're on yer own."

She distanced herself from him, though she was clueless as to who she might mingle with. The only person in the room she knew to speak to was Mrs. Donaldson, Grainne's mother, but Fionnuala hadn't had a civil word to say to her since two Sundays earlier, when the beast had cut her off at the holy water font to dip her fingers in first. *Self-centered cunt!*

Paddy inspected the ice sculpture, two hands reaching out in friendship and melting while they did it. He finished off his beer and grabbed another. A woman approached him from the Protestant contingent, and then another. And another.

Fionnuala lingered unaware behind a pillar, facial muscles aching from her fixed grin, and listening in on the filth a trio of self-important Protestant men were spreading.

"...those former terrorists...what new jobs...have now?"

"What...mean?"

"...former lives...no education...lounging around...out of bed at crack of noon...no time card to punch...spreading...hatred...detonating the occasional bomb...threats...kneecapping...instilling...brute force...no brains...life of Riley indeed...money from the Yanks...Libya..."

Fionnuala's blood percolated. Every word might be the God's honest truth, but they had a bold faced nerve stating it!

"Now…"

"…put their skill sets to good use, but what skill sets…possess?"

Fionnuala wanted to push their heads into the punch bowl and skewer their eyes with the toothpicks from the cheese bits, but couldn't as an old man in an Armani suit materialized at her side.

"Hello, having a good time? Have you any hobbies?" he asked with one of those blindingly white smiles.

"Aye," Fionnuala barked, her lips sliding over her bank of teeth to hide their color. "Paying bills!"

She shoved through the crowd of overdressed twats, suddenly panicked. Her head hurt from all the West Brit accents, the violins screeching from the sound system, the hatred and misunderstanding she had overheard. From all sides of the room it was coming at her: an alternate reality existed across the River Foyle to which she was barred access by reason of birth and finance. Her life to that point had been useless; her body would rot then turn to bones then dust in its coffin, forgotten and upstaged by the shakers and movers of history. Her only legacy would be her grandchildren and their children and their children's children, she would live on only in the collective memory of the world in *Lotto Balls of Shame*, the hardened Nelly Frood, the obese layabout who had given birth to nine children in a row and whose labor stopped there, who went after poor Una Bartlett's lottery winnings and—

She spied Paddy at the ice sculpture, surrounded by cooing, preening women. Her fingernails gouged into the palms of her hands. Fionnuala could deny her man her maidenly pleasures for months on end, but in a crowd of a thousand pairs of female eyes stretched before her, she could hone in on the one pair focused on his behind. And here were many pairs. She felt her claws extend.

"…so I told the union rep, give me one of them bacon sandwiches of yers, and he *did,* foolish git!"

They tinkled with laughter, all tits and teeth, and Fionnuala felt faint. Then, to her horror, she spied Dymphna's fiance's mother, Zoë, tinkling along, a hand pressing into Paddy's arm. Fionnuala searched frantically for a door that looked like it might contain toilets and scuttled inside.

She locked herself in a stall, plopped on the seat, and sobbed into the toilet roll at the sorry state of her life. The night before, she was certain Padraig wanted her to erupt into shrieks of rage when he told her the news. He must have been disappointed at her reaction: resignation. Her husband of twenty-odd years was getting it off against the mixing and grinding machines with a buck-toothed common laborer scab, and a Commie-bastard foreigner at that, and she just wasn't bothered. The ranting in her mind was directed elsewhere: at Moira, at the distance of Malta, at the Lord Almighty, at the sight of Mrs. Pilkey's Catholic hands on the thigh of Mr. Skivvins, at Beethoven and his fecking violins.

She had paid Padraig a tenner to keep his mouth shut. She knew damn well she would get revenge on her cheating husband, but she had sampled many times in her life the deliciousness of revenge served cold; Paddy's would be served to him from the freezer.

The door creaked open, and two giggling women entered.

"…what are you doing here, anyway, Zoë? You've no children this age, have you?"

"I've two nieces in the competition. One's doing fencing, the other demonstrating how to cook croissants, in French."

"Anyway, back to what we were saying. What lovely huge hands he has. Big worker's fingers. And he absolutely reeks of sweat—you know the way they exude a more feral odor than we? What I wouldn't give to…oh, goodness! I do fear those apple-tinis have gone to my head!"

There was a bray of unladylike laughter.

"You've always had a thing for rough trade. If your husband ever found out! Pass me one of those tissues, dear."

"It would be like pairing up with a member of a lesser species! *Marvelous!* Oh, Zoë! Do be a dear and help me with my bra strap, it seems to have come undone in the back. And when he went on in that guttural minion accent about lifting all those crates of fish, heaven help me, all I could think of was he must be an absolute animal in the sack, all bestial grunting and raw, brute force."

"Ha! Under the sheets with the lights off, more like. That's the Catholic way, don't you know? He was almost family, would you believe? Do keep still, dear, I'll never get it fixed at this rate, and quit gawping at me like that. Yes, his daughter almost married my son. I soon put a stop to that. I must touch up my lipstick as well. On a more tragic note, did you see the hard-faced creature that passes as his wife? It's no wonder, I suppose, those working class women all look decades older than their years."

"A trip to the health club wouldn't go amiss, either, especially with that fat harridan. You see droves of them waddling through those Catholic housing estates, women barely out of their forties rolling prams stuffed with their screaming great-grandchildren, and you can't tell if they're ready to drop another any moment, ready to add to the litter."

"I blame it on genes, the lack of proper nutrition, and ignorance of the beauty products of the day. Or, more likely, the inability to afford them."

"It's quite a giggle. Sometimes I suspect the lower classes were put on this earth only for our amusement, don't you agree?"

"Oh, of course. If they didn't exist, somebody would have to invent them."

They shared a chuckle, and Fionnuala looked down at the shreds of toilet paper still clutched in her fingernails.

"The hours the poor dear must have spent on the sewing machine, putting together that God-awful outfit. DYNK indeed! And clumsily paired with that Burberry scarf, no fashion sense whatsoever, and that scarf is sure to be a knockoff."

"Or shoplifted. And she needs to run, and I do mean run, to the hair salon. My eyes are still stinging from the sight of her bleached ponytails. Why do they all seem to cling to their youth? How that brawny hunk of manhood sleeps soundly at night with such a revolting creature at his side, I simply cannot fathom."

Fionnuala threw open the toilet door in a rage. The women flipped from the mirror in shock, lipsticks aloft.

"You want rough trade, ye minging slapper? I'll rough trade ye in yer Botoxed face, so the Sephora mascara be's running down yer cheeks! And me Burberry scarf be's genuine!"

They watched her go, mortified for her. Zoë shook her head sadly: "And why are the heels of their shoes always magnets for loo roll?"

"Ye Orange bastards! Looking down yer noses at us! Thinking ye're better than the likes of us!" Fionnuala roared into the masses.

She grabbed a vodka bottle and flung it through the screams and scattering bodies at the ice sculpture. Shards of ice and shattered glass flew through the air. A finger speared Mrs. Pilkey's forehead and she collapsed into a bookcase. It toppled over and pinned shrieking, wailing bodies under its weight. Legs and arms shuddered under thick volumes. Fionnuala raced for a whimpering Skivvins, grappled him around the neck and wrenched his head into the chocolate spewing from the cherubs' mouths.

"Take that! Take that, ye nancy-boy Proddy stoke, ye! That's for sacking me!" Fionnuala growled as he sputtered and struggled and chocolate splattered all over the—

But then Fionnuala realized she was only clutching the lapel of Paddy's denim jacket in a quiet corner, the others chuckling and nattering around them, clinking martini glasses and enjoying the classical music.

"Let's clear the feck outta this tip," she said, "and leave them Proddys to their own miserable lives."

CHAPTER 45

"One Cowalicious-On-A-Bun, two Lambkebaahbs, three curry chips, extra large."

"Please?" Bridie demanded of the customer, but the hooded teen was knocked to the side by Dymphna.

"Yer woman's till be's wonky," Dymphna explained, patting a Keanu slung over her shoulder. "Go ye to that wee girl over there. More pleasant on the eyes, she be's and all."

"Dymphna!" Bridie said, eyes searching frantically for the manager. "What—?"

"Aye, what indeed! What in the name of feck happened at the Craiglooner last night?"

"What are ye asking me for? I wasn't there, sure."

Keanu turned to inspect the noise of Bridie's voice.

"Has that wane of yers got an eye infection?" Bridie asked.

"Och, I hope it'll disappear, magic-like. Anyroad, don't change the subject. Aye, ye was there. Don't ye try to deny it. I've a vague recollection of ye shoving me and Rory into the back of a mini-cab."

"Rory? He had left hours before, but. Ye told me so. A headache, or some such, he was suffering from. Ye said youse had made a dinner date for last night. Lasagne, ye said ye would cook for him. Och, ye were in one paladic state, I can tell ye, singing aul Britney Spears songs, especially that 'did it again' one, and throwing yerself at every lad that came into the pub. I tried to stop ye, tried to remind ye about yer date with Rory and how ye had to make up with him as ye've got that other wane of his inside ye begging for release. Ye paid me no mind, but. And then yer man Paul McCreeney showed up and yer legs shot apart so quickly ye knocked a pint onto the floor. Ye fairly did the splits on yer man with his crotch as the floor! I thought yer second wane was coming months premature, sure!"

"No need to go on about it. Who the bloody feck be's this Paul McCreeney?"

"Ye met him last night. I know him from the line-dancing"

"Are ye sure?"

Bridie, bristling, placed a hand on her hip and stared Dymphna down.

"If ye've forgotten, ye made up with me and all," Bridie said. "Ye said ye were me best mate again, and ye were sorry for all the insults ye flung me way."

"Are ye sure?"

Bridie's face gave the answer. Dymphna's brain struggled to make sense of what had happened. She toyed with a ketchup packet.

"Why are ye asking, but?" Bridie wanted to know.

"Och, me and Rory was sitting down to dinner, dead romantic it was, candles lit and all, and then yer man Paul barged in and claimed he was me dinner date."

Bridie made a show of picking at her cold sore, but she was really hiding the mirth begging to be set free.

"Ye mean, ye mean ye made a dinner date with Rory, then one with yer man, and forgot about the second? And both lads showed up?"

"Och—!" Dymphna shook her head, anger vying with sorrow. "That Paul McCreeney stopped being a 'lad' about twenty years ago. Blootered, I was, outta me mind with drink. I hadn't a clue."

"I'm wile sorry," Bridie said, trusting herself finally to remove her fingers from her mouth. She placed them on Dymphna's arm and gave it a rub of compassion.

"I've to see to this queue." She nodded at the line forming behind Dymphna.

"Aye, sorry to bother ye at work, like. I just had to know. Before I go, but…"

Dymphna missed the flash of irritation in Bridie's eyes.

"Me mammy swiped a crate of genuine absinthe from the 1920's, and I've a few bottles stashed away at me granny's. How about ye come over after yer shift here and we get legless together, hi? I need it, and I've paid me mammy a tenner to look after this minging wane, so we'll have the house to werselves. What time do ye clock off here?"

"Seven, like."

"See if ye kyanny nick some of them sandwiches from the reject bin before ye go. Nothing with curry."

"Right ye are, see ye at seven. Cheerio."

As Bridie's fingers clacked the next order in the till, she was at a loss as to exactly how she felt. The prospect of wasting time alone with Dymphna Flood in 5 Murphy Crescent's sitting room, the carpeting of which hadn't been hoovered in months and the net curtains which stank of the granny's wee, filled her with less than excitement, but she was desperate to try genuine absinthe, rather than the legal, watered-down crap they had been passing off as the real thing in the pubs the past few years.

She decided drink was more important than discomfort, even though she had just had a lucky escape. Dymphna was so dim-witted, and had indeed been so deranged with alcohol, she hadn't a clue what 'best mate' Bridie had done that night.

"Ten pounds fifty-two pee, love."

And Dymphna would never find out, so long as Bridie could keep her mouth shut while tripping on absinthe.

CHAPTER 46

MacAfee (New Wave) and Scudder (Thin Lizzie) were parked once again across the street from the house with the saggy fence and the brown weeds for a front garden. They sat in a fog of fags, a cloud of vinegar, scoffing down fish and chips, the newsprint further blackening their already filthy fingers, the bottles of lager further disturbing their already disturbed minds. The door to 5 Murphy Crescent opened. MacAfee nudged Scudder and turned down A Flock of Seagulls.

"Themmuns is on the move, boyo," he said.

They leaned forward and peered through the mud spatters of the windshield. Down the path went the pensioner with the cane and the lipstick, then the ugly poofter with the ginger hair, then the hunger-stricken girl with the pink handbag. The gate clanked shut, and the two rogue terrorists looked at each other.

"By my reckoning, that leaves only the wee girl from the Pence-A-Day lockups and her infant in the house," MacAfee said. "Once she clears out, we can rush in and get them explosives."

"Weeks, we've been trying to collect em!" Scudder complained, gnawing on an undercooked chip. "It be's two against one. Can we not just push through the door now and menace that daft bitch with a gun while we search for the case? I wouldn't mind getting me leg over her and all into the bargain."

"Don't be daft! She knows us, sure. She rented us the lockups. Even with balaclavas over wer faces, she's sure to recognize us."

"How, but? X-ray eyes, do ye think she has now?"

"We be's wearing the same gear, sure."

"Pwoah! Would ye look at the backside on that?" Scudder suddenly rejoiced, eyes agog. "That be's a whole lotta woman! Wane-bearing hips, if I've ever seen em!"

A girl in a Kebabalicious outfit had rounded the corner and was clumping down the pavement.

"What I wouldn't give to get me fill of that! Like going at it with an elephant, it would be!" Scudder continued, eyes crazed with sex.

Kebabalicious pushed through the gate, marched up the path and clanked on the letter box.

"Jesus H. Christ!" MacAfee moaned. "The comings and goings through that door!"

"Let's take em both," Scudder insisted. "I want the big one, ye can take the ginger one."

"Never gonna happen."

"Och, this be's wile daft," Scudder said, frustration rising. "The Top-Yer-Trolley annual sale be's next week, so it does. We've still to construct the bomb once we've collected the Semtex, and them instructions from the Internet be's dead complicated."

"Aye, translated from Arabic, they must be, and not very professionally, I admit."

"Why did we not collect them cans before we left for that training course in Libya?"

"We hadn't the time. Don't get yer knickers in a twist. Them wee girls is sure to be preparing for a night on the town. The Pence-A-Day one dropped her infant off somewhere, so that must be the plan. Then we can enter, so we can."

Scudder looked at his watch.

"One hour, I'm giving themmuns. Then, feck ye're touchy-feely shite. I'm barging in there and taking the tins, and giving themmuns pure tight with me meat weapon and all. One hour, just!"

CHAPTER 47

HALF AN HOUR EARLIER

Around the corner, a Fionnuala fresh from Xpressions hair salon approached the mirror and inspected her new—age-appropriate—hairdo. A bland creature stared glumly back at her, the frivolity of youth now stripped from her skull, replaced with a mousy brown flip. She was saddened that "age-appropriate" for her meant "middle-aged." The words of the women in the toilets still stung, and the bleached pony tails had been the second thing to go; she had already snipped the DYNK rhinestones from the back of her black jacket. Perhaps, Fionnuala considered by way of making herself feel better, a change of appearance had been on the cards for a while, if only for the event the coppers came calling to haul her in for a line up courtesy of Mrs. Ming and the older Mrs. Gee.

Keanu gurgled in his stroller in the corner, and Fionnuala turned her attention to the TV to make herself feel better. *The Iceberg That Sank The Titanic* was on in a few minutes; she had circled it in the newspaper earlier that morning and had been looking forward to it for hours. She wasn't one for documentaries, but for her this was must-see TV, considering her all-time fave film.

The amount of times she had curled up on the sofa with the sitting room drapes drawn, a hand stuck inside a jumbo bag of prawn cocktail crisps, the other clutching a flagon of cider, the vacuum cleaner leaning unused against the wall and the filth of the house forgotten, the VCR tape of *Titanic* whirring before her misted eyes, and the sobs dribbling from her lips while the twisted shards of iron sank to the freezing ocean depths and Celine Dion's beautiful voice swaddled her ears. She turned the TV on, tingling with excitement.

"Next on BBC Three, there's a change to the billed programming. We take great pleasure in presenting our heartbreaking investigative feature Can't Stop Eating: Supersized Teens.*"*

Dear God give me strength! Fionnuala seethed inwardly, flinging the remote at the screen.

It bounced onto the floor, the back popping off and the batteries scattering. Fionnuala heaved herself off the sofa, slipped on a battery and cracked her skull against the coffee table.

"For the love of God!" she moaned.

How would she spend the next hour instead? She spied the *Ab Fab Abs and Boulder Buns* video under an ashtray stuffed with spent cigarettes. Zoë and her hateful friend had also talked about the size of her. Fionnuala looked down at her body. Was it any wonder Paddy had sought comfort elsewhere?

She decided it was time she heave her exhausted form onto the floor and demand her limbs mimic the movements of the trainer on the screen. A brief trip upstairs, and she had stretched herself in a pair of pink leotards and matching legwarmers that had lain unused in a drawer for ten years, brown flip tied back with a dirty pair of tights. Looking around the sitting room to ensure there were no voyeurs, she closed the net curtains, then the larger curtains. She was bathed in darkness.

Perhaps a little warm-up? Her bones creaked as she positioned herself prone on the floor. She groaned as the concrete beneath the scant carpeting dug into her spine. She would slip a disk if she didn't cushion it somehow.

She grabbed the cushions from the couch and placed them on the carpet. Then she finally pulled the video out of its case. She was about to slip it into the VCR when she saw it had no label. Had Mrs. Ming placed the wrong video inside?

"Ye've got to be joking!"

Maybe a jumping jack or two before the silent television instead? Fionnuala felt herself struck by a sudden lethargy, and she knew her new workout regime had failed before it had begun. She would just slip the video into the slot just to make sure, but already her heart was sinking. She somehow knew whatever was on that tape wasn't the cure for her beer gut.

There came a knocking on the door, and Fionnuala froze. The only inhabitants of Derry who didn't use the letter box to knock were the coppers and bill collectors. She threw the cushions back on the settee and hid the tape between two of them, the panic rising within her. She tiptoed to the hallway and peered through the beveled glass of the front door. Her heart sank further. Sure enough, the twats in suits must be from the gas or electric collections agency. Nobody else with suits would ever knock on her door.

She slipped silently away from the front hallway and into the kitchen. She needed cold hard cash more than she needed a workout, both to pay the bills and fund that flimmin trip to Malta. The furious pounding on the door (as it was now) made that more than evident. She grabbed her handbag from the counter and tugged her change purse out. She glumly inspected the scattering of coins inside, then snapped the clasp shut, steely resolve on her face.

She went to the washing machine, before which were piled garbage bags filled with Dymphna's clothing; her daughter had brought them around as 5 Murphy no longer had washing machine. Fionnuala delved inside, and her eyes lit up as she scrutinized the regular stitching, felt the thread count and read the labels that spelled Money. There on the kitchen linoleum, she stripped out of her workout gear, hauled her hips into a denim mini-skirt, twisted her breasts into a bright pink halter top with spangly bits, and packed her feet into red stilettos. (How Dymphna thought her mother could wash those was a mystery to Fionnuala, but the girl had never been the brightest bulb.)

She ran upstairs and, before her vanity table, spruced herself up. She slapped on a garish shade of lipstick, brightened her droopy eyelids with sparkly emerald eyeshadow, then slapped some fake tan on her face. She squinted at her reflection in the mirror and gave a satisfied nod. Given the dim lighting of the town's pubs, she felt sure she would fit into the throngs of teenyboppers that went out of their minds with drink there.

She hummed what she suspected was a pop hit of the day to herself (it was actually "Mr. Vain") as she made her way down the stairs, wobbling uncertainly in the heels and relieved the knocking had finally stopped. She grabbed her Celine Dion satchel and screwed as many absinthe bottles into its depths as the stitching would allow. She seized the handles of Keanu's stroller and, satchel around her shoulder, handbag swinging at her elbow, made her way out the front door. Time to finally make money from her OsteoCare visits.

CHAPTER 48

Unaware of Scudder and MacAfee staring at the vast expanse of her backside from their van, Bridie clanked the letter box of 5 Murphy Crescent, her pockmarked face slouched under a grimy waterfall of hair. Her smock stank of garlic sauce and cheap meat cuts.

"Outta me way, you!" she panted the moment Dymphna opened the door. "I'm gasping with thirst!"

"And I'm slavering with hunger! Let me at them kebabs! Me stomach thinks me throat's been cut!"

Dymphna snatched Bridie's bulging handbag from her elbow, tore at the paper and dug her teeth into whatever happened to occupy its depths. Except for the noise from Dymphna's mouth, the house was deathly quiet.

"Where's yer granny and the wanes?" Bridie wondered.

"They've gone to the pictures to see that new film."

"Shrek 3?"

"Dear God, naw," Dymphna scoffed. *"Saw 4."*

Bridie scanned the room for the booze. Dymphna pointed at the corner. Bridie ripped off the yellowed newsprint of the bottles, and a look of wonder transformed her pimples.

"I always thought," Dymphna said, "absinthe was meant to be green. I don't give a shite, but. It's sure to be potent."

"Ye're not wrong there. And, *actually*, if ye really want to know," the Wonderbook of Knowledge that was Bridie began, "absinthe turns brown after it ages. It's to do with the degrading of the chlorophyll, which of course be's in the herb wormwood, and also the anise—"

"Enough with the blabbering, and let's get legless, ye daft cunt, ye! I'm gagging to get it down me bake!"

Dymphna tugged the bottle out of Bridie's hand, pried open the cork and made to guzzle down.

"I'm drinking for two now, after all!"

"Are ye away in the flimmin head?" Bridie gasped. "Gimme that, you. There be's a special ritual ye're meant to follow. "

She tugged a perplexed Dymphna, on her second kebab, into the scullery.

"We're in need of some sugar cubes, a jug of cold water, some matches and an absinthe spoon of sorts."

Dymphna's chewing slowed as her suspicion mounted. She slurped juices off her fingers. Bridie plucked two tea mugs from the cabinet, wiped the filth from them and pried a cluster of congealed sugar cubes out of a bowl.

"What the bloody feck be's an absinthe spoon when it's at home?" Dymphna asked.

"A spoon with holes in it. This'll do grand and lovely," Bridie decided, wiping away an old skin from a potato peeler. "Fill you that jug there with cold water."

Bridie gathered the makeshift paraphernalia, then moved back into the front room. Dymphna plodded behind her, jug sloshing water. Bridie threw the glossy celebrity magazines on the coffee table to the carpet, and Dymphna sat one cushion over. Bridie poured the brown mess into the glasses with the precision of a professional barmaid, balanced the potato peeler on the rim of one glass and daintily positioned a clump of sugar on top, then doused the sugar with a dribble of absinthe. Dymphna could keep silent no longer.

"So what chemistry professor from Magee College have you been shagging, then? If I had known a flimmin PhD was required to dive headlong into a bottle of this manky shite—"

"Och, catch yerself on," Bridie shushed her. "Sure, I only know meself as…Ye mind that film with Nicole Kidman and Ewan McGregor? *Moulin Rouge?*"

Dymphna tensed at Bridie's perfect French diction.

"Ye mean that musical with the song 'Lady Marmelade?'"

"Aye, and if ye recall that be's me favorite film of all time. Mind, ye were keeping a lookout for the security for me when I nicked the DVD from the Top-Yer-Trolley bargain bin? The hours I've spent pausing almost every frame. Yer man Ewan McGregor has a fine arse, him."

"God's gift to women, right enough. Not a patch on me heartthrob Keanu, but."

"Anyroad, ye mind that scene where Ewan and all his poofter poetry mates guzzle down the flaming absinthe, and the wee green Kylie Minogue fairy appears in front of em, singing and dancing before their eyes?"

"Aye." Dymphna nodded eagerly. "Outta their bleeding fecking minds, they was. Seeing things that wasn't there and the like."

"Well, that's soon to be happening to us and all," Bridie promised.

She flicked a match and held it to the sugar. The sugar spit with flames, dissolved through the slit and set the absinthe ablaze. She did the same with the next mug.

"Now pour you the water over the fire to put it out," Bridie instructed.

Dymphna did, and they held up the broiling glasses and clanked them together.

"To best mates!" Dymphna toasted, and they guzzled down. And spat up. And forced it down again.

"Tastes like shite," Dymphna said, shuddering.

"Och, tastes like licorice, sure."

"Aye, licorice that was pulled from an arse," Dymphna replied, but held her glass out for another round.

"Speaking of arses," Bridie said, filling Dymphna's glass, "this flimmin newspaper has gone up the crack of mines."

She reached under her and tugged out the paper that had been wrapped around the bottle, while Dymphna focused on balancing the potato peeler and prying a clump of sugar from the mound.

"Och, can we not just drink from the bottle?"

"Heresy, that would be!" Bridie scoffed.

"What the feck does that mean?"

"Never you mind that. What's yer mammy doing in this paper, hi?" Bridie asked, stabbing the paper with her finger.

"Wise up, ye headbin," Dymphna snorted. "What would me mammy be doing in an ancient issue of the *Guardian*? Nobody reads it but intellectual Proddy bastards. Feck knows what that old perv Mrs. Gee was doing with it in her attic."

She lit the sugar, watched the flames rise and crammed alcohol down her throat.

"I'm serious, but! Go on and have a gander at that photo, would ye?" Bridie said, filling her glass and chucking the drink into her throat. "It be's yer mammy as sure am I'm sitting here!"

Dymphna saw a woman with a shaggy bleached perm and an off-the-shoulder Flashdance top draped around a man in army fatigues. The eyes of both were concealed behind black bars to keep their identities hidden, and the woman was laughing for the lens. Dymphna nearly spit up the wormwood again.

"Mary mother of God!" she gasped. "Them...them teeth. That smirk. And them *calves*. Yer woman does look like me mammy, right enough. What would me mammy be doing with a paratrooper, but?"

Dymphna squinted at the headline as another flaming shot razed a trail into her gullet. *Orange Camouflage and Green Lace—They Slept With The Enemy!* It was an exposé of shameless Derry girls from the staunchly-Catholic Creggan Heights who had engaged in filthy relationships with the occupying British forces as the Troubles in Northern Ireland had dragged wearily on through the 1980's.

As the nausea of such forbidden pairings instinctively swept through her, Dymphna glanced at the date of the newspaper: ten months before she was born. While she struggled to do the math, a niggling sensation of unease swept through her, and the absinthe wasn't to blame.

She had long wondered at her mother's contempt of her, her constant put-downs and inability to compliment. The moment Fionnuala had discovered Dymphna couldn't abide the taste of curry, her mother had embraced the cuisine of the Indian subcontinent. Dymphna had labored through dinners of rice and curry, curry and chips, goat curry and, right before payday, just plain curry.

Dymphna had always put it down to typical maternal jealousy: as she had blossomed into a gorgeous young woman, Fionnuala with her sagging love handles and thinning bleached ponytails couldn't help but envy her daughter, as, Dymphna thought, she was now a more wrinkle-free, more intelligent, and more sociable version of her mother. But…if the real reason for the spite was that Dymphna was the product of a secret tryst with a British Orangeman? The filthy spawn of a hated Proddy paratrooper…?

She thrust the absinthe into her and demanded another.

CHAPTER 49

The orange glow of Fionnuala's face lit up the greyness of the city center streets. The Titanic sank under the weight of the absinthe bottles, and a slumbering Keanu jolted in his stroller as she hauled it over the cobblestones. The bouncer of the Craiglooner pub couldn't hide his shock as she wobbled in her heels towards him, apparently seeking entrance. She was his niece's cousin's brother-in-law's aunt, he knew, and twenty-five years too late for the pub.

"Are ye right there, Mrs. Flood, ma'am?" he managed.

"Don't you fecking 'ma'am' me," Fionnuala seethed.

He waved her through warily, holding open the door for the stroller to fit through. Fionnuala slipped into the pub, skirted the wheels over a pile of sick on the entrance carpet and scoured the teeming teenaged masses within. Bright young eyes all around her shone with boozy glee, the bass of the senseless techno music hammered into her skull, and the slurred shrieks of hooligans mindless with drink battered her ears. She ducked as a fist came hurdling through the air in her direction, tripped over a broken pint glass and found her nose buried in some bared cleavage.

Three old ones in a corner smiled and waved in her direction through the fog of cigarette smoke. Fionnuala was mortified. They had some nerve to think her one of their crew. She was oblivious to the looks of hilarity shooting her way from the youngsters around her, the drunken sniggers behind sweaty palms.

She fought to carve a path with the stroller through the jerking limbs, grateful to have had the good sense to lace the infant's pureed apricots that evening with her supply of OsteoCare barbiturates. She plowed into a quintet of teen girls with dangly earrings and pleather mini-skirts and smeared blood-red lipstick writhing against the jukebox, bottles of lager clutched in their claws. Fionnuala had to lean forward and shriek into their ear canals to make herself heard.

"I've some absinthe going cheap!" she hollered, the grin on her as fake as their IDs.

Their glazed eyes moved in her general direction.

"What are ye on about?" slurred one.

"Have ye lost yer way, hi?" slurred another. "The bingo's on at the church club down the street."

Fionnuala cursed them under her breath, and the stroller trundled on through the stomping slingbacks.

Finding a quiet corner of the pub to conduct her business deals would be useless, so she parked Keanu by the broken karaoke machine, scuttled into the seedy corridor of the toilets and entered the ladies room. Someone had vomited in the sink. Her teeth ground at the sounds of drugs and sex coming from the stalls.

"Would ye look at the state of these loos," she tutted; even she was repulsed.

She quickly reentered the corridor, where three shifty-looking lads in Derry Football Club jerseys and shaved skulls were staggering out of the men's room, tugging up their flies. All of them had smirky faces she would never tire of kicking, but needs must.

"Psst! C'mere a moment, lads," Fionnuala hissed. "Go on and have a wee gander at what be's inside me bag."

They gave her a look as if she had just tugged up her skirt and invited them to sample her wares, but one decided to humor her, nudged a mate, and gave a tentative glance inside.

"Loo roll?" he asked, confused.

Fionnuala tsked impatiently. She had swiped all the free standing toilet paper from the ladies when she had glanced inside. Every penny counted.

"Naw!" she snapped, shoving aside the toilet paper, unearthing a bottle and shoving it under his nose. He recoiled at the sight of it.

"What the bleeding feck be'se that?"

"One hundred percent genuine absinthe."

They exchanged a look.

"It's gone off, so it has," one said. "It's meant to be green."

"It turns brown when it's aged," Fionnuala snapped. "Makes it more potent. I learned it on the Internet."

"One moment, there," another said.

He grabbed his mates by the elbows and led them a few feet away. They had a hurried discussion in the corner, then turned to face her.

"Sorry there, missus," the first one said. "One sip of that and we'd be off to Altnagelvin Hospital, not to help with the hallucinations, but to get wer stomachs pumped."

"Och, go on away and shite, youse," Fionnuala hissed.

She slapped the door open, wrenched the stroller from its parking place, and tramped through the masses in a dejected fury. She would've had better luck shifting Ricky Martin CDs to a construction crew. The stroller caught on the leg of a bar stool, and Fionnuala shoved a girl to the side. She decided she had to address the odd looks the barely of-age barmaid was giving her over the shaved heads and waterfall hairdos that bobbled at the bar; Fionnuala knew solicitation in pubs was frowned upon if it was not fresh meats or vegetables.

"Och, would ye shove yer eyes back into yer skull," she barked. "I'm on the search for me daughter, just. Silly bitch lifted twenty pounds from me handbag and made her way down the town to fill her gullet, so she did."

She rolled Keanu out of the pub and braced herself in the silence of the cold night air. She adjusted the sagging satchel on her scrawny shoulder and looked around for the bouncer. Perhaps she could tempt him. But the bouncer had disappeared, and before her stood the three hooligans from the toilets, menace glinting in their eyes. Fionnuala snorted derisively at the sharpened screwdriver aimed at her eyeball.

"Have youse no idea who I am?" she asked. "Who me brothers are?"

Of course they did; it was Derry City.

"Give us that absinthe, ye filthy minger!" one growled.

"Och, catch yerselves on," Fionnuala said. "I'll set me brothers onto youse, the few brothers of mines who're not already locked up for grievous bodily harm in Magilligan Prison. They'll give youse a clattering so youse'll be whistling outta yer arseholes."

As they wailed with laughter, Fionnuala's slow-churning brain cells couldn't realize a corner in her life was being turned: after decades of threatening and menacing and clawing and slapping those against her all her life, the passage of time was now gleefully turning against her and casting her in the new role of victim.

"Ye haggard old crone!" seethed one with a spiteful cackle.

And then they pounced.

CHAPTER 50

Dymphna fought the urge to spew as she took another gulp. Her fingernails scrabbled over her flesh, the skin which encased her now seeming alien and bizarre. She felt more unclean than she usually did. She couldn't look Bridie in the eye, which was fine by Bridie, as the drink had taken affect and she was now rocking back and forth in a corner, wondering what people were.

"Och, fuck this for a game of soldiers," Dymphna snorted. She tore out the page of the newspaper and slipped it into her pocket. "Where's that spud peeler?" she roared, and reached for the matches.

They guzzled down.

"Where the bleeding feck have me fingers gone?" Dymphna shrieked even as she stared straight at them.

"I can feel the madness seeping into me brain!" Bridie screamed, gulping down her fifth glass. "The poison's fairly shooting through all me veins!"

"I'm outta me skull with insanity!" Dymphna whimpered, fingernails clawing at her scalp. "Me brains feel like they're oozing outta me ears."

Around their deranged minds and staggering bodies, the sitting room was a chaos of flung sugar cubes, half-smoked cigarettes, rolling empty absinthe bottles. They raced around the room clutching flaming glasses, bumping into the china cabinet, the fireplace, the television shoved to the side. Anything not rooted down by extreme weight due to the pull of gravity had been overturned. The pop hits blaring from the radio had long ago not made any sense to their minds. Deep inside their eardrums rang banging and thrashing and peculiar noises no sane human had ever heard before.

"Arggh!" Dymphna wailed, slurping down and clutching at her eyeballs. "Me eyes kyanny take it no longer!"

"What are ye seeing? What are ye seeing?" Bridie begged to know. "Can ye see the wee green Kylie Minogue fairy?"

Dymphna clutched Bridie for support, fearing for her own sanity.

"Johnny Cash, more like!" Dymphna wailed. "I'm surrounded by a burning ring of fire!"

"These flimmin hallucinations!" Bridie agreed. "They're bleeding desperate. All of them feel so real!"

"Och, me eyes are scalded!" Dymphna wailed.

"Aye, mines and all!"

"We be's entering the gates of Hell," Dymphna cried. "Flames! Burning flames, I'm seeing! All around me!"

She wiped her feverish brow and fanned herself with a hand.

"Wooh!" she gasped. "I'm feeling them flames as if the delusions was real and all! I'm soaked! The sweat be's fairly lashing down me body! Wooooh!"

"A-aye, me and all. And it's making me parched!"

Bridie took another swig, then shuddered as a sudden jolt of cold clarity electrocuted her brain. She looked around her, as if seeing their whereabouts for the first time.

"Virgin Mary Mother of God! The carpeting's on fire!"

"And the drapes!"

"Let's clear the feck outta here!"

They snapped up their handbags and raced out the door, shrieking with laughter.

"Shall we make wer way down the pub?" Bridie slurred.

"Aye, surely!" Dymphna slurred, staggering across the pavement and thinking she heard fire engine sirens, or maybe they were only in her brain.

CHAPTER 51

"Naw, naw!" Fionnuala wailed.

She kicked at their shins with Dymphna's spiked heels. Fionnuala was a hard-faced cunt, but no match for three teen soccer stars. She clutched her satchel to her chest, screaming and punching and clawing at skulls with no hair to pull.

"Help me! Help me!" she wailed to a group of kids scoffing down from Kebabalicious containers, but they just laughed through their curry chips and staggered around the corner.

"Fecking useless beings!" Fionnuala called out. "Help! Police! The Filth!"

Even as the words exited her mouth, she wished she could retract them. Begging the despised police for help? What would her mother think of her, sinking so low? A hardened Heggarty girl like her!

Fionnuala was using every weapon at her disposal: her claws, her heels, her acid tongue, but they were no match for their wiry, hard limbs, their agility, their *youth*. With one thrust to the breastplate, she was sent spinning to the cobblestones. They wrenched the satchel from her knuckles, and she gasped for air and lunged for a sneaker, noticing it was one of those expensive Yank ones. Rage overtook her, and she yelled abuse into the darkness at their receding backs.

"Hard men, youse thinks youse be's? Fecking arse-bandit cowardly bastards!"

"Effin Christ!" Padraig roared, racing from the shadows to his mother.

"After themmuns, wane!" Fionnuala screamed, pointing frantically around the corner. "They've nicked the absinthe! And me bag! Me Celine Dion bag!"

He was off in hot pursuit, and Fionnuala sobbed on the cobblestones, running jittery fingers over the scratch on her forehead and the bruise forming on her elbow. A trip to the emergency room was out of the question; the coppers would have to be called. Padraig came back a few moments later, panting, his lenses fogged.

"Them bastards is gone," he said. "Like into thin air. Couldn't find hide nor hair of em."

"I'm not a spastic. No need to tell me three times, like. Help me up, lad."

Padraig did his best, his little hands grappling as much of his mother's mass as they could, but there was so much of it. Finally, Fionnuala leaned upright against the wall and looked down at her son.

"What the bleeding feck are ye doing trawling the city center at this hour?" she seethed, smacking him around the head. His glasses popped off his nose and clattered to the cobblestones.

Fionnuala exploded with tears as she looked down at his hand massaging his reddening cheek and what she saw in his eyes; now they were bare she could see the hurt.

"I'm wile sorry, son, dear God in Heaven forgive me," she whimpered, stooping and sobbing into his negligible shoulder. "Themmuns took all the absinthe, but, and me designer bag and all."

"Ye mean yer *My Hate Will Go On* bag?"

"Heart, wee boy, *heart!* All I be's wanting be's the funds for to take us all to an exciting new land as a family, like other families does, and get some bills paid but now, *now…!* I haven't a clue how we're meant to get the money together."

Padraig looked around uncomfortably, hoping none of his mates would happen by.

"Don't ye worry, Mammy," he said, patting her mousy flip. "I've a load of gear in me room we can sell down the market. X-boxes and Wiis and the like. Wile dear, all them be's. We should be raking in the cash, and then we can afford the trip to see Moira after all."

Fionnuala was recharging her palm to slap him for fencing stolen goods—some pornographic ones at that, apparently!—and for mentioning the filthy beanflicker's name, but she didn't want to keep apologizing to the Lord. And Padraig had tried to help her, after all.

"Och, ye're a wee dote, so ye are," she said, fondling his locks, the color of which she hated so much. *I've to take a bar of soap to the little minger's scalp and scrub the filth offa it the moment we get to the Moorside,* she thought as he led her over the cobbles, *me fingers be's slick with grease at just one touch. If he's given me the lice, I'll throttle his scrawny neck! Wile civil, but, of the wee freak to sell the gear he lifted to help out the family, and to tell me about Paddy and his fancy woman and all. Where the feck, but, am I expected to find another My Heart Will Go On tote?*

Fionnuala hurried back ten minutes later to collect Keanu.

CHAPTER 52

"Happiness hit her like a bullet in the ba-a-a-a-ack…!"

MacAfee's boot tapped amongst the empty crisp packets to the Florence and the Machine song on the radio. Just as his drink-addled brain was surprised good music had been produced after 1982, the door to the perfectly-intact, non-burning 5 Murphy flew open. Pence-A-Day and Kebabalicious jettisoned out with handbags oscillating and hair unhinged, the lipstick on them like Heath Ledger's Joker. They ejected themselves through the gate and, clutching each other for support, maneuvered their heels around the corner towards the city center. Their shrieks of laughter lanced the nighttime drizzle.

MacAfee smacked Scudder to life.

"Game's on, hi."

Scudder jerked to a semblance of consciousness on the seat, sputtering and unaware of his surroundings.

"Och? Eh?"

"Rouse yerself! Them wee girls has finally cleared out!"

Scudder plunged a cigarette in his mouth, and his hands scrabbled across his denim for a light. MacAfee was already out the door, ski-mask on his face. Scudder threw his on as well, prised himself out of the van and joined his comrade, hunched and leaping across the concrete like an orangutan.

They crept through the weeds of the garden, Scudder struggling to quell the fish-beer-chips-nicotine nausea in his stomach. The girls had left the door open, so there was no need for broken glass. They entered the shambles of a house, barely registering the stench of female sweat, spent booze, burnt sugar or delinquent housekeeping.

"Ye search down the stairs, I'll search up the stairs," MacAfee said.

"Right ye are."

Scudder skipped over what he suspected was a pile of sick on the carpet and scanned the overturned furniture of the sitting room. No joy. He made his way to the spartan kitchen. He gripped the door frame as his head suddenly spun. Was it the alcohol or the sight of the way they lived? He couldn't imagine dining in such filth.

He realized through the fug of his mind he was still chomping the unlit cigarette, and went to the stove to light up. He pushed aside the dirty pots and rags, some sopping with the stench of licorice and liquor, to locate a burner. As he turned the knob and leaned in to the gas flame, turning so his face wouldn't erupt into flames, he spied through the eyeholes of his ski-mask a case of canned vegetables in what he guessed was their 'garbage corner.'

"MacAfee!" he called, making as much of a bee-line as his drunken feet would allow.

He pawed through the cans, but the labels were in English. He had seen the cans with the Semtex, and they had godless foreign letters which real people had no use for.

Perplexed, he turned and—

—shrieked like a schoolgirl.

"What the bleeding feck—?" MacAfee roared from the door. "The cooker's in flames!"

Scudder whimpered at the fire spitting across the top of the stove, the plumes of smoke pouring from the absinthe-soaked rags and the oven.

"Gas fire—water or no?" MacAfee wailed, running back and forth to the sink in indecision and sweat.

They screamed as the fire leaped from the oven and attacked the grill above, devoured the grease-spattered wallpaper behind and lunged for the ratty curtains above the sink. The curtains dissolved in sputters and flames as the oven door burst open and spewed fire onto the linoleum, slick with spilled absinthe. Amidst the bubbling of plastic and popping of wood, fiery trails raced through the kitchen and nipped at their toes, then bit at their kicking, stomping boots. The fire gobbled up the hallway carpet.

"Let's clear the feck outta here!" MacAfee wailed.

Yelping as his fingers clawed the scalding backdoor knob, MacAfee spilled into the back garden, Scudder on his rear. Behind them, 5 Murphy Crescent danced with flames.

Scudder turned to MacAfee as they tore through the sopping bedsheets on the clothing line and trampled through the hedges into the neighboring garden.

"I guess we'll have to use that new shipment of Semtex I picked up from the market yesterday," he said.

MacAfee stared, the flames of the house sparkling in his eyes of disbelief.

"Ye mean ye picked up more explosives and didn't tell me?"

"Aye, they was delivered in a case of pregnancy tests from Albania."

"Why the bloody feck did we just risk life and limb to— Ye eejit! Ye flimmin eejit!"

Scudder cowered as MacAfee's fists rained down upon the dullness of his skull.

Four and a half hours later, Dymphna and Bridie clomped through the dusk yelling out the chorus of Lady Gaga's "Bad Romance." Bridie wore one shoe and the inside of Dymphna's handbag was sopping with sick, someone's or her own she'd never recall.

"Ak, I luv ye, Bdie, ye're de bess maten th world, so y'r, an donche mind wha tht mingin geebag in de club loos ws sayin boutye. In…intnsv care, she's now, so…"

"Dmna, but…Dmna, luk a th state o yer hous!"

Bridie's finger poked through the air as if it were treacle. Her boozy eyes ballooned as much as they could to comprehend what they were seeing.

"Hw're we ment t sleep ther?"

Her mouth weeped with paralytic laughter.

"Hly Mary, muther o God!" Dymphna gasped, stunned before the charred frame of the house. "Dd we brn th hous dwn? Ws tht not a hllucnation, bt?"

"Yr mammy'llbe ragin!"

"Ak," Dymphna said with a shrug. "A wee xtra hous, soit ws. W've nother right round de cornr."

They held each other up from falling down from the force of their laughter as they staggered around the hedges to the remaining Flood family home.

"Rah-rah-ah-ah-ah-ah! Roma-roma-mamaa!"

CHAPTER 53

Fionnuala, Paddy, Dymphna, Padraig, Siofra, Seamus and Maureen trudged around the corner toward the stench of carbon, the water from the fire hoses, and the rocks the children had thrown at the fire engine. Standing before the shell of the Flood family home, Maureen made the sign of the cross and muttered an expletive-laden prayer to the Virgin Mary. Paddy bit his knuckles, and a strange whimper escaped his throat. It caused them all alarm.

"It must've been them gas pipes, Daddy," Dymphna offered. "Or some leak from the cooker in the scullery."

They inspected her with their eyes.

Fionnuala took charge and chased away the pre-pubescent scavengers who were picking over the remains of 5 Murphy, and then the family marched through the smoldering threshold to do just that themselves. They poked their heads into the sitting room. The only thing not burnt was the fireplace.

"Mammy, everything's burnt!" Seamus said, lower lip trembling.

"Ta for stating the obvious, ye daft git," Fionnuala snapped.

"Me clothes! Me toys!" Siofra whimpered, eyes brimming with tears.

"I've to save them electronics of mines!" Padraig said, disappearing into the sooty gloom up what was left of the stairs.

"Aye, me and all!" Fionnuala agreed, following him with a speed that made the others marvel.

The damage doesn't be too bad up here, sure, Fionnuala thought to herself. The fire had petered out as it reached the second floor, and as Fionnuala squelched up the fire-ravaged stairs carpet, she could make out more and more primroses in the wallpaper, until at the landing it seemed as new as it had fifteen years earlier. Siofra ran into her room, Dymphna to hers, and Maureen and her cane were on the second step but making progress.

"Them wanes from the neighborhood has nicked all me gear," Padraig seethed, inspecting the dust bunnies and much worse under his bed.

"Och, for the love of—!" Fionnuala despaired, Malta receding and disconnection notices looming.

They reconvened in the hallway, Dymphna holding a brown rattle that used to be orange, Siofra her Barbie that hadn't had a head in months, but now was headless *and* burnt. Maureen clutched her heaving chest and sobbed into the charred pant leg of the purple velour track suit she saved for special family outings and Holy Days.

"All me clothing!" Maureen sobbed. "Fit for the bin. What am I to wear now?"

In in their misery, the others couldn't help but stare at the woman; they were all sick to the back teeth of the green tracksuit that left Maureen's body only for the half-hour of her thrice-weekly bath.

"M-mammy, ye never change them clothes of yers, but," Fionnuala pointed out.

"That's as may be," Maureen sniped, her arms suddenly a fortress around the offending green item in which she was clad. "It's nice to have the option, but. And now that's been ripped from me."

"Thank the Virgin Mary I took me gear round yers for to be washed," Dymphna said, then bit her fist as they all glared.

Fionnuala, sick of their misery, hurried into each of the bedrooms, tore open the drawers of the wardrobes and made a quick inventory. The clothing inside all was crusty with sooty bits, smoke-damaged or waterlogged, or a bit of all three. She stepped back onto the landing, holding up the best clothing from each person.

"Grand and lovely, they'll be, after a spin in the washing machine and some love."

"I kyanny wear that minging gear," Padraig said. "A laughing stock, I'll be. Even more so than now."

"Och, we can get werselves down to Oxfam. The charity shop has loads of lovely—"

"Naw, Mammy, *naw!*" Siofra screamed, tears of frustration pouring down her sooty face. "Not clothing from Oxfam!"

"Watch yerself, wane," Fionnuala said, hand hovering to strike.

"It's not fair, but, Mammy!" Siofra sobbed with a stamp of the foot. "Why hasn't all yer gear and belongings gone up in flames? Why was we shunted to this house with no telly or radio while you and me daddy lived with all them things all others has."

Fionnuala pinched her lips.

"Ye mind the squeals of joy from youse wanes when we suggested youse move around the corner here? Like Christmas morn round Richard Branson's, so it was."

"That was before ye sold all the things what makes a house livable in, but," Padraig said. "We've not even toothbrushes that works now, Mammy."

Fionnuala was in shock.

"Catch yerself on, wane! When have youse ever gladly brushed yer teeth?"

Siofra touched her mouth; it suddenly seemed overflowing with filthy teeth.

"I want a non-burnt toothbrush now!" Siofra sobbed. *"Now!"*

"Dear God in Heaven give me strength," Fionnuala muttered. "New toothbrushes be's last on me list of necessities at the moment."

They trudged down to the remains of the kitchen. Paddy sat atop something crusty and black (he wasn't quite sure what it had been), and Seamus whimpered at his side. Seamus had located his shapeless thing, and it was now a singed shapeless thing.

"This was me childhood home," Paddy said in a voice that cracked. "All the days spent, the nights spent with me mammy and daddy and brothers and sisters. All the craic we had, the…"

He openly wept. His family didn't know where to look. They had been taught to treat the sight of man crying with contempt. Fionnuala hurried over to his side to place a restraining hand on his shoulder, while Dymphna felt the guilt gnaw at her.

"I see them tins have gone unscathed," Maureen noted, nodding to the corner where the fridge used to be.

"Och, wise up, ye daft cunt, ye, Paddy," Fionnuala said softly. "We've got through worse, sure. Ye mind the time in the 80's when there was a riot on wer street and a rubber bullet shattered the front bay window, and tear gas poured into wer home and the wanes was screaming outta them?"

"This be's a time of peace, but. What the feck do ye think Ursula's going to make of all this?"

Fionnuala's fingers dug into his shoulder blade. The sound of the name was like fingernails scraping a chalkboard, chewing tinfoil and the whirr of a dentist's drill combined.

"She give it us," Paddy continued, the tears rolling down his face. "Outta the kindness of her heart. And didn't ye say she be's on her way here for a visit soon? What she's to make of this, I kyanny imagine."

Fionnuala set her lips. It must be that Polish bitch giving her husband a heart, she thought.

By the innards of the exploded stove, Dymphna inched her hand into the pocket of her jeans and felt the folded newsprint still. She had forgotten about the article, but when she had spied an absinthe bottle during their search, it had all flooded back. That was something she hadn't hallucinated.

She saw her mother's hand on her father's back, the look of tenderness trying to force itself on Fionnuala's face, and Dymphna felt a rage swell in her. Her mother had shagged with a hated British soldier, and her father was none the wiser. He didn't even have a clue that his second eldest daughter wasn't his! She was furious at her mother, who had a secret worse than burning down the family house on her conscience. It took every ounce of restraint—and she didn't possess restraint as a natural personality characteristic, so it was very, very difficult—to stop herself from blurting out the sordid, sinful secret then and there in the soot.

"Och, well, at least there's sure to be the insurance money," Paddy said with a sigh.

"If them insurance gits find no sign of foul play, that is!" Maureen harrumphed.

"The investigation will take care of that," Paddy said.

"Investigation?" Dymphna froze. She thought the police only did one of those when somebody was murdered.

"Aye, signs of arson, they'll be looking for," Maureen said.

"It was the gas pipes, I tell youse," Dymphna insisted as unease filled her. "I smelled a terrible whiff of gas the past few nights."

"Would ye for the love of God quit chuntering on about flimmin gas pipes, wane?" Maureen roared. "This house stood for decades, and the moment ye stepped foot in it, it burned to the ground. I find that highly suspect."

Paddy's head whipped up.

"If I find out," Paddy seethed, "that ye were lollygagging about with lit fags dangling from yer mouth…"

Fionnuala eyes glistened with suspicion.

"Or making chips in the chip pan fryer when ye was gee-eyed with drink!"

"Where did ye say ye was last night?"

"At Bridie's!" Dymphna wailed. They had formed a semi-circle around her. "It was a leak in the gas, I tell youse!"

Every creak of the wounded house could be heard as six pairs of eyes scrutinized her.

"Let's shift this lot, shall we?" Paddy finally said, resigned.

"And scoop up all them leftover cans," Fionnuala said. "We can dust them off and sell them still. Every penny counts, ye know."

CHAPTER 54

Dymphna kept scrutinizing the picture of the slag on the soldier's knee until the dots of the pixels drove her mental. Why was there a black bar covering her face? Dymphna had tried to remove it time and again through scratching, and the page was now tattered mulch in her desperate fingers. She peered through the rain attacking the bus window and pressed the button. After almost a year spent at the Riddells on the Waterside, she still felt uncomfortable, an alien, in the mostly Protestant neighborhood, but she had a mission to perform. She exited the bus and searched the numbers of the well-kept houses of Connolly Lane for 23.

Dymphna knew that if she could see the original photograph, a glance would let her know if the scarlet Green woman with the Orange fancy man was indeed her mother. The byline under the picture read Photo By William Chesterton, and the day before she realized one of Zoë's bridge partners was Poppy Chesterton. Poppy had gone on and on one afternoon between rubbers and sips of Earl Grey (Dymphna had been hovering outside the door, wondering what Protestants talked about when they thought no Catholics were around) about her uncle William, who was a photographer for the Northern Ireland division of the *Guardian*. Dymphna had looked for his address in the White Pages (the Floods did still use them) and found it was 23 Connolly Lane. Dymphna hoped he was the right William Chesterton, and that he kept all his old photographs.

The rain battered her face as she walked up the lane to the front door and knocked frantically on it. A woman in an Yves St. Laurent bathrobe and a mudpack answered.

"It's yer fella I'm after," Dymphna stated.

Mrs. Chesterton's hand flew to her neck in fear.

"I've a photo here he took yonks ago that I need to discuss with him, like."

Dymphna held the mulch to the woman's face.

"My husband's not here. He's away off to the Amazon for a story, freelance. He'll be gone a fortnight."

She tried to slam the door, but Dymphna's foot was already inside. As the chain lock flew time and again at Mrs. Chesterton's mudpack, she stared further at Dymphna's face. Her eyes squinted with recognition. The door was still.

"You're that horrid little creature from the meat and cheese counter of the Top-Yer-Trolley."

Dymphna gave a halting nod. Long and winding was the list of disgruntled customers she had abused; that had been one of many reasons she had been fired.

"You short-changed me on half a kilo of Brin d'Amor last year."

"Aye, and what of it? Let me in, would ye, woman! I'm catching me death out here in the pelting rain!"

She burst into tears on the doorstep.

"I need to know if I'm the love child of me mammy and a paratrooper," Dymphna sobbed.

A tenderness and thirst for hot gossip crinkled the mudpack, and Mrs. Chesterton bid Dymphna enter. Over two cups of tea and a biscuit, the newspaper photo displayed on the coffee table, Dymphna told her the story. Mrs. Chesterton marveled at it all.

"You people seem to lead such exciting lives! I don't know what to tell you, however, dear. William moved all his old negatives and prints to our lockup. We needed the space, you see, as our first grandchild is set to arrive in eight months, and we turned his office into a nursery for when our daughter Gwyneth and her husband Trevor visit with their young one."

This evidence of planned parenthood gave Dymphna a wistful glimpse into a life she would never have, the babies popping unannounced out of her womb as they were. She stirred her tea sadly. Then a thought hit her.

"Yer lockup? That wouldn't be the Pence-A-Day, would it?"

Mrs. Chesterton seemed surprised that someone from the Moorside would know of its existence.

"Why, yes!" she exclaimed. "A member of the family is friends with the owner. But how...?"

"I used to work there. Not a word to her, mind, but Zoë Riddell be's me soon-to-be mother-in-law, and I know yer Poppy plays bridge with her every Thursday, like."

Mrs. Chesterton squealed in delight and grappled Dymphna's startled hand with brute strength.

"Why didn't you say so from the beginning, dear? It's *so* refreshing to hear of a mixed-denominational couple. Surely this is the Peace Process at work, a peek into the future of Ireland. A refreshing change from *this* sensationalist tat." She indicated the newspaper article with a lip curled with distaste. "'Green lace and Orange camouflage,' indeed! My William should be ashamed of himself for taking part in such nonsense. Pouring fuel on the fire. Still, it's a time long gone now, I suppose."

Mrs. Chesterton considered for a moment, while the usually dormant neurons of Dymphna's brain fired. She still had that copy of the Pence-A-Day office key, and, now that she thought of it, she remembered from the accounts that the name on Unit 13B was Chesterton. It was right beside Unit 12B, which she had rented out to the two layabouts who had saved her from Mr. Tomlinson's diseases, and caused Rory and her such estrangement. And Zoë had told her that, in case of an emergency in the storage units of row B—strange smells or noises or such—there was a secret crawlspace that could be entered through the ceiling of the men's room of the office to gain access into the units without cutting the lock. Also, as ex-office manager, Dymphna knew Pence-A-Day was closed for lunch from 1 to 2 PM, and whoever had taken over her position probably had the same schedule. She tried to look down at her watch, but her hand was still being choked under Mrs. Chesterton's squelching fingers.

"You know, dear," Mrs. Chesterton said. "Having a Protestant father doesn't make you the Frankenstein monster it might have decades ago. Today, it's all about multiculturalism and the bridging of the communities. Isn't there that Fingers Across the Foyle talent show going on in a few days? Whoever came up with such a delightful idea?! I'll be there myself, actually, cheering on the city to a brighter future. I wish I could help you with your current plight. Please feel free to contact my husband when he returns home, you're quite welcome to, but I really am of the mind that being a child of two religions is a blessing, not a disgrace."

Dymphna pried her fingers free.

"I think I've taken up enough of yer time," she said. "Ye've been wile civil, and for that I thank ye. I've to be on me way now, but. Cheerio, now."

The moment she was out the door, Dymphna saw it was 11:20. Pence-A-Day was a fifteen minute walk away. She looked up at ricocheting raindrops and thanked the Lord in His heavenly home. Perhaps He was finally smiling down on her for the week she had spent singing in St. Molaug's choir as a schoolgirl. She hurried off through the rain.

Dymphna grabbed the flashlight, locked the door to the office and ran to the gent's lavatory. She climbed the toilet tank and stared up, gnawing on her lower lip. The suspended ceiling was a t-grid of rectangular gypsum board panels held in place by beams of light steel.

She reached up and pushed the panel above the toilet tank to the side. Grasping the top of the stall for support, she hauled herself up and poked her head into the darkness beyond. She flicked on the flashlight and shone it into the space. Electrical wires, various odd piping and ductwork revealed itself through the cobwebs and dust. Dymphna glanced at her watch. In forty-five minutes the manager would be back. She had to work fast.

Grunting, she hauled herself into the space, her bloated stomach straining to pass the beam of steel. Each panel was two feet long, and Dymphna knew she would have to clear ten panels at least before reaching Unit 13B. She tenderly pressed against the beams, testing their strength and cursing herself for carrying the extra weight of a child, as the beams seemed flimsy. The drop space between the ceiling tiles and the real ceiling was only two feet tall, so she would have to crawl.

Balancing her elbows and knees on the beams, Dymphna propelled her body further into the darkness. She thrust aside the wires and breathed in the dust, her spasm of sneezes sending spiders and ants and God only knew what other types of insects scurrying. Beads of sweat blinded her as she pushed forward. She felt the beams straining under her. She shoved herself the length of one panel, three, seven, ten…

And froze at the sound of half the panel ripping under her legs.

And shrieked as it gave way under her, a chunk clattering to the floor below. Her legs fell into space. She heaved her chest atop the panel, cursing the weight of her breasts for once in her life, and her fingers scrabbled towards the side support, her legs flailing wildly in the air. She clung at the pole, her knuckles white, her palms aching. Her overgrown abdomen swung below the edge of the panel. Her hands scrabbled the length of the pole towards the left. If she could get a hold of that, she could haul herself back up to the next panel. Sweat trickled down her brow and she gnawed on her lower lip. She inched her fingers across the pole, aware of the gaping darkness of the storage unit below, a ten foot plunge into the unknown.

This new panel creaked and moaned as she inched atop it, shoving her stomach and the baby inside onto the panel and heaving her hips over. The panel creaked and moaned under the weight. She thrust her right leg through the air, her knee latching onto the vertical surface. Her lower leg slipped to safety. Her right leg shot up, and the panel gave way. Dymphna screamed as she plummeted to the floor of Unit 12B, thudding atop the mass of MacAfee and Scudder's weapons of destruction.

CHAPTER 55

Fionnuala crept up to the sitting room door and propped her ear against it. She routinely performed these checks on her children to see if they were talking shite about her, but hadn't been able to since their exile in 5 Murphy.

Now the children were back, and Heaven help them if she overheard whining about toothbrushes. For once, though, their mother, her bad temper and beatings seemed not to be the topic of conversation. Siofra was babbling on, to Padraig, Fionnuala guessed:

"Then ye take these wee circles of paper and glue them together, and ye've got yer daisy. Och, it's wile civil of ye to help me out, as I've two hundred more to make for the Happiness Boat. Friday be's only a few days away ye know. And, Padraig, ye understand what ye're meant to do on the day? Ye want me to go through it again? I'm wile happy them tins survived the fire, as…"

Fionnuala nodded righteously and was about to head off to do a load of laundry when Siofra wailed in fascinated horror behind the door.

"Eewww! What in God's green earth be's that? It's wile disgusting, so it is!"

"Lookit the bones stickin out!" Padraig gasped. "Effin magic!"

Fionnuala heard Seamus' muffled sobs, so she barged into the sitting room to investigate. Siofra and Padraig jumped, pipe cleaners in their hands, guilt in their eyes.

Forgotten were the paper flowers on the floor; they were transfixed before the television screen. Seamus cowered behind the couch, tears pouring down his face. The gore erupting from the screen hurt even Fionnuala's hardened eyes.

"What the flimmin feck—!" Fionnuala gasped, hand to her chest.

Them flimmin eejit Hollywood film people! she seethed, running to the VCR to wrench out the tape before any more of her children's innocence was swiped from them. It had happened many times during family trips to the movie theater in the past, Fionnuala hiding her eyes, horrified of the filth spewing from the projector, while around her the pre-teen audience squealed with glee. Her children would leave the cinema years older, and Fionnuala wouldn't eat for a day.

"Where did youse get that video from?" she demanded. "Down the market, I've no doubt, them eejits peddling X-rated slasher films from Japan to wanes…"

"Naw, Mammy!" Siofra protested. "We found it between the cushions of the settee."

Fionnuala didn't need to ask what her daughter had been doing poking around there; that was where the loose change fell. Siofra held up the case, and Fionnuala's face burned pink with mortification. It was *Ab Fab Abs and Boulder Buns*.

Fionnuala's eyes flickered from the case back to the TV screen. It looked like a movie in a *Blair Witch Project* vein, all shaking hand-held camera and shoestring production values, some independent piece of filth celebrating violence, viscera and offal and bucketloads of blood spilling and spattering out of human beings.

"What *is* that?" she screamed, dreading the answer. "A flimmin operating table?"

"Och, catch yerself on, Mammy," Padraig said with a lick of the lips. "I saw worse on the telly last night, sure."

The camera jerkily panned around the stark whiteness of the room, and Fionnuala's slow-trundling brain cells came closer to understanding what her eyes were witnessing. Those eyes bulged with equal parts repulsion and awe. She wished she could erase the images burned in her retinas forever, yet felt her chest heaving with joy.

"Can it be…is it…it kyanny be…"

It was.

"I'm *sickened!* Pure revolted!"

She raced to the broken karaoke machine in the corner and heaved the contents of her stomach on top of it. Seamus' wails grew more fervent. Siofra and Padraig were mortified at their mother's weakness.

"Virgin Mary Mother of God!" Fionnuala gasped, torn between nausea, outrage, horror and excitement. "Do youse wanes have any clue what this be's?"

"Aye, a video nasty," Siofra said, nodding sagely.

"Naw…naw…it's…"

Fionnuala wiped the sick from her lips and ripped the video cassette from the VCR. She held it to her breast with epileptic fingers. Her mind raced, desperately trying to make sense of what she was clutching. How did it exist? *Why* did it exist? It was similar to homosexuals, Fionnuala thought. They existed, didn't they, and they made no sense either. More troubling, what had the video been doing in old Mrs. Ming's attic? No matter; Fionnuala, pound signs flashing, knew she was holding the holy grail of the media industry the world over.

"We're set for life, wanes," she squealed. "We're to be flying to Malta first class!"

But Padraig had already popped another video into the machine, and they were goggling the opening credits of *Carrie*. Siofra reached for a pipe cleaner.

CHAPTER 56

"Merciful Jesus of Nazareth," Dymphna moaned.

Small cylinder-type things with pointy bits dug into her back, and she struggled to remove herself from them. Pain shot through her right ankle, and she squealed. She had already experienced childbirth, so she had felt worse, but still tears stung her eyes. She shuffled her body with little crab-like motions of the hands across the floor, until her fingers found her handbag and the flashlight. The beam cut through the darkness, and Dymphna gasped, shocked, at what surrounded her. The barrels and handles of assault rifles poked out of crates, grenades lay on the concrete. Dymphna realized she had been rolling around on rounds of ammunition. Handbag slung over her shoulder, she slithered through the twirling bullets towards the door, yelping in pain.

After five pain-filled attempts to place her right foot on the floor and stand, she finally knew her right ankle must be broken, and the laws of biology would not allow her to perform that act. She placed her left foot on the ground, grabbed a crate of handguns and pulled her body upright. She hobbled to the door and tried the handle, but of course it was padlocked from outside.

She whimpered as she dug through her handbag and located her cellphone. She punched Bridie's number.

"Och, Dymphna, ye wouldn't believe the day I've been having here at the Kebab—"

"Bridie, Bridie! Listen to me!" Dymphna squealed.

"Have ye found the negatives?"

"Feck the negatives. I've fallen through the ceiling and landed in a lockup two yobs be's using to hide their weapons," she wailed into the phone. "Surrounded by rifles and grenades and God alone knows what, so I am. Terrorists, themmuns must be. I've broken me ankle and all, and kyanny walk like others can. Hopping around like a right eejit, I've been, and the pain be's wile terrible. And I'm afeared the door's gonny open any second and it'll be them terrorist simpletons, and I'll get meself a bullet in the skull."

"Och, decommissioned in 1997, the IRA was," Bridie said, infuriating Dymphna with her knowledge. "Themmuns turned their guns in to the British government donkey's years ago, sure, and now be's respectable members of society with seats in Parliament and all."

"Ye jumped up cow, quit yer babbling on and get me the feck outta here! It must be some new terrorist group I've discovered."

"Now ye mention it, I do mind reading something in the paper online about some suspicions the Filth has about a new—"

"Come you now and free me!"

"Call the Filth."

"Catch yerself on!"

There was a pause, and surely Bridie realized her suggestion was ludicrous; was she all knowledge and no common sense?

"Call an ambulance, sure."

"I could've done that meself, ye headbin! No one kyanny know where I've been. Themmuns'll know I've discovered their secret with hospital reports and the like if an ambulance picks me up here. Marked, me entire family'll be. Tarred and feathered, kneecapped, all of us are sure to be. Ye've got to sneak me outta here, and the manager of the lockups'll be back from his break in..." She looked at her watch. "Half an hour."

"Ye kyanny walk, sure. How in the name of the heavenly Father do ye expect me—"

"Nick a trolley from the Top-Yer-Trolley car park Ye can transport me that way and park me somewhere far away, then call the ambulance. Och, the pain! The pain!"

"I've only another fifteen minutes left to me break. I kyanny get the sack."

"Please, Bridie," Dymphna said, tears rolling down her cheeks, pleading in her trembling voice. "Tell that manager git ye've a family emergency!"

"Och—!"

"Take a taxi and get off two blocks from the lockups so's the driver doesn't be any the wiser."

"A taxi? Are ye mad? The price of them the day! And how am I meant to board a taxi with a trolley?"

"Feck the taxi, then. Ye've to save me life, Bridie. Get an extension on yer break."

"For the love of God!" Bridie muttered down the line. She heaved a sigh. "The things I do for ye, Dymphna Flood! Right ye are, then. See ye in ten minutes. Cheerio."

She hung up, and Dymphna's tears of pain and anguish sprinkled the bullets and grenades around her as she waited for rescue.

CHAPTER 57

In the incident room of the Derry division of the Police Service of Northern Ireland, Inspector McLaughlin gave a rundown of the sad crimes that had recently surfaced. The troops sat, notebooks at the ready, scribbling down the details of the four pensioners attacked with rocks; the two young males who set fire to the ladies' toilets of the Craiglooner; the boy whose lower lip was bitten by a homeless dog when he tried to pet it; the elderly woman whose handbag was snatched as she exited the parish hall after making a donation to the church's weekly bingo draw; the man whose lung was punctured by a screwdriver while he was withdrawing money from an ATM; the five cases of whiskey stolen from an off-license; the receptionist at Altnagelvin Hospital threatened at knife-point for an empty prescription pad; the possibly intoxicated male singing loudly inside a vehicle in the Quayside Shopping Center parking lot, then yelling, using profane language and exposing himself at passersby.

McLaughlin took a deep breath as he came to the finale, glancing down at a fist-full of documents.

"And then there be's this, this...*woman!*" he spat, pointing to a blown-up artist's rendering of the unknown suspect: horsey head, overbite and bleached ponytails. "We've recently discovered yer woman probably be's responsible for a smorgasbord of crimes alarming in range and frequency. As youse can see, she be's distinctive physically, and, indeed, it was wer sketch artist down the station here that brought her to me attention; he seemed to be sketching out the same woman time and again. Most disturbing in her long list of suspected crimes be's the administering of barbiturates while posing as an OsteoCare volunteer to pensioners in Creggan Heights, a Mrs. Ming and Mrs. Gee, to what ultimate purpose or for what motive we be's still unaware. Mrs. Gee suffered an adverse reaction, and yer woman up on the board there is now wanted for attempted manslaughter. Hours, we've spent, interrogating Mrs. Gee, but she still claims she hasn't a clue who the woman be's. Youse is all aware of the culture of silence in this town what makes wer job so difficult. A woman matching the same description also be's wanted for inciting violence outside the Our Lady of Perpetual Sorrow primary school. Yer woman was also sighted by an undercover agent in the Craiglooner Pub, trying to solicit illegal vintage absinthe; to no success, but. She *was* attacked by a group of thugs outside the pub and the contraband stolen from her, but, needless to say, she did not file a complaint."

"Me neck be's exhausted from the rate me head be's spinning at!" gasped one younger copper, clutching his aching skull.

But further back in the incident room, a seasoned pro—one of the few Catholic coppers—nudged another, also a Catholic, and led him just out the room to the tea, coffee and oxtail soup machine that had been out of order for months. Lynch whispered to Briggs:

"I near shite meself when I looked up and saw that sketch of Fionnuala Flood from the Moorside on the board."

"Aye, me and all," Briggs said.

"Yer man, but," Lynch whispered on with a knowing nod toward Inspector McLaughlin (now ranting, posing his paunch to the right and then the left, about a new terrorist organization that apparently had sprung up, like a fresh outbreak of genital warts that refused to go away), "must be embarking on some personal vendetta against the poor aul soul."

"I thought it wile strange, aye. Most of the housewives we knows be's engaging in wee harmless crimes to make ends meet, like, and a blind eye always be's turned."

"Another promotion, the inspector must be looking for."

"What could be the reason he's chosen to single yer woman out, hi?"

"Och, ye've not a clue, have ye? Ye know how yer man there got his promotion to inspector?"

"Aye, locking away them McDaid brothers and putting an end to their drug cartel."

"Word has it the McDaid's drug-dealing all came to light at the inspector's daughter's first holy communion last year. The youngest daughter of yer woman Flood was selling Ecstasy in the front pew to all her mates. His daughter Catherine took one during the service and had a bad reaction, epileptic-like fits right there at the altar, like. The mortification of it all pushed the inspector's wife off her trolley with madness, so it did. Hasn't been the same since, so she hasn't."

"So what ye're telling me is this be's some form of revenge?"

"Suddenly Fionnuala Flood be's public enemy number one for trying to shift some dodgy bottles of absinthe down the pub?"

"What if one of them Orange bastards on the force chances upon her, but? She's doesn't be difficult to miss, like."

"I'm keeping me ears pricked," Lynch said. "If any of themmuns gets closer to finding out her identity, I've half a mind to inform her mammy, ye know Mrs. Heggarty from Creggan Estate?"

Briggs laughed, and admiration shone in his eyes. "Ye mean the matriarch of the Heggarty clan, the mother of all them hooligan sons that dealt in casual violence and petty crime and drug dealing all them years ago? This Fionnuala be's their wee sister?"

"Aye. Them hard men brothers of hers moved abroad years ago, so she be's all on her lonesome here in Derry. Passed the baton of crime over to her, so her brothers musta done. But Mrs. Heggarty be's the godmother of me cousin Carmel's seventh daughter." Lynch nodded, suddenly decided. "A tip-off, I'll be happy to pass into the aul one's ear, if the web of wer investigation closes around her daughter."

Briggs nodded righteously.

"Give us Mrs. Heggarty's number," he said. "Now there be's two of us ready to tip her off. I'll see if I kyanny get Gallagher and Tyrone and Connolly into the loop and all."

"That's set. Now, ye wanted to discuss yer Molly's christening next Saturday with me?"

CHAPTER 58

Her big bones drenched, Bridie fumed as she wrested the shopping cart with one wheel that stuck through the parking lot of Pence-A-Day. The sign on the office still read Closed Until Two. She looked at her Swatch. It was ten to.

Dymphna had phoned her again when Bridie was puffing her way across Craigavon Bridge in the rain, flinching at the honks and rude comments yelled from passing cars; they made her feel like a woman, though. Dymphna had told her that, now that she thought of it, there was a pair of wire cutters under the third dumpster Bridie could use to cut the padlock off the unit.

Bridie raced to the dumpster and dug them out. The wire cutters were rusty and mangled, but they'd do the job. As she peeled off the old sock clinging to them, she called Dymphna.

"What unit does ye be held prisoner in?"

"I'm of the mind it must be 12B. Just to be sure, but, I'll yell and ye listen until ye can locate me."

Feeling like an idiot, Bridie crept from one door to another, tugging the cart with the reluctant wheel behind her, until she heard Dymphna wailing in Unit 13B.

Even with her small portions diet, Bridie had all that extra weight to use as leverage on the handles of the wire cutters; she thrust herself into them, and the lock snapped and clattered to the ground. Bridie tugged open the door and bit back the bile at the fog of chain-smoking that escaped into the pelting rain.

"Bridie! Me savior!" Dymphna wailed, crawling towards her through the ammunition.

Bridie looked in wonder at the cases of arms piled higgelty piggelty, but there was no time to inspect them. She took hold of Dymphna under her arms and hauled her out.

"Let's get ye outta here sharpish. The front left wheel sticks a bit, but I think we can manage. Where do ye want me to place ye?"

She said this as she trailed Dymphna's limbs from the unit, hauled them through the rain and plopped them in the shopping cart

"Just get me outta here," Dymphna panted through her cigarette. "Och, och, och! Mind me ankle! Outta the Waterside. Over the Craigavon Bridge and leave me somewhere in the Moorside. We can phone for an ambulance from there."

Bridie grappled the handle and shoved the shopping cart, wonky wheel squealing in protest, out of the parking lot. The bridge was only half a mile through the wastelands of the dockyards, but it was half a mile in horizontal rain. Bridie huffed and muttered expletives, and Dymphna whimpered and puffed away on a cigarette, and soon the Craigavon Bridge was in sight on the horizon, the nettle-infested fields on either side sloping gently towards the fetid waters of the River Foyle. Only a quarter of a mile left. A car raced by, spattering them in mud.

"Jesus Lord in Heaven above," Bridie seethed, the muck lashing down her body and pouring down her face. Dymphna had a speckle or two on her right arm.

Another car sped through the mud of the road towards them, and Bridie struggled to maneuver the cart wheels to the side, but the car slowed as it approached. Three shaved heads popped out, two with hoods, and the drunken teens whooped and sneered as they passed.

"Would ye look at the shape of yer woman pushing the trolley!"

"Skiprat! A face like a bulldog licking piss offa nettle!"

"A face like a donkey's abortion, more like! Pure minging oinker!"

"Yer woman in the trolley, but! Phwoah!"

"I wouldn't mind getting me leg over that!"

Even in her pain, Dymphna ran fingers through her curls and smiled as the car trundled around the corner.

"Ye're one pure dick, so ye are, Dymphna!" Bridie roared. "What the bloody feck am I doing this for?!"

"Och, I'm wile grateful for yer help, Bridie. All the times we've spent together—"

"Aye," Bridie seethed, asphyxiating the handle of the cart, Dymphna squealing and jerking as the trolley bounced at Bridie's anger-fueled speed, "and when I look back now, they were the times of blootered, desperate slags! The gropings in the mini-cabs! The vomit in the handbags!"

"But—Ow! Och, mind yerself, Bridie, I almost popped out, och—Ow!"

"C'mere til I tell ye," Bridie hollered, the cart racing, "ye see you, Dymphna? Ye had a brilliant effin charmed life, a fella who loved ye, a wane ye knew the father of—eventually, I mean—a deluxe home in the Waterside, and ye threw it all away. For what, I haven't a clue, as yer mother's a lunatic, yer father's a drunk, ye've two brothers in the nick, a beanflicker perv sister—"

"That pervy sister of mines has a book published!" Dymphna wailed.

"Aye, all about the disgrace that is yer family! What does yer Moira call ye in it? Deirdre Frood, with the legs that snap open quicker than a Venus fly-trap, the manky quim crawling with more exotic diseases than an African refugee camp, aren't ye meant to be?"

"Where..." Dymphna gasped, clutching the rails of the cart for dear life. "Where did ye read that?"

"I chanced upon an excerpt of it at...one of me Internet classes. Ye, but, Dymphna, bleating on and on about how yer mother hates ye, and is it any wonder? I kyanny stomach laying eyes on ye meself! And, now that home truths is being spoken, it was *me* that arranged that date with yer man Paul McCreeney. I shoved yer paralytic limbs into the stool next to him and whispered into yer ear ye should invite him to dinner, as I knew ye had arranged one with Rory and wouldn't remember a thing, gee-eyed with drink as ye was!"

"Bridie!" Dymphna whimpered through her cigarette butt. "Why...why would ye do that, but? Ye know I be's carrying his wane, and—"

"Aye, and the good Lord help that wane when it pokes its sorry head into this world, with a mother the likes of ye, a gacky, self-centered, jumped up hateful slag!"

Dymphna yelped as Bridie suddenly braked at the top of the riverbank and thrust the shopping cart on its side.

"Briiidiieee!"

Dymphna toppled out, hands clawing the air, legs kicking. She screamed at a *crack!* in her second ankle as she rolled through the nettles and the muck, careening towards the river, her hands whipping instinctively down to her womb to protect her manicure. She wailed as she hit the churning sewage that, had it been deeper than two feet, would have carried her waterlogged body down the river, into Lough Foyle and out into the Atlantic Ocean.

I kyanny be dealing with this childish palaver no longer Bridie seethed at the top of the hill, punching emergency numbers into her phone. *I'm away off back to work, and I'm weak with hunger and all. I'll stop off for a portion of curry chips. The paramedics can fish the silly bitch outta the water. Serves her right.*

Off she stomped through the rain, a smile crinkling the cold sore on her hungry mouth as Dymphna's screams rang out.

"I've just seen a wee girl in the river," Bridie barked into the phone, realizing it was going to be one long stint in the confessional that Wednesday at St. Molaug's. Even if her penance was to say the rosary at each of the Stations of the Cross (a very long penance reserved for the most exceptional sins), it would be a delight.

CHAPTER 59

Fionnuala slunk off the mini-bus at a stop in the Waterside, feeling stripped of her clothing. To mark their territory, the indigenous Protestants had painted the curbs red, white and blue—the colors of the British flag—and Fionnuala attacked them with discreet little kicks as she passed. But she had chosen this location as she was sure nobody would know her; certainly not the pawnbroker she had looked up in the Yellow Pages. She stood before the pawnshop and marveled at how clean their windows were. She slipped Dymphna's sunglasses on and hustled inside.

"C'mere you a wee moment," Fionnuala said, sidling up to the bald man with the salt-and-pepper goatee behind the counter. "I've something here that I think ye might like."

He looked through his bifocals in alarm as she popped open the buttons of her jacket. He took a step back.

"What are ye gawping at me like that for?" Fionnuala demanded to know, then reeled in her tongue. She plastered a smile on her face, but that seemed to disturb him more. "Och, I must look a right state. Small wonder, the sights me eyes have been subjected to thanks to this."

The man seemed relieved she was clothed under the buttons, yet looked skeptically at the VCR tape she unearthed from beyond them. Fionnuala looked around the shop, then slid it onto the counter, her fingernails shackling the case. The man smirked.

"It's all DVDs around here the day, love," he said.

"Aye, of that I'm well aware. Ye've no idea what be's on *this*, but."

She whispered in his ear, then stood back to watch in satisfaction as his face transform into one of shock.

"Ye and me be's the only two in the world that knows of it," she said. "And I'm wondering how much ye want to give me for it."

"Does such a thing really exist?" he sputtered. "Why has it taken this long to surface? And where on God's green earth did you get it?!"

Fionnuala looked him straight in the eye.

"Me son worked there."

He moved his hand toward the video, but Fionnuala inched it closer to her body.

"How much are ye prepared to hand over? Or I'm taking it over to yer competitors. It's now or never."

He ran his eyes over her, tried to peer through the dark lenses, and his demeanor suddenly changed. Fionnuala couldn't comprehend what caused the change, but his lips disappeared as if pulled by a string, and it was as if the helmet of a suit of armor clanked over his face. She looked behind her, but saw only a shelf of acoustic guitars with no strings.

"This is indeed a remarkable find," he said, but there was something strange about his delivery. "And I am certain you will be more than satisfied with the amount I am prepared to pay for it. It is a national treasure, after all, and demands the top price worthy of its historical importance."

It was as if he were reciting lines somebody had forced him to memorize. He went on: "I just need to check with my partners to see how much money we can get together."

"Six figures?" Fionnuala barked. "At least. Could you just wait there a wee moment, love? I'll give them a call now."

He flitted through the door to the back of the shop.

Fionnuala stood at the counter, her fingernails clanking nervously on the lacquered veneer. He was certainly a queer old bat but, Fionnuala considered, he *was* a Protestant. And he was probably stricken with the same amazement and disgust she had been. An unease began to fill her, though she didn't know why. She briefly considered sneaking up to the door to listen in on his conversation. But then it hit her like a bullet to the sloth-like cells of her brain: he was overcome with thoughts of all the notoriety, the accolades, the TV interviews, maybe even the knighthood, that were sure to come his way as the one who had introduced it to the world. And she had been about to hand it over like a simpleton, just to fund a trip to Malta!

Fionnuala had always felt she was destined for greatness. As the lone daughter in a family of ten, attention was heaped upon her by her brothers, the drunks and hoodlums notorious for cracking beer bottles against heads, torching post offices and other official buildings they didn't like the look of, trading a cornucopia of drugs and smuggled alcohol and cigarettes and cheap pantyhose. As Fionnuala grew into a repellent teen, however, it became apparent to her brothers she had no special skills save the acidity of her tongue and the speed with which she could down alcohol. The novelty of being a female sibling faded, and she was seen increasingly as a liability.

She had expected, as most her classmates in that battleground of teargas and rubber bullets did, that she would emigrate the moment she turned 16 and become an actress in Hollywood. But then she had met Paddy and settled for Derry; the Troubles were becoming less troublesome and she knew the best pubs and which stall in the market sold the cheapest lipstick, after all.

After popping out all her children, she thought the elusive fame would come to her through one of them, but she had spawned disappointment after disappointment. When the Barnetts won the lottery a year earlier, it was no wonder Fionnuala thought she was the rightful owner of the millions, though she had not selected the numbers, not bought the ticket (the £500,000 Jed had won had ballooned into endless millions in Fionnuala's mind).

Now, however, the video still clenched in her fingers, Fionnuala realized fate worked in meandering ways, and this was how her date with immortality was to be played out. Already selecting her TV interviewers and which tasks she would get her PA to perform, Fionnuala crept around the counter and peered through the door. The man was hissing into his cell phone, hand clutching where his heart was, eyes crazed.

Effin Christ our Lord! The Filth! The hateful Proddy bastard's calling in the coppers!

She hightailed it out of the shop, her heart and feet pumping quicker than they had that night in the '80's she and Paddy had tried amphetamines. She arrived, wheezing, at the bus stop.

"Never trust a Proddy bastard," she hissed to herself, then yelped as her phone vibrated against her thigh. "Aye?!"

"Get yerself to Altnagelvin now," Paddy said. "Wer Dymphna was attacked and tossed in the Foyle. She be's laid up with two broken ankles."

"Och, Paddy, I've something to tell ye about what I found the other—"

"I kyanny speak. The orderlies and such be's shooting daggers at me for using me mobile in the corridor, sure. She'll be outta the doctor's soon, I expect. See ye at Altnagelvin."

Fionnuala hung up and saw the mini-bus rolling towards her. She slipped the video next to her bosom and buttoned up, cursing her stupidity at even leaving the house with it. The video could have been wrenched from her by thugs, like her Titanic bag. She would have to make a pit-stop at the house to safeguard it, then she'd make her way to the hospital.

If that wee bitch Dymphna be's expecting grapes...! she thought as she heaved herself up the steps of the bus.

CHAPTER 60

Dymphna cranked her eyes open, then wished she hadn't. Eyes of concern and relief peered down at her, haloed by scalding fluorescent light. It hurt to look and it hurt to think.

"Are ye right there, love?" asked a nurse.

"Och, go on away and lemme sleep."

Dymphna tried to roll over and block them out, but discovered it was a physiological impossibility. Her right leg was weighed down by a monstrous cast, her left leg, also in a cast, was suspended above her in a pulley. Dread invaded her. "What the bleeding feck happened to me legs?"

The other nurse answered:

"It's not yer legs. Ye suffered a…fall into the River Foyle somehow and have sustained bimalleolar fractures both left and right."

"What in the name of Christ be's a bimalleolar when it's at home?"

"Yer ankles, dear," put in the first nurse.

Dymphna's lower lip trembled.

"B-but…I need me ankles for dancing!" she sobbed.

"Och, ye won't be able to *walk* for six weeks."

"And I'd give it another month or two before ye attend any raves."

Dymphna's nails dug frantically at her stomach.

"And what about me wane? How's me wane?" Dymphna begged to know, dreading what the answer might be. "How's me wee…" She had heard it bad luck to utter the name of an unborn child, so she spelled it out: "…me wee B-E-E-O-N-S-A-Y?"

The nurses swapped a startled look.

"But, surely that doesn't be the way it be's spel—"

"Yer wane be's fine," the other nurse cut in, tenderly mopping Dymphna's forehead.

It was the wrong answer.

Paddy and Fionnuala burst into the room and shoved through the nurses as if there were a two-for-one sale on lager under the mattress. Padraig trailed in behind them, and at the sight of him the nurses made a mental inventory of the all the items not bolted down.

"I'll wring the life outta the bastard that did this!" Paddy fumed.

"Me poor wee girl!" Fionnuala sobbed, then whipped around to the nurses and glared accusingly. "Why've ye her toenail fungus exposed for all the world to see?"

"What in the name of feck happened?" Paddy wanted to know. "Who caused ye harm?"

"The pain! The pain!" Dymphna sobbed, her eyes begging either nurse for morphine.

It wasn't needed for the pain, rather to knock her out and clear her family out of the room. Dymphna needed time to get her story straight. She didn't know how she could explain being dumped in the river, but it certainly wouldn't be the truth. And she knew from a lifetime of living under Fionnuala's "care" the crafty workings of her mother's mind. Her story was going to have to be detailed and airtight if it was to fool her mother.

"When can we take her home?" Paddy asked.

"We'd like to keep her in overnight for observation, like."

"What's there to observe?" Fionnuala barked. "Ye can see her now, sure!"

"How can we take her home?" Paddy wondered. "She kyanny walk, sure."

"The hospital'll give youse a lend of a wheelchair."

"A wheelchair?" Dymphna wailed. "Och, the mortification! Two broken ankles *and* two months up the duff!"

Dymphna clamped her hands around her mouth. Fionnuala's handbag clattered to the floor. Paddy gawped, and Padraig giggled. One nurse inspected the stitching of her shirt sleeve, the other the path to the door. They all screamed as Paddy's mobile erupted with the chorus of "Crazy Little Thing Called Love."

"Ye kyanny use a mobile—"

The other nurse cut her off again with a grip to the wrist. "I do believe we should make werselves scarce. I'm of the mind themmuns has a few wee things to discuss as a family unit."

The nurses hurried out as Paddy answered the phone.

"Aye?"

"Why the bloody feck hasn't Fionnuala got around to purchasing her own mobile?" Maureen snapped at him. Paddy was surprised at the panic beyond the rage. "Put her on, Paddy, would ye?"

"We've a bit of a—"

"Put yer wife on now! It be's a matter of life and death!"

Paddy handed the phone over and stared in dismay at his newly-pregnant daughter, who was sobbing uncontrollably into the axle of the pulley.

"What are ye after, Mammy?" Fionnuala snapped.

"I don't know what shenanigans ye've been playing at," Maureen harrumphed. "I've just received a tip-off from me friend in the Filth, but. The inspector's got ye and some of the wanes bang to rights on some sort of crime or another, and the troops be's getting a search warrant issued even as I speak so's they can swoop down on the home and clamp handcuffs on the lot of youse. Must have some wane-sized ones, I'm thinking, and what the neighbors is gonny make of it I haven't a clue! Pure red, so I'm are!"

"What are ye on about, Mammy? What crimes? The wanes...? *Padraig?*" Fionnuala seethed at him across the room.

"Och, I hadn't the time to give yer man an in-depth investigative interview, so I hadn't. He was hissing down the phone to me in the loos of the precinct. All I know, but, be's youse're to get yerselves over here sharpish, like, fling some frocks and socks in a bag and we've to catch the next ferry to Malta, or it'll be the inside of a cell youse'll be writing postcards from!"

"Malta? We haven't the money yet, but—"

"Never you mind about that. Leave you that to me. I've a wee errand to run to gather together enough hard cash to transport us most of the way. I'll meet youse at the house at half-four. Hours, it takes, for the coppers to get their fingers outta their lazy arses and cobble a search warrant together. Youse've got to get yer running shoes on, but. Splurge for a taxi, sure."

As much as Fionnuala wanted Dymphna to rot in the hospital bed, she was afraid of the police interrogating her and what the silly cunt might reveal without knowing.

"Get up! Get yer lazy arse outta the bed now!" she screamed, tugging at the sheets while Dymphna shrieked in pain. "Och, how do I dismantle this pulley? And youse, search the corridor for a wheelchair! We're away off to Malta! Yippee!"

CHAPTER 61

HALF AN HOUR EARLIER

Fionnuala had raced in and flung the video on the sofa, hissing: "Don't let that video outta yer site, Mammy. Millions, it be's worth. And wer ticket to a better life—in the sun of Florida, if I've anything to do with it. If hooligans burst in and demand that video or the wane, hand ye Keanu over with a smile on yer face."

"What…?"

But her daughter was already out the door. Maureen sat alone before a blank TV screen, Keanu gurgling in the corner. She got up and made a cup of tea, milky and sweet, then unearthed Fionnuala's secret stash of luxury Belgian chocolates. She popped one in her mouth and stuck the video in the player. She wanted to see for herself what all the fuss was about. She hoped it was a romantic comedy.

Maureen heaved herself back onto the groaning couch, located the remote somehow, and rewound the video. She pressed Play.

It was the panorama of a large city, buildings reaching up to a hazy sky; London, if she wasn't mistaken. The camera panned across the skyline, and Maureen bemoaned the lack of music or words on the screen to tell her what the title was and who the actors were. She wondered with a sinking heart if there were no actors. Nothing set her dentures on edge like a documentary.

Just as Maureen began to fidget with boredom, the camera pointed down and focused on a newspaper in the foreground. It was held in someone's hand; it seemed like the hand belonged to whoever was shooting the 'film.' She could tell the person filming was standing on a balcony of some sort looking over the city. The camera ran over the newspaper, but Maureen's elderly eyes couldn't make out the headline or the date, as she was sure they wanted her to see, like one of those videotapes of prisoners captured by the Taliban to verify the date.

She wiped the fingerprints off her lenses with the bottom of her track suit top and squinted at the screen, but there were a few squiggles of static as the camera was turned off, and the newspaper was gone. The framing was now fuzzy, and it seemed the person was filming from the hip. Maureen had once suffered through an exposé on flight attendants working for Ryanair, so she knew undercover filming when she saw it. The camera must be hidden under the person's clothing. She took a sip of tea and saw a sidewalk and the building the person was walking towards. The camera flashed on the name Hammersmith and Fulham M— She couldn't make out the last word, as it was obscured by the whipping branches of a tree. There were the squiggles again, the scene changed, and then they were inside, that building Maureen supposed, and the person with the camera (she would hardly call him a cinematographer) focused on the long hallway he was walking down.

"The shite that passes for entertainment the day!" she muttered to herself.

Maureen slurped cherry juice out of a chocolate and licked her fingers. She caught a glimpse of a water cooler, a potted plant, and *there isn't much of a story, is there?* she wondered. The squiggles again, and the camera panned awkwardly around the stark white tiles that formed the walls of a room. The camera jerked upwards, as if it had been hit by mistake, and the ceiling flashed onto the screen, massive lights hanging. She heard muffled voices, and saw the hips of people passing back and forth, doctors or some sort of medical staff; she had seen enough episodes of *ER* to know the hems of scrubs when she saw them.

Maureen leaned forward, her interest growing, but unease also creeping up the curvature of her spine. Maureen strained her ears to make sense of the voices.

"Is the mic on?"

"Not yet. Hold on one moment, would you please?" The male voices had upper-class British accents.

"We have here a…"

The camera zoomed in and Maureen saw cloth and flashes of steel, strange mechanical tools, blood and offal. Maureen wished her lenses weren't covered with so many scratches.

"…internal hemorrhaging…right lung and heart…"

Maureen nibbled on a Coconut Eclair

"…single lesion, a partial rupture…"

and on a Caramel Swirl

"…left pulmonary vein…contact with the left atrium…"

on a chewy berry-type thing

"…sutured…due to…major chest trauma…"

and a Hazelnut Cracknell, her favorite.

"…phenomenon of deceleration…"

Maureen screamed as her cellphone rang.

"Maureen," PC Lynch whispered. "What about ye?"

"Och, watching a shite video. Ready to flick it off after ten minutes, so I am. No bloody story, and I kyanny make head nor tail of what they be's blathering on about. More difficult hospital words than a seasons-worth of *ER*! Not me cup of tea."

Lynch cut her off, which she thought very rude, but when she heard what he had to say, she forgave his lack of manners.

"Ta very much for yer help," Maureen said.

She hung up, realizing the family had to flee the city, and she lunged for her handbag, never far from her elbow. She counted all the money she had been saving from her bingo wins for the past few years. £964.12. And surely Fionnuala and Paddy had managed to secure a few hundred pounds more.

But they would need more for the bus to Belfast, the ferry to Liverpool, the bus to London, the EuroStar through the Chunnel to the bottom of

France, and whatever sort of transportation would get them from there to Malta. Maureen had to pay a visit to someone she had been itching to for the past few days, ever since Padraig had come to her, his ugly and tear-stained face looking up at her as he told her about his father's infidelities in the fish factory. Maureen's fingers were like tendrils through every part of the city, even extending to the management of the Fillet-O-Fish. She had phoned up Lois, who she knew passed out uniforms to the new temporary workers, and had Lois' niece Fiona give her the slattern's name and address from the employee records.

From what Maureen could tell, Paddy had been keeping his todger in his jeans since Padraig had caught him at it, but it still rankled—a foreigner trying to tear her family apart!—and the woman responsible would now have to pay. If someone had asked her the day before what she planned to do to Agnieszka Czerwinska, Maureen would have said she only wanted to strike the fear of the Lord in the Polish woman's heart. But she realized that 'having to pay' now meant having to *pay*. And everyone knew the recent invasion of foreigner workers to their town never kept their money in banks.

Maureen hobbled to the kitchen, rifled through some drawers until she came across a faded pamphlet—instructions to the microwave oven nobody had ever read—and rolled Keanu's stroller out the door. She made her home visit, and the taxi was halfway back from the whore's house when what was on the video hit Maureen.

CHAPTER 62

Padraig cackled as he raced a squealing Dymphna up the sidewalk, his mother and father scurrying ahead of them towards the house.

"Would ye quit popping them fecking wheelies, Padraig! Me neck's gonny be fractured along with me ankles!"

"It be's the manky wheelchair!" Padraig said. "Something be's up with the front wheels, sure!"

Paddy hurried into the hallway after Fionnuala, his head spinning. He knew Moira had to be confronted, and that the trip was an opportunity to buy cigarettes in bulk, but he was clueless as to why they all had to flee the country so quickly. Endless overtime at the plant, avoiding Aggie at every turn, avoiding Fionnuala at home and Padraig on the street, he had been out of the loop in family matters the past few days.

"What the feck have ye been playing at, love?" he asked.

"It must be that video I nicked from an aul one's attic. The most important video of the century, sure," Fionnuala explained as she rushed it into the kitchen.

"What are ye on about? What be's on the video that makes it so special?" Paddy asked.

Fionnuala chewed on her lower lip as she tugged open a cupboard and rifled through the mayhem inside. She had yet to tell Paddy about the contents of the video, had yet to tell anybody, actually, as she couldn't trust anybody but herself. Padraig and Siofra had seen it, but they were too young to realize the importance. Fionnuala wanted to luxuriate solo in the excitement of this final period of privacy, before she was catapulted to celebrity on the world stage. She imagined opening the door to the family home to a barrage of blinding flashbulbs from an army of reporters. She hoped they wouldn't catch her in her bathrobe and curlers. And as a bonus, she mused, perhaps her renown would make her daft idiot of a husband see sense, make Paddy realize she was still worthwhile as a person and a wife.

"Fling some clothes in these, you," Fionnuala barked instead, dragging the big black garbage bags out. "We've not the time nor money to purchase luggage, and after that fire most haven't many clothes left in any event. Can ye unearth some clean socks and smalls to shove in?"

Siofra clumped down the stairs, her charred, headless Barbie clutched in her hand, wondering what the commotion was.

"Dymphna!" Siofra gasped as Padraig finally wrenched her older sister through the door. "What's up with ye?"

"Gather some clothes together now, Siofra," Fionnuala said. "We're away off to Malta."

The Barbie fell from Siofra's hand.

"Och, pick yer jaw off the floor, wane, and quit gawping at me like that or ye'll feel the force of me hand on—"

"Naw, Mammy! *Naw!*" Siofra wailed. "I'm not gonny go to Malta now! The morrow be's the talent show, sure!"

"Feck yer talent show! The Filth be's on wer tail, and ye were part of causing that aul Mrs. Ming to keel over, don't ye forget! Attempted murder, themmuns'll want yer wee arse for and all. There be's special units for wanes in the prison, ye know."

Paddy sidled up to his wife. "I've sent Padraig upstairs to do the packing. I'll nip to the off-license on the corner for some lager. We kyanny make a journey without drink, sure."

Fionnuala considered. "Mind ye pick up one of them flagons of cider for me mammy and all."

Padraig slipped gratefully out the door, out of the firing line. Fionnuala turned her attention back to Siofra, and Dymphna sat stranded between a furious Fionnuala and a sobbing and now foot-stamping Siofra.

"Naw! *Naw!* Weeks, we've been working on wer act! All them flowers and fishes we made for the Happiness Boat, and the wee song I wrote and all! Days, it took me! I can stay at Grainne's, sure. Och, Mammy, please, Mammy, please! Grainne's mammy's sure to say aye!"

"Would ye stop yer endless yammering, wane?! We kyanny hear if sirens be's coming down the street for us!"

Siofra's pleading turned to anger. She bellowed up at her mother: "I don't wanna go! I don't wanna travel to some strange land to harm wer Moira. I love me sister! And I hate *ye!*"

Dymphna gasped into the handle of the wheelchair as Siofra lunged forward and attacked Fionnuala's stomach with her little fists. Siofra yelped as Fionnuala snatched a handful of her hair, a barrette pinging off and ricocheting against Dymphna's cheek. Siofra's feet lashed out at her mother's shins, and Fionnuala roared and threw her against the wall. Siofra landed with a thud and looked up at her mother like a wounded dog. Then tears erupted from her eyes.

"A traitor, ye be's!" Fionnuala seethed, hand twitching in the air to strike. "First this palaver about loving yer beanflicking perv of a sister! And ye think I haven't spied ye skipping hand in hand down the town, all palsy-walsy with yer flash new mate, the police inspector's daughter, Little Miss Mini-Filth Catherine McLaughlin? Her collapsing at yer First Holy Communion on them drugs ye took from yer brother Eoin be's responsible for the poor wee boy being locked up! Consorting with the enemy, so ye are, wee girl! Next ye'll be telling me ye love yer auntie Ursula and all! *Traitor!*"

Smack! Smack!

Siofra screamed and sobbed in the corner, and Paddy returned, laden with drink. Padraig lumbered down the stairs bearing bulging garbage bags. With her father there, Dymphna felt safe to utter:

"I kyanny go, either, Mammy! Look at the state of me. I'm two months up the duff with two gammy legs."

"Ye want two gammy arms and all?" Fionnuala threatened.

"This wheelchair, but," Dymphna pleaded. "It flips up all the time, and I'm afeared I'm gonny fall over."

"Och—!" Scorn creased Fionnuala's face, and she raised her hand again.

"It be's true, but, Mammy," Padraig put in. "It took all me strength to stop it toppling over on me."

"Why," Dymphna said, cringing under her mother's hand, "couldn't we wait until themmuns at the hospital issued us a wheelchair that functions properly? Nicking it from the corridor like that, wrenching me from me bed and dumping me in—"

"Ye haven't a third ankle to break, ye daft cunt!"

"Love," Paddy said, grabbing Fionnuala's hand and maneuvering it to her side, "a malfunctioning wheelchair does be a problem. We've to leverage it down at the bottom with something heavy. Doesn't there be that aul case of tinned vegetables propping up the shelf in the cupboard? Padraig, go on and grab that case and shove it onto that...tray-like thing under the wheelchair."

"Och, ye've the lager, grand!" Fionnuala said as Padraig plopped the 'luggage' on the carpet and hurried into the scullery.

She reached into the liquor store bag, popped open a can, swigged down, then proffered an accusing finger at Dymphna.

"And ye see you, wee girl, ye've never had an ounce of family loyalty in them disease-ridden limbs of yers. I'm saddled with the mortification of a half-Orange bastard for a grandson, and now ye've another on the way! Dear God in Heaven alone knows what religion the father of this one might be!"

"What's that wane doing bawling in the corner?" Paddy asked.

"Och, the daft eejit doesn't want a holiday to Malta. Doesn't know what's good for her, how good she has it. I was twenty-seven before I stepped foot out of Derry. And then it was just a bus with no shock absorbers down to Dublin. Five hours of Hell on Earth, it was."

Paddy and Padraig forced the case of vegetables under the wheelchair, then Paddy gave a few pushes up and down the hallway to make sure Dymphna didn't flip back.

"That's grand," Fionnuala said. "And we can sell them veggies in some foreign market when wer funds run out and we're in need of spending money. I hear the prices of souvenirs on the Continent be's shocking. And would youse believe a quid for a tin of fizzy lemonade, them Frenchy-Frog bastards charge!"

Their eyes goggled at this information. Maureen sailed in with Keanu.

"Right! We've wer funds now," she said, opening her handbag and flashing the bills around.

Dymphna, Padraig and Siofra (who had dried her eyes but still glared at her mother, her hand accusingly caressing her cheek time and again) stared at the money. They had never seen so much together in one hand in their lives.

"Mammy!" Paddy said. "Where did ye get all that cash from?"

"I've me methods," Maureen said, eyes boring into him. Actually, a few more affairs, and Paddy's penis could fund her pilgrimage to Lourdes and maybe one to the Holy Land. "I've no need to pack as, sure, all me gear be's burnt. Let's be on wer way, shall we?"

Fionnuala searched them wildly for an appropriate place to hide her special video. She shoved Keanu to the side and hid it in the seat of his stroller. Nobody in their right mind would want to glance at that hideous infant, she thought.

"Out! Out the door now!" Fionnuala demanded.

As they left, Fionnuala hissed at the scowling Siofra: "And the day after the morrow be's the Top-Yer-Trolley annual sale, wane. Ye think I want to miss that? Highlight of me year, so it be's! But I'm sacrificing that for wer freedom!"

CHAPTER 63

HALF AN HOUR EARLIER

Maureen splurged on a taxi as time was of the essence. She hid Keanu in the hedges and banged on the door with the force of a woman scorned. She hoped the husband of Paddy's fancy woman wasn't home. Maureen knew the foreigner workers never invaded their country alone; they always came in pairs, or with a litter of children they sought to raise as Irish nationals, as they were embarrassed to be Polish/Filipino, and for that Maureen couldn't fault them. Her gnarled knuckles continued their banging.

"Czym mogę służyć?" Aggie asked, poking her head out. What can I do for you? Maureen instantly hated her blonde hair, blue eyes and voluptuous breasts.

Pronouncing Agnieszka Czerwinska was impossible, so Maureen had prepared, scrawling the name in capital letters on the back of a final disconnection notice from the electricity company. She forced it at the woman.

"Does this be you?"

Aggie looked down, surprised, and nodded, which was her first mistake.

"Immigration!" Maureen barked, flashing her ID from the church social and shoving her way in. Allowing Maureen in was Aggie's second mistake.

"I'm undercover," Maureen explained as Aggie looked the pensioner's track suit doubtfully up and down. "And still in service. Budget cutbacks have forced us to retire at 80. May I see yer papers?"

Aggie was confused at the torrent of English.

"Paper?" she asked, handing over a binder where she had scribbled her ESL notes. "You want pen also?"

"Naw, yer *papers!*"

Aggie, trembling, handed over a newspaper, her eyes shining with hope that that was what the scary woman wanted.

"*Yer work visa!*"

Aggie hastened to comply, opening the drawer of an end table and rummaging within. Maureen inspected the spartan furnishings of the living room, her eyes falling on the unframed photo curling on the mantelpiece of the woman with her arm wrapped around a wimpy blonde man who must be her husband at Giant's Causeway, the two of them beaming their unsightly overbites at the camera.

Aggie handed over her passport with jittery fingers. Maureen flicked it open, found the visa and inspected it.

"And yer husband's?"

Aggie scurried once again to the drawer.

"Fakes! Obvious fakes! Where did ye get these made? How much did they set ye back?" Maureen demanded to know, brandishing the passports in her claw. Aggie reached for them, but Maureen's cane smacked the fingers away.

"But..but...real! Real!"

"Do you know it's expressly forbidden under EU law to fornicate with a married national?"

Aggie's brow winkled with incomprehension.

"Ye kyanny shag yer Irish fancy-man!" Maureen seethed. She waved the instructions to the microwave oven at Aggie; she figured Poles would never be able to tell what the pamphlet was, so long as she kept her fingers blocking the illustrations of how to open and close the door. Maureen pointed to the Care and Cleaning section. "It's all written in this clause here. I won't report ye to me superiors. For a price."

"What you say? What that meaning is?"

"That meaning is ye won't be going to prison if ye *pay* me! Money!" Maureen ruffled her thumb and fingers together in what she hoped was the international symbol for money, all the while wondering how Paddy had wished this foreign creature an understandable good morning, let alone that he wanted to commit the sin of adultery with her. "You-pay-me-money." She said it as if to a spastic child.

"We have few monies! Work long hours, few monies."

"Right! I'm calling back-up!" Maureen announced, slipping the passports in her pocket and pulling out her cellphone. "That meaning is *more police in yer living room.*"

Maureen motioned the overturning of tables and chairs, and then pressed the numbers for the soccer results hotline. Maureen's eyes, magnified to the size of owl's eyes through the lenses, bored into the terrified immigrant as a bright female voice rattled off the scores.

"Big, angry, strong policemen!" Maureen intoned menacingly.

"Stop! I give money! I give money!"

Aggie rummaged through the drawer again and handed over a handful of rumpled bills. Maureen hung up and totaled them quickly in her mind.

"More!" she barked.

Aggie whimpered as she reached into the drawer again and tugged out bills of higher denomination. She handed them over, pleading on her face. Maureen's wrinkles lit up with delight.

"And I thought ye said ye worked long hours for little money?"

She handed over the passports.

"Husband taxi-driver," Aggie admitted.

"Ye've been wile civil, and ye've seen sense at last. Keep yer quim away from yer betters in the future."

That infuriating look of incomprehension once again.

"Don't shag Derrymen!" Maureen clarified.

Maureen hobbled as quickly as she could to the door, grabbed Keanu's stroller and rolled it down the path. Inside, Aggie picked up the pamphlet that was supposed to contain the rules of EU immigration, and saw instead an illustration of a hand wiping out a microwave oven with a soft, damp cloth. She hurried to the door and flung it open, but Maureen was already gone.

"*Ty suko! Ty suko!*" Aggie yelled into the rain. You bitch!

As Maureen settled herself in the taxi, £675 richer, she reflected over what she had done. There was, of course, the reputation of the Heggarty name to consider; regardless of their smorgasbord of crimes, no Heggarty had ever spent time in prison, and Maureen didn't want her flighty daughter Fionnuala to blemish that record. But it was less the hassle and mortification of the prison visits that had made Maureen visit Aggie, nor the need to make the woman pay for straining her daughter and son-in-law's marriage, more the misery of the past two weeks' non-stop rain. Her pallid flesh was begging for a little Mediterranean sun.

The taxi was zooming up the Lone Moor Road, the factory walls towering, when Maureen went back to the video in her mind. There was nothing on it that screamed controversy. She wondered if Fionnuala were going mental; perhaps it was the strain of putting on a brave face while her husband dipped his meatpole into Polish pleasure fields. And then it hit her: the pearl earring she had seen on the screen.

Maureen's brain froze, and her eyeballs felt as if they had been skewered with knitting needles. She desperately needed to reach for a sick bucket, but there wasn't one in the back of the taxi, and she knew the drivers charged a £25 Sick Cleanup Fee, highway robbery, so she kept it in her throat and swallowed. Then the taxi stopped. Shaken, she paid the fare and weakly tugged Keanu's stroller out. She looked up and down the street for a police car, understanding completely why the coppers were after them. If she were a copper, she'd be after them too.

CHAPTER 64

In a locker room of the precinct, the seven men of the Armed Response Unit suited up in helmets and bulletproof vests, checked their Tasers, 9mm Glocks and MP7 rifles. They had been preparing to storm the Flood's house once McLaughlin received the search warrant and gave the go-ahead, but plans were changing. Two Armed Response Vehicles and a Tech Vehicle waited outside, engines running, to now ambush the bus en route to Belfast the family had boarded.

The regular troops in the police incident room sat, stunned, at Inspector McLaughlin's announcement, the information phoned through to the station by the owner of the pawn shop. Lynch and Briggs did their best to look concerned, but their minds were urging the Floods on to success.

"How could a common housewife get her hands on such a thing?" the same young copper asked.

"I kyanny say stranger things have happened in me fifteen years on the force; only equally strange things. But there youse have it; the facts speak for themselves. More disturbing, but, be's the recent intelligence from wer flash new satellite-detection-and-tracking system that this 'common housewife' be's now on the move, planning to flee the country with it in her possession. Without that technology, we wouldn't even have a clue where on God's green earth it be's."

The door opened and an officer raced in, breathless. "I've checked with the Foyle Travel agency, and the granny has them booked on a ferry to Liverpool, a bus to London, and from there the EuroStar to France."

McLaughlin stared.

"What sort of bloody shenanigans does themmuns be up to?" he sputtered, as behind him a door opened, and the Armed Response unit clamored in.

"Should we not get the Secret Service, MI6, or maybe even Interpol involved, sir?" an officer chanced, gnawing on a fingernail.

Murmurs of insubordination rippled through the troops, and McLaughlin trembled with irritation, though he had briefly considered this himself. He wanted the glory of the arrest all for himself, however.

"Och, catch yerself on, ye daft cunt! It's serious, aye, as if the media get their filthy paws on this and the threat to National Security it be's, right enough…Are ye clueless, but, to the outrage it's sure generate throughout the international community, let alone the shame it'll bring upon wer precinct for letting something of such magnitude slip through wer fingers? Set yer tiny brain at rest, but, as I've called in a helicopter to transport me and the Armed Response unit over to Liverpool in the unlikely event themmuns evade us at the ferry terminal in Belfast."

Someone marched in and handed the inspector what they all, save Lynch and Briggs, had been waiting for.

"About bleedin fecking time," Inspector McLaughlin said, search warrant clutched in his fingers. "Right, men, on wer way!"

They burst out of the precinct and into the ARVs, McLaughlin hauling along a computer equipped with the satellite images of the family's whereabouts. McLaughlin and his second in command handed out copies of Fionnuala Flood's likeness to the unit, but that meant the ARU would be scanning the crowds at the ferry for the bleached ponytails burned on their retinas. The new helicopter would have to be put to use.

CHAPTER 65

The plane droned over the Atlantic Ocean, ETA at Belfast International Airport in five hours. In the dark calm of the cabin, Ursula sat under the lone shining reading light and nibbled at the free peanuts, wondering why the bag was so small and replaying the differing scenarios in her mind as to what she was going to say to Fionnuala and the entire Flood clan once she set eyes on them. There was the angry scenario, the compassionate scenario, the violent scenario...*Och, I haven't a clue if I be's going there to wrap me arms around them or claw their eyes out.*

Jed snored boozily at her side, *Counting Cards...The Math to Blackjack Success* rising and falling on his chest, drained mini-bottles from the drinks cart vibrating on his tray, his plastic glass empty save melting ice cubes. Ursula knew the prospect of entering the Flood battlefield was driving him momentarily to drink again; she couldn't complain, as he had been collateral damage before. She thanked him in her heart for approaching the firing line with her.

Ursula crumpled the peanut bag and groaned as she contorted her body to locate the carry-on bag shoved under the seat before her. She tugged out the skeins of yellow and green yarn, and the crocheting hook that had given her so much grief at security. She needed to complete the onesie for Keanu before they landed.

The crocheting hook attacked the yarn, and her left fingers leading the yarn started to strangle it as they curled into a fist, as if the gift were being made not with love but in anger.

A hometown was meant to be a hometown, especially Derry, where those who had fled to find jobs abroad were always welcomed back with open arms and a thousand smiles, regardless if some of those smiles curled with disgust the moment a back was turned and those arms ended in fists with accusing fingers attached.

Ursula never thought she would return to her hometown a refugee. Scrabbling for a place to stay, she had called her life-long friend Francine, her hairdresser at Xpressions, Molly, and even Father Hogan from St. Molaug's. She had received three answering machines. Ursula was mortified of being seen walking down the steps of a hotel in her hometown, and such a posh one at that; the need to rent a room showed she had failed as a family member, could only be coming home in shame, and the price tag of a night's stay a clue to the reason: too much money, a lady of luxury looking down her nose at others. Like a Protestant, the town would treat her. Her brow bowed in shame, Ursula held up the onesie in the beam of the reading light. She hoped the child had three arms.

A person of great mass lumbered down the aisle, and Ursula flinched as something sharp sliced the air an inch from her ear. She rotated her head slowly to the left. Foot-long fingernails scraped down the darkness of the aisle. The plane plunged into turbulence, all in Ursula's panicked head. *Casino Woman!* Heading to the restroom!

Jed sputtered awake as Ursula dug her claws into his arm.

"Jed! Jed!" she hissed, eyes crazed with fear. "She be's on wer plane! She be's here to attack and kill me! Och, Jed, Jed, I'm heart-scared!"

"But…?" Jed's eyes were heavy with drink and doubt.

Ursula brandished the crocheting hook as a weapon and frantically jabbed the call button. Then, to Jed's horror, Ursula opened her mouth. Wide.

"Stewardess! *Stewardesssss!*"

Around them passengers woke angrily, and one of the cabin crew materialized above her in the gloom.

"We are now called flight attendants," he said stiffly.

"There be's a madwoman in the loo!" Ursula screamed. He looked at her as if there were another in her seat.

"What is a loo?" he asked.

"Och, ye eejit! A toilet, sure! She be's trying to murder me!"

He looked at her doubtfully.

Ursula stood up, clutched the headrest before her and wailed down the length of the plane: "Does there be a marshal on board? I need a marshal to break down that loo door and arrest the madwoman within!"

"Ma'am—"

She threw the restraining hand to the side.

"Don't ye 'ma'am' me! Get her! Get that lunatic woman before she gets me!"

"My wife," Jed said weakly, "has been going through a bad patch, but she *was* viciously attacked by a crazy woman recently. Maybe you really should check the passenger out."

The flight attendant nibbled his lower lip in indecision.

"I'll help you," Jed offered, trying to get up from his seat.

"Jed, *naw!*" Ursula begged, shoving him back down. "She'll claw the eyes outta ye with them fingernails of hers!"

"She's never met me."

"Aye, but, Jed, if I lost ye—*Help us! Help us someone else!*"

As babies through the cabin erupted into fearful screams at Ursula's voice, and pockets of passengers trembled with irritation, the marshal finally decided to reveal himself. He pried himself from his seat, flashing his badge and brandishing his gun.

"*I'll* deal with this," he promised.

The flight attendant rolled his eyes without rolling them. The marshal crept through the rows of goggle-eyed passengers, muting their headphones at the in-flight entertainment for all. The marshal rapped on the door of the bathroom. Ursula wrung her hands, Jed caressed her shuddering shoulders.

"US Marshall! Out with your hands up! Out now!"

"Dear God in Heaven above, save us," Ursula whimpered, crossing herself as the handle of the door rattled.

The door opened and the woman stuck an angry head out, the roar of the toilet in her wake. She raised her hands, the nails like skyscrapers, and took a step out. The marshal threw her, screaming, against the handle of the emergency door, one of her nails popping off, and he clanked the cuffs on.

"Fucking motherfucker fucker!" the woman screamed. "Can't I take a crap in peace?"

The marshal manhandled her up the aisle, rows of eyes boring up at the struggling, expletive-screaming woman with suspicion and excitement.

Ursula cringed, tears trailing down her cheeks, as the woman approached. It wasn't Casino Woman. She was too old, her eyes too large, her fingernails the wrong color, the designs rainbows.

"I-I've made a mistake," Ursula admitted.

Jed, the marshal, the flight attendant and ninety-seven passengers stared in disbelief. The babies kept crying. Glaring at Ursula as if she were next for the handcuffs, the marshal released the passenger.

"I'm terribly sorry, ma'am, but, you know, post 9/11…"

"Post 9/11 my ass!" spat the woman. "I'll be suing! Suing!"

"Please forgive me," Ursula said. "Ye looked like someone who's made me every waking moment a misery. Och, please, I'm begging for forgiveness!"

The woman looked her up and down, her anger subsiding.

"Damn crazy white bitch," she finally said, then marched to her seat and landed on it with a thump. The man beside her moved his laptop closer to him.

"Make sure that doesn't happen again," the marshal said. "We are here for serious incidents only."

Ursula nodded weakly, and soon the flight was back to normal. Crisis over, Jed adjusted his neck pillow and collapsed into sleep against the curvature of the window again.

As Ursula sat alone in the one beam of light, the neurons of her brain were alive. She had only met Casino Woman for two…three? minutes, but it equaled a lifetime of change. She now knew what it was like to see her life ending. Being on death's doorstep was trauma best shared with the support of a loving family behind her. But she had none. And perhaps it was her own fault. Fionnuala maxing out her credit cards from afar paled in comparison to death.

Ursula's lips softened as she now saw it clearly: her mission to Derry had started as one of retribution, but it should be one of reconciliation. And the only language the Floods spoke was money.

When the Barnetts thought the security of Ursula's identity had been compromised by Casino Woman, they had withdrawn all the money from Ursula's account and placed it in a new one under Jed's name. As Jed muttered in his sleep, Ursula slipped her hand into his jacket pocket. She tugged out his checkbook. She briefly considered asking the flight attendant for the loan of a pen, but thought better of it. Her fingers slipped again into Jed's pocket and found one. Leaning the checkbook against the flimsy eating tray, Ursula pressed the tip of the pen on check 234, filled it out, then wrapped it inside Keanu's onesie.

Three and a half more hours, and she'd be back in Derry to see the Floods.

CHAPTER 66

Five minutes to departure, Padraig's eyes danced with glee at the rats jumping to and from the ferry, his little hands clapping. Siofra vomited into the water at his side. Rain attacked them both. Fifteen feet down the deck, it seemed every adult passenger was squeezed into the tiny sheltered smoking section, elbows gouging into stomachs, knees into thighs, hoards of smoke billowing. Wiping lager from a chin smeared with cigarette ash, Fionnuala yelped at something attacking her arse.

"The torture we're meant to endure for the God-given right to have a fag," Maureen harrumphed behind her, wondering what mass her cane had just come up against.

So many were bunched on the bow to smoke, Maureen feared the boat would capsize before they pulled out. If they didn't get arrested first.

But the horns rang out, the gangplank rose, and the ferry pushed off through the filthy water as cigarette-accessorized hands clapped. Paddy, Fionnuala and Maureen felt relief in their alcohol-addled brains, but they couldn't pull their eyes from the shore. Half a mile out, they heard sirens over the babbling voices of the smokers pressed against them, could see the flashing lights through the pelting rain as the ARVs invaded the pier.

"Dear God, there they are!" Paddy said.

Fionnuala clutched his arm.

"The Filth can't make the ferry turn round, can they?" she hissed in his ear.

"It's happened before," Paddy said.

Maureen gulped the last of her cider, then reached for one of their beers. The three puffed away in suspense for a few knots, but the ferry continued churning through the billowing sea, foam spraying up and meeting the pelting rain. Fionnuala flipped the police off over the waves, and she would've flashed them as well, but knew the state of her knickers.

"We're free! We beat the Filth!" Fionnuala rejoiced.

Paddy and Maureen seemed less joyful.

"Och, wipe them looks of gloom offa yer faces. What is the Filth gonny do?" Fionnuala spat scornfully. "Jump into a helicopter and meet us on the other side, hi?"

This seemed unlikely, so the worry disappeared from their brows.

"Could someone finally please tell me what the Filth be's after us for, but?" Paddy slurred.

Fionnuala placed her fingers on her lips. "Me lips be's sealed. *I've got a secret, and I'm gonny keep it!*" she sang, tapping the side of her nose, the excitement and booze filling her.

"Shall we not make wer way inside?" Maureen asked. "And see how the invalid and her infant be's faring in the lounge?"

"Aye," Paddy said. "I'm soaked to the bone and can feel the death forming in me lungs from all this fag smoke."

"I suppose we should have a wee gander inside," Fionnuala said, eyes goggled with drink. "I'll have youse know, but, me heart sank as we approached this floating rubbish dump. It doesn't resemble the Titanic in the least. Gather you up the wanes, Paddy."

"Has anybody seen Seamus, hi?" Paddy wondered.

They found him gnawing off the lead-based paint from a railing halfway down the deck.

The ferry pitched and rolled in the tumultuous sea like a drunk trying to make her way up Shipquay Street. Paddy, Fionnuala, Maureen were the drunks grappling at the walls as they wobbled through the corridor, trails of beer and cider in their wake. The children's bright young eyes (even Siofra's in a brief stint of wellness) devoured all the new things around them during their first trip out of Derry.

"C'mon, wanes," Fionnuala urged. "The ferry be's wer own private disco, so it does. *I've got the key, I've got the secret, ah, ah, ah, ah-ah-ha!* Sing along, youse! *I've got the key, I've got the secret...!*"

She banged on the wall, a drumbeat accompanying the decades-old dance tune, her shouting a drunken version of singing. Paddy and Maureen didn't know the song, but they beat the walls and attempted to sing as they staggered along, Maureen banging her cane, Seamus squealing with joy and clapping like one mentally unhinged. A fire extinguisher popped off the wall at the force of their collective blows. Maureen knocked it to the side with her cane.

"Hand ups, baby, hands up!" Fionnuala sang. *"Give me your heart, give me give me your heart!"*

"Me stomach feels wile strange again," Siofra sobbed, the greenish tinge reappearing on her face. She made a sharp left down a corridor.

"Where are ye away off to, wane?" Fionnuala demanded. "To cry in a corner about that piggin talent show again?"

"To the loo to boke again."

"Would ye all look at Little Miss Dainty Stomach, la-de-dah!" Fionnuala threw her hand out, limp wrist. "I thought ye was made of sterner stuff, wee girl."

"I'm desperate for to take a slash and all," Padraig said. "I'll go with wer Siofra."

"Fine," Fionnuala said. "Mind youse—"

"Och, we know, sure," Padraig cut her off angrily. "Nick two loo rolls when we be's inside and bring em back to ye."

"The evil in that wane has moved from his eyes to his mouth, so it has," Fionnuala said, nudging Paddy's lager-bloated stomach. "Sarky wee cunt! Och, I clear forgot, but…"

She unshackled her handbag and pulled out a five pound bill.

Padraig and even Siofra's eyes shone with joy.

"I'm feeling wile peckish," their mother said. "I want youse to go to visit the snack bar or on-board mini-mart or some such."

As if they were at Wimbledon, both children's heads moved back and forth, following the trail of the money in their mother's hand. *Vacation Mammy be's nicer than Home Mammy!* they thought as a team.

"Padraig, I'm putting ye in charge of this fiver," Vacation Mammy continued, "and I want this back in me fingers, untouched. One of youse is to wave it at the man behind the counter at the till, pretending ye've money, like, and distracting him while the other nicks as much as ye can from the shelves. Ye've seven mouths to feed, mind. And an infant. Take Seamus with youse. He has two empty hands that can be filled and all. Cheerio."

The children stomped glumly off, the sheen gone from their eyes. Fionnuala clapped her hands and banged on the wall again.

"C'mon, Mammy, c'mon Paddy, *She is D, desirable, She is I, irresistible, She is S, super sexy…*"

This one Paddy and Maureen knew, and they banged along as they sang: *"D-I-S-C-O, she is D-I-S-C-O…!"*

Dymphna had been deposited in the passenger seating area; it was non-smoking and a ghost-town. Apparently, the Floods were the only family that hadn't splurged on a cabin.

Dymphna was clutching a can of beer and guzzling down, the wheelchair (they had discovered it also had no brakes) clanking from one table of the passenger seating area to the other. The family had used her wheelchair as their mobile coat check and left luggage, handbags and outerwear swinging from one handle, plastic bags with more booze from the other. Keanu's stroller hadn't fared much better, the handles also straining. The sole non-smoking passenger had long since vacated his tattered plastic seat due to Keanu's shrieks and the stench from his diaper.

Dymphna drained the dregs of the beer from the can and tossed it on the stained carpet. She kept leaning over in her seat, her body straining, her feet two useless lumps in plaster, her fingers clawing the air to snatch a handle of the stroller to change the dirty diaper. Keanu rolled to one end of the lounge, Dymphna to the other. Whimpering from grief and the physical strain and the ever-increasing stench, Dymphna wondered if she should make an abortion pit-stop during the trip; it was legal across the water.

Paddy and Fionnuala burst through the doors, Maureen in their wake.

"Help me, Mammy!" Dymphna implored. "The wane needs his nappy changed, and I kyanny reach him."

Fionnuala recoiled in disgust.

"Are ye outta yer bleedin fecking mind?"

"I'll help ye," Maureen said.

"Naw, Mammy," Fionnuala ordered. "Don't help that one. The Orange bastard's her wane, after all. And, just to let ye know, wee girl, what this trip is gonny be like for ye, *I'm* not putting me back outta whack, wheeling ye around the transportation hubs of the EU! And straining me eyesight scouring the countryside for ramps to push ye up and down."

Paddy would've protested—it was an outrage, after all—but the lager and the guilt of Aggie and knowing he had to keep on Fionnuala's good side kept his lips shut. The three children came into the lounge and laid the toilet paper stash and loot from the mini-mart before their mother.

"Let's see what ye've got for wer sustenance," Fionnuala mused. She grabbed at the items with increasing confusion and repulsion, while behind her Maureen nudged Keanu's stroller closer and closer to Dymphna's wheelchair.

"What the bloody feck be's *soy* milk?" Fionnuala roared. "I wouldn't drink anything that didn't come from a cow, sure! And *flushable wipes with aloe vera?* Are youse wanes outta yer minds? And ye've brought me *bottled water?* While it pours from the taps worldwide for free? What sort of deranged shop for useless gacks with more money than sense did ye dredge these up from? Where's wer food, sure?"

"We couldn't reach the shelves with food," Padraig explained with a scowl.

"We did manage to get these, but," Siofra put in, slipping out of her jacket a can of Vienna sausages, three apricots and a pack of gum, teeth-whitening, "when I had Seamus on me shoulders."

"For the love of Christ almighty, what are we meant to eat? Paddy, can ye not have a word with these wanes? Och—!"

Fionnuala stared in horror as Dymphna snatched Keanu out of his stroller, brown streams rolling down his struggling legs.

"I'm warning ye, wee girl, so help ye God, if that wane has shite on me video, there'll be pure hell to pay!"

Fionnuala staggered to the stroller, wrenched out the video and inspected it. It was clean. She clamped it to her chest.

"How can a flimmin video mean more to ye than yer grandson?" Dymphna wondered as she dry retched and cried into Keanu's bared bottom.

"Shall I tell ye how? I'll tell youse all, shall I?"

"That would be a plan, aye," Paddy conceded.

Fionnuala cleared her throat and announced to the family around her in a teetering, wavering semi-circle what was on the video. She wouldn't have done it if she hadn't been legless. Those older than eleven were stunned, yet stared at her as if she had announced she was converting to the Church of England. Those eleven or under simply stared.

"I know it's shocking. It's true, but. Pity I kyanny see a VCR in this lounge, or youse could all have a look and see for yerselves. Now youse can understand why the Filth be's after us with such force. And I'm warning youse all now, when themmuns from the telly comes to interview, ye're to tell them it was me that found it! Now! Back to you!"

She turned to her favorite punching bag, Dymphna, who was still crying into the screaming and squirming mess she tried to balance on her legs and change.

"And, sin of sins, now ye've another half-Orange freak on the way. Ye're a disgrace, wee girl, popping them half-Protestant monsters outta yer manky womb..!"

"I'm half-Proddy meself, ye heartless bitch, and ye're to blame!" Dymphna yelled, then gasped in horror at her revelation.

Maureen dropped the anal wipes.

"The claptrap spewing from yer mouth!" Fionnuala snorted. "Must be them hormones of yers. What ye're saying doesn't even make no sense. And if ye ever call me a bitch again, I'll clatter the life outta ye, ye ungrateful cunt! I gave birth to ye, don't ye forget! Back me up, Paddy,"

"Do as yer mother says," Paddy hastened to comply, "or ye're no longer me daughter."

"I'm not yer daughter, but!" Dymphna blurt. "That be's the problem!"

The children gawped, and Maureen knew she should be horrified, but was distracted by the sound of a helicopter hovering over the roof that kept out the rain.

"Hi, youse'uns—!" she warned.

"Daddy, I'm mortified to let ye know, I've found out I'm the product of that *bitch* there—" Dymphna singled out Fionnuala with a brownish-yellow finger, "getting her leg over with a filthy, Proddy bastard Brit soldier!"

"Och, catch yerself on, ye simpleton," Fionnuala sneered as Paddy goggled her. "As if I would ever lay a finger on a Brit bastard paratrooper!"

"I hear a chopper—" Maureen attempted.

"I've the proof, but!" Dymphna contorted her seated form so she could reach the tattered newsprint in her back pocket. Keanu squealed on her left knee.

"Paddy, ye believe me, don't ye?" Fionnuala demanded.

Paddy's mouth was like a goldfish's on a floor again.

"The Filth be's hovering over us!" Maureen squealed, searching the lounge for exits.

Fionnuala tore the newsprint from her daughter's fingers, and Paddy peered over her shoulder, his quickly-sobering eyes drinking in the image.

"Och, that's me cousin Una, sure!" Fionnuala spat. She whipped her head to Dymphna. "Ye traitorous cunt!"

Fionnuala pushed a squealing Dymphna the length of the deck. The shit-filled diaper sailed through the air and spattered on a table. The wheelchair crashed into the picture window. The plexiglass pane popped out and clattered onto the deck. Dymphna screamed as torrents of rain poured through the window atop her. Siofra vomited on the apricots.

Eying Dymphna and the damage, a wave of guilt swept over Fionnuala; she had just realized it was a Holy Day and they weren't at mass. Wondering if there were a chapel on board, she turned to Paddy, but—

"The Filth! The Filth!" Maureen screamed, her cane pointing at human figures dangling from ropes that materialized behind Dymphna's drenched, screaming body.

Five officers rappelling from the helicopter overhead threw themselves through the window frame and landed on the carpet, machine guns aloft.

"Secure the perimeter!" one of them roared.

The Floods tried to scatter and escape, but it was useless: Fionnuala and

Paddy were too drunk, Maureen too old, Seamus too young, Siofra too sick, Dymphna wheelchair-bound and Keanu not even clothed. They captured Padraig halfway down the corridor to the video arcade and dragged him, kicking and squealing, to the rest of the family, handcuffed around their garbage bag baggage. Fionnuala had spat on the officers as they cuffed her.

The one in charge barked into his walkie-talkie: "We've got her, Inspector, but we've a few more suspects here than we expected. It's not gonny be possible to haul them all into the helicopter. They wouldn't fit, and I don't know how we'd propel the girl in the wheelchair up there in any event."

He listened, nodding.

"Right ye are, sir."

He turned to the Floods.

"We're locking youse up in the drunk tank here aboard, then transporting youse all back to Belfast on the next departing ferry. And from there to the precinct in Derry for questioning."

Maureen was surprised, as she hadn't seen a drunk tank in the brochure listing on-board amenities.

"When's the next ferry leaving for Derry?" the malnourished-looking little girl asked.

He was surprised at the question.

"Half-four. We'll be in Derry just after midnight."

"Yay! We'll be back in time for the talent show, sure!"

Siofra couldn't clap with glee as she was handcuffed.

They sat, hands bound, in the drunk tank, their rage long having subsided, and the intoxication of the adults as well. At least the coppers had fed them. Most were dozing. Maureen whispered to Fionnuala:

"I happened to have a wee watch of the video back home. Now that ye've explained it, I'm still trying to get me head around it. Didn't it happen in Paris, but?"

"Everybody knows that, sure, Mammy."

"What was themmuns in the video doing speaking with posh English accents, then?"

"Och, ye think I know everything, you!"

"I can assure ye I don't."

They fell silent, Fionnuala hoping Paddy never found out the coal delivery man was Dymphna's father, Maureen remembering the time she had taken a very young Dymphna down to the Top-Yer-Trolley back in 1997. Not that Maureen would reveal it to a living soul nowadays, but after doing the rest of the shopping, she had, like everyone else then, placed ten copies of "Candle

In The Wind," 5 on CD single and 5 on vinyl, into her shopping cart and rolled it towards the checkout.

The ferry chugged towards Belfast.

CHAPTER 67

"Take off yer cowboy hat, Jed," Ursula hissed. "It be's poking out, sure. Themmuns is gonny spot us!"

Ursula and Jed crouched behind the Coyle's ratty hedges, gawping at the police cars parked willy-nilly outside the Flood house.

"Some things never change." Ursula murmured.

She had wanted to have tea with Fionnuala, and then she wanted to go around the corner and visit 5 Murphy Crescent. Tea with Fionnuala wouldn't be forthcoming.

Police officers kept coming out with boxes they loaded in their cars, uncomfortable looks on their faces. Ursula was sure the looks had less to do with what they were hauling down to the precinct as evidence and more to do with the filth inside Fionnuala's house.

"What on God's green Earth has that family been up to now?" Ursula wondered.

Jed couldn't hazard a guess.

Ursula had replayed her triumphant return to Derry many times in her mind. The reality was proving very different. Their plane had flown through an electrical storm, and it had to make an emergency landing at Saint Angelo Airport in Enniskillen, County Fermanagh. It was a one hour drive to Derry, and the rental car broke down. Ursula sat fretting in the car while Jed puttered about outside with an umbrella attached to the hood and wobbling uncertainly in the downpour (the umbrella, not Jed). Once he got it started up, they were stopped for half an hour by a herd of sheep crossing the road. But they finally made it to Derry.

After checking into the hotel in shame, they had wandered around the familiar city center within the ancient walls and the cannons that poked out of them. Ursula had only been gone a year, but marveled at how clean and fresh the city now seemed. But they had yet to venture to the Moorside. All around her, Ursula relaxed at the accent and the Derry words that were to her so familiar, but to the rest of the world so strange...wane, flimmin, skegrat... They were the accent and the words that spelled Home. None of these words, however, were being directed towards her. She had become a stranger.

The comings and goings of the police soon bored her, and Ursula stared up at the gray clouds that always seemed to press down upon the town, shrouding the citizens in a perpetual feeling of being trapped, as she thought perhaps many here in the Moorside were. After a year in the health-obsessed US, however, Ursula now wondered if those clouds were less a phenomenon of nature and something to do with all the smoking going on in the town below.

"Right, let's be on wer way," Ursula and Jed strained to hear one officer say. "We've enough here, I think."

"What exactly do we have, but?"

"A few knock-off DVDs and some bottles of absinthe that was illegal years ago. That be's it, but."

"No sign of all them weapons the inspector was insisting was here?"

One of the officers quickly boarded up the door they had broken down, and the police cars zoomed down the road. Ursula made to leap across the street, but Jed dragged her into the bushes.

"I'll go first, honey," he said.

He crept across the street, looked around the Flood's 'garden' to ensure there were no police left, then motioned for Ursula to come across. She did, eagerly.

"What do ye see?" she asked.

"Nothing much."

They peered through the grime on the windows into the living room. Drawers hung out, tables and chairs were overturned, but ashtrays were still piled high with ash and butts. They didn't know if it was the state of a crime scene, the mess left over from the police search, or Fionnuala's lack of housekeeping.

Jed tried the door, but the officer had hammered the nails into the board across it tightly.

"I don't think there's much more we can do here, dear," he said.

Ursula agreed. "Let's just be on wer way around the corner to see the house, then," she said.

They walked around the corner. Ursula stuck her hand through Jed's arm and shivered with anticipation. Home. She would finally be there. Ursula could smell it in the ozone that threatened rain, see it in the forty shades of green, the familiar broken lager bottles, the menace in the eyes of the teenagers lounging on the corner.

"Och, Jed, it's wile exciting to see 5 Murphy again. Like meeting an aul friend, so it is."

Jed smiled. Ursula screamed. They both stared at the charred debris of what had once been the family home. She reached out a frail hand for support. Jed took it, and briefly debated removing his cowboy hat in reverence, but then realized it was only a house. Such a thought never entered Ursula's mind. Her sorrow turned to rage.

"That Fionnuala's had her hand in this, mark me words," she ranted. "Compensation for fire damage comes to mind. *This* be's the crime scene! When I see that Fionnuala...!"

"It appears she might be locked up," Jed said. "I don't think you can barge into the police station."

"They won't be keeping her there for long, Ye heard what the coppers said. There wasn't much evidence of a crime. I know, but, where I'll find yer woman sure as the day be's long."

Jed looked at her in surprise.

"Really? Where?"

"Ye mind that wee girl gave us the leaflet down the town? About the Top-Yer-Trolley annual sale the day after the morrow? Fionnuala would never miss it. Even if she has to break outta the cell she be's locked in, she'll be there, first in line. And I'm gonny be second."

Jed led a fuming Ursula back towards the city center and the empty hotel room that awaited them.

"Should we pop in here for a pint of Guinness?" he asked, motioning to the Rocking Seamaid pub.

"Naw," Ursula said. "I want to take a shower and cry in it. Then we can go out and ye can fill yer gullet with drink with me blessing. I'll be right at yer side knocking em back and all for once."

They walked on.

Inside the Rocking Seamaid, MacAfee and Scudder sat in the nook, eyes shining. MacAfee hissed down the pay-as-you-go cellphone:

"The day after the morrow, there'll be a huge bomb in a big shop in the city center."

He hung up, tossed the cellphone in the garbage and took a gulp of beer.

"Do ye think I gave the Filth enough clues as to the location?" MacAfee asked Scudder.

"Och, I always thought it wile daft, planting a bomb and then ruining the surprise by placing a warning call. What's the bloody point of planting the bomb in the first place, hi?"

MacAfee nodded in agreement. Scudder rubbed his filthy hands.

"The bomb's all set," he said. "Thank feck for that new shipment. And what I kyanny wait, for, be's the outrage that's gonny be unleashed when ye phone back after the deed be's done, the Top-Yer-Trolley in smithereens, like, and lie to the Filth by telling em we be's a Proddy terrorist group what done it. That's sure to make the Yanks come running with their dollars to help fund us, hi! I wonder, but, what that Flood woman ever did with the first shipment of explosives. Do ye think she be's starting her own freedom fighting group, like?"

CHAPTER 68

Dymphna buried her hands in despair as her unborn child kicked away at the walls of her womb. It was like poor Beeonsay was trying to escape from the family even before she entered it. Dymphna knew how Beeonsay felt. Since she could remember, she had blindly followed her family, treating the twisted venom that spit from her mother's mouth as the wisdom of the world. Sitting in the cell now, terrified the coppers might somehow question her about the cache of arms she found in the lockup, she was realizing how wrong Fionnuala was about many things.

Dymphna turned her attention to her three younger siblings passed out around her wheelchair. It was propped back against the wall as the coppers had taken the case of vegetables from the bottom tray, though why Dymphna couldn't fathom. Perhaps they were hungry. Dymphna wanted to yell at Padraig, Siofra and Seamus, "Run, youse! Run as fast as yer legs can take youse!" If they had still been on the ferry, she would've added: "Jump overboard, youse, and swim to shore sharpish, and never be seen from again!"

It had taken her brain long enough, but Dymphna was now catching a glimpse at what Bridie had meant, understanding why Bridie might be sick of her, and Zoë and Rory as well. All her nineteen years, Dymphna had been trusting the one who had given birth to her, blindly following the Flood party line, resenting and hating those outside the family, and where was she now? Friendless and man-less, with a six-month old bastard and another on the way, two broken ankles plopped on a wonky wheelchair, and locked up in the slammer with the threat of being an accomplice to a terrorist group she knew nothing about. Well, the coppers could add treason to the list. If Moira ever came to Derry for a book signing, and Ursula somehow stopped by to get a signed copy, Dymphna would be the first of the family to commit that crime and offer both Moira and Auntie Ursula the hand of peace. Just to spite her mother.

Keanu stirred, and the dark corner where his stroller was parked filled with squawks and gurgles. If she had been able to roll the wheelchair towards him, Dymphna would have cradled him in her arms for once and sung a lullaby to send him back to slumber. The song would be, of course, that one about the halo by Beyoncé (the diva one; her daughter was as yet unborn and had still to record any songs). As it was, Dymphna couldn't reach Keanu, so she ground her teeth at the unbearable racket instead.

Fionnuala was inspecting her teeth for lipstick in the mirror when she realized it was probably one of those high-class two-way ones she had seen on TV. The officers on the other side were probably fiddling with themselves as they checked her out! she thought.

"Youse filthy pervs!" she mouthed, lips stretched in disgust, then scuttled back to the hideous metal chair at its matching table. The strip of light on the ceiling kept crackling and flickering. They could have had the decency to give her a room with functioning electrics, she thought, arms crossed, foot tapping impatiently.

Inspector McLaughlin and one of his minions entered the room. Fionnuala searched their hands for the video, but they held only files. The minion was a hard-faced wee cunt barely out of diapers. Her brown hair was pulled so tightly on her skull she looked Asian. A Protestant, Fionnuala presumed, climbing the corporate ladder of the day's police force with her legs spread wide.

"Finally we meet, Mrs. Flood," Inspector McLaughlin said as he sat, and Fionnuala longed to slap the smarmy grin off his mustache. "I'm Inspector McLaughlin, and this be's PC Morrissey."

Fionnuala smirked. She knew a wife and mother should ask where they had hidden her husband and children, but she couldn't be bothered wasting the breath. She decided to play the game.

"I'm innocent!" she barked. "What've ye chased us the length and breadth of Europe for?"

McLaughlin delved into a file and pulled out the artist's sketch without looking at it; his eyes still smarting from the memory. He held it up to the suspect in the chair.

"Ye will agree this bears a remarkable resemblance to ye, aye?"

"Ach, looks more like me cousin Una, so it does. Sure, I haven't them God-awful ponytails, so I haven't. And bleached and all! What the bloody hell was she thinking, hi?"

"Actually, Mrs. Flood," Hard-Faced Cunt said, "we've interviewed…" she glanced at a note "…Molly, the stylist at Xpressions hair salon, and she told us you had your hair, er, your look—remodeled—the other week. So we know this is you."

"Aye, and? What of it?"

"We've had complaints that a woman matching this description, that is, *you*," Hard-Faced Cunt's eyes bored into Fionnuala, her promotion more secure with each sentence uttered, "instigated a riot outside the Our Lady of Perpetual Sorrow Girls' School the other week. You caused thousands of pounds in damage to windows and other building parts."

"Och, if that was me, and I'm not saying it was, mind, me fingers never clutched a rock. Youse kyanny bang me up for what eejits in the crowd decides to do in the heat of the moment."

"And," Inspector McLaughlin put in, "is it true ye be's an OsteoCare provider?"

"Och, I'm too busy, sure, I've wanes aplenty, and an aul dottery mother of me own that needs constant care." Fionnuala was confident her mate Aileen at OsteoCare, and even Mrs. Ming and Mrs. Gee, would never grass her up to the police. "Even if I was, since when does it be a crime to show Christian compassion to teetering aul folk what has one foot in the grave? If youse've no evidence, go on and release me now. The hunger be's gnawing a hole in me stomach, sure, and I'm twisting me legs for a slash."

PC Morrissey continued: "Not only do we have evidence taken from you at the ferry," Fionnuala tensed; *now* her video would be revealed from whatever hidden pocket or nook it was stashed, "we also searched your house earlier—"

"Without me permission, like?"

"We had probable cause," Inspector McLaughlin explained. "The lot of youse was fleeing the jurisdiction."

"Och, trying to intimidate me, are ye, with them big words of yers, like ye've gone and swallowed a dictionary whole. Our trip on the ferry, is ye on about? We was on wer way to a family holiday in Malta, just, to visit me eldest daughter. She's written a book, ye know." Fionnuala wondered if this might suddenly make her not guilty, but they didn't seem impressed. "And I'll have youse know, I'm to be filing for compensation for all the money we splashed out on wer holiday. Highway robbery, the price of that ferry was for the state it was in."

"What we've confiscated has now been entered into evidence, and our forensic lab will soon be going over it," PC Morrissey said. She suddenly jumped up and exited the room.

Inspector McLaughlin touched Fionnuala's hands. "Give yerself up, Mrs. Flood," he said. "There's only so much I can do, what with all the Proddies on the force I'm surrounded by."

"Och, don't ye good cop, bad cop me," Fionnuala spat. "I've seen more episodes of *Law and Order* than ye've had hot dinners."

Hard-Faced Cunt came back in, struggling under the weight of a box clutched in her hands, the fingernails of which, Fionnuala noted, were unpolished. She wondered if PC Morrissey might be the secret lesbian lover of the caterer who had given her the tomato sandwiches with no tops.

"These are just a selection, mind," PC Morrissey said. She pulled out a bottle of absinthe swaddled in a plastic evidence bag. "There were many more in a crate found in the scullery of your house."

"I found that absinthe down an alley in Creggan, so I did," Fionnuala said. "Finding things doesn't be a crime, sure!"

"Aye, but solicitation in pubs be's," Inspector McLaughlin said. "And the barmaid at the Craiglooner has identified you from the sketch. We might haul her in for a lineup."

"Och, a misdemeanor, sure!" Fionnuala said, proud at using a four-syllable word and already planning her revenge on the snitch bartender bitch. "Ye surely wouldn't send the chopper halfway across the Irish Sea for to arrest me for that, sure!"

"That is true," PC Morrissey said. "But now we come to the matter that threatened national security, the reason we almost got the Secret Service and Interpol involved. You see, as serious as it is to be in possession of what you were, it is an even more serious crime to attempt to transport it across international borders, even borders between EU states—"

"Ye see, Mrs. Flood," Inspector McLaughlin cut her off, his hand delving into the box. Fionnuala knew he was going for the video.

"It be's mines! *Mines!*" Fionnuala screamed.

"And now it is ours." McLaughlin smirked.

"I know the way youse work!" Fionnuala seethed, a trembling finger singling him out. "Ye've nicked it to snatch all the glory for yerself! Ye're in a position of power, a disgusting, hateful Filth-master, and think ye've the right to trample over decent, God-fearing members of the down-trodden class the likes of me. Yer position in the Filth-force, staring down yer nose at us, allows ye to nick what ye like and claim possession of it for yerself. I'm warning ye, but, I'll be on the phone to every newspaper the country over if ye claim that video be's yers!"

Her body shuddered, her eyes crazed with rage atop a blood-colored face, spittle trailing down her chin.

The inspector and the minion exchanged a look of confusion.

"Video?" PC Morrissey asked.

"I don't know about any video, love," Inspector McLaughlin said. "We've hauled ye and yer family down here for these."

Inspector McLaughlin drew his hand out of the box, and in a plastic bag were clustered three cans: brussels sprouts, new potatoes and carrots.

"Are ye having me on?" Fionnuala asked. "Where be's the video? The video that's to be the most-watched video of wer time? The media sensation of the century?!"

McLaughlin stared.

"What are ye on about?"

"Ye daft cunt! The secret illegal videotape of Princess Diana's autopsy, sure!"

"Princess…!" McLaughlin sputtered, while the shocked PC Morrissey could no longer look anywhere near Fionnuala's eyes, ashamed for the delusional creature across the table as she was. "I've never heard anything so ludicrous in me life! And, anyroad, what's this media blitz ye're on about? Ye're talking out yer arse, woman! Who in their right mind…*sputter! Sputter!* Only the mentally deranged or severely depraved would want to look upon such a *thing!* If it existed. I feel unclean just imagining it! Naw, we've hauled ye in for smuggling dangerous contraband across EU lines."

"Aye, and doesn't the dangerous contraband be the video of one of the world's most beloved icons being sliced into?"

"It be's the pigging Semtex explosives in these flimming tins of vegetables! An entire case of em, ye were trailing along on the ferry in yer daughter's wheelchair! Enough to blow the town to bits three times over!"

"Och, wise up, ye!" Fionnuala gnawed on her lip, her brain struggling to comprehend. "But…but youse started trailing me after that eejit at the pawn shop made a call to youse. After I told yer man what be's on the video, like. And quit gawping at me like I be's deranged! And ye and all, ye lesbo-perv!"

But neither of them could quit gawping at her. McLaughlin tried to comport himself to normalcy.

"Naw, yer man at the pawn shop recognized ye as his mother bought mushy peas from ye at the Sav-U-Mor weeks ago, but when yer woman opened the tin at home they were anything but. She told her son, and they brought it down to the station. After forensics had a look, we realized the tin was filled with Semtex. We approached the owner of the Sav-U-Mor, Mr. Skivvins, and he told us about yer switch-and-bait, but yer man has been doctoring the books for years and had no real employee records, like, so he couldn't tell us exactly who ye was. A Mrs. Flood, just, he hadn't a clue as to yer first name, and there be's hundreds of Floods in Derry, like. We hauled Skivvins in for tax evasion, but that be's of no concern here."

"How did youse find me, then?" Fionnuala had the intelligence to ask.

"We had a new satellite explosive-detection system installed the other day, been asking for it for years, like, but the budget was never there for it as the powers that be thinks the Troubles be's at an end, like. Anyroad, we turned it on, and that case of tinned Semtex of yers was shining out all sorts of red signals. We just followed yer trail. Heart-scared, we was, when we saw youse had mobilized and was traipsing through the countryside. Now, Mrs. Flood, to the point. I do believe ye hadn't a clue what be's in them cans. Are ye of the same mind, PC Morrissey?"

PC Morrissey bobbed her head like a dog giving its balls a spring cleaning with the tongue.

"So where did ye get them cans from?" McLaughlin asked.

Rule number one in the Moorside was never grass anyone up to the Filth, never ever. Ever. Fionnuala opened her mouth and wailed: "Down the Mountains of Mourne Gate market, from a lad with hollow eyes and shaky hands. He's the stall next to the one with the dog collars. Late-twenties, just under six foot, blue eyes, sandy blonde hair parted on the left, a wee scar just under his left nostril, wears plaid shirts and rolls up the cuffs of his jeans. Size thirty waist. Does I be free to go?"

"Ye're free to go, aye."

"About bloody time, hi!"

"Ye're released on yer own recognizance. Mind ye don't try another wee trip to Liverpool, but."

"Why?"

"We need ye to identify yer man from the market. And let's just say ye still be's a person of interest."

This made Fionnuala feel important. She adjusted her brown flip and smiled.

"And what about me video?" she demanded.

"The video be's in the evidence locker with all yer other gear. We'll have wer technological forensics team look into them…startling…allegations of yers. However unlikely they seems. If nothing comes of it, we'll hand it back to ye."

Fionnuala got up to go, but turned to them. "I wonder if one of youse might tell me. Didn't she die in Paris?"

"Still this babbling about Princess Di!" McLaughlin's eyes were weary of staring. This woman and her delusion: it was like a pitbull with its jaws locked around an infant. "Aye, she died in Paris. But—"

"Why, then, does themmuns be speaking English in the video? Surely themmuns would be speaking French? It was me mammy that brought it up, and I've been worrying over it ever since."

McLaughlin opened his mouth, closed it, then opened it again.

"Sir, if I may," PC Morrissey came to his rescue. "I've read up on it. If you must know, Mrs. Flood, the family had her body shipped to London a few days after the French autopsy was done. There was another autopsy at the Hammersmith and Fulham Mortuary. They didn't trust the French results. And who could blame them?"

Fionnuala brimmed with excitement. So it was the real thing!

"Ye've been wile informative. Ta, like. And what about me family members?" she asked, hoping the police would keep them overnight so she'd have the house to herself for once.

"Them has already been released. Useless, they was."

"Och, I could've told ye that, sure, and saved ye loads of taxpayers' money."

As Fionnuala walked down the hall, and McLaughlin and PC Morrissey exchanged a look in silence that said many things, there was a banging on the door. A head poked in.

"Sir, we've received an anonymous tip-off that a new terrorist group is planning to detonate a bomb somewhere in the city center the day after tomorrow."

McLaughlin and Morrissey stared.

"I wonder," McLaughlin said, "If this be's the same terrorist cell that left that cache of weapons we recovered from the Pence-A-Day lockup last week."

"I thought, sir," Morrissey said, "they had made a run for it. The door to the lock up was wide open, after all. As if they were consumed with guilt over the horriblel activities they were planning and wanted their arms to be confiscated."

"How credible is the threat?" McLaughlin asked the PC who had told them the news.

"Credible, sir. They didn't give a location, but. Might I suggest they will target the Top-Yer-Trolley's annual sale? That seems most likely, given the day chosen."

"Hmm, well, we don't really know."

"Should the public be warned, sir?"

"Are ye mad, boyo? There'd be city-wide panic, so there would! Naw, I've got the situation under control. We'll have groups combing the area, and bomb-sniffing dogs and whatnot in place. And hopefully themmuns will call again and give us more info."

CHAPTER 69

"I'm wile happy ye made it in time," Grainne said backstage to Siofra, and Catherine bobbed her head at her side. "We've been thinking, but."

"Out with it!" Siofra said.

"How is we meant to win the contest and become mates with Hannah Montana when we're to cause such destruction?"

"Och, I've that all planned out. It's wile easy. We'll say I hadn't a clue me brother was above us. What wee girls knows what their older brothers be's up to, sure?"

Catherine was an only child, so she was no authority.

'Fresh' from the holding cell, Siofra took command, adjusting the jellyfish and pipe-cleaner seahorses of the Happiness Boat they were about to roll onto the stage the moment the twenty-fourth girl wrapped up the Irish Dancing segment. But now worry creased her brow.

Siofra was so hell-bent on revenge, she hadn't paused to consider the fact that humiliating Pink Petals might make them lose. It was too late now. She had already sent Padraig up the catwalk that held the lights over the stage, and he had the instructions he was only too delighted to follow, and the motherload. It had been heavy to carry, and he had trouble hauling it up the ladder, but Siofra glanced up and saw him shoving his body across the catwalk. He gave her a wave with his free hand, and she could see the menace and delight beaming behind his urine-colored specs even at this distance.

Miss McClurkin hurried up to them, clipboard clamped to her chest, as the lackluster applause beyond the curtains petered out. She twittered down at them with unbridled excitement.

"The audience was bored senseless with all of them," she whispered, nodding slyly at the twenty-three girls sweating in a field of velvet, green sashes and black tights against the pulleys and boxes of the backstage. She grappled all six of their hands in hers. "You girls are the only chance we have of beating How Great Thou Art, especially after that croissant cooking lesson in French. We've kept you specially for last. Give it your all, girls, and the fingers of the Foyle will not only reach out for each other, they will *touch!* Do it for the future of the city, where Catholics and Protestants can live in harmony. Do it for a united, happy Ireland!"

"Aye, Miss," they chorused.

"Oh, this will be *historic!*"Miss McClurkin bubbled. "Give me a few minutes to clear the last girl off the stage and to introduce you."

She hurried back onstage, microphone in her hand, and Siofra, Grainne and Catherine rolled the Happiness Boat towards the stage.

"What hell hath *Riverdance* wrought?" Mr. Skivvins was murmuring to Mrs. Pilkey at his side at the table on the end of the stage reserved for the judges. Even Fionnuala in the back row of the auditorium, as proud as she was of Celtic culture, was wishing the coppers had kept her in overnight. She was still wondering about that Proddy girl who had spent five minutes on stage in a peculiar beekeeper-looking hat shoving a skinny sword through the air at nothing that Fionnuala could see. But, she had noticed, Zoë Riddell had wriggled her way onto the panel of judges. And that Mr. Skivvins as well, and the headmistress of How Great Thou Art. There were three Protestant judges versus the Catholic madwoman Concepta McLaughlin and Mrs. Pokey or Plinkey or whatever her name was. Typical. The contest was rigged. Her little girl would never win. Mrs. McLaughlin looked like she didn't know what timezone on Earth she was in, and the Our Lady of Perpetual Sorrow headmistress looked like she might convert to Protestantism for a feel of Mr. Skivvins' manpole. Fionnuala wanted to spew.

"And now, esteemed panel of judges, now, girls from both schools," Miss McClurkin yelled over the feedback of the microphone, " I'm proud to present our final act from Our Lady of Perpetual Sorrow, and it's a great one. We've Miss Siofra Flood, Miss Grainne Donaldson and Miss Catherine McLaughlin and their delightful journey on the Happiness Boat!"

There were a few suspicious claps as the Happiness Boat was rolled onstage by the three girls. Catherine and Grainne propped bricks against the wheels to keep it stationary as Siofra grabbed the microphone from Miss McClurkin. The teacher scurried offstage, clapping gleefully.

"Welcome youse all to the Happiness Boat!" Siofra yelled out at the crowd. The girls and their parents were seated How Great Thou Art on one side of the auditorium, Our Lady of Perpetual Sorrow on the other. Siofra scanned for PinkPetals, and her heart beat with dread. She couldn't see her. What if PinkPetals had called in sick?

"We need a volunteer," Siofra hollered, eyes begging themselves to land upon PinkPetal's face. "A girl from How Great Thou Art, please, a volunteer… er, with blonde hair! Which of youse would like to ride in the Happiness Boat with us?"

A smattering of hands went up, but Siofra finally zoned in on PinkPetals. How she had missed the Hannah Montana earrings framing Victoria Skivvins' sneer she didn't know. Siofra singled her out with a finger.

"You, there!" she insisted. "Come and board the Happiness Boat."

Victoria was horrified, but her school mates slapped her on the shoulder, and her teacher almost wrenched her arm out of its socket.

"Get you up there now," the teacher ordered. "And plaster a smile on your miserable face while you're at it. The school's reputation for being the friendliest in the North is on the line."

The smile Victoria plastered on her face would sour milk, but she forced her Jellies to climb the steps of the stage.

"Music, Miss McClurkin," Siofra instructed. A dancey-techno beat filled the auditorium. After so many fiddles and Irish reels, Mrs. Pilkey nudged Mr. Skivvins and they exchanged a delighted, approving look.

"Grand Prize," Mrs. Pilkey mouthed, and under the table she massaged his knee.

Mr. Skivvins felt himself stir at her touch and touched back, his free hand making as if he were scribbling a note or two.

The change in music, and something every child in the audience recognized, made them go mental. If the contest were judged on audience reaction, Siofra had won before she had even started. She could see herself curtseying before Hannah, could already taste the hotdog Hannah would offer her. Siofra smiled at Victoria and guided her up the plank of wood that led to the deck of the Happiness Boat.

"I know you," Victoria hissed, still beaming from ear to ear. "I stole these earrings and this watch from you. What are you up to?"

"Nothing," Siofra hummed, her own face the picture of ecstasy. "The coming together of the communities, just."

Victoria gasped as Grainne and Catherine hauled her atop the row of milk crates that was the deck of the boat.

"What am I supposed to do on this," Victoria sneered. "ridiculous *Happiness* boat of yours?"

"Stand and wave," Siofra instructed. "And look happy."

"I feel very foolish," Victoria said.

"Keep yer mouth shut," Siofra hissed. "If we win, we'll invite ye along to the concert and all." *As if!*

Victoria's hand shot up in the air, and she waved it from side to side. Siofra, Grainne and Catherine scampered off the boat. Siofra ran to the front, Grainne to the port, Catherine to the starboard. They shimmied and bounced and kicked and flung their arms in syncopation. Then the song began.

"*We be's Green,*" Catherine, Grainne and Siofra sang, pointing at their chests, "*and youse is Orange*"—they pointed at Victoria, who was grinning and smiling and waving away.

"*We be's Coke,*" pointing at themselves again

"and youse is Pepsi," pointing into the audience.
"Take a drink of Coke.
Ugh!
Take a drink of Pepsi.
Yuck!"

Miss McClurkin was alarmed at the vulgar thrust of the hips, and Mrs. Pilkey massaged the nape of her neck in worry. Zoë had already given them 10 out of 10.

"Pop open the tins and pour them together.
Yum, yum, delicious!
What tastes better?
Both together!
We are better together,
Green and Orange together,
Orange and Green.
The best two colors Ireland's ever seen!
Yum, yum, delicious!
Pour them together,
Coke and Pepsi,
Pepsi and Coke.
The two best sodas Ireland's ever seen! What tastes better?
Both together!
We're better together, better together…
La di dum dum,
la la,
dum de dum!"

Mrs. Pilkey squeezed Mr. Skivvins' arm, and even Miss McClurkin, having gotten over the filthy thrust of the bodies during the Ugh! and the Yuck!, was caught up in the excitement, her right foot trying in vain to find the beat and tap along to the devil's music, her hands clapping haltingly.

Siofra pointed to her classmates' side of the audience.

"What color is youse?" she hollered.

"Green!" they bellowed.

"And youse?" she demanded of the alien side.

"Orange!"

"What do youse drink?"

"Coke!"

"And youse?"

"Pepsi!"

"And what tastes better?"

"Both together!"

Siofra, Grainne and Catherine erupted into dance and song again: *"We be's green, and youse is orange..."*

Stood atop the Hapyness Boat, Victoria's smile blossomed at the roars and claps erupting in the auditorium and,

"We be's Coke and youse is Pepsi..."

as she squinted through the harsh spotlights, she saw the dancing in the rows and then the aisles of the two rival schoolchildren,

"What tastes better? **BOTH TOGETHER!"**

felt the coming together of the communities, the bridging of the religious, brimmed with pride at the youth of the day showing their elders the way, casting aside generations of segregation and mistrust and what in the name of God was that smell of artichoke and urine, that slimy glop she felt trickling down her back?

Victoria was aware of fingers in the audience pointing at her. Padraig's aim, with his laser-sharp new vision, was spot on. The glutinous, rank glop from the cans spilled from the catwalk onto Victoria's well-conditioned locks, upon her designer dress—

Siofra stared in delight at the mass of filth spewing from above. She had no idea Padraig had hovered over the cauldron and emptied his bladder and bowels into the mix to up the wow-factor. He had even stuck his finger down his throat in an attempt to add some vomit, but there was no food in his stomach.

Victoria's pert blonde flips sagged under the weight. She clamped her eyes shut in terror, and felt the offal weighing down her eyelids, oozing over the bridge of her nose and plopping from her chin to her neck and from there down her favorite yellow dress.

"What on Earth!?" Victoria roared, forcing her eyes down to look upon her fingers, which were covered with things that looked like cauliflowers, but her horror-stricken eyes realized weren't. And then the screaming started, first from her mouth, then from the mouths of the scrabbling audience.

The stench attacked Victoria's little nose, an alien half-human, half-animal stench of decay and repulsion. She gagged and gagged and finally gave up gagging and heaved the contents of her stomach down the side of the Happiness Boat.

Mrs. Pilkey raced forward, only to stop in her tracks as the odor hit her and the closer sight of the viscous mess made her think twice about saving the girl. She had her heels to consider.

"My Vicky! My petal!" Mr. Skivvins gasped, rushing across the stage where all feared to tread.

Above their bobbing heads, Padraig wiped his lips with delight, and dragged his granny's cigarettes and her lighter from his pocket. He lit one, puffed away, coughed, and held the burning ash up to the sprinklers. Torrents of water poured from the ceiling.

Through the downpour, Mr. Skivvins spied two of the Happiness Boat girls skipping off, just made out their cackles under the shrieking from the audience and the screaming of his little girl and the spraying from the ceiling. He thought he heard the skinnier, more evil-looking one cackle, "Pepsi-slurping bitch!" before she disappeared.

Fionnuala saw Padraig scurry down the ladder and across the stage. She raced up the aisle, shoving through the stampede of sopping, screaming children heading for the exits. As she reached the steps, she saw Mrs. Pilkey's hand on her ex-boss' shoulder as he wiped the slop off his daughter's face and tried to quell her shrieking. Zoë stood by them, wringing her hands, horror beneath her Burberry frames.

Fionnuala tiptoed up to the drenched trio around the little bitch (a glance and she could tell). She squelched through the pigs' blood and seal brain fritters and vomit and urine and child feces in the relentless downpour and confusion, and all it took was a simple shove from Fionnuala on the smug bastard's shoulder to send Mr. Skivvins tumbling over the stage and into the orchestra pit. Mrs. Pilkey and Zoe Riddell soon followed. Fionnuala giggled with victory as she scampered off.

The paramedics saw to them, after restraining Concepta McLaughlin and her now even more fragile mind.

CHAPTER 70

For this sale, Fionnuala was especially chomping at the bit to shove through the Top-Yer-Trolley's revolving doors (she hoped they had fixed the malfunction which made them stick the year before; it had been a trial maneuvering through them laden with bargains). This year, she had decided, it was out with the chain-link belts, the flowered tights and the skimpy stripy tops. She had lain awake in bed the night before, tossing and turning fitfully, as she imagined snapping up pants-suits and anti-wrinkle creams and sensible loafers for pennies on the pound, things that would transform her into a sophisticated woman aging with dignity and grace, as befitted a player on the world media stage.

The annual sale was a family event, if only because Paddy and the children all had hands which could carry. The Floods had dragged themselves out of bed at 5 AM, Fionnuala hovering impatiently over them, so she could bag her place in the front row. Maureen had cried illness, and Fionnuala was enraged, but she allowed her mother to stay in bed as long as she looked after Keanu; the old woman had languished hours in the holding cell, after all. Even Dymphna had been rolled towards the superstore's front doors. She would be useless in the crowds inside with her wheelchair, but Fionnuala could use it to haul the purchases back to the Moorside and save on a taxi.

They parked Dymphna next to the drinking fountain. The rest of the family were pressed against the shatterproof plexiglass window (real glass hadn't been used since 1980; the Top-Yer-Trolly had been blown up and rebuilt three times during the Troubles before they got the message). Seamus' snot and tears smeared the window, Padraig was hacking into it with a pocket knife, Siofra banging her headless Barbie against it so they would let the doll in. Paddy was transported back to the smoking section of the ferry as the body parts of rabid shoppers shoved into his back, his neck, his arse, his heels. Fionnuala's feet pawed the cobblestones before the window like a bull preparing to charge, her elbows gouging into anyone who looked like they had more credit on their cards. The only good thing about their truncated trip to Malta was that Fionnuala now had hundreds of pounds to shove eagerly into the Top-Yer-Trolly tills.

"The annual sale has now begun!" said a voice from a loudspeaker somewhere, and a roar went up from the churning, desperate masses.

The doors were unlocked, and the employees scampered to their places, fear in their eyes. The hoards erupted through the doors, elbowing and kicking their way through the aisles, eyes shimmering with deranged delight, claws shooting out for dented cans and battered boxes.

"Grab it! Grab it, wanes!" Fionnuala hollered through the screams and flailing limbs.

"Grab what, mammy?" Seamus asked, tears of fear rolling down his face as he dodged the legs and knees and feet that threatened to trample his young form.

"Aye, what?" Siofra echoed.

"Och, for the love of—!" Were her children mentally challenged? Hadn't they gone through this last year, and the year before, and the year before that?

"Anything!" Fionnuala barked. "We can sort out what be's the best buy after everything be's in wer trolley! Possession be's nine-tenths of the law, don't youse forget!"

The children scattered into the screaming masses, hands reaching for anything they could. Paddy had only been inside for less than a minute but already had to escape. He jettisoned himself upstream of the frenzied bodies, catching glimpses from eyes shooting by that told him he was mad to be making his way *out*. Paddy thrust himself through the doors of the din and collapsed, hair tousled, nerves begging for a cigarette. Puffing away, he went to Dymphna, and was shocked to see her talking to Jed.

"It's wile lovely to have ye back in Derry, Uncle Jed," Dymphna nattered on. "And, aye, me mammy be's as mental as ever. Had the Filth chasing us on wer way to Liverpool. We was banged up the lot of us all night long, then she drags us outta bed at the crack of dawn to traipse down to this pigging sale!"

Paddy felt no betrayal to the Flood family from Dymphna; he felt the same. He walked over and stuck his hand out.

"Jed! Right man ye are!" he said. "Welcome back to Derry, hi!"

Suspicion glinted in Jed's eyes, but the friendliness pouring from Paddy's—Jed could detect it even through the bloody veins—put him at ease. They threw their arms around each other and hugged. Dymphna nodded in satisfaction.

Her wheelchair was turned the wrong way, Jed's cowboy hat had fallen over his eyes, and Paddy had closed his during the hug. The three of them couldn't see Scudder and MacAfee sneaking out of their van and lurking behind a tree next to the public toilets. Their faces were bright with booze and excitement, turned towards the Top-Yer-Trolly doors and all the victims shoving through them to their early graves.

"Not a word to Fionnuala about this, mind," Paddy said. "She'd have me bollocks in a vise."

"And Ursula?" Jed asked.

Paddy and Dymphna exchanged an uncomfortable glance. Jed was a foreigner and didn't really count as a person, so he could easily be forgiven. Ursula was another matter. Paddy twiddled his cigarette, Dymphna inspected a crack in a cast.

"I guess I better get inside," Jed said, "and find her."

"Them shoppers be's deranged," Paddy said. "Good luck to ye in there, mucker."

"I think I already found it out here."

Jed removed his hat, took a deep breath and forced himself through the doors.

Against her plans and better judgment, Fionnuala found herself fending off fingernails and elbows at the deep discount bargain bin selections, scrabbling through returned toothbrushes and defective toilet bowl scrubbers. Her shopping cart already held a three-tier document organizer, an extendible snow broom, an elevated toilet seat with arms, a bruised cabbage and a case of pâté de foie gras past their sell-by date.

"Mammy!" Seamus said, rushing towards her with the fear still in his eyes. "I've me hands full!"

"Right ye are, wane. Dump it all in mammy's trolley and off ye go for more."

As the child struggled to throw his loot into the very high cart, Fionnuala was aware of Siofra and Padraig approaching, but couldn't face them as she had just spied at the bottom of the bin a cracked bottle of Liz Taylor's White Diamonds for 70% off. Her hand shot out—

—and was clawed into by another hungry shopper, fingernails gouging into Fionnuala's flesh to snatch the perfect bargain.

"That be's mines! *Mines!*" Fionnuala snarled. "Ye grabby, hateful cunt—!"

Fionnuala gawped.

"Fionnuala!" Ursula gasped, White Diamonds clutched to her chest.

At the sight of his auntie Ursula, Seamus held his hand out, Pavlovian-like, for a gift. Was it Ursula's generosity or Seamus' greed?

The children jumped up and down excitedly.

"Auntie Ur—!"

"Don't youse take one step towards that *woman,*" Fionnuala warned, the spittle spraying from her lips.

Like automatons, their faces became blank and their outstretched arms collapsed to their sides. But it was too late. Ursula had detected the glint of recognition in their eyes and the glee that had followed. It only registered for a second amidst the melee of shrieking shoppers, but it would have to suffice. She could go to her grave knowing that, secretly, she was missed and loved. She held out the perfume to Fionnuala.

"That's all I bloody well need!" Fionnuala seethed. "The Lady of the Manor swanning back into town, her nose so high in the air it's a wonder she doesn't drown from the rain. Feck this!" She grabbed Siofra and Seamus by their heads, lunged for her shopping cart of treasures, snatched the perfume out of Ursula's hand, and headed through the foliage department. Ursula shoved through the crowd to follow.

"Mammy, but—" Padraig began.

"C'mon, c'mon, wanes," Fionnuala said, snapping her fingers and picking up speed. "That madwoman's after us all!"

As they hurried through the dying trees and ferns, Siofra turned to Padraig, swerving the bodies and carts barreling towards them.

"I wish Auntie Ursula was wer mammy," Siofra said.

"Aye, me and all," Padraig replied.

The rounded the aisle, puffing after their mother, Seamus now screaming tearfully, and found themselves in the food department.

"Grab at them goods, wanes!" Fionnuala barked.

They hurried to obey, Siofra running to the chips shelves and grabbing as many as she could. She froze, mid-grab, in horror.

"Och—!" Siofra gasped.

One shelf over, PinkPetals was inspecting the nutritional information on a pack of salt and vinegar potato chips. She looked up in alarm. It dissolved to rage.

"You filthy little creature!" Victoria screamed.

Fionnuala spied Ursula by the pyramid of Spaghetti Hoops, her back to them, head bobbing up and down and back and forth as she searched through the crowd. Fionnuala cackled under her breath and rolled her cart towards her. It rammed against Ursula, who yelped and sailed through the air, hands clawing at nothing. She flew into the Spaghetti Hoops display, cans raining down on her eggplant-colored bob.

Fionnuala knew she should scamper off, but the sight of Ursula under the cans was priceless. She ground her fingers into the handle of her cart and wriggled with laughter. She should buy a camera.

"Look at yer auntie Ursula, wanes!" she said. But the children weren't at her side, and Fionnuala saw to her disappointment Jed's cowboy hat winding through the crowd towards them. Spoilsport!

Splayed on the tiles, Ursula pushed her arms through the rolling cans. She tried to lift her head and saw next to her packets of cookie dough piled together under what was left of the pyramid. Even as she simmered with anger over Fionnuala and wondered how long she might struggle to pull herself upright in a field of cans, Ursula wondered why they had placed packs of cookie dough there. Nobody could see them to buy them, hidden under the Spaghetti Hoops as they were. And what drunk shelf-stacker thought cookie dough belonged with Spaghetti Hoops in any event? Shouldn't it be in the Home Baking section two aisles over? Then she saw the brightly colored wires that decorated the cookie dough. And the wee clock on top. And the numbers counting down: 01:59, 01:58, 01:57.

"There be's a bomb here!" Ursula roared just as Jed made it to the rolling cans. "A bomb, I tell youse! Clear on outta here! We've only one minute fifty-three, fifty-*two* seconds to live!"

"AARGGHHHH!!"

Panic spiked through the food section and the foliage and beyond. People raced and goods flew and feet trampled those already pushed to the floor. Siofra and Victoria clung to each other as there was nobody else to cling to. Whimpering, Fionnuala pushed Jed towards the bomb.

"Ye've military training, sure! Get ye under them cans and fix that bomb before we be's blown to bits!"

"But I never dismantled a bomb in my life!" Jed gasped.

"Och, didn't ye attend a course or some such?"

At the front door, people's bodies were proving more dangerous than the bomb as they clawed and kicked and shoved each other to get through the revolving doors, which seemed to have stuck. Screaming women threw themselves against the windows for escape, but bounced onto the floor, the plexiglass rippling.

"Not much use trying to flee, then," Fionnuala observed. "May as well meet me maker here by the Spaghetti Hoops."

She crossed herself quickly.

00:44

"Jed! Pass me me handbag!" Ursula yelled in a hysterical voice, her eyes those of a raccoon from the teary mascara.

"What on Earth—?"

How could she think of touching up her make up with only 48, 47 seconds of life left? Surely God wouldn't care what she looked like—

"Och, give it to me, just!"

00:36

Brain percolating, fingers quaking, Jed fiddled under the cans and dragged out Ursula's handbag. He passed it to her and Ursula, having finally hauled herself into a sitting position, grabbed it and scrabbled at the disarray inside.

"I'll see if I kyanny dismantle this bomb meself," she said.

00:31

"Honey, I love you." Jed needed to say the words before they died.

"Aye, and I love ye and all, ye kind, daft creature!" she yelled. "Quit distracting me, but, would ye?"

Fionnuala finished her prayer and yammered strange sounds. Ursula wondered which would be most use: her toenail clippers or the bottom of the cross on her rosary.

00:23

She grappled the rosary and hacked into the bricks of Semtex.

"Och, would ye quit the wailing outta youse?" Ursula yelled into the tearful, keeling masses around them. "I'm trying to concentrate here, sure!"

Fionnuala found herself clutching Jed for support. Jed hoped Ursula wouldn't see him clutching back. They shuddered in fear over Ursula's bobbing purple bob. Her rosary didn't seem to be doing much; the clock was still counting down. Now it was on 00:11. She reached for her toenail clippers, her head racing, and tried to figure out which wire she should cut. There was the green one

00:10

the red one

00:09

the yellow one

00:08

the bluish-sort of-purple one

00:07

"I kyanny make the decision!"

00:06

"Och, Jed, och, even ye, Fionnuala, help me, would youse! Which one should I cut, then? Och, it's worse than choosing lotto numbers, this!"

Jed and Fionnuala whimpered and trembled and hugged above her. The toenail clippers shuddered in Ursula's aging hand. She would never look down upon that hand again. Ursula inched the clippers closer and closer to the bluish-purple wire...

00:02

Snip!

00:01

00:00

Even in the screaming, there seemed to be silence. They waited for the blast

and waited

and waited some more.

The seconds really do stretch out when death is imminent Jed thought, teeth digging into Fionnuala's shoulder. *It seems like we've been waiting forever to be blown to bits!*

Ursula finally pried her eyes open and looked down at the bomb. It just sat there. Scudder had bought the wires from the Mountains of Mourne Gate market.

As her mother dragged her past the electronics department on the way out, Siofra slipped three iPods in her pocket. Victoria giggled and swiped three as well.

The Floods sat outside around Dymphna's wheelchair, drugged to the eyeballs and wrapped in those foil capes they always seemed to place around the shoulders of accident victims; nobody was sure what their function was. Police milled around. Jed was calming Ursula over by the public toilets.

"Och, dearie me, aye," Paddy said. "What a day!"

Dymphna struggled around in her wheelchair and spied her uncle and auntie.

"Don't youse think we should invite—"

Her jaw dropped. Rory was making his way through the fleet of ambulances and the rocks being thrown at them, but that was not what had caught her attention.

"It was themmuns! Themmuns!" Dymphna screamed, jumping up and down, her mother's handbag jumping off the handle. "Coppers! There be's the culprits! Sneaking into that van there! They rented the lockup from me, so themmuns did! Here to see their handiwork, so themmuns is!"

Police raced to Scudder and MacAfee, and as they struggled, Bridie materialized from the crowd and pointed at Dymphna.

"Traitor!" Bridie roared. "Grassing to the Filth! A shame to the nation! And I know why, youse! Yer woman in the wheelchair there be's preggers with a Proddy bastard's bastard!"

The crowd stared, and Paddy and Fionnuala buried their heads in shame. Rory looked sadly at Bridie.

"Aye," Dymphna said to all the accusing eyes. She would have stood if she could. "Persecute and crucify me all youse want with them gacky eyes of yers! I'm grassing up the culprits to the Filth! I'm a traitor, I'm well aware, so tar and feather me if youse must! Themmuns almost blew youse to bits, but! And if youse must know, I've a half-Proddy wane, a demi-Orange bastard, growing inside of me and excuse me youse if I want that wane to have a world to grow up and get drunk in!"

Rory was suddenly at her feet, massaging her casts.

"I never knew ye had it in ye, Dymphna," he said.

"Ye mean, the courage to say what most doesn't dare? I was happy to do it, sure."

"Er, aye, that and all. I meant a new wane from me in ye, but."

Dymphna blushed.

"Och."

"A wane I'm happy to be the father of."

"I'm gonny spew," Fionnuala said, burying her head in the foil in shame.

After the police had hauled MacAfee and Scudder away and taken a statement from Dymphna (Fionnuala glared with every traitorous word that exited her lips), Fionnuala cursed under her breath as Ursula approached slowly over the cobbles.

"Am I now expected to apologize to this jumped up cunt for trying to save wer lives?" she hissed, but the family had no answer for her, and post-near-death-event Fionnuala was even starting to tire of her relentless hatred toward Ursula.

"Would youse mind if I had a wee word with Fionnuala?" Ursula asked. "Alone, like?"

Confusion and curiosity brimmed in their drugged eyes, but nobody minded. Paddy nudged Fionnuala away from him and towards Ursula.

"Fionnuala," Ursula said, wiping a smear of Semtex from her forehead, "I see even the drama of the day hasn't softened yer anthracite heart. Anthracite, just so's ye know, be's a very, very hard type of coal. I looked it up after it was in one of me word search puzzles. Anyroad, as I say, ye've still not got a civil word to say to me, so me and Jed will steer clear of ye wer last few days of wer visit to Derry. I've something to give ye, but."

Fionnuala tensed as Ursula delved into her handbag. To her relief, Ursula pulled out only a brightly-wrapped box.

"I've crocheted a wee onesie for me new…"

Ursula got lost in the family tree as to exactly what relative Keanu was to her.

"…family member," she settled on. "I want ye to wait until I leave the city before ye open it."

"Could ye not give it to wer Dymphna?" Fionnuala asked in a stilted voice. "The bastard be's hers, after all."

"Ah, but I want *ye* to open it. Promise me ye'll not toss it in the bin. And that ye'll open it after I leave."

"Och, that I will do, Ursula. That's wile civil of ye," Fionnuala said, managing an upward configuration of her lips.

Ursula took this as a smile.

"Make sure ye open it," Ursula repeated.

Fionnuala's 'smile' faltered.

"I've said I would, haven't I?" she snapped.

She took the gift, and Ursula walked back through the crowd.

She should just throw it in the garbage. The old Fionnuala would have. But the old Fionnuala had bleached pony tails and wore chain-link belts and…had a husband who loved her?

The new Fionnuala tossed it over to Dymphna.

"From yer auntie, traitors the two of youse," she said.

Dymphna tore it open, held up the onesie, and the check fluttered out.

"Mammy!" Dymphna gasped. "Would ye look at all them zeroes?"

The Floods huddled around the check and marveled.

"What a daft eejit that Ursula Barnett be's!" Fionnuala snorted. "Imagine, handing over a sum of money like that to us, after all the persecution we put her through. Mind you, it doesn't half rankle, knowing her Ladyship there has this much money in her account to hand over just so's she can make herself feel superior. Never youse mind, but, as we can now fly to Malta as the Lord intended. More money than sense, that foolish cunt Ursula Barnett."

She looked around at her family for the nodding heads she was used to, but their heads weren't nodding. Eyes inspected cobblestones and cuticles, wheelchair wheels and the stitching of pockets.

"Och, whose funeral did I just miss?" Fionnuala sneered. "Have them boyos gone and planted another bomb I'm not aware of, hi? What be's up with youse?"

When Paddy's head rose to meet hers, his eyes bored into hers and a peculiar expression was on his face. Fionnuala hadn't seen it since that night in the '80s when he caught her in the nook of the Rocking Seamaid with her hand up the coal delivery man's chunky sweater. It was anger.

"Get ye over there now," Paddy said with quiet rage, "and thank the woman."

"Och, catch yerself—" Fionnuala was cut off mid-scoff.

"What the feck am I after saying? Naw, not 'the woman,' me *sister.*"

Paddy's eyes promised all sorts of menace if she didn't comply. The children stared in wonder. Had Maureen been there, she would've clapped. There was silence as they all looked at her. Fionnuala, one part of her brain alerting her to a free-floating anxiety, another part projecting a scene on the back of her eyelids where Paddy lived in Warsaw and she sat alone in a house empty of offspring, nodded haltingly.

"If ye insist," she said stiffly.

Running fingers self-consciously through her brown flip, Fionnuala hurried off through the crowd. Behind her scurrying back, the children smiled. Paddy tried to place his hands on their shoulders, but there were too many.

"Ursula! Ursula!" Fionnuala called into the foil capes and bobbing heads. Her voice croaked, and she felt quite anxious about the new Paddy.

But Ursula was gone, looking forward to the next cribbage game with Slim and Louella in her new home of Wisconsin. The old Fionnuala was now part of Ursula's past as well, and Ursula would never again care if Louella cheated. At least she was friendly while she did it.

WEDNESDAY NIGHT CONFESSION AT ST. MOLAUG'S

Father Hogan sat in the dark stillness awaiting the next confessor. He loved this game, trying to match the voices with the faces he saw every week in the congregation. The door opened and a wee one sidled inside.

"Och, Father, I've wile terrible sins to reveal," Catherine began. "I'm scundered, so I am, with all the sinful shenanigans I've been part of. I've an excuse, like, but I know that doesn't make any difference to the Lord. I must tell ye, but, as I haven't been able to sleep nights. There be's this horrible beast of a girl at me school, a grabby, mouthy monster, so she be's. And she and her wee mate embarked on a campaign to torture and persecute me, so they did. They forced me to steal from me mammy and daddy. I had to lie and all to get them me mammy's press pass. Nights, I couldn't sleep, thinking of all the commandments them hooligans demanded I break. I wised up one day, but. I decided to get me own back and I devised a plan. The horrible wee creature insisted I get me iPod for her. I lied again and told her it was me daddy's. As if me daddy would have use for an iPod! I told her as well that me daddy beats the shite outta me all the time, and that he'd beat me bottom with his belt if I lost his iPod. Ach, I feel so ashamed now, me poor aul kind daddy, and there I was telling awful stories about him! Anyroad, I deleted all me own songs from the iPod and put in horrid aul ones that me daddy might like so's she wouldn't catch on the iPod belonged to me. Then I paid Tommy Coyle a visit. He's me cousin Brendan's best mate and he lives across the road from her. I paid him a pound to round the corner and smack the iPod outta wer hands and jump up and down on it. He was happy to do it even without the pound as he hates her and all. He took the pound from me, but. I don't mind, as he did as I asked and smacked me iPod outta her hand. Then, but, car rolled over it, and it was really broke. The look of shock on her face was priceless, so it was. But I feel bad about that now. Anyroad, the wee girl scrimped and scrimped and saved for weeks and weeks, and finally she gave me me new iPod. I'm happy to have it; I feel bad, but. What's me penance?"

"That's quite a story, wee girl. Tell me, but, are ye heartfully sorry for all these many sins of yers?"

"Aye," Catherine lied. She was adding another sin—and to a man of the cloth!—to her long and winding list, but she could easily get it erased next Wednesday in the confessional.

"Three Hail Marys, in that event," Father Hogan said.

Catherine couldn't help but stifle a giggle as she skipped towards the pew to rattle off the few prayers. Her soul would soon be shiny and clean again. Her father always sat her down at night and told her of the many scams run by criminals. Many were fascinating to Catherine, but how she really loved the long con!

MANY MONTHS LATER

"Mammy, would ye please shop in another aisle for a wee moment?"

Maureen eyed her daughter with suspicion, but took her body and cane to visit the pyramid of dented cans of pigeon peas that was the manager's special.

Fionnuala had spied Mrs. Ming at the frozen foods section. The old woman dropped the chicken tikka pizza in alarm as Fionnuala raced towards her.

"Why are ye smiling at me like that?" Mrs. Ming asked.

"Och, how are ye, Mrs. Ming? Terrible bad weather we've been having, aye? C'mere a wee moment, say if ye had an aul video round yers, a strange aul film with blood and guts on it, where do ye think it might have come from?"

The police had given Fionnuala back the video tape two weeks before; forensics had shown it was made in the mid-2000s. Fionnuala's hopes for fame were dashed. It couldn't have been Princess Diana's autopsy. But what was it? She had stared night after night at the ceiling of her bedroom as Paddy dozed at her side, wondering how she could bring it up to Mrs. Ming without incriminating herself. The police trail on the Flood family had grown cold, and she didn't want to start anything up again.

Mrs. Ming gave her an odd look as she rifled through the frozen peas.

"What are ye on about?" she asked.

"Ye've many questions, haven't ye? I'm only asking, like, as, I don't know if ye recall, I was yer OsteoCare provider once."

"Aye, the night I passed out. I mind."

She looked suspiciously at Fionnuala, then inspected a steak and kidney pie.

"Before ye passed out, but, ye had me look through yer videos, and we sat and watched this one, a blank one, it was, no case and no information on it, like. It put the fear of the lord into the wanes, I don't mind telling ye. Perhaps, but, ye kyanny remember as then ye blacked out."

Mrs. Ming wrapped her arms around her.

"Are ye saying I've mental problems?"

"Naw, naw," Fionnuala said quickly, massaging the old one's elbow. "I just wondered, like, what that film was."

Mrs. Ming seemed to be searching the cavern of her mind as she placed fish sticks into her cart. Her face lit up, then just as quickly as snort of scorn passed her lips.

"Ye must mean that video of me grand-nephew Eamonn. The fantasies of a disease-addled student mind, so it was. Ended up flunking out of that media course, so he did. A bloody fixture he was in the Student Union, propping up the bar, arsified with drink."

"But..the video…?" Fionnuala blinked.

"That was wer Eamonn's final project. I near shite meself at the first glance of it. Thought he'd conquer the cinema world as Ireland's answer to Steven bloody Spielberg. Load of shite, so it was, not even a proper story, just some scenes flung together of splattered body parts. Where they got them 'props' from, I don't want to know. Does these turnips look like they've gone off to ye?" She sniffed them. "Smells like death, so they do. He came round ours years ago, looking for that flimming thing. Who knows where it got to. Probably tossed up in me attic, never to be seen from again. Thank the Lord for that, as the world's better rid of it."

Breinigsville, PA USA
08 February 2011
255114BV00001B/2/P